joy Smith Aiken lives in Texas with her husband. *Solo's Journey* is her first novel.

JOY SMITH AIKEN

Solo's Journey

GRAFTON BOOKS

A Division of the Collins Publishing Group

LONDON GLASGOW
TORONTO SYDNEY AUCKLAND

For Scot, Terrie, Bo, and Mr and Mrs T.,
but especially for the real Solo –
I'm so sorry for what I did.

Grafton Books
A Division of the Collins Publishing Group
8 Grafton Street, London W1X 3LA

Published by Grafton Books 1990

First published in Great Britain by
The Bodley Head Ltd 1988

Copyright © Joy Smith Aiken 1987

ISBN 0-586-20686-8

Printed and bound in Great Britain by
Collins, Glasgow

Set in Optima

Contents

Glossary

AURA:	electromagnetic field surrounding all things, seen as colour
BARD:	male cat
BLACKROCK:	street pavement
BRING OUT:	challenge to battle
CALLING:	courtship ritual
DARKFALL:	night
DOM:	from 'dominant,' used as a title of respect or to denote the leader of a Quorum
DWELLING:	any Owner habitation
ENFORCER:	high-ranking bard in the immediate service of a Dom-cat
FEY:	a trancelike state brought on by great duress or illness, usually causing complete withdrawal or mindless combat
FEY-WEED:	a wild plant which, when eaten, causes a druglike sense of euphoria and increase in appetite
FUGUE:	long, continuous feline call, used in battle or as the vocal embodiment of a feline's history
GELT:	male scent produced in special glands under the tail that can be sprayed
GRAILLE:	food
GREYROCK:	concrete
GYPSY:	feline not associated with a specific Quorum or territory

7

KEEP:	large commercial refuse container
LEGENDS:	general term for feline instinctive knowledge and collectible memory
OWNER:	human
PERLL:	female mating time
PRILL:	female cat
QUORUM:	organized society of felines inhabiting a particular territory
RACK:	odour or scent
RAKSHA:	special scent given off by prills during mating time
RAUWULF:	any motorized vehicle
RAUWULFEN:	plural of rauwulf
ROGUE:	see Gypsy
SILT:	excrement, also used as an expletive
SILTAA:	urine
SPEAKER:	Wise One or Prophet
SURROUND:	intangible sensory mechanism extending outside the body with which felines sense or 'feel' the immediate environment
TAME-CAT:	any feline who has lived within Owner confines
THIRP:	soft throaty call, almost a spoken purr
THRAILLE:	mother's milk
THRILLE:	feline song, usually reserved for mating
WATER-DOWN:	rainfall
WOLFEN:	wolf, coyote, or fox
WHITEFALL:	snow

1

Rescue at the Keep

Even in his sleep, deep within the hidden thickets, Solo could sense that something was wrong. As he roused himself to the surface of wakefulness, he remembered what it was that made him feel so unsettled. He was alone. And he was very, very hungry. The second darkfall was approaching and still his mother, along with his two sister-kits, had not yet returned. She had never been gone for more than a few hours before, and though he still listened for her footfalls and thirping call, he intuitively knew there was little hope that she would return. And he knew, too, that if he were to survive, he would have to shake his despair and begin to fend for himself.

He could tell by the thin slashes of sunlight that flickered through the brush that it was still much too early to go outward for graille; the proper time for feline activity was after darkfall, when a cat could meld with the shadows and move about unseen. Curling tightly again, Solo forced his thoughts back into the borderland of sleep, where dreams and memories could at least temporarily forestall his paralyzing sense of fear. He sniffed longingly at the fading rack of his mother and sisters, and waited for night.

The den in which Solo slept was a small cavelike clearing hidden within a heavy overgrowth of thicket and weeds. Lined with soft old leaves spread over hard-packed earth, it had been his home since birth less than two circles ago, providing good protection from weather, and dogs, and from a myriad of dangers that Solo couldn't even begin to name yet. The thought of leaving the safety of the den alone was frightening. Since mother had been gone, he hadn't traveled farther away than a few cat-lengths, and then just long enough for siltaa.

As the sunlight gradually faded to grey, the kit determinedly roused himself again. His hunger had become a gnawing pain, and he knew that if he didn't find graille soon he would sleep straight into Shadowland. Solo knew where to find his food; he had been there with his mother several times before. Nervously he traced the route over in his mind as he prepared for the expedition.

Very carefully he licked the dust and dirt from his long blond fur and sparse whiskers. This was more than just simple hygiene. Dirty fur, his mother had taught him, would interfere with the auralike 'surround' that is a feral's early-warning system and first line of defense in the wild. When on full alert, Solo could actually 'feel' the atmosphere around him, sensing any movement or foreign vibrations that might warn of danger in the area. With his surround, Solo could read the outward conditions like a map.

Coat preened and relatively smoothed, Solo stepped timidly through the thicket. He stopped halfway, extending his surround to its maximum distance, but he sensed only stillness and quiet. Lifting his head, he read the many overlapping racks with his sensitive, if still inexperienced, nose. He caught the vague, musty scent of a possum den, the cool hint of coming waterdown, and, of course, the intimidating yet reassuring power gelt of Dom Bryndle, laid thickly and frequently over the bushes and weeds of the field. The size and strength and great age of the old warrior were woven into that gelt, warning anyone in the vicinity that this territory was firmly held by a feline who had fought and won many battles to keep what was his, and who would be more than willing to fight a few more to maintain that control.

Satisfied that there was no overt danger nearby, the kit eased further outward, the fur around his neck frumped and raised in alert, claws fully splayed. Quickly but without sound, he crept out into the prickly hedges, using the ultrasmooth, tense catwalk that makes no noise or vibration to draw unwanted attention. The darkfall was cool and settled, and with a caution that bordered on paranoia, Solo navigated through the tall grass and brush toward the Great Fence.

The feral territory was bordered along its entire east edge by the Great Fence, or Wall, but stretched far beyond sight to the west. Many times his mother had warned him against straying out into the field until he was older and could recognize the rack of that which might be dangerous, and so far the extent of his travels was limited to the path he took now that lay between his den and the Wall. Before, with his mother with him, it had been an adventure; alone, it was an ordeal.

The field through which the kit crept was a relatively barren prelude to the forest that progressively deepened to the west. Populated only here and there by thin-trunked mesquite and post-oak (adequate for climbing but too thin for hiding), and carpeted with a mixture of browned, starved Johnson grass and tall, variously flowered weeds, it would have been considered unsuitable for creatures of greater size. But to the ferals, who could move unseen from border to border beneath the ground cover or disappear completely within the mazelike networks of evergreen hedges that thrived everywhere, it was more than simply adequate; it was their chosen territory, and it was home.

The field ended abruptly at the base of the Great

Fence – a long, high stone wall that stood in various states of disrepair, erected by Owners long ago. Solo didn't know where the Fence began or ended, but it stretched for many, many hundreds of cat-lengths from north to south and was the center point in the life of every feral in the territory. There were several crumbled openings along the Wall where a kit could sneak through, although the elder ferals preferred to jump over it in the more adult manner. Easing into one such access, the kit listened for the sounds of other Quorum members. It was early darkfall, and he knew there should be many others outward; but he could feel that he was alone. Perhaps it was not only his own family that had disappeared. Perhaps Solo was the only feline left in the Quorum! But no – Dom Bryndle's gelt was fresh and omnipresent. He could not be the only one.

The ground on the other side of the Fence was covered with a hard, smooth substance his mother called 'greyrock,' and not so much as a blade of grass grew from it. Along the edge of the greyrock stood many of the giant, roaring monsters the ferals knew as 'rauwulfen,' which had frightened him so badly the first time he had seen them with his mother. But they all sat quiet and lifeless now, though still reeking of smoke and fire. Solo took courage from how fearless the elders had been around the rauwulfen when they slept silently, as they did now.

Across the greyrock and fifty or so cat-lengths from the Great Fence was a vast complex of Owner dens known by the ferals as the Dwelling. An uncountable number of Owners and their young lived within its mysterious confines, and although none of them were outward now, Solo knew them to be magical creatures, wielders of unimaginable power, and able to control the very elements. Even now, he could see captured sunlight spilling out from open places in the Dwelling walls. His mother had told him many strange and frightening stories about the Owners, but he didn't know how much was really true and how much was just kit-tales designed to entertain her restless young ones or teach the caution so necessary for feral survival.

Solo was especially relieved to discover that no dogs were outward. Mostly, they were kept within the Dwelling area with their Owners, but sometimes they went running without purpose around the rauwulfen or out into the big field. While the dogs did not often bother the ferals – they might chase one halfheartedly if Owners were watching, but they quickly lost interest – they were nonetheless big and clumsy, and could be cruel without reason. Dogs were to be strictly avoided, as were the mysterious Owners themselves.

There were felines who lived inside the Dwelling (as his mother once had), called Tame-cats, but they were distinctly separate from the ferals. The Tame-cats were sleek and beautiful, pampered and fat, and most had odd bands around their necks worn quite sanctimoniously, as if a mark of upper-class. They were smallish and undermuscled beneath the fat, however, and they did not communicate much with the ferals. With surrounds that were very weak and thin, the Tame-cats seemed slow and lethargic compared with the natural alertness of the Quorum felines. They were lazy, too, and easily sent running to their doors. Many of the Tame bards lacked their adult gelt for some reason, along with their cobblers, and it was said that their females seldom came into Perrl. And stranger still, many of them lacked foreclaws. Perhaps, Solo thought, the Owners kept these poor deformed creatures out of pity. Or maybe such pampered and protected felines just lost what they no longer needed – their surrounds faded, their claws dropped off, and their cobblers fell away with their silt!

From his hidden vantage point in the Great Fence, Solo could now see his destination gleaming under the light that came from the Dwelling. It was an enormous Owner structure, at least as large as two rauwulfen put together, and it sat close to the Fence not thirty catlengths from where he hid within the dark Wall. Completely hollow, it was the color of grass on the outside and was made of a cold, very smooth substance. No one seemed to know its exact function, but it must have been of the utmost importance to the Owners, for they all donated much of their own graille and other nest materials there regularly. Solo assumed the donations must be for the Dominant Owner (what a being he must be!), but such things were not for kits to understand. It was simply known as the Keep and was the main source of graille for the Quorum, as well as being the center of Quorum social activity.

Assuming full stealth once again, Solo projected his surround to maximum range and skirted along the Fence toward the Keep. He began to make his way to the east side, where there was an opening low enough for a kit to scrabble over. This side was the most brightly lit, however, reflecting the Dwelling lights, and for a few moments he would be painfully and dangerously exposed. Exposed to what, he wasn't exactly sure, but the Legends taught that there were many dangers outward, especially for young kits.

Taking a deep breath, Solo leapt out and crossed the short open distance, awkwardly rabbit-hopping in the way of the very young. He paused briefly at the Keep's south wall, listening for any alarms his movements may have caused, but there was only the scraping of fallen leaves over the greyrock and the unintelligible call of insects. So far, so good, Solo thought, but his amber eyes were bright and round with panic. The thought of having to traverse such treacherous terrain every dark-fall for graille was petrifying.

Satisfied that the area remained undisturbed, Solo crept very lowly around to the east wall and wriggled over and through the doorway. The sound of his claws against the slick slides of the Keep was sharp and clear in the stillness of the darkfall. Pushing off and landing on his footpads inside, the kit was surprised that he had dropped nearly back down to ground level; on his previous visits with his mother it had been filled up to the edge of the entrance. It was now almost empty. But the donations that littered the floor smelled fresh and inviting, and made his mouth wet as he savored the strange, potent flavors. To his left, Solo caught the scent of meat, and soon found the carcass of a large dead bird that had been treated in some Owner way that made the flesh tender and easily shredded. Stand-ing nearly inside the excavated bird, Solo ate for the first time in two darkfalls.

Gradually, his surround closed tightly in around him, all his senses and attention focused on the much-needed meal. Absorbed in his food, the kit did not feel the practiced approach of the gypsy rogue.

Cautiously, gliding as if in slow motion, the bard moved across the hard ground from the Dwelling wall and headed toward the Keep, pausing nervously in the shadows and under rauwulfen. His hungry yellow eyes were darting and wild. Sensing the kit inside the Keep, he was confused that one so young was not under the immediate protection of a prill. He had no desire to cross a female guarding her kits, but as he scrutinized the area he realized that this one was alone. The gypsy was starved. The killing of the kit would be incidental and take only a moment.

Solo sensed the approach when the gypsy was but

eight to ten cat-lengths away. Even the most untutored kit knew enough not to be trapped by an enemy in an enclosure; instinctively, Solo jumped up and out of the low opening in a single twisting motion. He landed squarely in front of the startled bard, who stood but a few cat-lengths away, looking fully frumped and vicious. Solo reacted in the only way he could. He dropped to his side, wet himself thoroughly, and lay kit-spitting and hissing ferociously in a growing puddle of siltaa.

The surprised gypsy stared and backed away a step or two. Solo was very close to complete fey when rapid footfalls from the south penetrated his last fragment of consciousness — was there more than one gypsy coming after him?

The rogue, too, heard the approach and turned quickly to face the newcomers. He crouched low in full defensive posture and growletted a fierce warning fugue. Momentarily forgotten, the kit pulled himself upright and glanced toward the sound. It was Spanno, a Quorum bard! Relief and gratitude washed over him as he backed against the Keep wall and tried to make himself as small as possible in the slender shadow. Spanno was second in rank only to Dom Bryndle himself, and the kit watched in awe as the young bard slowed and stopped five cat-lengths from the gypsy, his calico head down almost to ground level, his eyes locked in challenge. The two bards faced each other in classic feral style, every muscle tense and ready, their tails twitching spasmodically as each tried to read the intent of the other. Two more warriors moved into the periphery of Solo's sight.

Very slowly and deliberately the gypsy began moving backward, but the move was not a retreat — he was simply changing positions without giving the calico an advantage. Spanno soon began his own fugue, singing even more forcefully than the gypsy. The rogue had backed away several cat-lengths toward the Dwelling wall and stood stone-still and tensed. Suddenly he gathered in and launched himself with an eerie, fur-curling battle cry, his stiletto claws unsheathed and splayed. Spanno dodged to the side and turned to counterattack.

The calico was the first to hear the growing roar that came at high speed from the north. Then the gypsy heard it too, and seemed to freeze with indecision. Aborting his leap, he jerked around in half-turn just as the bright lights of the screaming rauwulf bore down on him. The rogue jumped out and tried to sprint across the greyrock, back toward the Dwelling, but an instant later there was a sickening 'thud' as the smok-ing monster hit the gypsy and flew past the calico, who stood on the greyrock, still frozen in full-battle stance. The rauwulf had not even slowed.

Solo stared in disbelief at the dead feline. The surround of the twisted and broken warrior, now liberated and no longer bound to its body, exuded outward in ever-thinning waves; combined with the gypsy's powerful gelt and the rack of his silt, it told the story of his life – a story of hardship and a long battle for survival. Within moments his aura became a shadow and sought the place from which it had come.

Tearing his eyes from the bard's body, Solo turned to the shocked, tense calico and noticed for the first time that the majority of the Quorum had gathered, witnessing the entire affair. It was his first introduction to Quorum life and he had to do it with a wet rump.

'Dom Spanno,' Solo began in a kit voice that was made even softer and smaller by his deference, 'I . . . I thank you for saving my life . . .' But before he could finish his halting little speech, Spanno jumped the short distance between them and slapped Solo squarely across his ear. The kit rolled out into the light, a small blond ball no bigger than a rodent. He remained on his side with his soft underbelly exposed, the ultimate act of submission. The slight breeze that wafted across the territory told him that his bottom was wetter than ever.

'I ought to slap the siltaa out of you, if you have any left! A warrior died here tonight because of you – because you don't have enough sense to stay with your mother. Get back to your thraille, kit, before someone else gets hurts trying to keep your wet rear end in one piece.' Spanno nervously paced back and forth. 'I should have let him have you.' He leapt gracefully to the high Wall's ledge, his muscular body catching the light, ears and tail flicking tersely as he paced the ledge, adrenaline still flowing from the near-fight.

'Forget the kit,' ordered the deep, gravelly voice of Dom Bryndle. It commanded instant attention, even from Spanno, as the old Dom moved quietly along the ledge toward the assembled community. 'We have other business tonight.'

Solo had never seen Dom Bryndle up close before, and he was glad of being so inconspicuous in the shadows. Bryndle was a veritable giant of a feral, sleek and black and heavily scarred. One ear was half-missing, and because of that he was often called 'Shredhead,' though never to his face. His nose was hashmarked, and a few silver hairs of age glistened throughout the black fur. His green eyes radiated power and cool control, and no one in the territory questioned his absolute authority. It was even rumored that he had once killed a bard in combat, an extremely rare occurrence despite the frequency of feline battle.

The Dom stayed very much to himself, except when in Calling or when presiding over a Quorum council.

With his ranking bards, he guarded the territory from usurpers and thieves, making constant, solitary rounds and laying down his power gelt as warning to outsiders that there was room here for only one dominant feline. The privilege of his rank was specific and non-negotiable – he held the right of first to everything.

Solo was immediately forgotten at the Dom's first utterance. Spanno left the ledge and stood at the Great Fence's base with Ponder and Selvyn, his first lieutenants. The rest of the Quorum was scattered about on top of or under the sleeping rauwulfen, or balancing along the slender ledge of the Keep. The kit recognized only a few, and most of those gathered were bards; the prills in this season of early spring were with new kits. Dom Bryndle had said there was 'business' tonight. That must have been why he had been the only one at graille – there had been a Quorum council.

The Dom retraced his steps along the Wall, and soundlessly the younger bards headed in the same direction, leaving Solo behind. Solo had not been afraid while surrounded by the others, but now he began to tremble again and longed for the safety and cover of his den. His hunger had been satisfied, but he was still thirsty, and the only water he knew about dripped in a continuous rivulet from an opening at the base of the Owner Dwelling's wall – from the direction the gypsy had come. He wasn't *that* thirsty. Anyway, he could feel the coming water-down in the air, and soon the field beyond his den would have water everywhere.

Leaving the shadows, Solo glanced back for a moment at the still and empty form of the gypsy; so this was what death looked like. He then ran full out all the way back through the Great Fence to fieldside and the thicket-den. Pausing a respectable distance from his nest, he silted and very carefully covered it to prevent its pungent and telltale rack from attracting attention. Finally crawling deep inside the den, he relaxed at last, finding a familiar comfort there. Settling quickly into sleep, he dreamed of his mother and heard again the melodic purring that rumbled gently inside her chest as she kept watch and told tales of her own past as a Tame-cat and the spellbinding stories that were the Legends. He stirred in his sleep and mewed softly. What could have taken her from him?

Deep to the south, the council had broken up and the bards headed back to the Keep and graille.

'Do you think that gypsy was from the North Quorum?' Selvyn asked, looking at Spanno.

The calico walked and thought in silence a moment before answering. 'He was pretty thin and wild. I don't think that cat's part of any quorum. Even the North's in better shape than that.'

'You should have let me handle him,' Ponder grumped. 'Lately you've been taking all the good fights – I thought I was your main muscle around here.'

'Main mouth, you mean,' quipped Selvyn over his shoulder. 'And I wouldn't exactly call that a "good" fight. You're just upset because you didn't get a chance to slap the kit – '

'Don't start, you two,' said Spanno wearily. 'Let's go over to the north border and look around a little. Maybe we can find out what's going on over there.'

The three took off across the field, with Spanno, as usual, in the lead. They were the Enforcers of the Quorum, if it could be said that Dom Bryndle had such a group at all. The Quorum itself had long been peaceful and the need for such police-state tactics was minimal. There was also a tinge of rivalry between the Dom and the calico, and their relationship was slightly strained. It was assumed that at some point Spanno would inherit Bryndle's mantle, and the Dom kept the younger bard at a distance, although only slightly more so than he did everyone else; Bryndle by nature was a loner and remained aloof from the more social aspects of Quorum life.

Spanno had a great deal of influence over Ponder and Selvyn, as he did over most of the Quorum. The calico had both wit and intelligence, as well as those qualities of leadership that attract those of less intellect, and challenge those who already lead. He was strong and quick, and his talents lay in strategy and cunning more than in actual muscle. All he lacked was time and maturity to become a Dom-cat in his own right. His only drawback was his calico coloring and long, thick fur. Spanno would fight many extra battles because of the almost feminine luxuriousness of his heavy coat. It was difficult, Spanno realized, for a long-haired calico to look tough and street-wise. Ponder, on the other hand, looked the part; grey-striped and heavily muscled, he was the strongest of the Quorum. But he lacked the aptitude for real leadership. Scruffy and unkempt, he had the raw brawn but needed direction to apply it effectively. Although Ponder was not especially bright, his loyalty to Spanno was unquestionable, and it made the big grey an invaluable ally, as well as friend, to the calico. Though Spanno vastly outranked Ponder in the Quorum hierarchy, if Spanno were ever to become Dom, Ponder would surely be his right-hand Enforcer.

Selvyn was the quietest of the three, a short-haired, smallish orange tabby. He suffered socially because of chronic indigestion. His main asset was speed – there wasn't a faster cat in the territory. Selvyn, too, was completely devoted to Spanno and was the best hit-and-run fighter any cat in the Quorum had ever seen. Spanno and the orange had, in fact, been littermates, though such familial relationships had no meaning for ferals past kithood, and had no bearing on the closeness of the two.

The water-down came as Solo had expected. Its gentle rhythm against the leaves woke him from his sleep. It was a comforting sound, for there was safety in the water-down; very few predators hunted while it fell. The den was dry and warm and Solo felt better than he had in several daybrights.

He had not slept long – his nocturnal Timer would have prevented that even without the sound of water-down to wake him – and he could feel that it was now well into darkfall. Flexing and preening methodically, the kit waited until the shower had faded into mist before crawling to the mouth of the nest. Testing the area with his surround, he discovered it quiet and undisturbed, and he picked his way outward cautiously, nose and ears twitching. The air was clean, and the damp earth beneath his footpads felt soft and cool. The night sounds had the familiar, rhythmic harmony that indicated all was peaceful.

Drinking deeply from shallow pools of water that had collected in fallen leaves, Solo realized just how thirsty he had been. This time, however, he was careful not to lapse into the sort of satisfied fey that had nearly cost him his life at graille earlier. Crouching in full alert, he analyzed each sound and stirring, listening for possible warnings of danger.

His thirst quenched, the kit carefully made his way through the wet grass and leaves to a partially cleared space about fifteen cat-lengths from his thicket to silt, making sure not to get too much of his fur wet as he walked. Damp fur, he knew, had a strong rack, making it difficult to hide. It also, he knew, interfered with a feral's surround.

Solo had not entirely completed siltaa when he felt feline footfalls headed in his direction. He froze to the spot in a panic, and held his breath, hoping the approaching cats wouldn't detect him. Moments later, however, he picked up the racks of Spanno, Selvyn, and Ponder, and he knew he wouldn't be passed by.

The three young bards loped into the clearing where Solo was so ungracefully poised, and stopped, smirking among themselves as the shaky kit attended to his business and made entirely too much of covering the result.

'Well, if it isn't the little twit from the Keep,' said Ponder, snickering.

Solo dropped to his belly and tried to make himself look as small and unworthy of attention as possible.

'I thought I told you to go back to your mother,' said Spanno, sounding annoyed. 'Or do you enjoy being a target for everything with an appetite?'

'Yeah, go back to your mother,' said Ponder, glancing at Spanno for approval.

Selvyn said nothing as he moved toward the freshly turned earth beside Solo. He sniffed for a moment, then turned to Spanno. 'This kit's off thraille – not a trace of it in his rack.'

Spanno looked surprised. 'Where's your mother?'

Solo answered in the merest whisper, couching his words with respect and deference – some adult bards could be dangerous to kits, even if they were in the same Quorum.

'My mother's been gone three daybrights, Dom Spanno, and I am denned alone. I waited . . . but she never came back. I had littermates, but they've gone too. I only came out tonight for graille, because I feared Shadowland; I didn't notice the gypsy until it was too late; then you came and I – '

'All right, I get the general idea,' said Spanno in a

less harsh tone of voice. Solo's respectful use of 'Dom' had not been lost on the calico. No one had ever called him Dom Spanno before.

'Forget the kit, Spanno,' interrupted Ponder, restless after the water-down. 'Let's get out to the field.'

Spanno ignored him. 'Who was your mother, kit?'

'She was called Mercell,' Solo answered, still belly-to-the-ground. 'She was colored like yourself – except for the light spots.'

'Mercell? Wasn't she the one they found . . .' Ponder halted in mid-sentence after catching a hard look from Spanno.

Spanno visibly softened toward Solo. 'Listen, kit. Try to stay undercover. There are gypsies all over the territory from the North Quorum. Bryndle says they've been run out of their own territory by traps and poison, and they may try and take over here. So be careful. Stay in your den and wait till we're at the Keep before coming out for graille. We'll watch out for you as much as we can.'

Solo heard annoyed groans from Ponder and Selvyn, neither of whom was interested in watching out for a young orphan. But the kit was too swelled with pride and gratitude to have hurt feelings. Spanno was going to protect him – at last he had a friend.

Ponder and Selvyn grew more and more impatient to be off to the field. They had planned an evening of rat-batting and were anxious to be on with it.

'Come on, Spanno,' Ponder urged. 'You sound like a mother-cat yourself.'

The calico turned and led the gang of three outward without another word. Solo watched the young bards as they strode boldly westward and out of sight, imagining the day when he might run with them, and even fight great battles at their side. If Spanno liked him, surely the others would too, eventually.

* * *

'Mercell was the prill they found empty at the south border, wasn't she, Spanno?' asked Ponder as they moved across the damp field.

'Yes, but it won't help the kit to know about it,' answered the calico. 'At his size he hasn't got much chance of surviving anyway. Let's drop it.' Spanno sounded strangely upset, as if he knew something Ponder didn't know, but the grey didn't question him any further.

'Come on, guys, let's go after the Big One!' said Selvyn, streaking out ahead.

'Let's go, Ponder,' Spanno called, sounding less serious and ready for play.

'Yes, Dom Spanno,' chided the grey as they fanned out across the field for the hunt.

Solo sat alone in the clearing for some time after the three had left, thinking of Spanno's words about 'traps' and 'poison.' The Legends told of such things, of horrible atrocities designed for killing. He knew that horrors like that did not exist naturally, but were created by the Owners. And that brought Solo face-to-face with the Great Paradox. Everyone knew that feline existence was inextricably bound to Owner Culture, but the how and why of it were beyond him. These great and malevolent God-beings were feared above all else, and yet the Quorum itself was anchored to the periphery of their strange and incomprehensible world, seemingly without thought of leaving it. Clearly, the Legends had much to teach him. Taking the feline way out of an uncomfortable mental quandary, Solo returned to his den to sleep.

It was nearly daybright as Solo circled out his place and made ready for rest. Previously, the north-most corner of his nest had felt the most comfortable, but now, as he turned and tried to settle into it, he felt lopsided, as if he were pulled to his left. He moved toward the north wall, but felt like he was listing to his right. With a tired sigh, he pushed over to the west side near the opening. It was well balanced there and the only tugging he felt was straight downward. Sleep would come quickly; his first darkfall outward had been full and tiring. Coiled tightly, he closed his eyes and slept.

A short distance to the south, the solemn, reflective eyes of Speaker followed Solo's aura up through the hedge and into the early-morning sky. Reading its secrets, he shuddered inwardly with both anticipation and foreboding. The other Quorum cats thought of Speaker as a kind of feline mystic. He was older than anyone else in the Quorum, and as wise as any feline alive. It was even said that he could recite the Legends out loud in their entirety. Speaker kept to himself except when approached for advice or a Teaching, and his assent was essential to any Quorum matter that was left to a general consensus. Even when Dom Bryndle established a Law, the voice of Speaker was always allowed to be heard, and had once or twice even swayed the Dom's decisions. But Speaker never led or tried to lead, and he showed complete deference and respect to the Dom. In fact, he never asserted any rank in the territorial hierarchy. As far as anyone knew, Speaker had never fathered any kits, nor was he ever seen or heard in Calling. He did not have a bard's power gelt either, although his anatomy appeared unaltered. His past was obscure and his future seemed eternal in the Quorum. Speaker was a prophet.

The Old One, the prophet, kept watch over the thicket-den as Solo slept and the morning became full daybright.

2

The Traps

A penetrating sound invaded Solo's dream, bringing him gently back to consciousness. A moment later he recognized the sound for what it was – Dom Bryndle's Calling thrille, an eerie yet soothing cat-opera sung *a cappella* in deep, unstructured tones, speaking not only of the old bard's passion for a prill but also of things as they should be, and of a calm in the territory that would permit a Dom to turn his attentions to affairs of the heart.

The kit flexed and stretched himself full out inside the den, listening intently behind closed eyes, impressed with the sheer beauty of Bryndle's song. Solo didn't completely understand Calling, but he knew it was an extremely important adult activity. He could feel its meaning and basic felineness as the Dom sang his life into the timeless poetry, individualizing the ritual with his voice and spirit and wooing the prill as bards have done since felines came to be. Solo was mesmerized by the long, seemingly breathless tones, sometimes sad and mournful in minor keys, occasionally sharp and wild like a fugue of battle challenge. Gradually the kit's somnolence was replaced with a mounting curiosity; he decided to investigate the feline activity outward.

Threading his way out of the intricate thicket and through the weeds, he headed toward the Great Fence. He fought back the terror that had gripped him so badly the night before, knowing that virtually every Quorum bard was gathered not a hundred cat-lengths from where he stood. A gypsy would have to be completely fegin to risk an attack this darkfall.

Bryndle's thrille grew steadily as Solo neared the Wall. He located the same opening he had used last darkfall, but for a moment he lost his courage when his surround came into contact with that of several older bards; Spanno and the others weren't there. Controlling his trembling, Solo insinuated himself into the narrow crack and looked out the other side, just as the Dom reached an impassioned crescendo that reverberated and amplified over the greyrock.

Bryndle was poised on top of a rauwulf not thirty cat-lengths from Solo's dark vantage point, looking immense and statuesque against the dim sky. Head held high and back, ears almost folded forward, the old warrior looked powerful and intimidating. His black coat sparkled with the lights of his aura and his tail was arched gracefully over his back, weaving gently as if in rhythm with his Call. Seven or eight lesser bards were stationed in a ragged semicircle, upright and visibly affected.

Down on the greyrock, in the center of it all, was the prill, crouched and silent, watching Dom Bryndle's every move through wary eyes. She was lovely and white-coated, and her sweet, enticing raksha permeated the still air.

Solo was confused. While she was certainly pretty and perfumed, why a bard would want to sing to her was beyond him.

At last Solo spotted Spanno, Selvyn and Ponder just behind Bryndle, and they, too, paced with mounting frustration. The prill was now exclusively Bryndle's, and to vie for her honors one would first have to negotiate with the Dom. Bryndle, feeling the heightened emotional state of his bards, briefly assumed an offensive posture and growled a stern warning. When

Spanno and the rest stepped back and sullenly acquiesced, Bryndle resumed his supplications, his singing now soft and gently hypnotic. Suddenly, in mid-stanza, the Dom leapt from the rauwulf and landed lightly and silently five or six cat-lengths from the white prill: knowing a female in Perrl is very unstable and easily frightened into combat or a state of fey, Bryndle moved in a slow, unthreatening manner; softly, almost inaudibly at first, the prill began her answer. She would accept him. Encouraged, Bryndle circled her, gradually closing the distance between them. The prill turned to follow his movements, always facing the bard. His Call and her delicate thirp blended into loose harmony as they replayed the ancient ritual as it had been set down in the Legends, Bryndle adding his story of strength and triumph, exciting the small female into compliance. A chain of events had begun that was as old as the Legends themselves.

Without warning, Bryndle stepped toward the prill and bit quickly but gently at her ear. She responded with a lightening-fast swat of her forepaw toward his eyes, as was the custom. The Dom came back with a left to her neck, but she ducked to the side and bit hard into Bryndle's lower lip. With a yelp, he jumped backward. She had drawn blood, and the electric streak of pain in his mouth and the salty taste of his own blood seemed to excite the Dom even further. After a few minutes of the almost choreographed sparring, the prill broke the pattern and ran quickly toward the Great Fence, pausing to see that Bryndle followed before leaping to fieldside. Bryndle was behind her instantly and they were gone, leaving a tortured and twitching pack of feral bards behind them.

Fitfully flicking his stubby tail, Solo stayed within the

Wall, round-eyed and a little dismayed. Is that all there is? he thought.

At least he would have graille all to himself – every bard in the territory was glued to the prill's raksha. Nobody, including Spanno, had even noticed Solo's presence.

Solo crept from his hiding place toward the Keep. He glanced at the spot where the gypsy had gone down, knowing before looking that the body would be gone, though without knowing who or what might have removed it. Several cat-lengths across the grey-rock he sensed and then saw Speaker, perched on the Keep's ledge, aloof and solitary, as usual. Solo accepted his silent presence matter-of-factly, as everyone did, and scraped his way over the low opening and inside. He was glad that an elder was so close. The sage remained above him in silence while he ate.

The blond kit was nearly full when he heard the bounding footfalls of several cats coming from the south.

'That prill is beautiful!' said Spanno as he neared the Keep with Ponder and Selvyn loping easily at his side.

'She's a Tame-cat!' Selvyn replied, his voice staccato from running. 'Not only that, but old Bryndle won't let anyone close to her. Forget her, Spanno.' Selvyn hit the Keep wall at a dead run and was over before the others had reached its base.

'Droud, that little white prill is something, Tame-cat or not!'

The three sat rummaging for food as Solo watched in silence. Suddenly Ponder spotted him.

'Look who's here. It's the twit again! Did an Owner throw you in here?'

Solo opened his mouth to answer, but Selvyn spoke first.

'What's your name, anyway, kit? We can't go on calling you "Twit" all the time.'

'My name is Solo, Dom Selvyn,' squeaked the kit, edging toward the door.

'Don't pay any attention to those two,' said Spanno through a full mouth. 'They do well to know their own names.'

Solo made no reply, and looked at least as small and nervous as he felt. Ponder and Selvyn scratched and pawed through the crackly brown containers, absorbed in their work.

'Go on, finish your graille, Solo,' Spanno said gently. 'You're safe with us here. You had water lately?'

The kit was very flattered at the great Spanno showing such an interest in him, and he was feeling taller by the minute.

'I was just going when you got here, Dom Spanno,' he answered in a painfully kittenish voice.

'Better drop that "Dom" stuff – Bryndle would slap you fey. Just call me Spanno. Call those two anything you like, they'll answer.'

'A simple "master" will do,' offered Ponder.

'Okay, Simple Master,' roared Selvyn.

'Aren't they clever?' Spanno said dryly. 'Come on, Solo. I'm thirsty too, and I need a break from these two. Let's go to the Dwelling.'

Spanno leapt the high wall without another word, and Solo quickly heaved himself out and over the low door. Although it was considered juvenile to use the low east opening, Solo had no choice.

When they reached the Owner structure, Spanno drank from the water that had collected on the ground below a round silver opening.

'Where does the water come from?' Solo asked as he watched it steadily dripping down the wall.

The calico hesitated, as if he hadn't really thought

about it before. 'Somewhere in there,' he said, looking upward at the high Dwelling. 'Anyway, who cares? It's here.'

Ponder and Selvyn joined them, looking restless and fidgety. The kit could sense other Quorum cats gathering at the Keep, all equally pensive. The Dom was markedly absent, as was the white Tame-cat. There would soon be new kits in the Quorum, if Solo's limited knowledge of cause and effect served him correctly – and if the Tame prill chose to stay with the feral community.

Full of energy, Ponder pranced and pawed restlessly at the greyrock.

'Let's go rat-batting again, Spanno,' he whined. 'We can't hang around here all darkfall.'

'Yeah,' Selvyn agreed. 'Anyway, we didn't find much last time.'

Before Spanno could answer, a high-pitched commanding yowl stopped everyone in his tracks. It was Bryndle, signaling for the attention of the Quorum from atop the Great Fence. The urgency in his tone was unsettling, and after a moment of stunned hesitation the three bards quickly trotted back toward the Wall, the kit running to keep up with Spanno. No one spoke as they waited for the other Quorum members to assemble. Whatever had taken the Dom away from his prill could not be good news.

'Follow me,' Bryndle ordered simply, in such a way that Solo was tempted to go immediately to his den.

Silently and apprehensively the small band of ferals crossed over or through the Great Fence as the Dom jumped fieldside and headed westward into the weeds. Behind him the younger bards exchanged anxious glances, their surrounds strained outward in alert.

Several hundred cat-lengths into the westward field, they walked directly into a rack of stark terror and fey panic. As they neared its source, the scent of fegin fear became thick and nauseating. Then, in a semiclearing beyond a heavy growth of hedges, they saw a grey bard crouched in a fey stupor. His eyes were fogged and vacant of reason, and pink froth from his mouth was smeared across his face, glistening on his striped fur like threads of starlight. The odor of his silt was strong and uncovered. A shiny, toothed, jawlike object gripped him high on his foreleg, and it was wet with blood. A long, thinly twisted length of dried plant material tethered the thing securely to a small tree. The captured bard had been unable even to drag himself away. The heavy stench of pain sucked the breath from the terrified onlookers, who fought the urge to flee.

'It's Jesse,' breathed Selvyn in a whisper. But Jesse was beyond hearing his name.

'It's an Owner trap,' spoke Dom Bryndle evenly, but his tone gave away the helplessness they all felt.

'Stay alert. Where there's one trap there are usually more.' It was Speaker, and even he was showing traces of shock.

Jesse had begun a low, whining purr, something the ferals did only in times of pleasure or great illness. All the ferals knew that Jesse was dying.

'Let's kill the droud thing and get it off him!' hissed Ponder, ears laid back and downward.

'It's not alive, and we can't remove it. It would be too late even if we could. Jesse's close to Shadowland now.' Speaker had turned away, and most of the others did the same.

'I thought you were so wise, Speaker! We've got to do something!' Selvyn spat out his words in frustration, claws splayed and coat frumped. Ponder stomped his front paws in place, rocking his head and shoulders from side to side. Spanno looked at Jesse with an expression that mirrored the fear they all felt. Behind him, Solo trembled violently, staring in disbelief at the dying bard, unable to look away.

Jesse's pained purring was softer now, and came ragged through parted lips, revealing broken and bleeding teeth. He had obviously tried to gnaw the trap from his leg.

Dom Bryndle sat apart from the group. 'You heard Speaker. Where there is one trap, there may be more. We will return to the Great Fence exactly the way we came. Group up and let's go!'

Silently they turned and retraced their steps to the Wall, traveling more closely together than ferals did normally. Bryndle and Spanno assumed the outside and most dangerous positions, with Selvyn and Ponder and Speaker at the front. Solo stumbled within the group, shaken and numb. The labored, rattling purr of their wounded brother faded into the distance as they left him to finish his journey into Shadowland alone.

Back at the Great Fence, the little band fretted in silence, except for an occasional obscenity or frustrated growlette. Even the Quorum prills were outward now, having left their kits nested with stern warnings to stay put. The Quorum met in High Council, with Dom Bryndle presiding from the ledge and Spanno, Selvyn, and Ponder at the front of the swelling group below. Speaker sat on the Fence to the south of Bryndle, facing the field in studied thought.

'What are we going to do, Dom Bryndle?' demanded Ponder, frustrated at having nothing to fight. 'We can't just wait for the traps to bite off our legs!'

'Shut up, Ponder, unless you have a plan of your own to offer,' said Selvyn. He was suffering from a severe bout of indigestion, and several felines were repositioning themselves upwind.

Bryndle's green eyes flashed angrily. 'Shut them

both up or get them out of here,' he ordered, looking at Spanno. He paused. 'This is no gypsy intruder to be driven out. It's not a cat-killing dog to be outmaneuvered. These things are of Owner design. That puts the danger beyond anything we've faced before. We'd be better off with the Water Sickness.'

Hidden in the shadows, Solo sat dumbstruck. Owner design? Why would the Owners create such an unspeakable horror? He looked at Spanno, but the calico was lost in his own thoughts.

The Dom continued, 'We have seen what these traps can do; there may be more in the field, or even around the Great Fence – '

'I think the traps can be disabled.'

It was Speaker who had interrupted the Dom, an act of surprising disrespect. Speaker himself seemed shocked at his thoughtlessness. It was as if he had suddenly come to a truth and had spoken his thoughts out loud without thinking. 'Your pardon, Dom Bryndle, but I must speak. I believe we can disarm the traps.'

Silence, like a vacuum, followed. The feline nature was to deal with things as they were, not to try to effect changes. Speaker's words were foreign and unsettling to them; it was a long moment before anyone answered. Bryndle's eyes narrowed with thought, and not a little suspicion.

'Go on, Speaker,' he said quietly. 'What plan do you have for accomplishing these great things?'

Even Ponder and Selvyn sat wide-eyed on the grey-rock. Solo unconsciously edged his way out into the light to listen.

'These traps are small, and spring shut with weight, like the weight of a cat's paw. Then they close quickly and bite into the flesh. Would the trap not close just as quickly, and harmlessly, with the weight of something else? Loose earth, for instance?'

No one spoke. The ferals did not seem to understand. 'If we covered the trap with dirt,' Speaker explained patiently, 'just as we do our own silt, the jaw-thing might close under the weight and be rendered harmless.

All eyes turned toward Bryndle, who gave no reaction. Soft murmurings began again, none clear enough to be considered a reply to Speaker's proposal.

'Even if this idea of yours would work,' Spanno said, 'we don't know where the traps might be hidden. And how close would we have to get to cover them? We all know how wise you are, Speaker, but this thing sounds dangerous.'

Spanno had voiced the concerns of the majority, as usual. But Dom Bryndle's decision would be the final verdict; he had already begun pacing the ledge in deep concentration.

'We'll all get killed if we listen to that spook,' growled Ponder to Selvyn, though too softly to be overheard by the others.

The Dom became still and sat facing Speaker. 'There is much to Spanno's words. To disable the traps, we must first find out where they are. How do you propose to find these other traps?'

The Quorum waited tensely, but it was not Speaker who finally answered the leader.

'From the way they glow . . . we'll be able to find them from the way they glow . . .' Solo said, his voice trailing off into nothing. He, too, had spoken aloud without thinking – and in response to the Dom himself! Everyone looked at the kit in disbelief, shocked at his impertinence.

'Let me slap him, Dom Bryndle,' offered Ponder, mock pleading in his eyes.

'Droud, kit, have you got nothing but silt between

those ears?' Spanno hissed at Solo, who crouched and trembled on the ground.

Bryndle and Speaker conferred briefly on the ledge before the Dom leapt down to the greyrock and approached the kit. Solo promptly wet himself. The others backed away, giving Bryndle a wide berth, except Spanno, who stood uneasily beside the quivering kit.

'What did you say, kit?' asked the Dom, obviously attempting to keep his naturally gruff voice from further intimidating the young one. 'Speak up. You needn't be afraid.'

Solo's voice was a high-pitched quaver as he addressed the Dom. 'I . . . I . . . said . . . the traps g-g-glow . . . we'll be able to find them from the way they glow, Brin Domdle . . . I mean Bom Drindle . . .'

Spanno looked from Solo to the Dom and back again, uncomprehendingly. 'This kit was parted from his mother too soon. I think his brain has shrunk from lack of thraille,' he said, in an effort at levity. He was rewarded by chuckles from a nervous Quorum.

Bryndle ignored the remark. 'Tell me of this "glow," little one,' said the Dom, eyes narrowed with suspicion.

Solo hesitated in confusion. Hadn't they all seen it? 'I just meant the blue sparkles, Dom Bryndle. They were very bright around the trap that held Dom Jes . . . I mean, Jesse.'

Now everyone began to understand what Solo meant. While all felines see radiant, ever-changing colors around living things, only a very few could see the more static, monotoned emanations given off by inanimate objects, in this case metal, which sparkles electric blue. Solo evidently had such an ability.

'I didn't see any blue sparkles,' muttered Ponder.

'Shut up,' snapped the calico. 'Don't you understand? Solo can see the traps even if they're hidden! If he's right, I think Speaker's plan just might work.'

Solo was overwhelmed. Too much seemed to depend on him. He would have given his milk teeth to be back in the den, alone and out of sight.

The Dom resumed his position of authority on the ledge. 'We must make a plan,' he began. 'There will be a lot of territory to cover before daybright, and this kit won't be able to travel very fast.'

The council erupted with suggestions and strategies. Solo remained speechless beside his beloved Spanno. Oh, what if I fail? he wondered.

After a great deal of discussion, the final plans were set. With Speaker's help they determined that Solo's field of vision was effective for about six cat-lengths at the periphery and twenty or so cat-lengths directly ahead. They would cover the length and breadth of the field by crisscrossing from north to south in swaths no wider than the kit's field of vision. It could well take all of what was left of the darkfall.

Not all of the Quorum would be needed for the mission. Dom Bryndle, of course, would act as field commander, with Solo close beside him. Spanno, Ponder, and Selvyn would go, as would Speaker, and Ditto, Abalon, Babbot, and Rivalle, bards known to Solo only by name, to help with disarming.

Beginning northward and fieldside of the Keep, the company began the first sweep southward across the field, with Bryndle and Solo at the head of an almost single line of cats. The little blond kit had not spoken a word since answering Bryndle. He followed instructions from the elders in a semidaze: walk here, look there, slow down, go faster. Bryndle seemed oddly irritated and somewhat preoccupied, giving his orders curtly and bluntly. Spanno assumed it was because he had been unable to deal with the situation directly and was forced to depend on an orphaned kit to solve a dangerous dilemma. Too, Bryndle was a strict adherent of the old, conservative ways, and not fond of ideas or things that were new or different.

Spanno stayed close behind Solo and the Dom, with Ponder and Selvyn tight at his heels. Ponder acted more sullen than usual, feeling somewhat resentful at Solo getting so much attention. Selvyn openly distrusted the entire operation, hinging as it did on some sort of weird second sight by a kit still in his baby fur. But no one actively disputed the Dom once a decision was Law, and Speaker backing the scheme lent it credibility.

Solo's short life had been so circumspect that he really had no idea just how large a territory Bryndle ruled. They started from an area several hundred cat-lengths from the vicinity of Solo's den, so heavily marked with Dom Bryndle's power gelt that the kit knew it must represent the north territorial boundary. Staying within sight range of the Wall, they moved past where the Keep stood on greyrock side and at least two to three hundred cat-lengths beyond it, not stopping or turning until they reached an area where the foliage thinned into barren ground. This, Solo could tell, marked the south border, and beyond that were several Owner places, but unlike the huge territorial Dwelling – they were very small and widely spaced. In the distance, past the last of these Dwellings, the forest became thick and wild, and Solo could see mountains on the far horizon.

On this first pass, Solo had seen nothing that resembled the blue, sparkling aura that had hovered around the trap. But Jesse's body had been found much deeper into the field – there would be many treks from north to south border and back again before they neared that area. Even if they walked without stopping until daybright, Solo knew, they would be lucky to reach the westward forest edge in one darkfall. He was already tired, but Dom Bryndle had turned and headed north again, and Solo followed in silence. Slowly and cautiously the group moved forward, each one straining his eyes, hoping to see the mysterious 'blue sparkles' and thereby join the kit in the center ring. They were heading northward again for the third time when Solo saw it – a soft blue haze very close to the ground, with spiraling silvery-blue flecks sparkling within it.

'There!' he gasped, whispering as if the thing could hear him. Instantly, forty cat feet froze, many suspended in midair, for no one could see the aura but Solo.

'Where?' asked the Dom, using the same hushed tone. 'Exactly where do you see it?'

It's two cat-lengths from that center bush,' the kit replied, pointing with his ears and nose.

Bryndle inched forward slowly, nose twitching and head low to the ground. The others followed gingerly. Solo stayed rigidly behind.

'Get over here, Solo. We don't see what you see,' Spanno snapped at the kit; Solo moved forward past the larger bards, realizing that he was in charge from that point on.

Sneaking up nearly to the edge of the blue mist, the kit looked directly at its origin. It wasn't a trap at all; just a collection of rusting hollow containers left behind by some Owner.

'It's not a trap,' he said in a small voice, bracing for the anger and derision of those behind him.

Deep sighs of relief followed, instead, along with a few nervous giggles. Most had been holding their breath without realizing it.

'But it is made of the same material as the trap,' Speaker said, inspecting the objects more closely.

'Good work, Solo,' said the Dom expansively. 'Now we know you can do it.'

The cats regrouped into formation again and headed out, snaking their way across the weed-covered field. They were nearing the clearing where Bryndle had found Jesse when Solo yelled out.

'Stop!' he called, his voice breaking with fear. Another blue patch, like a misty fog, lay before them, this time larger and stronger. Solo's intuition told him that this was no false alarm. 'It's behind that rock pile, there!'

Once again the warriors halted in silence. Bryndle nodded a go-ahead signal, and they circled the little stone hill from the west. There it was, thinly disguised with dried leaves and broken glass. It was exactly like the trap that held Jesse. The base of the thing was made of tree material, and attached to it were narrow strips of the same substance from which the Keep was made. It was barely a half cat-length long, and although it didn't look at all deadly, everyone had already seen what its toothed cutting jaws could do.

'Well, Speaker, we found the droud thing. Now tell us how to kill it!' Ponder had kept silent as long as his nature would allow.

'Anyone who gets close to that thing is going to get bitten,' spat Selvyn, looking a little wild.

The others were milling anxiously, keeping a safe distance from the deadly trap.

'No one will get bitten if we're careful,' answered Speaker evenly.

'Let's get on with it, then,' said Bryndle. 'How is it to be done?'

Speaker said nothing, but moved in very close to the trap, placing his paws with careful deliberation. The

41

bards watched, round-eyed and alert. Solo went belly-to-the-ground, afraid to move.

Speaker was less than a cat-length away when he turned and began to scrape and dig at the loose earth beneath his hindpaws. He paused to adjust his distance several times, until the dirt was landing squarely on top of the trap.

'Well, *I'm* with you, Speaker,' said Spanno, a little too loudly, as he assumed a position at the prophet's side and began digging in the same manner.

Selvyn, Ponder, Ditto, and the others shortly joined in, leaving only Solo and the Dom to watch from the rock pile. It simply wasn't proper for the Dom himself to dig, and no one really expected Solo to help with this part.

On and on they dug, grim and quiet. The dirt continued to fly until each cat had made a small excavation behind him. Still nothing happened to the trap. Bryndle began pacing, frumped and rattled, when suddenly the jaws snapped together like thunder, 'Thwack!' All the diggers leapt simultaneously into the air, pedaling for traction. Even the Dom leapt backward. Solo wrapped himself into a fey ball and wet himself. Only Speaker had remained relatively unaffected. Gradually the bards collected themselves and regained their composure. 'Droud, Speaker! Why didn't you tell us that would happen?' demanded Spanno, shaking the dust and leaves out of his long calico fur.

Speaker didn't answer, absorbed in inspecting the dead trap.

'It worked well,' he said simply, after a few moments. 'Very well indeed.'

Bryndle went to confer with Speaker over their success.

'You should have seen yourselves!' laughed Ponder.

42

'Why, I wasn't scared at all! It takes more than a little noise to – '

'Oh, shut up, Ponder,' said Selvyn with a weary edge to his voice.

'Back it up, you two,' ordered Bryndle. 'This kit's nearly fey, and we need him. Spanno, see if you can pull him out of it.' The Dom had spoken, and silence prevailed.

Spanno nudged Solo with his nose. 'Hey, big guy! It's over! Hey, kit. Relax. I can't tell one end from the other.' (Actually he could. The wet end was easily identifiable.) 'Tomorrow this will all be over and we'll take you rat-batting, okay?'

'Silt, we'll be wearing the little runt from now on,' growletted Ponder, catching a sharp look from the calico.

'Like a second fur,' breathed Selvyn in agreement.

The lesser bards gathered together, straightening out their own fur, anxious to be done with the work. Speaker, too, sat waiting for Solo to collect himself.

The kit raised his head, and his eyes began to clear. Spanno licked his oversize ears and spoke soothingly.

'You'll take me rat-batting?' begged Solo, not really sure exactly what it was.

'Sure, Solo. Whenever you like. Are you okay now?' asked Spanno, sounding relieved.

'I'm sorry, Spanno, I'll do better next time.' Solo shook out his coat and tried to even out his head. When an adult goes fey he sometimes fights tooth and claw, without reason or even a specific target. A kit simply withdraws, almost to the point of unconsciousness. Solo just felt like he had been near sleep, and was terribly embarrassed when he realized he had been so fey in front of half the Quorum.

'We've got the rest of the field to cover tonight,' said Bryndle. 'Now group up and let's move out.' The

Dom's tone brought them back to the business at hand, and each bard prepared himself for a very long darkfall.

Encouraged by their success, the warriors regrouped and struck out across the field once more. Spirits were a little higher, though, and the heavy sense of danger and foreboding had lessened. Much of the mystery surrounding the traps was gone – they were, after all, defeatable.

They had walked north and then southward several more times and had reached the heavy line of briars that marked mid-field, but still there was no sign of any more traps. Bryndle and Speaker decided that it would be wise to snake through the midst of this thicket for its entire length rather than just checking along its outer edges. The prills nested there when they had new kits, and the bards could not chance missing the faint bluish glow within its heavy branches and leaves. Taking a winding path that crisscrossed the width of the briars, Solo walked uneasily beside the Dom. He could sense the presence of several prills and their kits scattered throughout the hedge, and he could feel their tense reaction to the presence of the bards. They would not dare to leave or move about, however, until the area had been thoroughly inspected and pronounced free of danger.

Seventy-five to eighty cat-lengths southward of Solo's own den, the kit saw a faint patch of blue, just barely visible in the heavy brush. He stopped in his tracks, and everyone behind him froze, knowing that Solo had found another one.

'Where?' asked Bryndle simply, trying to follow Solo's gaze into the hedge ahead.

'It's there, to the left, Dom Bryndle,' Solo whispered, 'about fifteen cat-lengths, I think. It's hard to tell in the bushes . . .'

Bryndle looked at Speaker and then began inching forward, motioning with his head for Solo to assume the lead. Cautiously and silently, the others followed.

'I see it,' said Speaker. 'Under those leaves.'

Again, everyone halted, then slowly crept forward, needing to have the thing visibly covered.

'There's not much digging room,' observed Spanno. 'How will we get enough dirt on it to make it close?'

Speaker didn't answer, but moved to within a cat-length of the partially hidden trap. It had been wedged into a slender space between two large bushes and lightly covered with fallen leaves. Digging would be difficult.

We'll have to surround it and try to cover it from all sides,' the old white prophet said, mostly to himself. Turning, he began scraping at the hard-packed ground as he had done before. Nervously Spanno, Selvyn, Ponder, and the others circled around and found places close to the trap and began to dig with Speaker. It was slow going, hampered as they were by cramped quarters and rock-hard earth. With each scrape of a hindpaw the ferals tensed in anticipation of the trap jaws slamming shut. Solo crouched behind Bryndle, nearly at his breaking point.

This time, when the sharp crack finally came, they were ready, and the sound was followed by relief and even mild, giggling hysteria. It had taken three times as long to disarm this trap as it had the first.

Spanno left the others at the trap and sat beside Solo. 'You're doing a good job, kit. We're all proud of you. We couldn't do this without you.'

Solo didn't know how to answer, but suddenly his weariness left him and he realized that he was anxious to get back to the search. Rising to his feet beside the calico, he squared his shoulders and resumed forma-tion with the elder bards. Spanno was proud of him!

By the time the little band returned to the Great Fence at early daybright, three more traps had been found and made harmless, and the ferals were weary right down to their footpads. The most difficult part of the evening, however, had been seeing Jesse's dead and empty body lying alone in the field. A young brother had died badly for no purpose they could understand.

The remainder of the Quorum had waited all darkfall at the Keep. They greeted the bedraggled warriors and the news of their victory with relief and congratulations. Everyone knew that something terribly important had happened that night, though no one could have put it into words. Something new had been added to the Legends, and there was a new hero within their Quorum in the form of a tiny, shy kit: Solo the Small.

3
The Giant Rat

'Hey, Kit. Are you going to be a weird like Speaker?' asked Ponder as the four broke away from the rest of the Quorum and headed southward on the greyrock.

'I'm going to be like Spanno,' said Solo, sounding very serious.

The calico smiled to himself, obviously pleased.

'And I want to run as fast as a rauwulf like Selvyn, and be as big and strong as Ponder,' added Solo diplomatically.

'The twerp's got a good head on his shoulders.' Ponder grinned. Flattery was not wasted on the grey.

'We might just make something of him yet,' Selvyn agreed.

'I don't know about anybody else, but I'm ready for a little sleep. How about you, Solo? Your tail must really be dragging. You can stay at the Woodstack if you want. There's plenty of room.'

Solo had started to ask what the 'Woodstack' was, but was afraid it might sound ignorant. He was only just beginning to overcome his shyness with the three larger bards.

If Bryndle's seat of authority was the Great Fence ledge, then Spanno's was the Woodstack. The Woodstack was really a huge collection of neatly sliced trees piled haphazardly against the Great Fence on greyrock side about a hundred cat-lengths south of the Keep. Spanno had denned there, with Ponder and Selvyn, since he had left his mother's nest four seasons ago, and much of the derring-do and general mischief the three had accomplished was plotted from this wooden hill. One would have thought that such a perfect feline fortress would have been claimed by Bryndle, but the old Dom felt it would be a tactical error for the Quorum leader to have such predictable behavior. Any sort of permanent address would make him an easy target. Bryndle preferred to randomly usurp the lairs of other Quorum members, other than prills and kits, for a night or two, and then move on to another.

Standing nearly as high as the Great Fence itself, the Woodstack was dark and catacombed, with several entrances and a relatively roomy open space near its center. It provided easy access to fieldside, and the tunnellike openings were too small for either dogs or Owner kits to follow. Solo was impressed.

As the four ferals circled out their places in the central area, conversation dwindled. Spanno did make it a point, however, to commend Solo for his bravery and courage during the mission in order to help the kit forget just how frightening the whole affair had been. He could imagine how intimidated Solo must have felt with Dom Bryndle breathing down his ears for an entire darkfall.

As they all found spots to lie down, Solo resisted his natural urge to curl up snugly to Spanno's side, and Ponder pretended not to notice when, during the long daybright, Solo rolled over in his sleep and plastered himself tightly against the big grey.

At darkfall, most of the Quorum had collected around the Keep. Not much was said about the heroic expedition of the previous night. Spirits were higher than usual, however, and everyone made it a point to speak to Solo and call him by name when he came with Spanno, Selvyn, and Ponder for graille. Ditto, a grey like Ponder, who had been one of the silent diggers on the mission (nonranking bards did not speak freely around the Dom unless addressed directly), joined them at water. He was loosely considered a friend of Spanno and the others, and sometimes went with them on prill hunts or other bardly quests. No one really trusted him, though, because he had no tail – from birth, not misfortune – and had been a Tame-cat almost until adulthood. He would always lack the true feralness that comes from maturing in the wild. Ditto offered to Relate with Solo – the formal feline gesture of friendliness and acceptance accomplished by exchanging exhaled air nose-to-nose – and the kit accepted, wondering why Ditto would invite so formal a ritual within his own Quorum. But Ditto was a little odd, he had heard, and Solo did not want to offend him, even if the tailless bard did hold so little rank.

At the Woodstack after graille, the four lounged in full feline satisfaction. Spanno had stretched out along the Great Fence's ledge, flanked by Ponder and Selvyn, watching Solo as he tried to climb the Woodstack.

'Will you really take me rat-batting?' asked the kit, tail and ears straight up with anticipation. 'I've never been rat-batting . . .'

'Yeah, Spann. The kit's got an idea there. We could use a little fun, and we could show the little twit how it's done.' Ponder was already up and flexing.

Spanno looked over at Selvyn. 'What do you say, Sel? Want to go, or is the old gut acting up again?'

'Sure, I'll go. And the "old gut" is fine, thank you. But if Ponder crums it up again like last time and the rat gets away, we're going to play a new game. We'll call it Slap the Silt Out of Ponder.'

'Me crum it up!' snapped the grey defensively. 'You're the one that ran it toward the rocks!'

'You were supposed to turn it!' hissed Selvyn, up on all fours.

'Listen, you two,' Spanno interrupted, 'we can stay here and argue, or we can go rat-batting, but we can't do both. Now, I'm going to the field. Who's going with me?'

Ponder and Selvyn continued to glare at one another, but followed Spanno as he jumped to field-side. Crawling through an opening at the base of the Wall, Solo still didn't know how much of this to take seriously and how much was just cat-banter. Wide-eyed and filled with pride at being with the three elder bards, the kit frumped his fur and tried to lengthen his stride to keep up with them without having to run full-out.

Past the central hedges and several dozen cat-lengths further into the field, the group stopped to plot their strategy for the hunt. Rat-batting was more a game than a serious hunt for food, but it represented a basic feline survival skill and was played very seriously. Well-fed ferals seldom killed and ate rats or mice, but they loved to stalk and catch them, sometimes literally 'batting' the rodents to death. At this point the dead rat became a trophy to be given to whomever the hunter decided to impress.

Like all creatures, ferals tend to learn their best lessons from their worst mistakes. Of all the many and varied such learning experiences Solo and the stalwart three would have, the Night of the Giant Rat was to be one of the most memorable.

The plan of action had been set. The Gang of Four set out into the mild, starlit field, their olfactory senses keenly alert and attuned to the slight vibrations that might represent their prey. It was Ponder who caught the rack first, far past the central hedges.

'Hold it!' he whispered; the others stopped, nostrils flaring, each searching to find the rack.

'There!' breathed Spanno, pointing with his ears. 'Under those rocks.'

Five or six cat-lengths ahead of the group was a mound of rubble and small stones. Spanno directed them with a nod of his head, rather than risk any sound that might frighten the rat. Ponder swung around wide to the south, while Selvyn circled the other way.

'Solo,' said Spanno in an inaudible whisper. 'You stay here and try to turn it toward one of us when it runs.'

Solo trembled with excitement, his heart pounding in his chest, and he felt a great surge of elation at having been assigned such a pivotal role. He crouched low in the thin grass, tail flicking in anticipation, determined to do his part well and impress the others.

Silently Ponder and Selvyn assumed their positions. The calico had passed Selvyn's post and came up on the rat's hold from the west. It was now fully surrounded.

As Ponder inched closer to the rat's position, he noticed that the rack upon which he was focusing so intently was just a little peculiar. While it smelled like a rat, stale and musky, it was different somehow. Selvyn noticed it too, and raised his head over the weeds to signal Spanno. But the calico was already sleazing toward the rat in total concentration. If Selvyn made a move now, he'd risk ruining the entire operation. Ponder, much too afraid of being wrong to say anything, reassured himself that Spanno, with his superior intellect, must surely know exactly what they were doing.

Suddenly, from the west, Spanno sprang and they were committed.

Out of the rocks ran the biggest, blackest rat they had ever seen. It had two wide stripes of white down its back, and a thick tail any bard would have traded his cobblers for. It scurried eastward, its black eyes wide with fear, nearly running over an astonished Solo. The kit backpedaled several steps without thinking as the huge rodent stopped and glared. It was almost as big as Ponder.

Spanno leapt over the rock pile, wide-eyed, then paused, but Selvyn and Ponder, farther away and with less grasp of the situation, were moving in toward the giant rat as planned, keeping it penned between Spanno and Solo. The kit was almost fey with shock as he watched the giant rat gather in and gracefully lift its magnificent tail, turning in slow circles and glowering at each of its attackers in turn as they moved in closer. Spanno quickly recovered and began to move forward again in full stalk, with Ponder and Selvyn, now visibly shaken themselves, admirably following suit.

'Droud, wait till the Dom sees this,' Spanno said to himself, his excitement returning as he thought of the reception they would get when they brought the giant rat home.

Solo hoped against hope that the thing wouldn't try to escape toward him. Ponder came from one side, and Selvyn from the other, as Spanno closed in from the rear. Moments later, they had formed a tight circle around the striped rat, each about four cat-lengths away. The strange animal began clicking its teeth and slowly turned its exposed hindparts to first one attacker, then another, in an odd, threatening manner. None of the hunters had ever been threatened with a rump before.

When Spanno yelled 'Now!' they all sprang for the kill – except for Solo. They were instantly bombarded with the foulest, vilest, thickest rack-stench they had ever encountered. Their mission was aborted in mid-leap. Coughing and sputtering, eyes watering, they didn't even notice the rat move leisurely out of the circle and away into the field, leaving the invisible fog of its rack behind to permeate the fur of the startled ferals.

Spanno shook out his coat and wiped his eyes with a lick-dampened forepaw. 'What *was* that?'

'At least you can't blame this one on *me,*' Ponder said triumphantly.

'I can hardly breathe,' Selvyn said, sneezing. 'We've got to get away from this rack.'

'Selvyn, it's all over *us,*' answered Spanno. 'Droud, we've got to find a way to get it off. We can't go back like this. Where's the kit?' The calico looked around and saw Solo sitting behind him, totally dazed. 'Come on, Solo. Don't get fey on me. It's just a smell; we'll figure out something.'

'I'm not fey, Spanno, but I don't think I want to go rat-batting anymore. Maybe I need to be older.' Solo began rolling in the dirt and shaking his body, trying to dislodge the heavy odor from his baby fur. 'What are we going to do now? You don't think that rat might come back, do you?'

Involuntarily the elder bards glanced around them.

'No, it's gone. We've got to find Speaker. If anyone will know how to get rid of this rack, it's him.' Spanno headed back across the field toward the Wall, the others following.

'We almost had him, Spanno. If he hadn't hit us with that . . . that rack, he wouldn't have had a chance.' Ponder suffered more from lack of a fight than from the overpowering gelt.

'As far as I'm concerned, that rat can have the whole field to itself. With a weapon like that, he's invincible,' grumbled Selvyn.

For Solo, at least, the strange experience had one decidedly positive aspect. He had been frightened nearly to fey, but had still managed to keep his rear totally dry.

The four disheveled cats carefully eased through the crumbling Fence south of the Keep to look for Speaker. As they approached, members of the Quorum appeared over the Keep wall and out from under sleeping rauwulfen, noses twitching.

'What do I smell?' someone asked.

'Has something died out here?'

'If it's something dead, it must have died a circle ago to smell this bad!'

Bryndle himself materialized on the Wall. 'What in droud happened to you?' he said, staring at Spanno and the others. 'You're fouling up the territory!'

The other ferals backed away, shaking their heads and trying not to inhale too deeply. Prills gathered their kits and hurried to their nests, as if the scent was contagious.

Hastily, Spanno told their story before the entire Quorum, though with a few little changes and embellishments; the giant striped rat had become as big as a dog, and Ponder recounted a heated scuffle that Solo didn't quite remember.

When they had finished their sad tale, Bryndle pronounced his verdict: banishment. They would not be allowed at or around the Great Fence until the smell had faded. Given the strength of the rack, that wouldn't happen soon.

A slightly less cocky band of felines than had set out that darkfall walked dejectedly away, suffering the catcalls of the other bards, and the first of many Striped Rat jokes that would soon become a part of Quorum culture.

They slowly made their way back into the field, deliberately avoiding the direction the Giant Rat had taken. Spanno felt the loss of face acutely, and his long calico tail dragged abjectly through the dirt as he led his fragrant band into the night.

It was too early for sleep, with daybright still hours away, yet hunting was out of the question now – it was difficult to hunt when your rack preceded you by fifty cat-lengths.

Solo followed behind the three, still a little dismayed over it all. 'Where are we going, Spanno?'

'Anywhere we want to. Anything with a nose on its face will give us lots of room,' Spanno answered dryly.

'We sure can't go to the Woodstack,' said Ponder.

'Dom Bryndle would have our ears,' Selvyn mumbled, fur well frumped to air it more quickly.

Solo longed to go alone back to his old den, but felt that would be a desertion of sorts, and knew he must suffer with his comrades.

There wasn't much breeze, which would have been nice. Although the kit was becoming accustomed to their strong gelt, his eyes still stung and teared. Presently their aimless wandering brought them to a thick growth of mustard-weed, and each circled out a place and sat, well-spaced, in silence. There was much fur licking and air drying to be done before they would be allowed back in the Quorum again, and they set to their work, except for Ponder, who only preened when in Calling and then only in spots. Having long fur, Solo and Spanno knew they could look forward to fur-ball hacking for weeks to come.

Trusting the others to warn him of danger, the kit was the last to feel the approach of the dogs. A soft vibration at first, it quickly grew to a thunder of pounding paws. From what he could tell, it sounded like four or five running in a loose pack as Tame-dogs often did when free. Spanno hissed hasty instructions.

'Don't run – stay together! If we separate, we don't

stand a chance, they'll go after us individually. Get under the bushes, and don't move.'

Solo leapt beside Spanno as the ferals dove for cover. If the dogs were already on a scent, they might pass the cats by. Twenty cat-lengths from where they hid, the dogs stopped, sniffing at the strange rack, unsure of exactly what kind of animal they had found. But the smell of fear was there, and that set them barking again with excitement.

In the bushes, the coiled felines huddled, their breathing shallow and rapid. They knew they were caught. The dogs approached cautiously now, sniffing along the ground, wagging their tails with anticipation. Solo felt close to fey again, and the term 'cat-batting' kept running through his mind.

'When I give the signal,' Spanno whispered frantically, 'jump out and hit them with everything you've got. Go for the eyes and make lots of noise . . . then take off for Solo's den as fast as you can. It's our only chance.'

The dogs were less than ten cat-lengths away, and closing fast. Slavering excitedly, they were almost on top of the ferals when Spanno gave the signal. The three bards leapt from the brush, claws splayed, hissing and spitting ferociously. Ponder landed squarely on top of the lead dog's head and dug in his claws, causing the dog to yelp with pain. Two of the other dogs jumped backward in confusion as Spanno attacked a third, biting a floppy ear as hard as he could and drawing blood. Selvyn rushed the remaining dog, and had bitten into its lower lip. Flying past the others, Solo ran toward his den, the sounds of the dogs ringing in his ears. Spanno was soon shaken off and landed on his paws at a dead run behind the kit. Selvyn, releasing the giant dog's lip, rolled once, spitting and clawing, and then took off like an orange streak against the horizon. Bleeding and startled, the dogs did not pursue.

Spanno and Selvyn crossed the hundred or more cat-lengths of open field and hit the den's slender opening at the same time. Selvyn squeezed through first as Spanno turned to look for Solo, who was coming up behind him, legs moving so fast they looked like a blond blur beneath his short body.

'Get in!' urged Spanno, and dove into the thicket on Solo's heels, breathing in loud gasps.

The dogs had turned in confusion and pounded off in the opposite direction, two of them leaving trails of bright red droplets glistening in the starlight.

'Where's Ponder?' panted Spanno, looking around the tight quarters.

'I thought he was behind us,' said Selvyn.

'You think he's all right? You don't suppose . . .' Solo didn't finish. He didn't have to – they were all thinking the same thing.

After a few moments Spanno said, 'I think they're gone. Let's go check on Ponder.' The calico's voice was tightly controlled.

Spanno poked his head out of the thicket and checked the area with his surround. The dogs were gone. With Selvyn and Solo close behind him, the calico strained his eyes and nose into the darkness. He felt a sickened tightness in his stomach when he failed to locate Ponder's rack. Selvyn, too, felt a sense of dread as they stood looking out into the dim field.

'Solo, stay here,' Spanno said. 'Selvyn, let's go find him.' Solo, heartbroken at having to stay behind, did not argue.

The calico and the orange made their way forward with all senses alert, moving soundlessly through the dry grass, not wanting to miss some slight sound or movement that might be Ponder. Solo strained to keep them in sight as they faded into the darkness, feeling guilty that he had not fought like a bard beside them, but had run to safety like a new kit to its mother. Perhaps if he'd faced the dogs with the others, Ponder might be with them now. Rocking his weight from paw to paw, he waited.

It was Selvyn who spotted the still grey form lying close to a small tree about twenty cat-lengths ahead. He nudged the calico and pointed with a twist of his head. Walking stiffly forward, they tried to put off seeing what they knew to be inevitable. Hearts racing, they approached the dark figure.

Suddenly Ponder rolled over and flexed with satisfaction, lying stretched out in the dirt. 'Have you ever had so much fun in your whole life? Droud, that's the best fight I've ever been in. There must have been twenty of them! Where'd you go?'

Spanno dropped like a stone, overwhelmed with relief at finding his friend alive.

'You silt-head,' cried Selvyn, looking at the grey, but the insult sounded more like a term of endearment.

The bedraggled three headed denward to tell Solo the news of Ponder's resurrection amidst silly cat-banter and giddy slapsticking – the elation and mild hysterics would soon give way to total exhaustion, both physical and psychological.

Solo knew that three feline forms approached long before they were in sight. He rabbit-hopped across the field to meet them, rushing at Ponder, who feigned losing his balance and rolled to his side as the kit straddled his neck and licked the grey's ear, an act of extreme affection.

'Someone get this silly twit off my face!' Ponder growletted sharply, but he turned his unlicked ear toward Solo.

'Ponder! Ponder, you're back! I thought you went

to Shadowland! I knew they couldn't stop *you*, Ponder,' Solo exclaimed happily, abandoning the last traces of shyness and introversion.

'Get away, kit! *You're* going to kill me if you don't let me breathe!' Ponder play-nipped at Solo's side without making any real effort to be rid of him.

Spanno and Selvyn watched the two, feeling a sense of camaraderie among them all that hadn't been there before. At last Solo and the bards found a safe, protected place to sleep, and the rest of the darkfall was passed uneventfully, with the three adults rotating the watch. Five darkfalls would pass before the four were judged acceptably aired out and allowed to return to the Quorum.

Their time of exile passed gently and without disaster. The skies remained clear, and there was just enough breeze to disperse the rat gelt that clung to the four. The sounds of life in the field still ceased wherever the little group congregated, and evidently their distinctive rack was just as unpleasant to the lower creatures. They lapsed into a silent boredom, passing the empty time each one to himself. Solo became Spanno's shadow, clinging to his every word and unconsciously imitating the calico's bold, easy walk and the tilt of his head in listening. As far as Solo was concerned, Spanno was everything a kit could hope to be: strong, yet gentle of heart, a leader, yet not aloof from those who followed. Solo dreamed that one day the calico would be Dom, and he would be one of his trusted Enforcers, with Selvyn and Ponder at his side. Spanno felt Solo's growing attachment and affection, and, as accustomed as he was to the respect and deference to rank, it made him feel proudly protective. Spanno's own kithood was not so far behind him that he couldn't take real pleasure in Solo's kit-games and endless questions. And Spanno felt that there was something different, something special about this kit, and he knew that behind their pretended indifference, Selvyn and the grey felt it too. The calico had always felt somewhat responsible for Ponder and Selvyn, but he knew that Solo really needed him, and he very much enjoyed that feeling.

Feral cats can handle languid inactivity gracefully for only so long before the nocturnal prowling instinct takes over and rest becomes restlessness. By the third darkfall of exile, the bards were irritable *and* restless.

Selvyn roused from a catnap, flexing and coiling several times, splaying his toes and unsheathing his claws repeatedly, appraising their fine, sharp points. 'Let's do something,' he complained. 'We can't just lie around all darkfall like a bunch of prills.'

'Wanna go rat-batting?' Ponder sneered.

'Funny. What do you feel like, Spanno?' Selvyn drawled, without turning.

'Well, we sure can't go chase prills; no one would get near us,' the calico sighed as he rolled over to inspect his own toes, gnawing fiercely at the itchy places between them he could never quite seem to get at.

'I know!' Ponder offered hopefully. 'Let's sneak into the North Territory and look around. Bryndle would love to know what's going on over there.'

'Ponder,' replied Spanno wearily, 'we're not going to sneak anywhere for a long time. They'd smell us coming before we crossed our own border. Anyway, its a half-darkfall's travel there and back. I'm just not up to it.'

'Well, let's go explore,' offered Selvyn, and he immediately began his preening and preparations. The other two soon followed suit.

'You coming, Solo?' asked Spanno, noticing that the kit had not started smoothing his long baby fur.

'I'm just a little tired, Spanno,' Solo replied. 'I think I'll stay here this time . . . if it's okay.'

'Had enough of our kind of fun, have you?' laughed the calico. 'All right, but stay near the den until we get back. At daybright we'll make a quick run to the Keep for graille.'

'I'll stay right here, I promise.' Solo was unsure himself why he had not wanted to follow the others.

The three turned to head out into the field, but Ponder hesitated and looked back around at Solo. 'You do like Spanno says and stay put. We've got enough to worry about without some kit running off and getting – '

'I won't leave the den. I'll wait right here until you get back.' Solo smiled. He had not missed the gruff concern in the big grey's voice.

As the bards headed westward, Solo settled back down on his haunches, his blond fur like a fuzzy halo in the starlight. He felt a peace and communion with the world that cannot be shared even with the closest of companions. His surround was on full alert as he read the sounds and feel of the night, and through it he picked up the distant vibrations of a solitary cat moving toward him. Presently, however, Solo could tell that they were the movements of a Quorum feral and he relaxed, although he had instinctively begun backing toward the entrance of his den. In a few moments Speaker came into sight range in the distance. The kit felt a twinge of excitement; he had never really talked to the prophet, and he hoped that Speaker was not on some important mission of his own and could stop with him awhile. Respectfully Solo stood and walked out a short way to meet the sage.

'Dom Speaker, it's Solo, of Dom Bryndle's Quorum,' he said, following the formal protocol.

Solo was extremely flattered and a little nervous

when Speaker proffered his nose to Relate, and he correctly followed protocol again and exchanged breath with the Wise One. He invited Speaker to sit, and the old white bard accepted without seeming haughty or aloof, although a world of difference lay between their respective ranking, Solo knew. He was a mere kit, and an orphan at that, while Speaker was the venerated sage who gave counsel to the great Bryndle, and countless Doms before Bryndle.

The kit nearly dropped with mortification when he remembered the rat gelt he still carried, and how he must smell to the honorable nose of the great prophet. His very presence must be an insult to Speaker! He began to back away self-consciously.

'Don't worry, little Solo,' laughed the Old One. 'The rack has faded and I'm upwind. You don't offend me, and there's no need for such formality between us.'

Speaker's voice was full of kindness and understanding, as were his eyes. His lightly yellowed fur shone and sparkled in the shadows where the two rested, belly-to-the-ground and head upright, but the kit couldn't be sure if the prophet's aura radiated a true light of its own or only reflected the scant starlight. The old bard's face had the serene look of true wisdom and a haunted quality of remembered pain, and the compassion that comes from such pain. And he was unbelievably old. It was said that Speaker had counted more than forty seasons in his lifetime, at least double the normal feral life expectancy. He had earned the right to be wise.

'Is it true that you can say the Legends out loud from start to finish?' Solo asked, remembering the first stories his mother had told him about Speaker.

'I know the Legends,' answered Speaker after a moment of thought. 'But not to their "finish." They don't really have an end, you know, just as history has no end. We write it as we live it.'

'Do the Legends tell about Owners? I don't understand at all about the Owners.'

'Something troubles you, Solo?' Speaker said, watching the kit closely.

'It's just that the Legends teach us to fear the Owners, and yet we live right beside them. The Tamecats even live *with* them.' Solo looked perplexed. 'Sometimes I can't tell what to make of it.'

'A wise observation from such a young one,' Speaker said, sounding pleased. 'Let me tell you a story.'

Speaker settled himself comfortably on the ground, his paws neatly forward. He closed his eyes for a moment, as if remembering, and then began to speak.

'Long, long ago, so long now that no one remembers the time, and in a place far away, where felines first began to be, there lived the Great Dominant Owner of the entire universe. This Dom Owner controlled the water-down, and whitefall, and the sunlight, and all the lesser Owners came and sat before him, bringing gifts and the finest graille to show their immense respect and fear. His Dwelling was larger and more magnificent than the Owner dens across our own greyrock. He loved all things of beauty, and gathered around himself the most wondrous and magical things. He saw beauty in the animals, too, and collected many strange, exotic creatures from all over the world. Inside his Dwelling there was row after row of brightly feathered birds kept in small enclosures, like traps, so that they would always be available if the Dom Owner cared to look at them.'

'Birds in traps?' Solo interrupted. 'How cruel he must have been to keep a flying thing in a trap.'

'It would seem that way to us, but perhaps not to the Great Owner,' Speaker replied.

'Of course, there were many dogs there too, of all shapes and sizes, to lick his hands and grovel before him. But all of this grandeur did not satisfy the Dom, for he had heard of an animal far eastward that was too swift to be captured, too wily to be trapped, and too proud to be made subservient to Owners. The Great One had sent out many expeditions to find this elusive creature, but to no avail. At last he sent forth his own Enforcer.

'Seasons passed without word of success, but finally news was received that the animal had been caught and would be brought to the Great Dwelling for the Dom Owner to see. Impatiently he waited, and at last the Enforcer came before the Great One bearing a golden trap. The Dom Owner rushed to see the object of his long desire. It was Shamalat, the Cat.

'A spirited and very wild bard, Shamalat spat and hissed and threatened the Dom Owner with his fierce, sharp claws and teeth. His angry yellow eyes were filled not with fear, but with hatred for his captors, and no Owner had been able to touch him. Shamalat was much bigger than felines are today, with black stripes marking his grey coat and silver tufts at the ends of his large, pointed ears. The Great Owner was pleased beyond words, and decreed that the wild feline be ensconced in the most sumptuous enclosure within the Dwelling itself, to be fed the choicest meats and all manner of wonderful graille.

'Shamalat, being vain and full of his own self-importance, began to enjoy his new life of ease. No longer did he have to chase and kill the lower animals for his graille. No longer did he have to be constantly on watch for his enemies. Even his silt was carried away by the Owner hands! Fresh mounds of soft, clean nest material were brought to him each daybright, and honored visitors came to look upon him with the greatest awe.

'Soon Shamalat allowed the Dom Owner to touch and stroke his fur, and the wild bard began to enjoy the gentle caressing and scratching from Owner hands. Within a season, Shamalat had the run of the Great Dwelling with no thought or desire to leave it. Why should he? He had only to call for graille and it was brought to him, and at his slightest whimper he was soothed and pampered. He learned to purr again, and he grew fat.

'At great length a prill was found and brought to Shamalat, and in due course there were kits born into the Great Dwelling. The Dom Owner, offering the kits as gifts, would send them great distances to the other Owners of high and dominant ranking. Sheltered and protected, the felines flourished and rapidly reproduced. Soon it was a mark of great status for anyone to have a feline within his Dwelling. Callings were arranged to produce the favored variations in color and length of fur, some being preferred to others for reasons unknown to us.

'As season upon season went by, virtually every Dwelling boasted of at least one feline member. Spoiled and overfed, underexercised and confined, they became the original Tame-cats. But when they were no longer wild and rare, they were no longer as valued or desired. Tame-cats were abandoned and left to fend for themselves again. They formed the first feral Quorums and scavenged as gypsies. Their instincts damaged, they continued to live in the Owner shadow and existed on their scraps.

'Now Owners seem to feel that all felines should be dwelling creatures, and persecute those of us who are free and feral. Shamalat changed the course of our destiny forever the day he yielded to the lure of an easy life. We will never be truly wild again.'

Solo sat in contemplation. He didn't know if Speaker had answered his question, or simply added new ones. 'But what about the giant cats of the Legends? They're still wild, aren't they?'

'They are not our kind anymore. We are descended from Shamalat, and we are damaged. We're damaged in more ways than can be explained in one darkfall. We call ourselves feral, but even the wildest among us return to the Owner community for graille. And not just for that, Solo. We're drawn to them. The Owner connection is strong now. They fascinate us, they frighten us, and sometimes they even kill us. But we're still here, aren't we?'

'What about the other feral Quorums, like the North, for instance?' Solo asked. The North Quorum was the only other one he knew of by name.

'They have their Keep, just as we do. All feral Quorums coexist with the Owners in some way. There are no more wild ones like us. Shamalat was the last.' Speaker sounded tired, or maybe resigned.

'Dom Speaker, no one else seems worried about all this. But sometimes I think about it, and it feels like something is wrong . . .'

'These are things that won't be settled in a darkfall, Solo, or even in a season. Continue to think on it. See what's around you – don't just accept without questioning things. Being tamed by the Owners did give us that one gift – the ability to question and think. It is the product of leisure and security, but the price we have paid for it was our freedom and our oneness with nature. And a dear price it was. What will become of us ultimately, I don't know; perhaps one day there will come a feline among us who will solve the mysteries and break the tie between felines and Owners, and lead us back into the wilderness and freedom.'

'*You* know everything, Dom Speaker,' Solo said, brightening. 'You could do it!'

'An old, feckless bard,' sighed Speaker, 'who recites ancient knowledge and adds nothing new, is not what our race requires.'

Speaker rose, and Solo knew the Teaching was over. He didn't know what to say, and remained silent as the Old One left without ceremony and headed into the night.

Watching the occasional light flickers from the high Dwelling far across the greyrock, Solo pictured pampered felines on soft bedding being fed from Owner hands. He remembered the Owners he had seen from a distance, walking upright on hind legs, surrounded by an aura of magic. He, too, was fascinated by them and their power . . .

Lapsing into sleep, Solo was haunted by Speaker's story. He felt as though there was something of terrible importance in it that he had missed. He wished for Spanno, Ponder, and Selvyn to return – they filled his thoughts and kept his mind quiet when they were near.

4

Invaded

Two circles had passed without catastrophe, and summer was now in full heat, heavy and stifling. Solo was in the process of shedding his blond kit-fluff for a coat of shining wheat-colored adult fur. His falsettolike kit's voice had begun to deepen, and his problem with wetting himself when under stress was long resolved. The kit still walked stretched up on the ends of his toes, trying to look taller, and Ponder still called him the 'twit,' but Solo was now accepted by everyone as a full member of the Brotherhood of Four, with all the rank and privileges thereof.

It was a time of plenty for the territory, though a boring time for the bards, with the females not even close to Perrling. The season's crop of kits had been weaned and were foraging about on their own, no longer needing a protective mother to supervise their widening activities. Bryndle's white prill had come into Perrl well out of season, as had a few others, and either hadn't settled or was still keeping her tiny ones nested and out of sight. She was called Kitty-Kitty, which was a very un-feline-sounding name, but she had been taken from her mother when very young and could remember no other. Kitty-Kitty said that Owners were very fond of this particular name, giving it to only their most prized and beautiful felines as a symbol of great affection. A very confident and strong-minded prill, she had adjusted to feral ways very quickly. But she still felt hurt that her Owners had moved their den and not taken her too, and was unsure of what she had done to offend them. Spanno watched Kitty-Kitty with what Ponder called 'that fegin lovesick look,' but even though the white prill was not bonded with Bryndle and no longer considered to be exclusively his, the calico had still not found the courage to make a move toward her.

It was particularly hot that darkfall. Ponder was working close-watch, patrolling the long ledge halfheartedly, making use of the time by practicing his famous 'fearsome look.' Ditto had been assigned to outwatch at fieldside, but the rounds were made casually and perfunctorily – life was secure in the territory. No gypsy rogue had been seen in a while, and there was graille enough for everyone. Even the Owners and their dogs seemed to be avoiding the sultry heat, staying mostly within the Dwelling and out of the ferals' way.

Although Dom Bryndle had not been seen on the Great Fence for two darkfalls, this was not unusual – he often went off on some unnamed personal business, returning perhaps with a few more scars and scratches to add to his collection, and they would all know that their leader had been out successfully asserting himself. Spanno was at full weight now, as were Ponder and Selvyn, and the calico was quite capable of managing the Quorum in Bryndle's absence. This darkfall, however, there hadn't been much to manage, and most of the bards lay about on the ledge or around the rauwulfen. Spanno preened himself on top of the Woodstack, watching Solo and Selvyn on the greyrock below.

'I'm old enough to go on an Explore!' Solo complained to the orange, prancing with eagerness.

'Forget it, kit,' said Selvyn with mock gruffness. 'You're not talking me into this one. You're not ready yet.'

Solo had decided to try begging, when he was

interrupted by Ditto, who sailed over the Wall and streaked toward the Woodstack like a low-flying bird. The tailless grey came to an abrupt stop directly below Spanno.

'They're coming!' he said, panting and huffing. 'From the North!'

Spanno jumped quickly to the ground. 'Who's coming?' He asked, becoming very tense. Where was Dom Bryndle? he thought to himself.

Ponder and Selvyn were silent beside the calico, eyes darting northward and then back to Ditto. The rest of the Quorum had gathered close to hear what had brought him in from watch in such a panic.

'The North bards!' Ditto huffed, trying to slow his breathing. 'Eight of them, maybe more. They've crossed our north border, moving fast.'

'Eight North bards running in a pack?' Spanno repeated in astonishment.

'Yes,' said Ditto, sounding very serious. 'It looks like the whole North Quorum just crossed our border, and they don't look friendly.'

Spanno looked out over the assembled group and took stock of the available warrior power. Several of their own bards were missing; Ponder and Selvyn were present, as well as Abalon, Babbot, and Rivalle. They were young, but Spanno couldn't be picky at the moment. Speaker was not among them, but he was no warrior anyway. Counting Ditto, they were only seven.

Already the few prills with kits were rushing for their dens to guard their young. If the gypsies scored on them successfully, they would kill any kit they found, making way for a Quorum of their own descendants.

'There are seven of us here now; they're eight,' Spanno said. 'Good enough odds against gypsies. Fan out at the Fence and hold a position. Let's find out what they're up to.'

For many of the bards, this would be their first real fight. Hopefully, thought Spanno, all the feline kit-play and rough-housing would pay off. The gypsies were seasoned veterans, though, and Spanno had deliberately lied about the odds for morale. But the attackers would probably not be as rested and well-fed as those from Dom Bryndle's Quorum, and that might given them an edge.

The North Quorum had been in chaos for several circles, with rumors of Sleeping Sickness and traps filtering southward. Bryndle had long expected that the North bards might try to infiltrate the territory. The feud between the two bands of ferals was fierce and of long standing, its origin obscured by time. Nonetheless, to attack an entire Quorum en masse was unheard-of. This wasn't simple battle; it was full-scale war.

Solo faded into the inner catacombs of the Woodstack, realizing that a disaster might well be at hand. He feared he would be more of a liability than an asset if he stayed in the open. The North bards would soon be within range; he could feel their vibrations through the greyrock beneath his footpads. They hadn't bothered with a surprise attack – they were confident and driven, and it felt like more than just eight of them. Where, Solo wondered, was Dom Bryndle?

Spanno jumped on top of the Woodstack, directly over Solo, claws unsheathed and ready, his long calico coat in full-battle frump, and snarling impressively in preparation. Ponder was almost salivating at the thought of a fight, flexing his jaw muscles in anticipation. Eyes narrowed to slits, he crouched on a rauwulf just behind the Woodstack. Selvyn was positioned on the ledge, guarding the rear approach, nervously jerking his head as he tried to watch both the greyrock and the fieldside of the Great Fence. Abalon, Babbot, and Rivalle waited for other rauwulfen, all in full crouch and radiating an ill-disguised fear that identified them as the amateurs that they were. No feline is born craven, and all ferals love a good fight, but true martial expertise and self-confidence come with experience and victories. One-on-one, as is the normal course of cat-battle, was a natural experience for any feline, but in a group brawl, not even Spanno knew how to handle it.

Ditto, fully recovered, seemed calm and collected, giving Spanno the impression that, tailless or not, he might be of greater value than anyone had guessed. But then, Spanno reasoned, a bard without a tail could not have reached adulthood without fighting for his honor a few times.

Everyone sensed the absence of Dom Bryndle, like a rent in their self-confidence, but the moment for such reflection was soon swept away as the North bards cleared the Great Fence some twenty cat-lengths from the Woodstack. Spanno counted twelve of them, all large and obviously long feral. They didn't look as scraggy and unkempt as rumor had led everyone to believe. Their Dom, or at least the bard who seemed to be in charge, was a short-haired white, moderately scarred and matted down, though surprisingly young-appearing for his rank. His name was Tanner, and he had tried unsuccessfully to bring out Bryndle within the last season. Somewhere on his belly he carried deep scars from Bryndle's hind claws. Very intelligent and street-mean, they had all known he would some-day try again. It was Bryndle he sought out now as he scanned the area, surveying the Quorum warriors silently, pleased with what he saw.

From his vantage point within the Woodstack, Solo watched in bewilderment. Cats traveling in packs and attacking as a group was unheard-of. He was beginning to understand what Speaker had meant when he'd spoken of felines being 'damaged.' No natural instinct was responsible for this. The kit wished for Speaker as much as for Dom Bryndle.

'I want Shredhead,' Tanner said finally, looking directly at Ponder and evidently assuming him to be the main Enforcer.

But it was Spanno who answered, matching Tanner's cool and forceful tones. 'Well, he doesn't want you. Didn't you get enough last time? Get back on your own territory, Tanner, and take your prills with you.'

Tanner ignored the insult, though angry growlettes could be heard from several of his bards. 'So it's the Great Rat Hunter who speaks for this army of kits.' He sneered, turning toward Spanno. 'We've heard about the big one that got away. Is the great Bryndle depending on that rack you carry to deter his enemies?'

Ponder leapt from the rauwulf and moved warily along the greyrock toward Tanner, stopping at the northeast edge of the Woodstack just in front of Ditto.

'Get off our greyrock or I'll whip the fur off you,' hissed the grey. 'I'm gonna turn you inside out, Tanner. You'll be silting fur for six circles.'

Even Solo was filled with awe at the sheer ferocity of the big grey, but Tanner seemed unimpressed. The North bards grouped in more closely around their leader.

Tanner turned back to Spanno. 'I said, I want Bryndle.'

'Well, you got him.'

All heads whipped around to the ledge behind them. Bryndle had surprised everybody, coming up noiselessly along the Great Fence from the north. Only Bryndle could sneak up on an entire group of cats on total alert. Speaker was several cat-lengths behind.

Solo breathed a sigh of relief, though they were still outnumbered and outweighed.

Bryndle moved along the Wall in the slinky, level-shouldered, head-down stride he reserved for use when approaching an enemy. 'You're in my territory, Tanner, and you're going to have to fight me to get out of it. Get your bards out of the way and let's get on with it.'

'Oh, no, Bryndle. This time we do it *my* way, by *my* rules.' Tanner sounded confident and slick. 'I've learned a few things . . . we're going to take on your entire Quorum . . . right now.' There was an odd sort of satisfaction spilling over in his tone.

Solo was rocking from foot to foot in frustration. He had felt the approach of the Quorum prills, fieldside and west of where he stood. They peeped through the crumbling Fence nervously. Prills seldom delved into Quorum politics, and never into territorial altercations, even though they were generally the ones most affected by the outcome. Bryndle's Quorum might lose this battle, thought Solo; yet there is a lot of wasted cat-poundage on the other side of the Wall. The prills of the Quorum well outnumbered the bards. But this battle didn't need spectators. It needed warriors.

An idea suddenly struck Solo with crystal clarity; it was all so obvious and simple. Silt on etiquette! Solo crept out the back of the Woodstack and through the Great Fence toward the prills. From the north, Speaker watched the kit with knowing eyes.

Bryndle, snarling with anger, realized at last what Tanner had in mind. Tanner had probably dredged up every gypsy rogue for miles to ensure enough strength to outnumber Bryndle's Quorum; for the first time since the Dom had risen to power, he stood precariously close to losing his territory to an archenemy. Lowering, his heavy body flush with the ledge and his head very low and thrust forward, Bryndle began his battle fugue with a deep, throaty hiss. He curled back his lips to expose his yellowed fangs, narrowing his eyes with concentration as he focused and gathered his power. Bryndle was magnificent; his tail arched and twisted around hard to his left, claws unsheathed and splayed, his black fur raised along his spine and around his neck. Tanner, knowing that the battle was now under way, nodded almost imperceptibly to his group of bards, several of whom began cautiously changing positions on the greyrock. Spanno and Selvyn exchanged glances. This would be no free-for-all brawl – Tanner obviously had it carefully planned.

Bryndle was in full fugue and his battle call was piercing and breathless in the darkfall. Ponder, too, had begun his battle song, deep and monotoned, as he focused himself completely on the enemy. Soon Tanner's planning became evident. He, and what appeared to be his Enforcer, stood beneath Dom Bryndle on the greyrock. Two other gypsies were approaching Spanno's position. Also moving in pairs, four of the toughest-looking North bards were headed for Ponder and Selvyn. The others were stationed about on the greyrock, ready to cover the rest of Dom Bryndle's warriors. Everyone was in full fugue now, and the mingled voices steadily grew to an overwhelming, discordant chorus. Speaker watched from northward on the ledge, nearly overcome by the realization that at no time before in feline history had so many sung together in battle.

Bryndle knew he was in trouble. He, and each of his Enforcers, faced two opponents, and the few that remained were young and inexperienced. Two more of his warriors had come in from field-watch, but even if all his bards were gathered, he knew, the odds were heavily against them. Without breaking his fugue,

Bryndle leapt from the Wall, and as he connected with Tanner, total chaos broke out on the greyrock.

Everyone leapt simultaneously into battle. Fugues became muffled growls as teeth found fur and hide and claws slashed and raked viciously. Ponder was just barely holding his own against his two attackers, but Spanno and Selvyn were already down, each under the combined weight of two gypsies. Bryndle was upright but backed against the Wall as he faced Tanner and the other.

Suddenly a different sound was heard over the din of battle. High-pitched and sharp, it was the combined fugues of many cats coming in fast from southward, but unlike any fugue any of the bards had heard before. Within a moment these new warriors were everywhere, and Spanno found himself flanked by two that he instantly recognized – Kitty-Kitty and Sondle. It was the prills! All thirteen of the Quorum prills were on the greyrock and bristled like true fighters. There was a moment of stunned hesitation and the battle sounds faded into complete silence. As Spanno recovered from the shock, his expression of amazement melted into one of proud triumph.

Bryndle stood fully upright, showing his typical cool control as he looked out at the brave company of prill warriors. Looking into Tanner's surprised eyes, he said, 'How does twenty-three to twelve strike you, Tanner? Seems you've walked into a little more than you planned on.'

Tanner backed away a few steps. 'I can't believe you'd crouch to bringing prills into battle. How will this look in your history?'

'How will it look in yours when they stomp you into the greyrock?' Bryndle growled with a sneer.

Solo eased out of the Woodstack, his chest filled with exhilaration, overwhelmed by the sheer drama of what was taking place before him. Glancing along the ledge, he looked for Speaker, but the prophet was nowhere to be seen.

Tanner realized he was in a corner, and he knew, too, that there was only one way out of it. Bryndle would never let them go with such an upper hand as this. Settling his head for the inevitable, the white gypsy once again assumed face-off position.

Bryndle began his song, joined by an eager Ponder and several others, when the first drops of water-down began to fall. A droplet hit Ponder directly on his lowered head, breaking his concentration. All eyes glanced skyward as more and more water-down splatted on the greyrock and onto the tense, poised ferals. They glanced around nervously among themselves, but no one retreated. Soon the water drops were falling faster, leaving depressed spots of wetness on frumpy fur. Solo backed within the Woodstack again to avoid the wetness, unsure of what would happen now.

Water-down in the middle of a battle? They had all been so engrossed in the fight that they hadn't even sensed its coming. And still they all stood, getting wetter by the minute, no one willing to make the first move for cover lest it be read as surrender. The water-down began to pick up, tapping a steady rhythm against the greyrock, and the cats were becoming panicky.

'Droud, don't just stand here!' Tanner yelled. 'Let's get the silt out of this water-down!' After a moment's hesitation, the entire North expedition was in motion, following their soggy leader around the Keep and over the Great Fence. 'Don't think you're saved, Shred-head!' Tanner called from a safe distance. 'We'll be back.'

With a scrabble of footpads on damp earth, they

were gone, headed for dry ground under thick brush and the nearest neutral border.

Bryndle didn't look especially worried at the parting threat. He took refuge in the Woodstack with Spanno, Ponder, Selvyn, and Solo. The kit winced at the strong rack of wet fur in close quarters as he watched the elders try to shake and flex the water from their dripping coats. The others in the Quorum had run for cover under rauwulfen, including the prills, who huddled together waiting for the water-down to slacken before returning to the kits left nested fieldside.

Inside the Woodstack, the bards were still trembling with adrenaline and nerves. No one spoke as Bryndle paced and spat distractedly. It was obvious that he was not thrilled with what had gone on this darkfall – especially the intervention of the prills. Yet he also knew they had saved his Quorum for him.

'Ponder, when the water-down stops, I want you on watch at the north border. I want to know if the North Quorum moves again tonight. Take Ditto with you.' Bryndle spoke in the clipped, gruff voice he used when deeply concerned, and no one argued or even made the usual after-battle small talk. 'Spanno, you and Selvyn keep the close-watch here. I'll take Babbot and Rivalle with me. We'll work double watch from now on, daybrights too. Stay on alert.' With that, Bryndle went out into the still-misting darkfall, barking orders at the other Quorum bards.

'Well, if I've got outwatch, I'd better get going,' Ponder grumbled. He didn't like working with anyone but Selvyn and Spanno, but understood Bryndle's reasoning, spreading the muscle around to best advantage, pairing his strongest warriors with a weaker backup. 'I don't understand this,' he added, speaking to no one in particular. 'They came in like a pack of dogs!'

'Speaker says we're damaged,' Solo said softly, but no one heard.

Ponder stomped outward as Spanno paced in a tight back-and-forth pattern. Selvyn fidgeted at the main entrance.

'Did you see those prills?' said the calico, shaking his head. 'Droud, I wonder how Speaker will explain this!'

'One thing's for sure – they pulled our tails out of a crack, however he explains it,' Selvyn said as he licked at his matted sides.

'Hey, kit. What did you think about that?' asked Spanno, realizing he had been ignoring Solo.

'With the prills there, I bet we could have beaten Tanner, if it hadn't been for the water-down.'

Before Spanno could say anything else, a faint, eerie sound from the field silenced them. Then it came again – a soft, distant, strangely unsettling Call. The three moved cautiously outward and stood silently at the base of the Woodstack. A little louder now, they could tell that it was the call of a prill in great distress. Spanno and Selvyn leapt to the ledge and perched on top, looking intently into the dark field. Solo crept through the Wall and waited beneath them fieldside. The sorrowful feline cry came again, and moments later they saw Kitty-Kitty stumbling out of the tall weeds, her eyes glazed and fixed. In her mouth she carried the limp and lifeless form of her single tiny kit. There was blood dripping from its nose and staining the thraille-white fur of its mother. She stopped, unable to go on, and laid her kit gently down, purring in anguish, licking its bleeding sides, encouraging it to breathe. Kitty-Kitty was obviously deeply in shock, and nearing total fey.

Spanno and Selvyn, after a lot of urging and nudging, led Kitty-Kitty away from the mangled kit and into the Woodstack. Inside, she sat numbly, front paws curled inward and staring at nothing. It was Spanno who went back outward and took her kit away, deep into the field.

No one spoke about it afterward. Evidently one of the North bards had come across Kitty-Kitty's nest as they fled through the field to their own territory and murdered the sleeping kit as an afterthought.

Ponder and Ditto crept through the deepest part of the field, wet and miserable, along the north border as instructed. Ponder was sullen and pouting, but kept his sensorium at full alert, sensing even the creatures that inhabited the dirt (and, occasionally, his own hide). Ditto was silent but effective, especially for a onetime Tame-cat, and tailless at that (what did he use for an antenna?), keeping his surround slightly over-lapped with Ponder's and prickling at a sound some-times even before Ponder picked up on it. The North Quorum, however, kept well within their own bound-aries and at the first hints of sunlight, Ponder and Ditto headed homeward, tired and sore but dry at last.

'Where do you den?' asked the grey. It was the first social sentence that had passed between them all darkfall.

'Nowhere in particular. I don't really have my own den yet . . .'

'Yeah?' answered Ponder. 'Well, there's room at the Woodstack, if you want. Unless you have someplace to go . . .'

'I wouldn't mind,' Ditto said. 'Just for one daybright – if the others don't mind.' Ditto was secretly flattered and pleased. He liked Ponder, with his rough, unpol-ished ways, and greatly admired Spanno, as did every-one. He didn't know Selvyn as well, and supposed Solo's opinion didn't count yet.

Selvyn was on watch as Ponder and Ditto approached the Woodstack, and scarely lifted a whisker as the two bards trudged past, shoulder to shoulder, into the warm recesses of the communal den. Spanno looked at them quizzically as they circled out a spot and flopped wearily down, but after the previous darkfall's doings, Ponder could have brought the Giant Rat home and not have caused much alarm.

The calico explained Kitty-Kitty's presence and fey condition in hushed tones, and even Ponder looked at the little prill with genuine sadness as he made ready for sleep. Spanno and Selvyn were to take the first daybright watch and left for their patrols. Solo curled up close to Kitty-Kitty, unaware of just how much the simple contact would help her overcome her loss.

And so they became the Gang of Six, an unlikely alliance of bards, prill, and kit, bound closely together by mutual need and unnatural circumstance.

Through the next several darkfalls, the Quorum, at least outwardly, remained quiet. Excessive caution, however, runs deep in ferals, and Dom Bryndle seemed to carry that caution to extremes. Talk was circulating that Bryndle had become obsessed by dangers that no one else could sense, and haunted by fears with no tangible foundation. Whatever was driving the Dom, the end result was that every inch of the territory had to be patrolled and checked according to a tight, unrelenting schedule. The double watches and long patrols continued for many darkfalls and daybrights. The bards began to grumble and spit among themselves, but Dom Bryndle showed no signs of a letup on the strict routines.

Solo remained with Kitty-Kitty constantly. At only four circles old he was still considered too young for patrol. Very gradually Kitty-Kitty pulled herself out of her depression and began to move about again, pacing along the greyrock with Solo at her side. Kitty-Kitty would tell Solo of her life inside the Owner Dwelling and of the great, magical things she had seen there. The kit listened raptly to the astonishing stories, and learned of the Winter-box, an object full of trapped winter coldness that produced graille without end, and of a little captive world that Owners would watch for hours and then destroy completely with the touch of their powerful hands. There was a hideous, roaring contraption that Owners would lead around the Dwelling, devouring any object it passed over. The white prill told Solo of a giant water puddle that the great beings would take turns sitting inside, wetting every part of their furless bodies, but the kit found this too fantastic to believe – why would they want to sit in a water puddle?

'The Owner culture is centered around water,' Kitty-Kitty explained. 'It's everywhere in the Dwelling. They even have a water holder that swallows and gurgles every time they silt. Owners love wetness – they put their hands in it, their graille in it, and once they even put me in the big puddle! I fought and scratched till they let me out, but they were very upset when I wouldn't stay in. I thought they were murdering me!'

Solo was totally captivated, and the more he learned, the more he was convinced that the Owner Dwelling was no place for a proper feline. Kitty-Kitty even said that they took their sleep at darkfall instead of day-bright, and had taught her to do the same; completely against feline nature.

Solo liked the white prill almost as much as he liked Spanno. She was strong and intelligent, and told her stories well, a talent for which few felines are well known. She also talked a lot about something she called 'prill evenness,' and from what Solo could gather, it meant that prills and bards should be of equal importance in the Quorum structure. The kit wanted to discuss this with Speaker, but lately he had seen very little of the old sage, and when he did see the prophet he was usually in the company of Dom Bryndle or looking so deep in thought that Solo was reticent to approach him.

It was now a half-circle since the North Quorum Confrontation, and still Spanno and the others were gone on almost endless patrols. Solo missed their company. He was surprised and excited one day when he heard the bards coming toward the Woodstack from fieldside. It was unusual during this time of alert to have more than one or two of them home at once. Presently the bards snaked their way into the Woodstack.

'I think Bryndle's finally lost his balance,' Ponder complained. 'If the North silt-heads haven't come back by now, they won't be back. They know better than to mess with us. Shredhead's got to back up a little. Of course, *I'm* not tired,' Ponder added quickly. 'I'm just worried about everyone else.'

'Right, Pon, that's why you've been dragging your tail through the dirt the last three patrols,' Ditto said wearily, his ears down and lax.

Reflectively Ponder turned and checked his tail. 'At least I've got one to drag, bare-butt.'

'I knew that was coming.' Ditto smiled, shaking his head.

'Well, Bryndle has no plans to ease up anytime soon,' Spanno said. 'He's already worked out the watches for the next four darkfalls.' Spanno circled out and slouched into his spot. 'I'd go for graille but I'm to tired to eat.'

'Maybe we ... I mean ... you could talk to him, Spanno,' Solo offered. 'He listens to you. Why don't you try it? Then we could all be together like before.'

'Solo's right, Spanno,' said Kitty-Kitty, rising from her place. 'Maybe you really should talk to him. You can't keep this up forever. You all look completely worn out.'

'Bryndle just can't accept the fact that the prills saved our hides,' said Selvyn. 'Granted, we got careless with security, but the Dom's really gone too far. Between the night we fixed the cat-traps and the prills' willingness to fight, it's more than he can handle. Bryndle never wants anything to change. He always does everything strictly according to the Legends.'

'Well put!' said Ditto appreciatively. 'But unhinged or not, this is still his Quorum.'

'All this moaning and complaining won't get us anywhere,' Spanno said soberly. 'Let's see if we can find him and talk some sense into him. We're going to be in up to our cobblers if he finds out we're all off watch at the same time.'

'Let me go too, Spanno!' Solo said, dashing to the entrance.

'No, Solo, you'd better stay here. Old Shredhead doesn't take suggestions too gracefully at the best of times. It will be no place for kits or prills,' the calico said with finality.

Solo sat back down on his hindpaws, as did Kitty-Kitty. There were sparks flashing in the prill's green eyes – after the North confrontation, the prill-bard distinction didn't feel quite fair.

Spanno and the others went outward, heavy-footed and exhausted, with Ponder still mumbling under his breath. They didn't have far to look for Dom Bryndle. The big black was coming down the ledge from northward, looking less than pleased. Rivalle was several cat-lengths behind him.

'You'd better have a good reason for abandoning patrol,' said Bryndle as he approached them. 'The

84

entire south field is unprotected. What's going on here?'

The strain of hard work was telling on the Dom too. The old bard sat back and glared at the younger bards below.

'Dom Bryndle, we were just looking for you. I think we need to talk.' Spanno wished he'd had time to plan his words. Bryndle was flipping his ears in the way he did when he'd already decided to hate whatever the other had to say.

The calico continued, worried at Dom Bryndle's expression. 'We've been on constant alert for a half-circle now. We all want to maintain tight security, but the North bards ran out of here defeated, and haven't been seen or heard from since. Don't you think it's time we let up a little?'

Bryndle's eyes grew narrow. Although he didn't raise his voice, his barely controlled, hissing tone left no doubt about his mood. 'We'll patrol until *I* say the danger is past. You'll stick to your watch from darkfall to next season if I think it's necessary. Any bard who leaves his post again without authorization can answer to me.'

'It's not worth it, Spann,' Selvyn whispered, feeling the calico bristle. 'Let's get back to the field.'

Spanno met the Dom's steady gaze without fear. Ponder came up even with the calico, his aura tingling ominously as he reacted to Dom Bryndle's words.

'With all due respect for your position, what we're doing doesn't make sense anymore. We're patrolling an empty field . . .' Spanno hesitated. Bryndle's ears were now laid back tightly against his head, his eyes filled with rage.

'This is not negotiable. Get back to your watch or get out of my territory!' The Dom spoke in a forced, halting tone.

'Bryndle,' Spanno began, shocked at the black's reaction, 'this isn't what we came here for. You are the Dom and we respect that, but I'm your Enforcer and I have a right to be heard. We just need to let up some on the patrols.' Bryndle had been known to be unreasonable before, but this was getting close to a face-off!

'One of us, at least, will patrol this territory no longer after this darkfall,' Bryndle growled, eyes narrowed to slits and head lowered.

Speaker materialized on the ledge over the Wood-stack. It was one of the very few times anyone would see the prophet genuinely upset. 'Dom Bryndle, think of what you're doing,' Speaker cautioned. 'Let's talk awhile, before things go too far.' It was clear from Speaker's tone that he'd tried to reason with the Dom before now, and had not been successful.

Suddenly the others realized it was true – the old Dom had lost his balance. The three bards on the greyrock exchanged brief glances. Things had already gone too far. Ditto was as worried about Ponder as he was about Spanno, and with good reason.

'If it's a fight you want, then hit the greyrock, Bryndle, because you've got one,' Ponder hissed, moving out ahead of Spanno, unable to stay out of the action any longer. Selvyn, too, had come up alongside the calico, orange fur standing out around his neck.

'Stay back, Ponder – I can handle this.' Spanno remained cool, his eyes never leaving the Dom, show-ing no sign of fear.

Bryndle was motionless on the ledge, looking like the wild thing that he had become. He didn't respond to Ponder. The battle he wanted was with the calico. And Ponder did not hold enough rank to challenge the Dom directly. In a proper feral hierarchy, Ponder would have had to dispose of the main Enforcer first, or the bard next in ranking to himself, working his way up to the Dominant cat. Feral rank was an intricate system of caste or class, depending on much more than simple size and strength. Other, more indefinable qualities and feline charactistics determined one's rank, counting as much as or more than basic brawn. A Quorum would not allow itself to be led by any feral bully who defeated its Dom. It would only disintegrate.

'I don't want to fight you, Bryndle,' said Spanno, sounding exasperated. 'I just ask that you listen to reason.'

'You have challenged my Law. Now defend that challenge or leave the territory . . . *now*.'

Spanno saw that there was no reasoning left in Bryndle's eyes. He realized that a fight was inevitable, though he was still not sure how it had come about. Ponder knew it too, and took another step toward the Dom.

'Ponder, get out of the way. I have the right of battle here,' Spanno said sharply, invoking his privilege as Enforcer in a rare display of rank. 'I'll have to do this one alone.'

Selvyn deferred and edged toward the Dwelling, but the grey stayed where he was, claws unsheathed. Ditto remained by the Woodstack, as did Rivalle. Their rank did not permit interference.

'Get back, Ponder,' ordered Spanno brusquely; and then, more gently, 'I'll be all right, my friend.'

Bryndle watched Spanno, and deliberately began his fugue. The big grey hesitantly stepped back two or three cat-lengths and sat on his haunches, still ruffled. There was nothing he could do now to stop this battle.

Spanno widened his stance for a broader base of support in preparation for the fight.

'Spanno! No!' Solo raced out into the open, his fear for Spanno stronger than his respect for protocol. 'We can leave! We can make our own Quorum, with all of us, and Kitty-Kitty, and maybe some of the others – '

'Solo! Get back in the Woodstack!' Spanno ordered, never taking his eyes from Bryndle. 'Selvyn, Ditto! Get him out of here!'

The white prill, too, had come out of the Woodstack, but had been unable to hold the kit back. Selvyn and Ditto hastily corralled the panic-stricken and wild-eyed Solo toward Kitty-Kitty, who had to nearly sit on the kit to keep him from running out to rescue Spanno.

When the arena was finally cleared again, Spanno lowered himself flat on the greyrock and began settling his head. The confrontation was unavoidable, but the first move would be Bryndle's.

Dom Bryndle's deep, vibrato fugue softly rolled from the depths of his chest, sounding as wild and near-fegin as the look in his dilated eyes. Shoulders level and ears hard back, the Dom moved along the thin ledge toward Spanno like a black, silky ribbon, muscles flowing like thick water under his coat. Each movement was premeditated with feral caution – even the lifting of a paw was designed to be easily converted into a fast leap if necessary. Bryndle was in his element; a fighting machine with a target.

The calico, too, was coiled and ready. His Call was choppy and spasmodic, more directly challenging and less descriptive or poetic than Bryndle's. It would take a lifetime to build a fugue like the old Dom's, and when it was finished, this night would be near its beginning. The combined fugues cut through the still darkfall, and where the voices intersected, the random melodies created a spine-tingling harmony that would have been beautiful had it not been so primal and fierce.

Bryndle positioned himself five or six cat-lengths from Spanno, above and to the left of the calico. Their eyes were locked together, their surrounds probing to discover a clue to the other's intent. Crouched and still as a statue, Ponder watched intently, sensing the gathering battle he ached to fight himself. Selvyn seemed to remain the more unaffected, but nervous eyes betrayed his apprehension. Kitty-Kitty, waiting with Solo in the shadows, realized that any loyalty she might have felt for the Dom was gone. It was Spanno she watched with worry and concern, and a gentle feeling in the heart known only to prills.

Only Ditto, watching from the periphery, saw Speaker jump from the ledge to fieldside. An adviser was of no use here.

In exaggerated slow motion, Spanno inched tightly forward, his extravagant fur shimmering with the lights of his charged aura. The calico was in the midst of a slow, careful step forward when Bryndle finally sprang in a flat, fast dive, his ear-piercing battle fugue echoing out behind him. Spanno reflexively dropped to his side and rolled, paws upward and claws poised, opting for the ground position that might give him access to Bryndle's soft underside. Landing heavily on top of the calico, the Dom buried his fangs deep into the fleshy part of Spanno's neck as the younger bard dug rapidly and effectively at the black's abdomen with his hind claws. The battle cries were muffled growls, and the occasional scraping of switch-blade claws against the greyrock was grating and sharp as they clawed at each other in an indistinguishable mass. After a few moments of frenzied battle, round one ended, with neither bard scoring significantly on the other.

Bryndle collected himself to one side of Spanno, and the battle songs began again. Tufts of fur were everywhere, floating like wisps of dandelion. Again it was Bryndle who tried for the advantage, springing straight upward in mid-chorus and coming down hard in an attempt to knock Spanno off balance. But the calico was too fast, and sidestepped the huge bard, who landed hard on the greyrock, losing his breath. Seizing the opportunity, Spanno curled around Bryndle's head, holding on to the side of the black's face with his teeth and clawing at the Dom's unprotected eyes. Bryndle lurched forcefully backward and dislodged Spanno, who rolled into defensive posture as Bryndle leapt at him again. The Dom hit Spanno hard, sinking his teeth into Spanno's abdomen and drawing blood. Arching and twisting, the calico tore free and ended round two.

Although Spanno was bleeding, he couldn't stop to lick the shallow wounds. Collected and coiled not four cat-lengths away, Bryndle sensed victory.

But suddenly it was Spanno who took the offensive, even before the singing had resumed. He charged, very nearly catching Bryndle off guard. Again he went for the black's face, biting down hard over Bryndle's eye ridge. Spanno felt the flesh give way and tasted blood, and he knew he had scored well. Bryndle, partially blinded by his own blood and enraged with pain, lunged wildly at the calico, but caught only an ear. Spanno ducked quickly and found a mouthful of Bryndle's throat, the best of all possible cat-holds. The Dom, however, raked his claws against Spanno's side and shoulder, cutting the calico in more than one place. Spanno stubbornly held on to Bryndle's throat, biting down until his jaws ached with the effort. Bryndle's saliva flew in stringy fibers as, unable to swallow, he jerked violently back and forth in a vain effort to dislodge his tormentor.

At last, now on the defensive, Bryndle found traction on the greyrock and heaved desperately forward, loosening Spanno's vise-grip but tearing away part of his underjaw as the price. The Dom, bleeding badly now, needed time to gather his strength if he were to go another round.

But time he did not get, for Spanno quickly seized the advantage and attacked again. Still half-blinded and gagging on his blood, Bryndle tried to step backward to gain a moment's respite. He stumbled and faltered awkwardly onto his side as Spanno leapt, and reflexively curled, covering his face. It was something no feline had ever seen Bryndle do. And in that moment, everyone knew that the old Dom was defeated.

Spanno aborted his attack in midair and landed to one side, still poised in case the black was feigning. Breathing fast and hard, the calico was very near his own limit. Bryndle righted himself, but did not look directly at Spanno. Protocol forbade any eye contact by the vanquished when the battle was over.

Without words or ceremony, the Dom stood and limped slowly to the south, past the Woodstack, his tail tucked under. He left a blotchy trail of bright red behind him as he walked. Moments later he was gone, and an era had ended.

Long minutes passed in total silence, except for the rasp of the calico's openmouthed breathing.

'Dom Spanno,' came a voice from within the crowd that had gathered before him.

Spanno, covered with blood and dirt, looked around with a dazed, quizzical expression, realizing for the first time the magnitude of what had just transpired. Absentmindedly he licked at the stinging wounds under his thick fur, buying time before having to respond to 'his Quorum.' What he wanted most to do was to go fieldside for a while to be alone. So much had happened; there was so much to think about.

At the Woodstack, Solo released his breath and relaxed his tensed muscles. Spanno was the Quorum Dom-cat! He was feeling so many things at once, he didn't know how to react. Kitty-Kitty, bubbling with her own pent-up emotions, finally allowed herself to be aware of just how much the outcome, and Spanno, had meant to her.

Ponder lay where he was, looking as exhausted as Spanno, eyes closed and face right down in the dirt. Selvyn, too, sat back wearily on the greyrock, but his expression showed his pride and constant faith in the calico. Unsure of how Spanno's new rank would affect him, Ditto paced on the sidelines and waited.

'Dom Spanno,' came another voice, solemn with respect.

Suddenly the entire Quorum exploded into activity. Everyone rushed forward to congratulate the calico with a genuine affection that Bryndle had never known from them. Embarrassed, Spanno sat amid the buzzing Quorum looking a little overwhelmed, finally realizing that he *was* the Dom. He had done it.

When the celebration had died down a little, Abalon began the ritual of Relating and pledge of loyalty that inaugurates a new Dom-cat. Walking stiffly up to the calico, he pressed his nose to Spanno's, briefly exchanged breath, and then formally gave his name and pledge.

'Dom Spanno, I am Abalon, and I will walk behind you.'

Spanno sat back on his hindpaws, looking frazzled but serene. He said his thanks as required, and waited in silence as the next Quorum member faced the leader.

'Dom Spanno, I am Rivalle, and I, too, will walk behind you.'

Again Spanno acknowledged the bard and gave his thanks. One by one each bard Related and addressed his new Dom. Then came the prills, who did the same. Only the youngest kits were exempt. Spanno's closest companions waited till last. Selvyn glanced around to see who would start, then took it upon himself, smiling nervously.

'Dom Spanno, I am Selvyn, and I will walk behind you.' Selvyn felt a little silly greeting his lifelong friend so formally, but there was real affection and great respect in his tone.

Next came Ponder. The big grey scratched for a moment, postponing his ordeal, before shuffling over to the calico. 'Dom Spanno, I am Ponder and I will walk behind you,' he said quickly and rather self-consciously. Ponder was not comfortable with such formal ceremonies.

'Ponder, you are my friend, and I ask that you, as well as Selvyn, walk beside me as my Enforcers.'

The big grey sat beside Spanno, both embarrassed and proud, relishing his sudden new position and importance.

'Dom Spanno, my name is Ditto. I, too, will walk behind you.' Ditto kept his eyes down after the required Relating, and turned to walk away almost before the words were out.

'Come back here, Ditto,' Spanno called, trying to sound exasperated. 'I'm going to need all the help I can get from now on.'

Ditto looked gratefully at Spanno for a moment before moving in between Selvyn and Ponder.

At last, blond, lanky Solo rabbit-hopped across the greyrock, ears and tail straight up.

'My name is Solo, and I will walk behind you too, Dom Spanno!' said the kit joyfully as he rushed the calico, licking Spanno's face like a new kit would its mother.

'Solo, please, get out of my face,' laughed Spanno, welcoming the relief from all the solemnity.

Kitty-Kitty stood waiting for Solo to collect himself,

her feline heart twittering with pride and an odd excitement as she looked at the calico. Walking gracefully over to Spanno, she lowered her eyes coyly.

'My name is Kitty-Kitty, and I will walk behind you,' she purred. And then, more softly, 'Or anywhere you want me to.'

Spanno looked at Kitty-Kitty with surprise and a sudden fluttering of his heart. He had forgotten, over the previous hard, exhausting darkfalls, just how beautiful and feminine Kitty-Kitty was. And until this moment, he had been unsure how much feeling the white prill had for the old Dom.

Ponder, seeing the infatuated look that passed between the calico and Kitty-Kitty, suppressed a twinge of jealousy.

Too young to understand what had transpired, Solo was confused. Had he missed something? He glanced at Selvyn, who suddenly became interested in the stars. Kitty-Kitty turned and walked back to the Woodstack. Why was she walking that way, swishing from side to side? Solo looked at Spanno, whose mouth was hanging slightly open, and decided not to ask.

Suddenly a new voice broke the embarrassed silence.

'My name is Speaker, and I will walk behind you.'

Everyone watched in awe as the Old One, the prophet, Related with the young Dom.

'Speaker! I was afraid you might have gone with Dom . . . with Bryndle. I'm going to need your counsel.'

'Bryndle no longer hears anything except the voice of his own mind. Felines are changing, turning from the old ways. Bryndle feared those changes. But he was a good Dom – he kept his Quorum well for many seasons. We must not judge him too harshly, and we must remember the good he did for the territory.'

A respectful silence followed. Speaker's words had sounded like a eulogy.

Spanno cleared his throat. 'In line with changes, I would like to propose one or two right now. First: no bard in this Quorum will ever kill a kit needlessly, whether it is our own or from another territory.'

From her place by the Woodstack, Kitty-Kitty winced at a painful memory. Murmurs of approval from the other prills and grudging assent from the bards rose from the Quorum. It was not a revolutionary idea; most bards had never hurt a kit anyway, the instinct having begun to fade long ago, as it was no longer necessary for survival.

'Second: it will be permissible for a bard to recognize his own kits.'

A shocked silence followed the second pronouncement. Recognize their own kits? But why? There is no feral word for 'father,' but cats long ago made the connection between Calling and the subsequent appearance of young.

'Next he'll have us producing thraille,' came a perplexed voice from the crowd, 'and denning up with prills and kits!'

'Why not recognize your own kits?' asked a disgruntled prill. 'They are of *you* too!'

'How do we know our "own" kits, anyway?' asked one of the bards.

In a flash, more than one growling prill answered. '*We* know whose kits they are! Try showing an interest and perhaps you'll recognize them!'

A chorus of complaints arose from the bards, but no one actively challenged the edict. After all, Dom Spanno had said it was permissible, not that it was mandatory, the bards reasoned.

Kitty-Kitty was overjoyed. Another small step toward equal treatment for prills in the Quorum. Ponder had his face in the dirt again. What did bards need with the little twits?

'If you're going to have us recognize our own kits, then you should start with your own,' Speaker said, eyes twinkling and looking directly at Solo.

The realization of what Speaker meant suddenly dawned on both Solo and Spanno simultaneously. The calico knew it was true – he had known Mercell, Solo's mother, very well.

'Solo, sit down before you fall over.' Selvyn smiled. He had come up beside the kit without even being felt.

Solo sat, feeling disoriented. So many things had happened so quickly. He was Spanno's kit!

Snickers rippled through the assembled Quorum. Just as Bryndle had been known as Old Shredhead behind his back, Spanno was instantly given the nickname 'Mother Spanno.'

The calico straightened himself quickly and turned back to the Quorum at large.

'That's all for now. I'll be at the Woodstack if anybody needs me. Banda and Sessel will work field-watch first half, Rivalle and Weldon will relieve. I'll be fieldside myself later.'

Dom Spanno started toward the Woodstack, then turned and added, 'Thanks to all you of. I'll try to be worthy of your respect.'

Banda and Sessel leapt the Great Fence and went fieldside for their watch rotation. Tame-cats who had recently come to the Quorum, they had never been trusted with the watch before. This represented a long-awaited acceptance into territorial activities.

Inside the wooden cave, the Gang of Six, as they had become known since the addition of Kitty-Kitty and Ditto, flexed out, each deep in thought over the events of the darkfall. Spanno was especially quiet. Not only was he the Dom-cat now, but Solo was *his* kit, and the knowledge gave him a feeling he could not name. He had always felt protective of Solo, and responsible for him, but now it was mixed with a very personal kind of pride, as if the kit were a literal extension of himself. The calico picked a spot close to Solo and the two sat together in silence.

The kit was still trembling inside. He wanted to run, and jump, and throw himself all over Spanno the way he had done when much younger. But instead he remained quietly beside the calico, holding his head high and feeling very, very proud.

Ponder could keep silent no longer. 'Not a bad piece of work, Spann. Not bad at all.'

'You liked the speech?' answered the calico, stretching broadly. 'Just some thoughts off the top of my – '

'Not your stupid speech,' Ponder groaned. 'The fight! I couldn't have done much better myself. I knew you could do it all along. Never had a doubt.'

'Where do you think Bryndle will go?' asked Selvyn. The question had been on everyone's mind.

'Bryndle?' Spanno said, thinking. 'He'll probably follow the old ways and establish a Quorum in another territory. Don't worry about that old scrapper. He's tough. I'm just lucky I beat him at all.'

'Thank you for what you did for the prills,' purred Kitty-Kitty. 'You're going to be a wonderful Dom.' The white prill's eyes had not left Spanno since they'd returned to the Woodstack; how strong and handsome he was!

'It was something we should have done a long time ago. After all, Owners themselves den up with their prills and kits.' Spanno avoided Kitty-Kitty's eyes self-consciously.

'I want you to know that I'm proud to be with you,' said Ditto. 'I didn't know if you'd feel differently about

97

me after becoming the new Dom . . . since I'm a Tame-cat and have no tail.'

'What's so important about a tail?' asked Spanno. 'Banda doesn't have any cobblers, but that doesn't mean he's any less feline.' Banda had escaped from the Owner Dwelling less than a circle past, but not before he was altered and mutilated.

'At least Banda won't have to claim many kits,' quipped Selvyn, catching a sharp look from Kitty-Kitty *and* Solo.

'I'd rather be without a tail,' muttered Ditto.

After a while Spanno rose and stretched himself luxuriously. 'Well,' he said to the others, 'let's hit the greyrock. We've got a lot of territory to cover.' It was time, as they all knew, for Spanno to lay down his warning gelt over Bryndle's.

The bards were instantly on their feet and preening, their weariness evaporating in the excitement. Kitty-Kitty stayed down – prill equality hadn't gone that far.

As the bards prepared to leave, Spanno turned to Solo. 'Take care of Kitty-Kitty, little one. When the work is done, we'll talk.'

Kitty-Kitty was a bundle of nerves during the bard's absence. She preened and paced, paced and preened, her surround fully extended, waiting for the first sign of Spanno's return. Feeling ignored, Solo began a much-needed fur cleaning of his own, and during the process noticed for the first time the beginnings of that which Banda so sorely lacked. Solo realized that this marked the halfway point between being a kit and an adult, and knew that within two more seasons he would be old enough to take his place at Spanno's side as an Enforcer. This darkfall had held many surprises.

Tired from the activity and filled with emotions that he needed to sort out in his mind, Solo curled beside Kitty-Kitty for sleep. He kept his surround on full alert, however. Spanno had asked him to watch over the white prill, and Solo had taken the request very seriously. After all, he was Spanno's kit.

Far to the west, hidden in deep forest cover, a large black cat lay in the shadows, breathing raggedly. His fur was badly matted, and there was sticky brown blood caked across his nostrils and over one eye. The pain was great, but he knew that if he lived until daybright, he would survive. And then, the old Dom vowed silently, vengeance would be his.

5
A Brush with Shadowland

The transference of power was accepted easily and without reservation by the Quorum. Spanno laid his gelt over the territory proudly and solemnly, and attended to Quorum business with the ease of one born to such rank and leadership. Basically unaffected by his title, he remained, at least to his friends, the same old Spanno, the quality of the bond between them unchanged. By far the youngest Dom the Quorum had ever had, Spanno sometimes felt as if he had been thrust into a position of great responsibility too suddenly, and often missed the carefree times that he had always taken for granted. But he was a true Dom-cat at heart, and accepted the changes and challenges as his destiny.

As the darkfalls became progressively cooler, Solo would often sit in the Woodstack before daybright with the calico, listening raptly as the Dom talked about his experiences as a bard or gave his viewpoints on feral life. Their relationship deepened as Spanno contributed all he knew to Solo's education, and in the process redefined the usual limits of feline paternal involvement.

The Quorum settled comfortably into the normal feral routines again. Fieldside was still patrolled and the territorial borders still guarded, but generally only one of Spanno's group was out on watch at a time; the duties rotated among all the bards more than four circles of age. There had been no alarms or threat of danger in the territory, other than an occasional Tame-dog or Owner kit loose fieldside. Certainly there had been no sign of Tanner and his band. Spanno, as befitted his rank, made nightly rounds and reinforced his gelt where needed, usually with Ponder and Selvyn or Ditto at his side. The last few darkfalls, though, he had taken Kitty-Kitty with him, and the excursion seemed to take much longer when the prill went with the Dom. Solo noticed the disgruntled snickers from the rest of the group when the calico and Kitty-Kitty left together. No one snickered like that when Spanno left with Ponder.

A true friendship had developed between the grey and the soft-spoken, unassuming Ditto, who was now as much a part of the group as any of them. They complemented each other well; Ponder coarse and tough, Ditto almost suave and reserved. Generally it was difficult to find one without also seeing the other.

With Spanno spending so much time with Kitty-Kitty, and Ponder with his tailless new friend, Solo found himself more and more in the company of Selvyn. The big orange had been having frequent attacks of 'indigestion' lately, and was forced to sleep outward more often than inside. With six felines in close quarters, an unannounced 'attack' could drive them all outward. Selvyn accepted his handicap good-naturedly, and removed himself from society when he felt an attack coming on. Solo would go with him to the top of the Woodstack during his exiles; sometimes they would go fieldside to Solo's old den, where it was cool and airy enough for even the orange to feel comfortable. The kit was fond of Selvyn, though he didn't talk much. Selvyn carried himself with a kind of quiet humility, approaching shyness. His speed was legendary – no cat could climb a tree faster or cross the field in less time than he. Although Solo had not realized it before, Selvyn outranked Ponder in the Quorum. But Selvyn didn't assert his rank, and was perfectly content to let the grey play the more dominant role.

There had been several additions to the Quorum population recently, all Tame-cats that had been left behind when their Owners did not return from an Explore. Their story was usually the same – heartbreak and confusion at first, followed by bewilderment and gradual acceptance, and a return to feral ways. They would always wonder, however, as Kitty-Kitty did, what great misdeed had turned their Owners against them. One or two seemed to love their Owners, and would wait daybright after daybright for their return, though always in vain. Some of the Tame-cats were deformed, missing their foreclaws or cobblers, and would never be able to assert much rank within the feral society. One young bard named Minit, who was almost as young as Solo, still had one of the Owner bands around his neck. It was gradually getting tighter as he grew, and it would soon be impossible for Minit to swallow without difficulty.

Sometimes it took several circles for a Tame-cat to remember the feral language properly, but most eventually did well enough. Speaker was always near the newcomers, helping them make the often difficult transition from tame to feral. Tame-cats fought frequently, but ineffectually, and most often among themselves. They seemed to spat over inconsequential things, such as who got to sit on which spot, or who went to graille first. It was baffling, but Ditto explained that it was all a natural reaction to being locked inside an Owner Dwelling for long periods without freedom. He called it the worst kind of bondage, not knowing that you have no freedom. Living in such circumscribed surroundings, Speaker said, little things began to mean a great deal.

Occasionally a bard would leave the Quorum on a

big Explore and simply not return, his fate unknown. Because of this and the ever-present danger from speeding rauwulfen, the Quorum census remained about the same, roughly thirty ferals in all, including prills, though not counting kits.

Speaker came occasionally to the Woodstack; it was as if he were making himself available should someone need to talk to him. Solo was unsure to whom this availability was directed, but the sage always made it a point to speak to the kit before he left. Solo had wanted to have another long talk with Speaker about the Legends, but there was so much on his mind that he simply wasn't ready for a deep, philosophical discussion with the prophet.

Early one darkfall, after a large meal and a denied request to accompany Spanno on rounds, the kit sat with Selvyn on the Woodstack, pouting and bored. A bored cat is a potential disaster on four paws, and this was no exception. Spanno had taken Kitty-Kitty on grand rounds . . . again, and Ponder and Ditto were up to some mischief of their own, leaving the watch to Rivalle and Banda. Selvyn had overdone it at graille and had stayed behind, feeling bloated and decidedly unwell with his usual problem.

'I've got to go fieldside and find some grass,' Selvyn said as he flexed and moaned. 'My stomach is killing me. I don't know what Owners put all over their graille, but they ruined a perfectly good dead bird. Makes my eyes water and my nose itch! Their Dom Owner must have a gut made of greyrock.'

Solo preferred to think of the Keep as an enormous feeding area set aside specifically for the Quorum. He didn't understand how or why it existed, only that it did; and although he knew the Owners were involved, he hadn't figured out why they brought graille to the Keep – no Dominant Owner ever seemed to feed from it. A gigantic rauwulf did, however, come every so often to take away whatever was left in the Keep, but what happened to the donations after that was a mystery – a mystery that Solo was determined to solve one day, with Speaker's help.

Selvyn was preparing to go in search of his grass, and Solo quickly pulled away from his thoughts. 'Let me go with you, Selvyn! I don't want to stay here alone. You can teach me about the grass and which kinds are good to eat.' Solo knew that the Legends were very specific about grass eating, but no adult can resist the opportunity to pass on his vast wisdom to an eager young bard.

'Yes, I suppose I could teach you a few things. With my condition, I know a lot about grass, you know. We'll make it a little Explore.'

Instantly up and preening, the kit was out of the Woodstack well ahead of Selvyn.

'We'll go to the westfield,' the orange said. 'Lots of the best grass grows out there.' He added playfully, 'Come on, kit. Let's see you take the Wall this time!'

Leaping to the ledge with his usual flair, Selvyn waited as Solo prepared for his jump. The kit backed away six or seven cat-lengths, gathered in, and ran lightly toward the Great Fence. Just before reaching the base of the Wall, he made his leap, beautifully executed, though about three cat-lengths short of the ledge. He struck the wall with all fours, legs extended. For a brief moment he remained suspended, like a wall-walker, a blank look on his face. Then he crumpled and hit the greyrock. Attempt number twenty-four: unsuccessful. The kit eased through the Wall without further comment.

'Next time, kit, next time,' Selvyn consoled, remembering his own attempts at clearing the same high Wall.

They traveled westward, with Selvyn on full alert and Solo well within the orange's surround. As the kit snooped his way through the now familiar thickets, he noted Spanno's gelt here and there with a feeling of pride. Occasionally Selvyn stopped to check out a clump of grass with meticulous care, teaching Solo as he did. 'No, not this kind,' he would say. 'It's rough and sticky in the mouth and hard to swallow. But it might be good for thread worms.' They walked further into the field.

'Selvyn, over here! How's this?' Solo waited as Selvyn came over to inspect his find.

'Good work, kit. It's the right kind of grass, all right, but it's old. Look for young, tender shoots.'

The search continued, and in a few moments Selvyn found his medicine.

'This is it,' he announced with satisfaction. 'Young, tender, moist – just right.'

'What's this over here?' called the kit from about ten cat-lengths away. 'Look at its pretty colors!' he said, referring to the multicolored aura of the plant rather than the color of the plant itself. Selvyn raised his head and walked over for a closer inspection. He sniffed the weed analytically.

'It smells strange, but good. It's got more color around it than any other grass around here – that's a good sign, you know. I'll try a little and see what it's like.'

Wrapping his mouth around a large piece, he bit into it. The kit watched for the elder's reaction.

'It's not bad. Not bad at all. Something like this is bound to be good for what ails. Try some,' he said through a mouthful of the stuff.

'Uh, no. I don't think I want any right now – it has a funny rack, Selvyn. With all those colors around it, maybe you should get some of the regular kind?' The

Legends said some grasses could make a feral very sick.

'Nonsense,' Selvyn replied, still chewing. 'This is great. Better than usual, as a matter of fact. My stomach feels better already.'

A little worried, the kit watched as the orange ate the grass. Selvyn seemed unaffected, and Solo felt relieved.

'It's time to go, Solo,' said Selvyn when he'd finished. 'Spanno and Kitty-Kitty should be back by now, and you know how they worry over you.' Selvyn flexed and burped with satisfaction, then headed eastward toward the Woodstack, with Solo at his side.

Halfway across the field, Selvyn suddenly began to giggle out loud. Solo couldn't remember saying anything funny.

'What's so funny, Selvyn?' asked the kit, perplexed.

'What's so funny?' The orange broke out into raucous laughter. 'What's so funny!'

'Yeah, Sel. What's so funny?'

The big orange fell on his side, doubled over in convulsive giggles. Finally he stood up, shaking with laughter, and ran toward a young tree. He leapt up onto its side and hung there by his claws, still giggling.

'Hey, Solo. This is you, trying to jump the Great Fence!'

Selvyn was laughing so hard at his own joke that he was gasping for breath. But the kit couldn't see the humor.

'Come on, Sel. Let's go back.' He was genuinely concerned now. Selvyn climbing trees?

Jumping down and continuing to laugh, the orange began to run rings around the kit, who had started toward the Fence.

'I feel like a kit again! Loosen up, Solo!' Selvyn was

having a wonderful time, but his defenses were completely down and the kit felt their vulnerability out in the open field. Solo began to trot toward the Wall, the orange still running wildly around him.

'You should have seen your face when the Giant Rat jumped out of the rocks!' Selvyn could hardly talk between paroxysms of laughter. 'I thought he had you there, but you put up a tough fight!'

As they neared the Woodstack, the other four heard the ruckus and lined up on the ledge, gaping in disbelief as Selvyn and Solo approached.

'Hi, guys!' called the orange lightly. 'Oh, excuse me! And hi, prill, too!' He rolled onto his side again, still giggling.

'What in droud has happened to Sel?' demanded Spanno, finding it difficult not to become infected with the hysteria himself.

'Nothing's wrong, your Domship,' said Selvyn, trying to straighten himself. 'I feel great!'

'Maybe he's sick?' offered Kitty-Kitty, looking a little worried.

'He ate some funny grass out in the field, and he's been acting like this ever since,' said the kit, finally getting a word in.

'Fey-weed?' the calico asked himself aloud. 'If it's fey-weed, he'll be getting – '

'Droud, am I hungry!' interrupted Selvyn. 'I'm going to the Keep!' Seconds later he was in motion, sailing over the Wall toward the Keep and graille.

By now, most of the Quorum had gathered, snickering among themselves.

'I didn't eat any,' said Solo in a small voice, but no one seemed interested.

'Someone had better go with him,' sighed Spanno, smiling. 'In his condition, if he were attacked, he'd probably roll over and laugh. Ponder, stay with him.'

'I don't want to listen to that fegin nitwit,' Ponder grumped. 'Droud, he deserves to have the silt slapped out of him!' But he was already walking toward the Keep as he grumbled.

'Where exactly is this grass he ate, Solo?' Spanno asked. 'We should know exactly where it is . . . just so no one else eats it accidentally.'

'It's due west, just past the central thickets . . . I'll show you.'

'No, Solo. You and Kitty-Kitty stay here. We bards will find and mark it.' The calico sounded a little too nonchalant.

'Come on, kit,' said Kitty-Kitty with exasperation. 'Let them go play bard-cat. We'll stay here and wait for Selvyn and Ponder.'

The Dom and his entourage disappeared into the brush. Solo slipped through the Wall to greyrock-side, where the prill was waiting.

'Selvyn was kind of cute, don't you think?' she asked.

'He was laughing at everything – and at nothing!' Solo was disappointed in the orange – kits like to depend totally on their elders. Kitty-Kitty understood his feelings.

'Don't be too hard on him,' the prill said gently. 'Even grown bards need to play sometimes. Come and sit with me inside. We haven't talked for a long time.'

They had barely taken their places inside the Woodstack when Kitty-Kitty tensed, her surround on full alert. A cat was nearing the Woodstack from the south. The approach was bold and familiar, however, and both Solo and Kitty-Kitty relaxed; it must be a Quorum feral. Before the prill could stop him, Solo bounded outward.

'Solo! No!' called Kitty-Kitty, knowing better than to go out without being sure of who was there. But the kit had already darted through an opening, running directly into Bryndle.

One of his eyes was swollen completely shut, and his other eye was glazed and wild, empty of any trace of the old Dom Bryndle. The fegin bard was breathing through his mouth rapidly, and he held his head very low. He looked at Solo with black hatred, and suddenly the kit knew that Bryndle had come for his revenge.

Solo opened his mouth to call out, but not much more than a thin squeak escaped from his throat before Bryndle lunged forward and knocked him over sideways onto the greyrock. The kit tried to right himself, but already the black was on top of him, pinning him to the ground. Unable to even turn his head, Solo didn't hear Kitty-Kitty's blood-chilling scream from behind, but Bryndle heard it and in response he quickly snatched up the kit in his teeth. Like a bard possessed, he began to shake the kit violently, snapping the small head back and forth until at last Solo hung limp and unresisting. Again Kitty-Kitty cried out for help, and then sprang onto Bryndle's back, trying to use all her weight to knock the bard off balance. Sinking her teeth into his head and digging in with her claws, she tried to hurt Bryndle enough to make him loosen his hold on Solo. But the black only braced down and growled against her attack as he continued to shake the young kit.

Ponder and Selvyn heard the horrified call, and instantly the two were on the greyrock racing toward the Woodstack. As they approached, they could see Kitty-Kitty on top of the black bard, but the old Dom seemed unaffected by the prill's frantic attack. Bryndle growled a senseless, muffled fugue, his eye fegin with madness. Solo hung from his mouth, bloodstained and misshapen.

Deep into the field, Spanno and the others too heard

Kitty-Kitty's call. The calico remained motionless for an instant as a hollow, icy dread squeezed at the pit of his stomach. Suddenly he leapt out, racing toward the Great Fence with Ditto at his side.

Without hesitation, Ponder broadsided Bryndle with his head and shoulder at a full run. Kitty-Kitty barely managed to leap clear as the two bards collided with a loud thud and a whoosh of expelled breath. Ponder's momentum sent them both skidding across the ground and into the side of the Woodstack. Knocked from Bryndle's grasp, Solo's limp form rolled several cat-lengths away, still and motionless. Selvyn leapt forward and stood guard protectively over Solo as Ponder attacked Bryndle, tearing into the black with a frightening fury. Still dazed from the flying tackle, Bryndle made only feeble and ineffectual attempts to defend himself. With a lethal grip on the left side of the black's throat, Ponder slashed again and again with his razor-sharp hind claws, drawing blood with every cut, but Bryndle did not cry out in pain or challenge. In only a few moments it was Bryndle who hung limp and passive. With a final powerful jerk of his head, Ponder snapped the black's neck and dropped him.

Trembling visibly, Ponder stood over the dark form on the greyrock, prepared to attack again. But it was obvious that Bryndle would fight no more.

All eyes turned to Solo, who lay on his side, spine curled inward, his neck hyperextended and one leg tucked under his body in an awkward position. Blood colored the kit's blond fur in several places. Looking for some movement or sign of life, they watched the kit with a heavy sense of dread.

Spanno and Ditto leapt to the ledge together and then hesitated, frozen with shock as they took in the scene before them. Ponder stood over Bryndle's body, shaking with rage, while Kitty-Kitty and Selvyn paced helplessly beside Solo. It was obvious what had happened.

'Is he alive?' cried Spanno, quickly jumping to the greyrock with Ditto beside him.

They all gathered closely around the kit, watching him intently, not knowing what to do or how to help. Spanno's eyes were wide and panic-stricken, but he could find no words.

'He's alive!' Ditto said softly, astonishment telling in his voice. 'He's breathing!'

But they knew it was not necessarily good news when an injured feline still lived; in the feral world, serious injury usually meant slow death.

With the others in close attendance, Kitty-Kitty very gently sniffed and touched the kit's body, carefully checking the obvious injuries: possible broken neck, bleeding gashes to the left shoulder, puncture wounds on the left side, nosebleed. His sides still rose and fell as he breathed, however shallowly, and his eyes were closed. Felines, they knew, always die with their eyes open.

Finally, Kitty-Kitty backed away, and Spanno took her place, licking gently at Solo's ears.

'I couldn't help him!' Kitty-Kitty sobbed, breaking down as she lay on the greyrock.

'You did all you could have, Kitty-Kitty,' Ditto said in a whisper. 'I know you did.'

'We should have been with you,' Spanno said quickly, his voice tight with fear.

'It's my fault! We would have all been here if I hadn't gotten silt-faced on fey-weed!' Selvyn's eyes mirrored his self-loathing and despair. 'It's all my fault.'

'It's no one's fault, and now's not the time to think of blame,' said Spanno. 'We've got to get this kit inside and under cover, and send for Speaker. We'll have to be very careful – we don't know where he may be broken inside.'

Ponder turned back to Bryndle, hissing, 'I want to kill him again!'

'Ponder, it's over,' Ditto said. 'We need your help with Solo.' Ditto knew they didn't really need help, but wanted to get Ponder's mind off Bryndle and get him away from the body.

Searching for safe areas to grip the wounded kit, they carefully pulled and dragged him, inch by inch, back toward the Woodstack and then through its largest entrance. Solo made no sound or movement throughout the lengthy process. The slow trickle of blood from his nose left a trail of red behind him.

'Ditto, find Speaker and bring him here, fast,' ordered Spanno without looking up.

Ditto turned and was outward without a word. Kitty-Kitty stayed closely beside Solo, talking soothingly into his ears.

'You'll be all right, little one. I'll take good care of you. You'll be as good as new in no time,' she sing-songed over and over. 'Speaker's coming, and you'll be just fine.'

Spanno paced and brooded. The sense of helplessness filled his chest and choked his heart. Selvyn and Ponder sat off to the side, silently pleading for Speaker to hurry.

'Why did he do it?' Spanno asked of no one. 'Why did he hurt Solo? He should have come after me!' But they all knew that Bryndle had hurt the calico much more by attacking Solo than he could have in a simple fight.

Presently the sounds of feline claws clicking rapidly on the greyrock brought Spanno to a standstill and Selvyn to his paws. Speaker entered without formalities and went directly to Solo, the concern obvious in his uncharacteristic haste. Ditto followed closely behind, out of breath, an anxious question in his eyes.

'Is he . . . ?' Ditto asked, not able to finish.

'He still has breath,' answered Kitty-Kitty as she stepped back to give Speaker room.

'Bryndle did this,' said the calico, knowing that Ditto had surely told Speaker the details.

'Yes,' said the prophet as he, too, sniffed and inspected the little kit, assessing his injuries.

For a long time the white bard bent over Solo in silence and concentration. The others huddled closely, restless for Speaker's diagnosis. Finally Ponder could stand it no longer.

'Well? Tell us!' blurted the grey, waiting for the prophet's response. 'Will he live, Speaker?'

'It's bad. Very bad. I can't tell if he's hurt inside or not, but I don't think he'll die from what I see here. His neck is not broken.'

Sighs of relief filled the inner Woodstack. That's what they had been waiting to hear.

'He'll need care,' Speaker continued hastily. 'And time. I can't say how long.'

'We'll given him care,' whispered Kitty-Kitty, with Spanno beside her. 'Oh, we'll give him care!'

Selvyn's head was down, his face covered with his paws. Ponder tried to control his trembling. Ditto, too, was down, and very quiet.

'You killed Bryndle?' asked Speaker, looking evenly at the grey.

'I killed him,' answered Ponder in a strong voice, meeting Speaker's gaze with a defiant look.

Speaker hesitated. 'You did what you had to do,' he said, looking again at the kit. There was an expression of concern and hurt in his face, and no one was sure whether that concern was for Solo or for Bryndle. 'Let's talk outside.'

The bards followed Speaker outward; Kitty-Kitty remained with Solo, thirping softly and sharing her warmth. She was a mother again, and her baby needed her.

The Quorum had gathered around the Woodstack, waiting for word of the kit's condition.

'Is he all right?' asked Banda, speaking for everyone. 'He's not . . . gone, is he?'

'I think if he lives through this daybright, he'll not see Shadowland,' Speaker told them all. 'But the damage is great.'

Whispers rippled through the assembly. The same question was on everyone's mind. 'Why did Bryndle do it?'

'Why Solo?' asked Mondy, a young prill. 'We owe him so much! First the traps, then the North invasion . . .'

'What about the North invasion?' asked Dom Spanno and Ponder in a single voice.

'I meant about Solo giving us the idea to fight with the bards – '

'*Solo* gave you the idea?' Spanno sounded surprised, and it was obvious that he hadn't known. In fact, the kit had mentioned it to no one, and the prills had spoken of it only within their own group, assuming it was general knowledge.

'Droud,' muttered Ponder. 'What kind of a kit is Solo, anyway?' Spanno said nothing.

Speaker broke the silence that followed. 'A once-great warrior died badly here this darkfall. But it is important for us to remember this: the bard who lies empty on the greyrock is not the Bryndle that led us and governed our territory for so long. I don't know what stole his reason and took his mind, but it made him empty and blind. This was an act of vengeance directed toward an innocent, and it is an example of the very thing that Bryndle hated and feared most: felines leaning away from the Legends and acting with forethought ... and selfishness. I think the changes pulled him apart.'

The Quorum was reflective and respectful. This time Speaker's words really were a eulogy.

Some of the lesser bards had dragged Bryndle's body farther down the greyrock to the south and away from the Woodstack. It would soon be gone – an Owner would find it and carry it away. Owners didn't like such things cluttering up their Dwelling environment, the ferals knew from past experience. Dom Spanno and his council went back inside to check on Solo, while Speaker kept his vigil on the ledge overhead.

'Go to your dens,' the Old One instructed. 'There's nothing to be done here.' And reluctantly the Quorum members left, speaking together in whispers, as if not to waken the kit that slept inside.

There was no change in Solo's condition, though he still breathed. Ditto volunteered to take the watch, and Ponder went with him, gently nuzzling Solo's neck before he left.

Ponder wanted to run, hard and fast and far. Run he did, as if chased by Shadowland itself, until he finally fell, out of breath and spent, in the weeds. He remained there alone for a long while as Ditto kept his distance and let the grey vent his grief in private, which was his way.

During the next two darkfalls, Solo remained asleep and motionless, with Kitty-Kitty supervising every aspect of his care. Water was brought in the only way they knew, one mouthful at a time, and dribbled between the kit's parted lips. Ponder himself scratched loose earth over what silt and siltaa Solo made, and Kitty-Kitty swept it outward with her own paws. The least ear-twitch or kit-whine from Solo brought them all instantly to their feet with anticipation, but still he slept. Spanno would sit with the kit for hours, talking of the times they would have together, making promises, and praying for an opportunity to keep them. Ponder grew more sullen and gruff, and Selvyn, too, withdrew into himself, consumed with guilt. With his calm coolheadedness, it was Ditto who really held them together, encouraging Spanno to attend to Quorum affairs, forcing Ponder to run off his frustrations fieldside, and trying to reason with the despairing Selvyn. Speaker was always near, frequently coming in to check on Solo and looking for signs of progress. But he always declined the invitation to stay.

Solo felt trapped inside a dream, a long dream from which he could not waken. Was this Shadowland? Were his eyes open or closed? He couldn't tell. Had he eaten Selvyn's funny grass too? Sometimes he felt dissociated from his body and seemed to see things as if from high overhead; this was the only time the pain was completely gone. Strange voices ran together in thick, gurgling noises. Solo wanted to wake up so badly, for always the narrow green eyes of a giant black cat chased him through his dreams, and Solo knew that if he were finally caught, he would find Shadowland waiting.

Solo could feel Kitty-Kitty's soft tongue licking and soothing the fire in his wounds, and felt the warmth of her body close to his. No, not Kitty-Kitty – it was his mother, returned to him at last. The others must be his sister-kits, lost for so long . . .

'Listen!' Kitty-Kitty cried. Spanno and Selvyn rushed to her side. Solo was purring, but so softly that it was impossible to identify what kind of purr it was.

'Get Speaker!' snapped the calico, leaning close to Solo.

Kitty-Kitty raced outward to call the sage, returning almost instantly. Speaker entered and went quickly to the kit, listening for the faint sound.

'What does it mean?' demanded Spanno, eyes wild with uncertainty.

Selvyn was rocking from paw to paw and shaking his head, driven almost to his limit.

'Is it good, Speaker?' asked the prill, holding her breath for the answer.

'It is good,' the prophet said at last, not turning from the kit.

Collapsing with relief, Kitty-Kitty buried her face in the way of prills. Spanno and Selvyn stood trembling, trying to maintain their composure.

Someone had evidently sent for Ponder and Ditto. They dashed into the Woodstack and braked in a cloud of dust.

'He's purring and Speaker says it's good!' Selvyn blurted in answer to their questioning eyes.

Word was passed to those waiting outward, to an immediate cheer of relief and gratitude. Solo would be back with them.

'The kit will live – to lead us,' said Speaker. But the last part of his statement was lost in the elation of the others.

'I knew the little twit would make it!' said Ponder. 'He'd live just to torture me!' The grey was obviously trying to hide the tenderness he felt for the kit.

'Well, someone has to do it,' Selvyn laughed. 'It's a dirty job, but – '

'I'm hungry,' said a parched, cracked voice.

There was numbed silence as all eyes turned back to Solo. His head was slightly raised, his eyes still clouded and matted with sleep.

'I'll go!' echoed five voices simultaneously in the confusion.

'I'll go,' repeated Selvyn, alone, as he quickly left the Woodstack and headed for the Keep, hoping to find some tender morsel fit for a weakened kit. He needed to do this thing.

The others rushed toward Solo, and found themselves facing a very determined-looking Kitty-Kitty, barring their way.

'Get back,' she hissed. 'This kit is still too sick to have you clumsy bards swarming all over him!' No one argued.

When Selvyn returned, Solo ate for the first time in over two darkfalls. But it was two more before he took his first shaky steps outward. Ponder accused him of dragging out his recovery deliberately; Kitty-Kitty told him he was going too fast. The best tidbits of graille were brought to the Woodstack by various Quorum members, more than an army of healthy kits could have handled.

Solo never asked about Bryndle or 'that darkfall,' and no one was sure whether or not he remembered, but the bond between Ponder the Grey and Solo the Small was obvious, if unspoken.

'I love you,' whispered Solo early one daybright as they all lay circled and ready for sleep. But none of them knew exactly to whom the words of affection were directed.

6
The Dwelling

In the darkfalls that followed, Solo recovered and quickly regained his strength. He was filling out and growing taller, looking and feeling less like a kit and more like a true feral bard. Soon the giant night-star would be completely round again for the fifth time since his birth, and at five circles he had nearly half his adult size and weight.

Although he had been at a disadvantage, having lost his mother at such a young age, in reality Solo had acquired five 'mothers,' each seeing to his feral education from his or her own unique perspective. Spanno, of course, was Solo's chief role model, and the elder was well aware of how much influence he exerted by example alone. From him Solo learned about fairness and 'gentle' strength, and that real class meant never looking down on another, regardless of rank. Ponder taught the kit the more practical aspects of feral life – how to fight, how to bluff, and that being brave didn't mean simply 'not being afraid.' Selvyn helped Solo learn the secrets of nature itself, and as he walked with the orange, the kit learned to feel the life in the trees and hear the silent melodies of the world around him.

Humility was a natural gift to Solo, but Ditto showed him a different kind of humble courage. A walking monument to nature's inequalities, the tailless bard exuded an inner pride based on an acceptance of himself not grounded in his acceptance by others. Kitty-Kitty, needless to say, became the mother he had lost. She fretted and worried over Solo, and taught the kit about selfless caring and belonging together. The white prill insisted on absolute cleanliness (except for Ponder, who had successfully resisted) and fastidiously kept coats. There were ear inspections and lectures about felines being the cleanest of all species. Kitty-Kitty said that dirt was for dogs.

All in all, his education was rounded and complete. With his Quorum family, he grew to be strong, courageous, humble, and tidy, and well-versed in every aspect of feral life.

Although Solo's life was full and happy, and he was indulged by his elders and respected by the Quorum, he was plagued by the restless curiosity so indigenous to youth. Each new darkfall was a blank place to be filled with wonderful adventures and discoveries. One darkfall in particular was to become one of his more memorable kithood experiences, when Solo persuaded Spanno to take him within the borders of the Dwelling itself, to look around a little and spy on the Owners.

'We won't mention this to Kitty-Kitty,' said Spanno, trying to sound casual. 'There's no reason to worry her over nothing.'

'Right,' agreed Solo quickly. 'We'll just keep this between us.' He enjoyed sharing a secret with the calico.

'I was just about your age when I first explored the Dwelling. Ponder and I used to go over there and pick fights with the Tame-cats. But of course, we were younger then.'

Solo was thoughtful as they crossed through the Wall and looked at the Owner lights sparkling around the Dwelling. 'I don't see any Tame-cats outward these days. The Owners must be keeping them inside . . . I'd hate to be trapped in there.'

'They like it,' Spanno said. 'And the ones that do get out are too afraid of us to even talk.'

'Can we go now, Spanno?' Solo was up on all fours and ready to explore.

'Okay, but remember what I told you – at the first sign of danger, run back to fieldside as fast as you can. If you see an Owner, though, just keep still where you are – they probably won't even notice you. They usually don't.' They both knew the chance of actually encountering one of the great beings was slight; very few Owners were ever seen outward this far into the darkfall. That was just as well for the ferals, who weren't interested in seeing them at all.

The two cats crossed the greyrock in exaggerated full-out alert. Spanno saw the excursion as a teaching opportunity, while Solo was determined to show the calico how crafty and mature he'd already become. The kit was both anxious and excited – the Owner Dwelling was not officially part of the territory and technically constituted an Explore.

Pausing under one of the thin, squat bushes that lined the Dwelling's outer edge, Solo crouched beside the Dom and listened to the muffled sounds that filtered through the great walls. There was the familiar assortment of sporadic, garbled noises and something that Solo assumed must be the Owner form of music. At times it was almost like a Calling fugue, beautifully pure and unbroken, but now it was just rattling and complicated, with too many sounds put together at once and a rhythm that sounded like heavy running. As he listened, the harsh voice of an Owner itself pierced the wall not far from where he stood, and Solo could feel that it was angered.

Undaunted, Spanno nudged the kit back to the business at hand. 'Follow me, kit, and I'll show you something that you won't believe.'

'What is it, Spanno?' Solo's curiosity was tempered with just a touch of trepidation.

'You'll see.' The calico smiled. 'Brace yourself.'

They crept through a brightly lit canopied walkway, moving quickly to be out of the light, and emerged into a large uncovered open space that was completely surrounded by Owner dens. Most of the ground had been turned into greyrock, with very little grass or even dirt left showing. The ferals supposed that Owners didn't like grass and that's why they covered up so much of it with greyrock.

Solo was overwhelmed by the immensity of it all, but Spanno, who did not want to linger there, urged the kit southward across the clearing and through another walkway. Following very closely behind the calico, Solo found himself in a second clearing, except that this one was larger and what he saw near its center nearly took his breath away.

'What in droud is that?' gasped the kit, staring in disbelief.

Spanno smiled and looked pleased with himself. 'Go and take a look. It won't hurt you. Just be careful.'

Solo took a few cautious steps forward. On the other side of a see-through fence was the biggest water puddle he had ever seen. Kitty-Kitty had told him that Owners collected water, but she hadn't told him about this! It was at least twenty cat-lengths wide, and longer still, and appeared to be very, very deep. The water had a sharp, unpleasant rack, but it was incredibly beautiful, with multicolored lights sparkling and reflecting across its surface.

'What's the puddle for, Spanno?' Solo whispered, unable to take his eyes from the greenish water.

'The Owners play in it. Even their kits. I've never actually seen them do it, but some of the Tame-cats swear to it. Don't try to drink any, though. It tastes just as bad as it smells.'

Solo was utterly fascinated. The Legends told of such things – unimaginable places where there was no ground at all, only water. They were called oceans and were inhabited by strange legless creatures that could be eaten. 'Let's go closer,' said the kit, not wanting to go on alone. 'Does anything live in there?'

'I've never see anything in it, other than bugs. They can walk on it. Abalon says Owners can walk on water with their hands, but I don't believe it. Ditto says they just lie on it.'

With Spanno comfortably at his side, Solo shimmied over the little fence and slowly neared the water, stopping a respectful distance from the edge. 'You can see all the way down to the bottom,' he observed. 'And there's nothing down there.'

Frumped with fascination, the kit eased even further toward the water's edge. As he watched, he began to relax, mesmerized by the random movement and the shimmering lights on its unstable surface. Hesitantly extending a forepaw, Solo gingerly reached out to the water. Perhaps it *was* special water and it *was* possible to walk on it. As soon as he felt the cool wetness on his footpad, he jerked back. No, it was the regular kind. Mindful of Spanno's warning about the taste, he resisted the urge to lick his damp paw and settled for a few quick shakes.

'It's really something, isn't it?' Spanno said, mostly to himself. A veteran of many previous expeditions, he was still amazed by it. 'Come on, kit. There's something else I want you to see.'

Solo preferred to stay at the puddle and finish his investigation, but he didn't want to be there alone. Reluctantly he followed the calico around the water and across the artificial ground to the east. Back in full stealth, they climbed over the short fence and went across the clearing toward the Dwelling wall. About fifteen cat-lengths from the Owner structure, Spanno slowed into a hunting gait, signaling for Solo to follow suit. They crept toward a row of wooden enclosures that were attached to the Dwelling. In some places the enclosures didn't come all the way to the ground and there was enough room beneath them to crawl through. Spanno stopped and sniffed at several places in turn, as if he were looking for something in particular.

'What are we doing?' asked the kit, still tight at Spanno's side.

'Hunting,' Spanno answered mysteriously, as he inspected the next structure.

Unceremoniously Spanno bellied under one of the fencelike walls. Solo laid his ears down and crawled in behind the calico, not quite sure what they were doing. They had entered a walled-in area about the size of the Keep, though not as tall. There was the scent of cat-rack everywhere – a Tame-cat must live there. Many strange Owner objects lay strewn about within the confines, but Spanno ignored them and went directly to the main wall of the Dwelling. Suddenly the kit picked up another rack, and its sweet flavor made his mouth water. Joining the calico, he sniffed at a round, shallow container that sat on the greyrock close to the wall. Solo recognized the contents instantly – it was thraille! Not the warm, fresh thraille of his mother, but thraille nonetheless. Could this be Owner thraille? No, it was overpoweringly animal. The kit took a small taste while Spanno watched with amusement. It really *was* thraille!

They couldn't both get their faces in the container at the same time, so they took turns and finally licked the little dish completely dry. Solo was glad that he wasn't sharing with Ponder – the grey's idea of equal portions was computed by body weight.

'Where does this come from?' asked the kit, wiping at his whiskers with a forepaw and wishing for more.

'It probably belongs to some Tame-cat who couldn't eat it all,' answered Spanno, not quite understanding Solo's question. 'Come on, we should be able to find more in the other enclosures.'

They crawled back out into the clearing and started southward, but before they had gone five cat-lengths the unmistakable sound of adult Owner footsteps froze them in their tracks. It was coming from the west directly toward them with loud, deliberate strides. The two ferals crouched in full alert, feeling the ground echoes beneath their footpads. They waited in silence for the steps to turn or fade. A feral could easily outrun any Owner, they knew, but it was best to avoid being seen whenever possible. Solo wasn't really afraid, for Owners often came and went around the Keep or rauwulfen, and he was used to seeing them from a distance.

'If it spots us, just do what I do,' whispered the calico, tense and ready beside the kit.

Solo nodded his answer, for the Owner was already coming out through the south-most walkway. Surely it would disappear into one of the many doors of the Dwelling and they could continue their mission. But the Owner didn't turn and was now so close that Solo could tell that it was a prill.

The Owner crossed the greyrock and walked straight toward the cats. With their bright coats, they would soon be spotted and have to make a run for it through the clearing. The Owner stopped short not fifteen cat-lengths away and looked directly into the dark-widened eyes of the ferals. Solo could feel the eye contact, and it made him vaguely uncomfortable, as if

125

the Owner 'knew' him. Bending down almost cat-fashion, the great being began a soft, high-pitched call and held out one of its hairless paws in a beckoning manner. Solo knew that it wanted to touch him.

Spanno had gathered down and Solo automatically did the same. When Spanno hissed 'Now!' they leapt out and ran wide to the surprised Owner's left, retracing their path out of the Dwelling complex at a full, bounding run.

Several minutes later, feeling brave and adventurous, they crossed the greyrock, only to stop abruptly at the base of the Great Fence. Kitty-Kitty was perched on the ledge, looking down at them with a stern, disapproving expression. Grinning guiltily, Spanno leapt up beside her; Solo tried to make himself invisible on the ground below.

'Hi, Kitty-Kitty,' the calico said innocently as he settled beside her and tried to slow his breathing.

'Don't "hit" me! I know where you two have been. It can be dangerous in there – '

Spanno laughed. 'We're all right. See? Every hair in place.'

Kitty-Kitty paused and leaned down to inspect the kit. 'That place can be like . . . like a kind of trap. You should stay away from it. I know – I lived there.'

'You shouldn't worry about us so much,' said Solo, trying to sound mature. 'We're feral; we can take care of ourselves.'

Harrumphing, Kitty-Kitty made it obvious that the subject was not open to further discussion. She and Spanno leapt to fieldside, but Solo hesitated before crossing through the Wall and turned toward the Dwelling. He would have gone back if he'd been alone, and a little bigger.

* * *

Nothing else very exciting happened that darkfall, and before the night gave in to the hazy beginnings of daybright, everyone was assembled at the Woodstack and languidly preparing for sleep. Kitty-Kitty was absorbed in a major preening, trying to get every last knot and bur out of her field-matted tail. The others watched absentmindedly, lost within their own thoughts, and unconsciously began licking and smoothing their own coats. Fur licking, like yawning, is incredibly infectious, and even in a large group, if one feline begins to preen, within a few moments every cat within sight range will be concentrated on his personal hygiene.

It was not yet daybright when Murdok brought the news that another Quorum kit had been found dead at the southern limits of the territory, evidently hit by a speeding rauwulf. The kit was Pensey's; only a few darkfalls ago another of her young kits had been killed in the same way. Murdok said that Pensey was deeply fey and couldn't make thraille for the single kit she had left in her nest. Kitty-Kitty quickly left the Woodstack and went to the central hedges to try to console her friend.

Ponder was already grumpy and upset. A Tame-dog had siltaa'd over his favorite side of the Woodstack. In addition, his ear-grunge was bothering him, and earlier he'd fallen asleep under a rauwulf that had dripped a black, sticky substance all over his fur. Even Ditto had long since given up trying to improve the grey's disposition.

Ponder clawed at an ear with a hindpaw. 'I'm going to the Keep,' he announced, flexing and shaking his head till his ears slapped against his skull. The grey slouched his way outward, making it quite clear that he didn't want company.

'The graille will do him good,' observed Ditto. 'He'll

over-eat and be miserable, and drop off to sleep somewhere.'

A few minutes later, an enraged, fegin-sounding feline call echoed out over the greyrock and silenced them all. It was the unmistakable sound of a cat in pain.

'Ponder!' the four exclaimed in a single voice.

Spanno, Selvyn, Ditto, and Solo raced out of the Woodstack and ran northward toward the sound of Ponder's voice. But the grey was nowhere to be seen. As they came closer to the Keep, they felt Ponder's bristling surround, and realized that he was inside.

Spanno hesitated. 'Ponder. Are you all right?'

'Get me out of here,' Ponder barked from inside the hollow structure.

'Look!' cried Solo, and everyone followed his eyes to the topmost corner of the Keep. A scraggly tuft of grey was sticking through a slender crack where two sides of the Keep came together. It was the tip of Ponder's tail.

Exchanging apprehensive glances, the elder bards leapt up to the thin ledge and looked down into the darkness as Solo climbed through the lower doorway. Ponder was hanging upside down by his tail, his forepaws braced against the inner Keep wall, his face twisted with pain and not a little embarrassment.

'Don't just stand there,' hissed the grey. '*Do* something!'

Spanno jumped down into the Keep's interior beside Solo. 'How did you get your stupid tail caught in a crack?'

'It wasn't easy,' growled Ponder. 'And do I look like I want to talk about it right now? I'm in pain!'

The Keep was less than half-full and Ponder was unable to reach the donations with his forepaws to take some of the weight off his sensitive tail. He couldn't go up because the walls were too slick for a decent toehold, and he couldn't go down with his tail painfully and tightly wedged into the crack above.

'Droud,' muttered Selvyn. 'Let me see if I can pull it out. Hold on – this will probably hurt a little.'

'I don't care what you have to do. Just get me out of here before anyone else sees!'

Ditto backed away to give Selvyn room, and Spanno watched with Solo from below. Gripping Ponder's tail fur with his teeth, the orange pulled with all his might, but without success. The grey was heavy and most of his weight was supported by the end portion of his thick tail.

'This isn't going to work,' said Selvyn at last. 'Not unless we can get some of the weight off.'

'Two or three darkfalls without graille ought to do it . . .' Ditto giggled, but was cut off by Ponder's low growl. Ditto straightened his face and looked down at Solo. 'Can you think of a way to get his tail out, kit? I think we're in trouble here.'

Solo began to investigate Ponder's situation. After a few moments he brightened. 'Spanno, try standing under Ponder and let him put his paws on your back. That will support some of the weight, and Selvyn might be able to pull his tail out of the crack.'

'It might work, Solo!' said Ditto, impressed. He was glad that Ponder wasn't going to stand on *his* back.

'Just *do* it,' whined Ponder.

Spanno picked his way through the donations to position himself directly under the grey.

'Oh, no,' said Selvyn from above. 'Here comes the rest of the Quorum.'

Several cats were nearing the Keep, having sensed the activity. Selvyn, Ditto, and Solo sympathized with Ponder's mortifying predicament. A feral is entitled to his pride.

'Hurry up!' groaned Ponder. 'Silt! Don't let them see me like this!' The grey had his reputation to uphold.

Spanno balanced on the Keep donations and Ponder gingerly put his forepaws on the calico's shoulders. But before the rest of the plan could be put into operation, the Quorum ferals who were gathering outward hesitated and then bolted for fieldside or under rauwulfen. After a moment's confusion, everyone understood their hasty departure; an Owner was approaching from the north, and in its hands was a large brown container. It was coming to make a donation.

'It's an Owner!' said Solo, and they all froze with indecision. Should they run for cover and just leave poor Ponder hanging there, or should they stay out in the open with the incapacitated friend? Spanno made the decision.

'Ponder,' he whispered hurriedly, 'just stay quiet and still and I don't think it will see you. If it does, we'll rush it from fieldside.' The calico looked up at the others. 'Let's go!'

Selvyn and Ditto leapt to the greyrock and cleared the Great Fence, while Spanno and Solo scrabbled out and through the Wall behind them.

Ponder held his breath and pulled his surround in tight. He was in agony, and the base of his tail felt like it was on fire, but he remained motionless and silent, hoping the Owner wouldn't notice the bit of cat-tail sticking out over the ledge. The Owner deposited its donation and turned back to the north, apparently oblivious of the feline hanging inside the Keep. When the Owner was a safe distance away, Spanno and the others returned and hastily resumed their positions.

'Ponder?' Selvyn called. 'You okay?'

Ponder growled a string of cat-obscenities, and there was true rage in his aura. The calico jumped inside,

130

landing below the grey, and immediately understood Ponder's fury. The Owner's donation had fallen on the overturned feral, decorating the frumpy coat with strings of white, slippery dead wormlike things that hung from the grey's ears like dirty winter icicles. Solo wanted to laugh, but instinct told him this wouldn't be the proper time.

'Get me out of here!' spat the grey through clenched teeth.

Spanno hid his smile and climbed onto the donations under Ponder, trying to place his paws on fairly stable areas that wouldn't give way under the combined weight of two ferals. Ponder carefully braced his forepaws on Spanno's back, at last relieving a little of the pain in his tail. When the calico cried 'Now!' Selvyn and Ditto each grabbed a mouthful of fur and pulled upward. With a final, all-out heave, the two bards jerked the grey's tail free and Ponder crumpled heavily onto Spanno and Solo within the Keep. Selvyn lost his balance and tumbled inside, bringing Ditto down with him, and there was a momentary panic as five cats tried to untangle and right themselves among the soft mounds of donations.

Ponder wasted no time in getting clear of the Keep. He leapt out and stood bristling on the greyrock, trying to collect himself.

'How's your tail?' Solo ventured. 'It's not . . . damaged, is it?'

Ponder glanced around the area to check for witnesses, but said nothing.

'You okay, Pon?' asked Ditto, trying to find something acceptably neutral to say. Ponder grunted in Ditto's direction and walked toward the Fence. He looked awful. There were Owner donations all over him, not to mention the black sludge from the rauwulf, and his tail was badly kinked and tucked protectively under his belly. He went over the Wall and disappeared fieldside, presumably to care for his wound in private.

'I knew there was some advantage to not having a tail.' Ditto smiled as he headed back to the Woodstack with Spanno, Selvyn, and Solo.

The others, too, were smiling, but as much as they might laugh about the incident among themselves, not one of them would ever mention it again to Ponder the Grey.

7

A Time for Love

Summer was behind them and the darkfalls became progressively colder as the season of winter approached. No longer did the ferals have to suffer through water-down – though there was an occasional and much more acceptable whitefall, soft patches of white fell gently from the sky and covered the greyrock and field. It caused water drops to appear on their warm fur, but whitefall was easily shaken off and didn't soak through the way water-down did. Solo occasionally sat in the Woodstack with the calico or one of the others and watched the tiny white flakes float down and fill in the rauwulfen tracks, and he would wonder at the origin and purpose of the strange, fascinating substance.

The coming of the first whitefall marked the beginning of the fourth and last season of the feral year, but more important to the bards, it meant that Calling time was near.

It was now two circles into winter. Solo eased out of the Woodstack, flexing his muscles as he checked the outward conditions with his surround. It was pleasantly cold but the sky was clear. There were several felines to the north in and around the Keep, with two or three more southward, all restless and excited. Calling explained that, though, and every bard over nine or ten circles was half-fey with passion. Solo, however, took pride in remaining above that sort of neurotic behavior. At eight circles, he had eighty-five percent of his adult size, but only about one percent of the interest needed for Calling.

His coat, still strawberry blond, had shortened some-what and lay smoothly in place now in the adult style. He carried several long scars on his left shoulder and leg that an older bard might have worn proudly, devising heroic tales about their origin to impress others. But to Solo the wounds brought back only ominous, shadowy memories. Solo was destined to be large and powerful, even among ferals, who are five to eight pounds heavier than their Tame-cat counterparts. But he was still known as the kit.

Spanno had gone fieldside on rounds, taking Kitty-Kitty with him for a 'talk,' although what they could possibly have left to talk about was beyond Solo – they had 'talked' every darkfall for an entire season. Ponder and Selvyn were nearly fegin lately as the sounds of Calling interrupted the silence and serenity of the territory. They, along with Ditto, were probably out courting prills, or trying to. Passion was in the air.

Solo headed for the Keep, as much for company as from hunger, and as he neared it he was surprised to feel the presence of Ponder and Ditto. Selvyn, he assumed, had gone out after Mondy, a smallish orange prill he had been stalking of late. At least it would be easy to recognize their kits, Solo thought, for Mondy was colored and marked exactly like Selvyn.

Leaping the tall south wall of the Keep – a recent accomplishment and a source of great satisfaction – the kit joined the elder two, who were picking halfheartedly through the donations.

'Hey, twerp. Finally decided to get up?' asked the grey without looking up.

'Hi, Pon. Hi, Ditto. Where's Selvyn?' answered Solo, rooting around for his own dinner.

'Fieldside with what's-her-name. You won't see him

for a while. The Orange Flash has finally fallen. Want some of this?' Ditto pointed with his nose to a shredded brown container of indeterminate contents.

'Thanks,' said Solo between mouthfuls of his own find. 'Seen Dom Spanno?'

'The Great Dom combineth his business with pleasure, as usual,' answered Ponder dryly. 'He and Kitty-Kitty went to check the west border.'

'West border? We don't have a west border.'

'Right, twit, but they're checking it anyway.' Ponder chuckled, pleased with himself.

Suddenly they heard the low, melodic sound of a bard's Calling thrille, coming from southward beyond the Woodstack. Pricking their ears forward, Ponder and Ditto listened and tried to identify the bard. Soon another bard joined in the Call, adding his voice in an off-key whine-sing.

Without another word, Ditto and the grey cleared the Keep wall and hit the ground together. Solo followed rather than stay behind alone.

Twenty to thirty cat-lengths past the Woodstack, three bards were circling a crouching prill. She must be a Tame-cat or a gypsy, Solo thought – he didn't recognize her rack. The prill was lovely, with short black and white fur and beautifully tufted ears that reminded the kit of Shamalat in Speaker's story. Her raksha filled the air like the perfume of a thousand fieldside flowers, but it was offset by the sharp rack of fear and confusion. Again the bard's thrille resounded into the darkfall, and Solo saw that it was Rivalle who courted her, with Abalon and Murdok joining in.

Ponder and Ditto stopped at the periphery, tingling in response to the prill's raksha.

Moving in closer to her, Rivalle Called again, his voice rising in both pitch and volume as he neared the prill and waited for her answer, but the sound she made was no Calling thirp; it was a shrill and incoherent wailing. The prill was fey! Badly frightened and shaking, her eyes glazed and fixed, she remained motionless. But still Rivalle advanced on her, with Abalon and Murdok closing in from behind. Solo turned to complain to Ponder, but the words stuck in his throat when he saw the grey's face. He stood wide-eyed and staring at the little female, his tail limp, his ears standing out at silly angles.

Ditto, too, had noticed his friend's condition and was looking with confusion at Ponder, then back at the fey female.

Without any warning, Ponder began a Call of his own, but this was no thrille of love; it was his war cry, his most fearsome battle challenge! Every hair on his stocky body stood out fully frumped as he leapt over Rivalle, past Ditto and Solo, and landed directly over the unseeing prill. Turning toward Rivalle with ears laid flatly back and eyes narrowed to threatening slits, he hissed, 'If you touch this prill I'll snatch you bald, hair by hair.'

Shocked, Rivalle quickly backed away a few paces. Abalon and Murdok fell all over each other in immediate retreat as Solo and Ditto stared in wonder.

'I mean it, rag-tail. Back it up right now or you'll be wearing me, and I promise you, you'll hate it.' Ponder sounded, looked, and smelled pure mean. The little prill was still fey-whining, and hadn't flicked an ear.

'Uh . . . Ponder, you can't just come in here and take – ' began Rivalle, partially recovered.

'I can do whatever I droud well please. This prill is fey. She hasn't answered your Call. Now clear out of here before I stomp your head down flat between your shoulders.'

Ponder advanced a step toward the surprised suitor. The grey vastly outranked Rivalle and the other two, not even counting his position as Enforcer. Muttering, Rivalle backed away a safe distance and disappeared over the Wall to fieldside. Murdok and Abalon faded away southward without protest.

Solo was transfixed. He didn't like seeing Ponder like this, especially toward another Quorum member. But what he liked even less was seeing Quorum bards taking advantage of a fey prill. Ditto remained calm and unruffled.

Ponder's fierce expression melted into one of tender concern as he turned to the almost unconscious female. Slowly and unthreateningly he moved to her side, speaking with soft, soothing words that were in sharp contrast to his vicious manner with Rivalle.

'It's all right now. No one's going to hurt you,' he repeated over and over, gradually coming up to her side. 'Ponder's here. Just try to relax.'

Solo could see Ponder's nostrils twitching as he read the prill through her rack, and slowly the grey reached out and nuzzled her stiffened neck, talking in comforting tones, being very careful not to make any sudden movement that might frighten her and send her more deeply within.

Flopping back down on his haunches, Solo realized that Ponder was in love. Rough, gruff, street-fighting Ponder had managed to fall head-over-paws in love with the fey prill. Solo glanced at Ditto, who barely managed to hide a smirking grin as he watched the Dom's great Enforcer encourage and comfort the female with all the tenderness of a mother with new kits.

'There, now, small one. Ponder's here. They've all gone. You'll be safe with me.'

Slowly, with Ponder's encouragement and gentleness, the black-and-white prill began to regain herself. She stopped her soft cry-whining and looked up into the grey's gentle, moon-struck eyes, moving closely against the large bard as if for protection.

'I was so scared,' she said finally in a high, kitlike voice. 'They were all around me . . .'

'It's all over now. I'm Ponder, Enforcer to the Dom of this territory, and I won't let anybody hurt you,' he crooned.

Then he began to lick her face and ears. Ponder never even licked his *own* fur.

Her name, they discovered, was Rosen (pronounced Rahsen), and she had wandered for two darkfalls before finding Spanno's territory. She came, she told them, from a Dwelling far to the north. She had been taken away in a moving rauwulf, and had been thrown from it while it ran.

Ditto and Solo returned to the Keep, leaving the great Ponder towering over the prill.

'I've never seen Ponder look like that,' said Solo, shaking his blond head.

'Calling brings down the best of them,' laughed Ditto. 'Next season it will be you groveling before some cute prill.'

'Never! I'm going to keep my head on my shoulders like you, Ditto.'

'Sure you will. And Calling hits me as hard as anybody; I've just never been a big favorite with the prills. I think they worry about how the kits would look.'

It took a moment before Solo realized the Ditto was referring to his having no tail. Would the kits be tailless, or have half a tail? Solo had no answer, so they walked on in silence.

They had just passed the Woodstack when Dom Spanno appeared on the Great Fence ledge, quickly followed by an irate Rivalle. Solo assumed that Rivalle had taken his complaint and wounded pride to the Dom.

'Where's Ponder?' asked Spanno, sounding slightly irritated.

'He's down on the greyrock southward, Spanno,' said Solo uncomfortably.

News travels quickly through the territory, and already several Quorum cats had materialized around them.

'Okay, kit. Go get him,' sighed the Dom.

Solo reluctantly turned to go, but sensed the grey's approach and stopped in his tracks. Ponder had felt the assembling felines and was approaching with determination and firm resolve in his stride. Close behind, well within his surround, was Rosen.

'You wanted me, Spanno?' Ponder asked as he drew near, his tone deliberately bland.

Looking nervous but triumphant, Rivalle sat on the ledge directly behind Dom Spanno. Solo moved eastward next to Ditto and a few others, into what was obviously the neutral corner.

The calico looked at Ponder. 'Rivalle here tells me you interrupted his Call and took that prill away by force.'

The grey didn't bat an eye. Most of the Quorum was gathered now, and it had become a true council. 'I have the right and the rank, Dom Spanno,' said the grey, using the formal address. 'It was no Calling I interrupted, anyway. This prill was fey and Rivalle knew it.'

Kitty-Kitty had joined the group, along with a number of other prills, and stood uneasily at Spanno's side. She, like Ditto and Solo, felt uncomfortable at the conflict between two lifelong friends.

'She went fey because he jumped in and started

pushing me around!' blurted Rivalle. 'Ask Murdok or Abalon!'

Shocked at Rivalle's blatant distortion of the facts, Solo turned to Ditto, who signaled him to keep quiet. Everyone had looked around for Murdok or Abalon, but neither bard was present.

'I'm going to pound you into the greyrock, you limp-tailed excuse for a cat – '

'Hold on, Ponder. Just answer the charge. Did you or didn't you take that prill by force?'

'Has anybody thought about asking "that prill" what happened?' said Kitty-Kitty angrily.

Rosen's eyes showed her surprise at hearing a female interrupt the bards at council. But Spanno hesitated only a moment before turning toward the young female.

'Don't be afraid – you can speak freely here. Try to tell us what happened.'

Haltingly, and looking to Ponder and Kitty-Kitty for encouragement, Rosen began. 'I. . . I . . . the black bard and two others surrounded me . . . I couldn't get away . . . I tried to run. I don't remember anything else until Ponny came . . . the other bards were gone . . . '

Rosen's voice had faded into a whimper, and Ponder quickly nuzzled her face and whispered soft words of comfort into her ear.

'*Ponny?*' Someone giggled, immediately silenced by a flash of the grey's eyes.

Spanno looked hard at Rivalle. 'The charge you brought against Ponder is empty. On the weight of your words I have questioned my friend and my second in command. Now you can settle directly with him.'

Rivalle's jaw sagged and his eyes grew frightened and glossy.

Underscoring his decision to leave Rivalle's fate up

to Ponder, Spanno turned and headed northward along the ledge.

Solo fully expected Ponder to jump on Rivalle and pound him into the greyrock. Ditto just watched with his usual objectivity, possibly knowing the grey better than anyone else.

Standing beside his trembling prill, Ponder spoke with an uncharacteristic calm. 'You can either leave the Quorum or fight me for the right to stay.'

It was obvious from Rivalle's expression that before daybright the Quorum census would be down by exactly one.

Kitty-Kitty followed Spanno, and the others gradually dispersed, talking excitedly in small groups. Solo and Ditto went back to sit on the Woodstack.

'Why didn't you let me tell Spanno what happened?' asked the kit, remembering Ditto's hard, silencing look.

'Spanno can handle things well enough,' said Ditto quietly. 'And Ponder didn't need our defense.'

'I thought for sure Ponder would slap Rivalle fey, but he just let him go . . . '

'Ponder had better things on his mind.' Ditto laughed, secretly pleased with the grey's handling of the situation.

Spanno and the white prill came back to the Woodstack just before daybright. Kitty-Kitty remained especially attentive to the calico, even though her raksha had faded and gone. Although felines do not pair-bond in the usual sense of the word, the relationship between the two of them transcended the simple, basic allure of Calling.

Ditto lay quietly and pretended to sleep, but remained awake long after the others had settled into themselves, deep within his own thoughts. He was

141

lonely, and felt a separateness that even Ponder could not have quieted.

The following darkfall brought Selvyn home, looking bedraggled but none the worse for wear. Ponder remained fieldside and was not really expected anytime soon. Banda and Minit had eagerly volunteered for outwatch, and after Spanno's gelt-reinforcing patrol, the group met for graille at the Keep. Ditto was still pensive and withdrawn.

'Ditto! Come here, quick!' Ponder yelled as he thundered up to the Keep, shadowed closely by Rosen.

The grey was wild with a sort of gleeful excitement, but no fear or fury showed in his surround. The others stood curious and alert, wondering what could have taken Ponder away from his Calling.

'Hurry, Ditto!' he panted, out of breath. 'Come on, follow me!'

Ponder turned and headed back the way he had come, Rosen barely managing to keep up. Ditto and Selvyn leapt out ahead and raced to follow the grey, with Spanno, Kitty-Kitty, and Solo behind them in confusion.

Well over a hundred cat-lengths south of the Woodstack, Ponder stopped short and waited for the others to catch up. Grinning, he pointed to the Dwelling wall.

'Look over there!'

Sitting in one of the see-through places in the structure's wall was a Tame-cat prill. She was very dark grey without any markings at all, and had large, outsize ears. Everyone remained silent. Were they looking in the right place? Ditto turned to Ponder, who watched the Tame-cat with a pleased-with-himself expression.

'Well? What's all the fuss about, Pon? That? A Tame-cat sitting in a Dwelling?'

'Just keep watching,' said Ponder, smiling.

They turned back toward the Dwelling just as the

Tame-cat prill stood and flexed, looking bored and oblivious. Everyone soon understood Ponder's excitement – she had no tail. Like Ditto, she had not even the hint of one.

Ditto stared, unblinking. His ears looked exactly like Ponder's had when he'd seen Rosen for the first time. The dark prill, unaware of her audience, settled back down.

'Droud,' said Ditto at length.

'There goes the last unaffected bard in the territory,' sighed Solo.

'She's okay, but you'll never get at her.' Selvyn yawned expressively. 'Not unless you can walk through walls.'

'Okay? She's perfect!' said the grey, still grinning. 'Old Ponder takes care of his friends. Now, go on over there and talk to her. Go on! Try it!'

'And just what am I supposed to say to her?'

'Just go over there and tell her your name and show her your . . . I mean . . . let her see that you two have something in common,' Solo instructed authoritatively.

'Go on, Ditto. What have you got to lose?' Spanno said, nudging the tailless bard with his shoulder.

Looking around nervously, Ditto took a deep breath and bravely strode across the greyrock to the Dwelling wall. There was a slender ledge under the transparent square, and he jumped lightly up onto it and landed facing the Tame-prill. She seemed surprised, but didn't withdraw.

No one could hear what Ditto was saying, but the prill was apparently interested. Settling into a full sit on the ledge, he was right next to her, though he might as well have been a thousand cat-lengths away.

'Just look at them!' Ponder beamed proudly.

'Well, we can't just sit here and stare,' Kitty-Kitty

said, turning toward the Woodstack. The others did the same.

Rosen stood within the grey's shadow, looking a little lost.

'Rosen, when you're ready,' said Kitty-Kitty as they walked, 'I'll introduce you to the other Quorum prills and help you get settled.'

Rosen looked at the ground and only glanced at the white prill in reply. But Kitty-Kitty understood. She, too, had been an abandoned, frightened Tame-cat.

Most of the darkfall had passed before Ditto returned. Solo and the orange were lounging on the Great Fence ledge as Ditto leapt up to join them.

'How did it go?' asked the kit. 'Do you like her? What's she like?'

'She's beautiful! And she's intelligent, and very sophisticated. Her name is Doeby, and –'

'And she's a Tame-cat, and locked up, and unavailable,' interrupted Selvyn. 'I'm sorry, Ditto, but I just don't want you to get hurt over this. You'll never get her out of there.'

'Don't the Owners ever let her out?' Solo said hopefully.

'No,' sighed Ditto, 'never. Selvyn's right.'

Ditto was miserable for the next few darkfalls. Almost every waking minute he was on the Dwelling's little ledge, talking to Doeby, watching her, and finally, late one darkfall, he sang to her.

Solo had gone with him and sat on the Great Fence, watching the would-be lovers from across the grey-rock, deeply moved by their plight. Ditto called and sang to Doeby passionately as she leaned against the square and pressed her face close to his. On and on he sang, his heartfelt thrille clear and beautiful in the cool darkfall stillness, gaining momentum and volume with every chorus.

Suddenly an entranceway not six cat-lengths from where Ditto stood opened wide and a huge, growletting Owner charged outward. It carried a long, thin sticklike object that was bushy on one end, and whatever it was, it looked lethal. Calling out loudly in the choppy, grunting speak of Owners, the great lumbering being advanced toward Ditto, waving its fierce object threateningly. Ditto swallowed his last few notes and scrabbled from the ledge just as the Owner's weapon came down on the very spot where he had been. Tumbling onto the greyrock below, he narrowly escaped two more violent swats before gaining traction and bounding away.

Solo, however, had sensed an opportunity, and acting on impulse, charged across the greyrock to the open Dwelling entrance.

'Doeby! Run! Hurry!' he called as he raced by, distracting the Owner's attention.

Inside, the prill hesitated only an instant before diving through the doorway to freedom. Ditto was halfway to the Great Fence when he heard Solo's call to the prill. When he turned, he saw the Owner angrily brandishing the long stick and Solo herding the tailless prill Fence-ward as fast as he could get her to go. The three squeezed through the Fence and continued well into the field before stopping, out of breath and winded.

'Solo!' gasped Ditto. 'I can't believe you did it! You were fantastic! Doeby! You're free now! We can be together and you can join the Quorum!'

Doeby looked worried, as if she already regretted her hasty, unplanned escape. She glanced around and assumed the same expression Kitty-Kitty used when Selvyn had one of his attacks.

'Well, I certainly hope you've made some arrangements for taking care of me,' said Doeby, collecting herself. 'Surely you won't expect me to live in this . . . this wilderness!' A shy, retiring creature she was not.

'I don't understand, Doeby . . . but don't worry about a thing . . .' replied Ditto, a little taken aback.

'I've never been that close to an Owner before!' panted Solo. 'Droud! They're big!' He was just beginning to realize exactly what he'd done.

'This place is filthy!' interrupted Doeby, sounding disgusted.

Spanno, Selvyn, and Kitty-Kitty were coming from the north and had seen the whole thing.

'Droud, Solo! Taking on Owners now, are you?' asked the calico, but there was genuine respect in his tone.

Busily straightening out her beautiful coat, Doeby was quiet. She seemed haughty, and was very careful not to touch any of the ferals. Nonetheless, Ditto watched her every movement, totally enraptured.

'Everyone, I'd like you to meet Doeby. Doeby, these are my friends: Dom Spanno, our leader; Selvyn, one of the Enforcers; Kitty-Kitty, Dom Spanno's . . . uh . . . friend; and Solo, your rescuer.'

'Yes,' murmured Doeby absently, looking out across the field.

Nervous silence followed. Ditto was smitten beyond all reason, however, and fawned over the grey prill shamefully.

'Solo,' Spanno said, turning to the kit, 'you could have gotten hurt over there.'

'We appreciate what you did for us,' Ditto added quickly. 'We can't tell you how much.' Ditto looked at Doeby for confirmation, but none was forthcoming.

'Well,' said Spanno, clearing his throat, 'I guess we'd better be going and leave these two alone.'

'Right,' agreed Selvyn, relieved, and everyone quickly got to his feet and headed out into the field.

'I think you should have left that one to the Owners, Solo,' Spanno said after they were out of hearing range.

'Maybe she's just nervous after being inside the Dwelling for so long,' Kitty-Kitty offered generously.

'Nervous, my hindpaw,' snapped Selvyn. 'That prill looked at us like we were dirt.'

'At least Ditto seems happy,' Solo said as they walked.

Ditto's love affair, however, lasted less than half the darkfall – as long as it took Doeby to discover that the entire outward was covered with 'dirt.' She scratched and whined at her Dwelling door and was taken back inside, while Ditto watched dejectedly from the Great Fence.

'What happened?' asked Solo when Ditto came back to the Woodstack alone.

'I don't want to discuss it,' he answered. And he never did.

8
A Final Journey

Calling time eventually passed, and sanity, to Solo's point of view, returned to the Quorum. Ponder came back to the Woodstack, worn out but happy, though Rosen refused to come with him. Shy and overwhelmed by so many ferals living together so closely, she preferred to den in the prill-hedges with Mondy and the other females. Ditto was recovering from his 'situation,' as Selvyn called it, with Doeby, and even the normally tactless Ponder was careful not to tease him about it. The Gang of Six was intact again, and Solo couldn't have been happier.

New whitefall covered the territory, falling silently during the daybright, transforming the fieldside into sparkling, starlit whiteness. Solo like the whitefall, the way his paws crunched into it when he walked across the greyrock. But he found it uncomfortable to sit on for very long, and he had to either remain upright on all fours or find a protected space where it hadn't collected to sit for any length of time.

Fieldside and just north of the Keep, Solo settled within the bushes, watching a pair of last season's kits diligently practicing their stalk and pounce on a partially disabled insect. Solo could remember perfecting that same maneuver on an unsuspecting Ponder only a few circles before. Spanno and Selvyn had taken outwatch, and Ditto and the grey were inside the Keep at graille.

Through his surround, Solo could feel Banda and Minit nearing him. The two young bards had become

close companions and, as both were recently abandoned Tame-cats, had a lot in common. Banda would
never talk about his experiences inside the Dwelling
or how he'd lost his cobblers, but Solo had learned
enough about such things to give up his notion that
cobblers just fell off from lack of purpose. He now
supposed that the Owners had taken them away
because of unattractiveness, although they weren't at
all ugly to felines.

Banda was well-liked and willingly took his turns at
patrols and watches, and appeared to be unhampered
by his lack of power gelt. White with large black
blotches, he was shy around the ranking bards, but
had a ready smile and was never heard to grumble.
Minit, a young white about Solo's age, hardly ever
spoke except to Banda. He was extremely self-
conscious about the Owner band that had been left
around his neck, even though it was mostly hidden in
his thick fur. Minit seemed to think that it 'branded'
him, and in a way it did, just as Banda was branded in
another way.

The two young bards came directly into sight range,
gingerly high-stepping across the whitefall-covered
ground. They seemed hesitant, and glanced around
the area; spotting Solo, they quickened their pace.

'Have you seen Speaker, Solo?' Banda asked. 'We've
been looking all over for him. It's important that we
talk to him.'

Minit stood slightly behind Banda, a worried expression in his eyes.

'I haven't seen Speaker since Calling time,' answered
Solo, becoming curious. He wanted to ask them why
they sought the prophet, but didn't want to intrude. 'I
could help you look for him,' he offered, hoping for an
explanation. 'Is there anything I can do?'

'Let's ask *him*,' whispered Minit.

'I will, I will,' shushed Banda over his shoulder.

Solo looked from one to the other, baffled. 'Ask me. What?'

'Well,' Banda began, 'it's the band around Minit's neck. It's getter tighter, and he's having trouble swallowing. If we don't get it off soon . . . I mean . . . if he grows much more . . . he might choke.'

'And you're so good at figuring out problems,' Minit added softly, 'that we thought since we couldn't find Speaker . . .'

Solo stood and moved closer to Minit. The band was just barely visible in his fur. It was brownish-colored and had a strange animal rack. There were gnawed places all over it – evidently Banda had already tried chewing it off.

The little black-and-white read Solo's thoughts. 'I couldn't bite through it. It was already so tight I couldn't get a decent grip with my teeth.'

Minit looked miserable under such close scrutiny, as well as desperate. Solo was absorbed, inspecting the band from every angle.

Just then, Ponder and Ditto approached from the direction of the Keep. 'What's up?' asked the grey as they joined the others.

'We're trying to think of a way to get this band off Minit. Any ideas?'

The two elder bards sniffed and inspected, but offered no suggestions.

'That's been put on there to stay,' Ditto said finally, shaking his head. 'All I can say is, you'd better not grow much more.'

'You're on your own with this one, kit,' added Ponder.

Minit looked as if he might bolt for fieldside any moment.

'Well, we've got to do something, and soon.' Banda sighed, looking at Solo.

'You know,' Solo said thoughtfully, 'if it wasn't for his coat, it wouldn't be so tight. If we could just get his fur off, the band might come off over his head.'

'Sounds great, kit,' Ponder said skeptically, 'but how do you plan to get his fur off?'

'Maybe we can't get it off,' Solo answered slowly, mainly to himself, 'but I think we can get it out of the way.'

'What do you mean?' asked Minit. 'What are you going to do to me?'

'Listen,' said Solo finally. 'If we got you wet and flattened down your fur, the band might be loose enough to pull off over your ears.'

'Wet?' squeaked Minit. 'With water?'

'Right. Then we'll try to pull it off.'

Although Minit was horrified, Banda looked hopeful. Ditto and Ponder were trying to picture Solo's plan.

'Remember that last big water-down,' Solo explained, 'when Tanner and his bards came? Remember how everyone looked when their fur was wet and plastered down?'

'You're going to make water-down?' asked Banda, half-believing the kit could do it.

'Wet?' Minit repeated in a shocked whisper, looking dazed.

'Come on, Ponder,' Solo instructed. 'Help me get Minit to the Dwelling.'

'This is crazy,' mumbled the grey, but he was already helping Solo herd the little white toward the Owner Dwelling, with Banda and Ditto close behind.

Pushing and nudging, they finally brought Minit close to the wall where the Quorum drinking supply dripped steadily from a round spigot. Minit's eyes were panicky as he looked at the trickle of water.

'Now,' ordered Solo, 'stick you head under the water and get good and wet.'

Minit didn't move.

'Minit! Do you want the band off or not?' Solo tried to sound impatient.

'Isn't there another way?' asked Banda. 'Are you sure this will work?' Everyone sympathized with Minit.

'No, I'm not sure it will work, but it's the best idea I've got.'

Staring at the water, Minit gradually began to go fey.

'Minit! It's just a little water. You'll dry. I promise!' It was becoming easier for Solo to sound impatient.

'I'll freeze!' Minit whined. 'I'll freeze and die!'

'You'll choke and die if you don't do something,' Ditto said softly.

'I can't watch,' moaned Ponder, turning his head.

'Ponder!' Solo called. 'Help me get this kit's head wet.'

The grey hesitated a moment, but then he very deliberately began rearranging his face into his famous 'fegin threaten' and hulked toward Minit.

'Get your head under that water or I'll slap that band down around your skinny little butt!' he hissed right in Minit's face.

Holding his breath and squeezing his eyes tightly shut, Minit sidestepped hesitantly to the wall and forced his head toward the dripping water. Then he stopped, frozen with fear. Ponder reached out and nosed him hard against the Dwelling and directly under the silver opening, and the water ran down over Minit's stiffened neck and across his chest. Every dry hair on his tense, trembling body stood straight up as he braced himself against the little deluge.

'Now I've seen everything!' gasped Spanno, coming up from the Great Fence. 'What in droud is that kit doing under the water?'

'They're torturing him!' Selvyn cried from behind Spanno, wide-eyed.

Hastily the operation was explained to the disbelieving bards. It was best that Minit's eyes were closed, for many other Quorum members began to gather, staring in horror as Minit stood dripping wet under the water.

'That should do it,' said Solo at last.

Minit didn't move.

'Minit! That's enough!' repeated Solo, but Minit remained motionless, completely fey.

Ponder reached out and jerked the sopping white away from the Dwelling, grabbing him by a mouthful of fairly dry fur. Minit began to shake violently, his face pinched and drawn.

'Okay,' said Solo, 'now to get the band off.'

Positioning himself at Minit's head, Solo grasped the Owner band in his teeth at the back of the kit's neck. He braced his forelegs against the little bard's shoulders and pulled and wrenched the band up to just behind Minit's ears, and then with several twisting tugs he slowly worked it first over one wet, slick ear, then the other. It was now ledged over the top of Minit's head in front of his ears, and very tightly under his jaw. The kit could neither talk nor swallow, and had trouble even breathing.

'This is it!' cried Solo.

Gathering down and straining backward, Solo gave a great final heave that pulled the band free and sent him rolling over backward with the momentum.

'It's off!' yelled Banda. 'Minit! Open your eyes and look!'

Minit, crouched down and braced for back-traction, opened one eye and saw Solo sitting back on his hindpaws, the band hanging from his mouth, looking victorious and proud. The band *was* off!

153

The Quorum breathed a collective sigh of relief, and Banda bustled around Minit gleefully.

'You're awfully good at figuring out things,' Minit said quietly, looking at the ground. 'Even better than Speaker.' It was as close as he could come to a thank-you.

Solo, too, looked at the ground, uncomfortable with the comparison.

'I knew you could do it,' said Ponder as Ditto rolled his eyes heavenward. 'Never had a doubt.'

Dropping the Owner band, Solo stepped back over to Minit to check for damage, but found none.

'I'm sorry we had to get you wet,' he said. 'Let's get you inside the Woodstack. It's warmer there and you'll dry in no time.'

Minit was still trembling, and looked grateful for the invitation to the Woodstack. He looked at the Owner band lying on the greyrock. 'I've never seen it before,' he said to Banda. 'It's been around my neck for most of my life, and I've never seen it. I still don't know why they put it on.'

The elder bards went back to fieldside, and Solo, Banda, and Minit made their way to the Woodstack. Solo was glad to have an opportunity to talk with them alone, to see what new information about Owners he could pry out of them. He sat back expectantly as Banda helped lick Minit dry.

'Kitty-Kitty has told me a lot about when she was a Tame-cat,' Solo prodded. 'What was your experience with the Owners like?'

'It's all well and good if you have nice Owners, like she did, that scratch your ears and give you good things to eat. But if you live with cruel ones, it's a different story!'

'I'm sorry, Banda,' Solo said, surprised. 'I didn't

realize it was bad for you. It's just that I don't understand about Owners and felines . . .'

'Well, I don't understand either,' Banda said more
softly. 'But I know what they did to me, and so does
everyone in the Quorum. And I thought my Owners
liked me . . . I did everything I knew to please them – '

'I certainly didn't!' interrupted Minit with unusual
forcefulness in his normally timid voice. 'Our den had
two Owner kits and they took turns abusing me. I had
my tail tied in knots and my ears pulled until I finally
had to fight back. I think they've moved their den now,
and I'm glad! I was scared at first, being alone, before
I knew any of the ferals.'

'At least you've still got your cobblers,' sighed Banda.
'I don't think mine will ever grow back. I keep hoping
and checking, but it's been so long now . . . still not
even a bump.'

'Dom Spanno says that you're not any less feline
without them,' offered Solo, not really sure if that
was the right thing to say. 'Did it hurt a lot when they
came off?'

'Came off? They were chopped off! And they stuck
sharp things in my skin, and I couldn't cry out or move
. . .' Banda was close to breaking down. Minit looked
helpless as he watched his friend suffering.

'One of *my* Owners put me in a big water-holder
and closed it shut on my head; then the water started
going down into a dark hole at the bottom and made a
terrible loud noise. I almost went down the hole too,
before they took me out. Then they held me under a
hot windmaker until I thought my skin would burn off,
and when I finally clawed and scratched and got away,
I hid under the Winter-box and didn't come out for
two darkfalls.'

Stunned at Minit's story, Solo sat back, assimilating
this new information. He had heard of such atrocities

155

as a kit, but hadn't actually believed that Owners would commit such cruelties. It was time to talk to Speaker again, just as soon as the sage returned from whatever had kept him away for so long.

Solo felt Ponder and Selvyn nearing the Woodstack from the west, and knew their arrival would end the conversation. Banda and Minit got to their feet, upset by the reverie and anxious to be outward before the elders came inside. Ponder usually managed to intimidate younger felines, however inadvertently. Minit looked at Solo and started to say something, but instead only lowered his eyes and followed Banda to the exit.

'May you always find cover,' Banda said, turning self-consciously toward Solo and bidding a formal good-bye.

'And may the daybright never dawn on your hunger,' answered the kit in kind.

The two scurried outward, narrowly escaping an encounter with Ponder. Trying to think of an excuse to be outward himself, Solo listened to the two elder bards trade insults and suffered patiently through their gentle teasing about his 'heroism.' He had almost edged his way to the tunnellike exit when Ponder noticed he was leaving.

'Going somewhere, are we?' asked the grey suspiciously.

'Oh, I just thought I'd go out for a while to be alone,' Solo answered. That, he knew, was something any cat could relate to. He wished Ponder wouldn't be so protective. Once or twice he even suspected the grey had followed him out on patrol to watch over him, but he hadn't actually felt him close by.

'Well, stay within range. I don't want to have to lie here and worry about your skinny rear. Spanno and

Kitty-Kitty would have my hide if anything happened to you.' Of course, *he* wasn't concerned at all . . .

'I'll just be fieldside a little ways. Don't worry,' Solo said, and quickly darted outward. How he loved those cats!

Over the Great Fence and heading westward, Solo rambled through the weeds, thinking about Banda's and Minit's experiences with their Owners. Why hadn't they run away . . . far away? Why did any of the Tame-cats stay? For that matter, why did the ferals stay? Why did this feel so much like 'home' when it was so very much the Owners' territory? He needed to talk with Speaker again. There was so much he didn't understand.

Solo hadn't gone far when he suddenly came upon the white prophet sitting almost out in the open. Why hadn't he felt the sage's surround? he wondered.

'Speaker,' said the kit, surprised, 'I was just coming to look for you.'

'And I have been waiting for you, little one.'

'Waiting for me? Why were you waiting for me, Dom Speaker?'

Ignoring the question, Speaker only smiled at Solo's confusion.

'Do you come to tell me some great news?' asked the Old One.

Solo forgot his confusion over the Owners and eagerly recounted the removal of Minit's band, watching for Speaker's reaction. The white bard listened with interest and nodded his approval, but Solo suspected that he had already heard. Solo was noticing that Speaker looked . . . different somehow; he seemed whiter and more filled out, and felt 'vibrant,' and very powerful. Solo realized that Speaker was really beautiful, and wondered why he'd never noticed it before. It was an illusion created by starlight shining against a

white coat, Solo knew, and it would have been dis-
quieting had it been any other cat.

'. . . and now Minit won't have to worry about
growing bigger,' finished the kit. 'Of course, I'm sure
you could have found a better way, without the water,
if you'd been there.'

'A job well done.' Speaker smiled. 'And a good
reason for pride. I can think of no other way it could
have been removed. When I am gone, the Quorum
will have a wise Speaker to take my place.'

For the first time, Solo realized that 'Speaker' was a
title and not just a name. Flustered, he hesitated before
answering. 'Me? I couldn't possibly take your place! I
don't even know all the Legends!'

Knowing how to solve problems, Solo thought, was
rewarding, but he had no plans to be a prophet, a
Speaker! He was Spanno's kit; he wanted to be an
Enforcer. Speaker watched the kit with gentle, affec-
tionate amusement.

'Anyway,' Solo added, 'you're not going anywhere
for a long time. There's still a lot I need to learn about
the Legends, and Shamalat, and the Owners.'

'You'll learn from what you see, much more than
from my words. One day you'll solve all your mysteries.
I know you will.'

'Well, I sure haven't solved any yet,' Solo sighed.
'I'm just finding more and more of them. Do you know
that Banda and Minit were tortured by their Owners?'

The kit settled back, hoping he had opened the door
to a Teaching. He had procrastinated long enough.

'I know, Solo. But think on this: a *cat* tortured you,
yet we don't judge all felines by it. The Legends tell us
that Owners are the only beings with complete Reason,
and that there is nothing which is outside their capa-
bilities. We cannot begin to comprehend their actions.'

'But why do we live in the shadow of their Dwelling?

Why don't we go far away from the Owners and live like cats did before Shamalat? We don't need Owners . . .'

'It was from Owners, and our connection with them, that we learned how to think. Perhaps we're still learning. That might explain what binds us here.'

'But we're not Tame-cats, we're feral. We can think and reason, and we have no direct contact with the Owners,' said Solo thoughtfully.

'Many of our number began their lives as Tame-cats. You know how eager everyone is to learn all we can from the Tame-cats who join the Quorum. Gradually, our association with Owners is changing us as a species – we're intelligent now, but it hasn't always been that way. Long ago, most of our energy was spent hunting for graille, or protecting ourselves from enemies. There was simply no time for introspection and learning. Now we take our graille from the Keep, and the presence of Owners deters our natural enemies. We have time and leisure. We can think, and learn, and change. We have taken a path that none of us truly wants to leave. We think we hate the Owners, but in truth we want to be like them, even though these great benefactors have become our enemy. They kill us with their rauwulfen, they set traps for us, their kits throw stones at us, yet others of our kind live inside their dens, loved and protected. It is a paradox, a great contradiction. The Owners are powerful and unpredictable, and I feel a danger here I've never felt before . . .'

Speaker's eyes had wandered out into the field, as if he were talking mostly to himself. It made Solo tremble inside.

'I think that we should leave, and find our own place far away from them,' said the kit softly.

Turning back to Solo, Speaker smiled. 'I have pondered these things for my entire life, and I think you will do the same. You might find the answers for us one day.'

Solo sat in silence, remembering the great Owner he'd seen inside the Dwelling complex with Spanno. Part of him, deep inside, had wanted to be touched by that Owner.

'I'm proud of you, kit,' Speaker said finally. 'Keep to your path.' It sounded very much like a good-bye.

Picking up on the sounds of cats moving along the Great Fence, Solo looked around for a moment, trying to identify the surrounds. When he turned back, Speaker had vanished without a trace. 'How do you *do* that?' asked Solo of the empty space where Speaker had been. The prophet had a flair that was hard not to admire.

Disappointed at Speaker's departure, Solo headed back to the Woodstack. He felt uneasy over what Speaker had said about 'taking his place' and feeling a danger, and avoided the other Quorum members as he slipped into the Woodstack and tried to sleep.

The following darkfall, Solo crept away from the others at the Keep and furtively crossed the dark field. He was headed for the central hedges where the prills denned with their kits, and didn't want to be teased about it, especially by Ponder and Selvyn. Sometimes he just needed the feminine company of the prills with their high-pitched, excited conversation that was so different from the bardly atmosphere of the Woodstack. They were so completely absorbed in their Quorum life – they had their kits season after season, talked about each other viciously, and fell into complete, eye-averted acquiescence in the presence of ranking bards. It was just this 'empty-headed, passive acceptance' that

Kitty-Kitty hoped to eradicate forever in the hearts of the prills. At least that's what she said – Solo wasn't quite sure he understood exactly what she meant. But she seemed to be making headway; the bards now had to announce their intentions and wait for acknowledgment before entering the feminine stronghold of the central hedges. Solo, of course, as a ward of the Quorum, was free to visit the quasi-communal lair unannounced.

Solo was nearly across the field when the southern edge of his surround touched with that of another feline. It was not a Quorum feral; the surround was foreign, and the bard traveled with the hesitant caution of one unfamiliar with his surroundings. It was a gypsy, Solo realized. He reflexively pulled in his surround and turned eastward toward the protection of his elders.

'No,' Solo thought to himself, 'I'm a bard now – and I've got to start acting like one.' Eventually he would have to face his first battle, and it might as well be now.

The gypsy was about twenty cat-lengths away and had surely felt Solo's presence. Creeping ahead, Solo tried to interpret the stranger's emanations. The bard was young, about Solo's age, and definitely feral – his surround was extended and functioning to the limit. He didn't feel as coarse and hardened as gypsies generally are; there was an openness and gentleness of purpose that was out of character for the typical rogue.

Solo began a low, throaty warning, trying to sound experienced, and was surprised at the sound of his own voice in battle fugue. The gypsy responded with his own call, though he seemed careful not to sound too openly challenging; he was in another Quorum's territory, which put him automatically on the defensive. A few paces more and Solo broke through the weeds, staring directly into the tired eyes of the intruder. The bard was smaller than Solo, and grey-colored like Ponder. He looked completely exhausted.

The gypsy watched Solo with cautious respect – he had noticed Dom Spanno's power gelt in the area and picked up traces of it on the blond bard. He assumed that Solo was a young Enforcer out on patrol.

Solo knew that the stranger would expect to have to fight his way through, as was customary in feline culture. He watched the gypsy adjust his stance and settle his tired head. There was an odd quality about this cat that Solo liked, a certain affinity he felt for him. Did they *have* to fight? Surely they could at least discuss it first. Solo hesitated, hoping the gesture wouldn't be interpreted as cowardice.

'Well,' Solo said, feeling his shyness returning, 'do you really *want* to fight?'

The gypsy looked thoughtful and relaxed a bit. 'I guess we're supposed to, aren't we? It's . . . expected, isn't it?'

'I suppose so,' said Solo, beginning to fidget. 'It might look bad if we didn't . . .'

'Well, that's true. Maybe we should, then . . . I guess.'

Sighing, Solo looked at the young bard. 'Do you want to start, or should I?'

'It's your territory. I think that gives you the right of challenge, doesn't it?'

How could Solo do battle with a bard that was being so polite? 'I really don't know. I've never . . . never had to talk about it before.'

'Oh, listen,' said the gypsy with a weary shake of his head. 'We both know you're going to win. Why go through all this trouble?'

'Y-yes,' stammered Solo, 'why go through all of that . . .'

The little gypsy was obviously relieved. 'Why don't we just cut out the fight and let you simply run me off? You can tell the story any way you want to . . . later.'

Solo really did like this cat, and he knew that he was no coward. He was just a young bard, like Solo, out on his first Big Explore and had better things planned for it than fighting every feline that crossed his path.

'Why don't we just forget that too,' offered Solo, 'and you go your way and I'll go mine?' Solo felt better than if he'd fought and won a great battle – although he might not mention this to Ponder and the others.

'That sounds fine to me,' said the grey bard. 'You know, I've heard about this territory. It's said that you have a calico Dom, and prill warriors, and a Speaker-kit. Is any of that true?'

Solo smiled self-consciously. 'Some of it.'

The gypsy looked at the ground and seemed vaguely reluctant to leave. 'May you always find cover,' he said finally, breaking the uncomfortable silence.

'And safe journey to you, my friend. If you keep straight northward, you might not run into anyone else from my Quorum, but watch out for the territory a half-darkfall's run to the north of ours. It's full of gypsy rogues, and they're rough.'

Looking at Solo for a moment longer, the bard finally crept back into the weed-cover and was gone. Solo turned and headed for the central hedges, pretending that he, too, was on an Explore, alone in unknown territory . . .

'Solo?' Kitty-Kitty called as he approached the main hedge. 'Is that you? Come in and sit with us.'

Threading his way through the prickly briars, Solo found Kitty-Kitty with several of the prills in a cavelike den. The hedge was dark and warm inside, and had a cozy, lived-in feeling. Solo's old den was in part of this very same hedge, a little farther to the north. The prills twitched their noses and craned their necks toward the kit, reading the racks he brought from outward. Likewise, Solo sniffed at the heavy, sweet rack of the prills, and the fading wisps of raksha.

Solo settled onto his belly across from Rosen, who looked calmer now and more in control of herself. Mondy sat next to Trivet, and Sondle, a big orange-and-white, was curled up on Solo's left. The surrounds of several other prills could be felt from elsewhere in the bushes.

'No new kits in the hedge yet?' asked Solo, exaggerating his sniffing.

'Not yet.' Kitty-Kitty smiled. 'But soon. Maybe less than a circle. I think Trivet will be first.'

'I'm going to be first!' said Sondle, looking down her large nose.

'We'll see about that,' snapped Mondy, looking aloof. She was very, very proud of being Selvyn's chosen prill. Rosen remained silent beside her.

Solo couldn't imagine what difference it made which prill had her kits first. Soon enough the whole territory would be crawling with them.

A young prill named Pardie came into the main den and settled across from Solo. She was white and looked a lot like Kitty-Kitty, with the most beautiful, bouffant tail the kit had ever seen. She carried it straight up and plumed out when she walked, and it had a delicate little crook at the tip that flicked around incessantly. Solo's insides squeezed together as Pardie fluttered her lashes and circled out her place. Why hadn't he noticed how lovely she was before?

'What brings you here alone?' asked Kitty-Kitty. 'Did the bards abandon you?'

'No, it's just so nice way out here,' answered Solo, inhaling deeply. 'Sometimes I wish the Woodstack was farther away from the Dwelling.'

'I know,' Kitty-Kitty said. 'The burned rack of the rauwulfen is so heavy at times it hurts my throat.'

'It's not just that,' replied Solo. 'Everything seems to be touched by the Owners – the greyrock, the Wall, even the trees for the Woodstack. I don't think we should live so close to them . . .'

'You're starting to sound just like Speaker.' Sondle yawned.

'Dom Spanno's coming!' cried Trivet, looking at Kitty-Kitty.

'And he's not alone,' purred Sondle, twinkling her eyes at Rosen and Mondy.

Instantly the prills began their frantic preening. Solo couldn't see much difference before and after, but the females seemed to feel better. Forgetting his embarrassment at being caught curled up with the prills, Solo followed Kitty-Kitty and the others outward.

Spanno, Selvyn, Ponder, and Ditto stood five cat-lengths from the hedge. Solo sensed that something terrible had happened. Spanno touched Kitty-Kitty's nose in greeting, but only briefly, before turning to Solo.

'Kit,' the calico began, hesitating, 'I've been looking for you. We thought we might find you out here. Selvyn and I . . . well, we just got back from outwatch, and . . . uh . . . we found Speaker in the west field. He's . . . empty.'

Solo felt suddenly hollow inside, and very, very alert. 'Speaker?' he whispered. 'Speaker's dead? How? When?' Solo sat back on his hindpaws, drained.

'I'm sorry, kit,' Spanno said. 'I know you had a special feeling for him, and he had a special feeling for you.'

'Droud,' breathed Kitty-Kitty. 'I thought Speaker would live forever.'

'What happened?' Solo asked, looking at Spanno.

165

'We don't know. I think it was just his . . . time.'

Ponder stepped forward. 'There were no marks, and he looked . . . peaceful.' The grey seemed uncomfortable and fidgety.

'Show me where he is.'

'You don't need to see him, kit,' said Selvyn quickly. 'There's no reason to . . .'

'Spanno, please. I want to see him. It's . . . important.'

'Let him go,' Kitty-Kitty said softly, looking at the calico.

Ditto looked as if he wanted to say something, but kept his silence. Solo was prepared to go on alone, but Spanno nodded his assent and turned toward the hedge. Followed by what was now a good part of the Quorum, Solo and the young Dom nosed through a relatively sparse stretch of thicket and walked westward into the field. In a heavily weeded area several hundred cat-lengths from the central thickets, several ferals milled about in silence. Solo knew that Speaker must be close by.

Walking out alone ahead of the others, Solo saw the prophet's body partially hidden in the grass. The moment he looked at him, he realized that the white bard had been empty for at least two darkfalls, possibly more. Yet only one darkfall since, he had walked and talked with the Old One, and he knew, with icy certainty, that it had been no dream.

Speaker lay on his side, neck flexed and legs stiffly out. His face was peaceful, as Ponder had said, and his eyes were open. His lips were parted, but not pulled back in the grotesque feline 'face of death.' There were insects on him, but that was as it should be.

Solo sat alone for a long time, silently grieving for the enigmatic, cryptic Speaker. The old prophet was dead. Yet who was it that had talked with Solo only one darkfall ago?

9
The Big Explore

Solo had decided to wait until the shock of Speaker's passing had lessened before making his announcement, but as it turned out, it was several darkfalls until he caught everyone together and in reasonably good humor.

'After the next daybright,' he said firmly to the others, 'I'm leaving for my first Big Explore.' It was like dropping a bombshell.

'Solo!' Kitty-Kitty said, recovering. 'You're too young!'

'I'm over ten circles now, and that's not too young, Kitty-Kitty.'

'Why now?' asked Spanno. 'Does it have anything to do with Speaker?'

'I don't know. Anyway, it doesn't make any difference. I want to go . . . I need to.'

All feline bards, at some time before achieving full weight, must make a great solitary venture outward into the world past their territory. This journey might last anywhere from several darkfalls to a half-circle, and is the universal rite of passage into adulthood. Young bards are drawn to it, feeling the strong, instinctual wanderlust pull them from wherever might be home to uncharted territory; their destination unknown.

As happy as Solo was living in the home territory with Spanno and the others, he was acutely aware that there was an entire world out there that he knew nothing about. The Legends told of other creatures he had never seen, and thick forests to be explored; but most of all, Solo wanted to get far from the Owners for a while, and see what life would be like without their influence. As adulthood bore down on him and his instincts matured, Solo's need to venture out on his own became an obsession that could not be ignored.

'Hey, twit,' Ponder said brightly. 'I'm a little restless lately too, so why don't we just go together? In fact, I'm glad that you thought of it. I need – '

'No, Ponder,' interrupted Solo, 'it won't work. You know I have to go alone. You can't protect me forever.'

'Why do you have to go alone?' snapped Kitty-Kitty. 'Because it's the *bardly* thing to do? A bardly deed done in a bardly manner?'

Selvyn was pacing. 'Do you know how dangerous it can be out there? Alone and away from this territory? There are gypsies, and dogs, and . . .'

Selvyn didn't finish, looking to Spanno for agreement. The calico remained silent.

'If it's Solo's time to go, then we shouldn't stop him,' Ditto said. 'It's just hard for us to realize that he's not a kit anymore. We've all been out on our own Big Explore, and we know why it's important. Even the Legends say – '

'Legends!' hissed Kitty-Kitty. 'One minute you talk about giving up the old ways and living by reason, and the next minute you talk about the Legends!'

'Kitty-Kitty,' Spanno said patiently. 'He's a feral bard now. We've got to let him go. And living by reason and thought doesn't mean giving up the Legends or our instincts – it means we can try to understand them.'

'That's right, Solo,' muttered Ponder. 'And when some wild dog starts chewing on your butt out there, just explain all that to him.'

Ditto smiled. 'He'll be all right. He'll come back to us from his Explore. We won't lose him.'

'He'd better,' said Selvyn. 'Someone has to keep Ponder in line.'

'Where do you think you'll go?' sighed Ponder grudgingly. 'I went east . . .'

'I'm going west.'

'West?' Spanno echoed. 'Why west? There isn't anything out there . . .'

'It's nothing but fieldside, forever,' Selvyn added.

'What do you think you'll find westward?' asked Ditto, sounding worried himself.

'Well, we all know that beyond the north border is another feral territory. Southward, past the field, there are smaller Owner dens, and eastward is the blackrock strip where the rauwulfen go to run. But west is still unknown. That's what I want to see.'

'What will you eat?' Kitty-Kitty asked quickly.

'What did any cat eat before Shamalat? What do truly wild animals eat?'

'They eat uppity, silver-tongued kits,' grumbled the grey to himself.

'Listen,' said Spanno, interrupting. 'Solo doesn't have to explain himself, and he doesn't need anybody's permission. This is his *right*.' Spanno's pronouncement was silently accepted as final.

It was now fully daybright, and Solo curled beside Kitty-Kitty, who tucked her head under her forepaws and tried to hide her concern. The bards only pretended to sleep, and the kit felt guilty about causing so much worry. But this was something he had to do, and he knew that beneath their concern, the others understood.

That darkfall, Kitty-Kitty herded Solo to the Keep and supervised while he ate. When he was finished, she took him to the Dwelling for water.

'I'm not going to Shadowland,' Solo complained. 'I'm just going on an Explore!'

169

'Get a good drink and clean up that coat,' the white prill answered curtly. 'Someone's got to get you off to a good start.'

Solo dreaded saying good-bye to his friends, and knew the others were waiting for him across the greyrock and fieldside. As he preened, a tiny out-of-season kit approached, his eyes lowered with respect. Solo watched the little ball of black fluff move hesitantly toward him, and finally stop several cat-lengths away.

'Dom Solo,' said the kit, looking up at his elder. 'Is . . . is it true . . . that you can say the Legends out loud . . . start to finish?'

Stunned, Solo sat in silence for a long moment before answering, remembering another kit, and another time. 'I know the Legends, but not to their finish . . .'

Unable to go on, Solo stammered and turned to the Great Fence. He hesitated, and looked back to the Dwelling for the mother-cat that should be close by. She was there, watching from the north, and Solo was relieved that the kit was not an orphan.

Jumping over the Fence to fieldside with Kitty-Kitty, Solo saw that most of the Quorum had gathered to see him off. Spanno came forward to meet him.

'I guess this is it,' said the calico, trying to sound light. 'Our kit has become a bard, and now he leaves to see the universe.'

For the first time, Spanno formally Related with Solo, thereby acknowledging him as an adult and an equal. Solo was very proud.

'You caused my birth, Dom Spanno, and when I was young you guarded my life. I will always walk behind you.' A moment had passed between them that Solo would always remember.

One by one, the Quorum ferals stepped out and

Related. There were cats there that Solo knew only by name, and one or two kits his own age that he had never run or played with. Spanno and the others had always been everything he'd needed, but he resolved that when he returned, he would get to know all of his feral brothers. Now, though, it was time to go.

Solo turned westward and headed out into the darkness.

A short way into the field, Solo paused to collect himself and make his final preparations. From this point forward, he was on his own and would have to rely completely on his natural defenses and wiles. He was determined to make no mistakes. Clearing his mind, Solo concentrated on his physical senses. He extended his surround to its fullest, testing the outer limits of its reception by focusing on the trees that formed a semicircle around him. Satisfied, he flared his nostrils out wide and inhaled deeply, drawing in the various racks and defining them through a sense so highly developed that he could identify every creature that had been in the area for the last three darkfalls. He held one ear slightly forward and the other down and to the side, positioned to gather in the greatest possible spectrum of sound vibrations. His ears would be in constant motion during his Explore, moving independently and distinguishing the safe, natural sounds from that which might warn of discord or a predator's movement. Widening his stance, he stood well down on his footpads, feeling for the ground tremors of any nearby animal activity. He adjusted his eyes to enhance his peripheral vision, acutely alert for any movement in the brush. Streamlining himself, Solo lowered his head in line with his shoulders, carrying his tail straight out behind him and curved around slightly at the tip. Finally, he confirmed the direction in the way Ponder had taught him, turning in a slow circle and feeling for the gentle tugging from northward. When he'd found the north pull, he was ready. He began his westward trek, his sensorium so perfectly fine-tuned that he blended with the cool, dark outward and became a part of its feel and rhythm.

The darkfall was still, with very little wind, and just cold enough to feel stimulating. Solo was glad that the giant night-star was round and bright – when part of it was missing it gave far less light and the ferals had to use the forced, misleading dark-sight that can make it difficult to judge distance and object size. Using his regular vision, he carefully picked his way through the tall clumps of Johnson grass and dried, prickly brambles, headed for the inviting denseness of the westward forest. Although he was still well within the boundaries of the territory, he walked with watchful, cautious purpose, using the silky adult glide that causes the least disturbance in the immediate atmosphere. He narrowed his eyes and pulled back at the corners of his mouth to make himself appear more mature and fierce. Ponder had said that it was very important for a feral to look 'mean and hungry' when outward alone, and had advised him to get rid of his kittenish expression and to cultivate the appearance of true 'feral nastiness,' adding that one could never be sure who might be watching. Ponder, who could look nastier than anybody else, would have been proud of him now.

Feeling a newfound sense of self-sufficiency, he crossed the quiet, empty field. The brush thickened and closed in around him as he moved gradually into increasing wilderness. His body, accustomed and tuned to the particular feel of the Quorum territory, sensed the change and tried to pull him back; it was this same pull that would help him find his way home again when the adventure was done. Solo kept to his westward course and wound a path through the trees that now towered over him like giants, with large branches that nearly covered the starlight-speckled sky. Very little grass grew beneath them, and the ground was uneven and strewn with rocks, hiding the clicker-crickets that kept time with the darkfall. Their strange calls fused into a muted backdrop for his thoughts – there was balance here, and it excited him to know that his presence did not upset it.

The darkfall passed with the passing territory and Solo became involved with his surroundings – everything was a new discovery. Even the smell of it was foreign and sharply different. Solo tasted the racks of recent water-down and damp, rotting leaves, and he occasionally stopped to investigate the fading traces of jackrabbit or armadillo. But what he noticed most were the things that he could not smell – no irritating, burned odor of rauwulfen, no stench of wasted, unclaimed donations decomposing in the Keep. The static, dull smell of the greyrock was gone, as was the cool majesty of the Great Fence. The air here was pristine – nothing had been added to it by the Owners.

Slipping steadily through the wilderness, Solo imagined himself a feral scout, sent out ahead to clear the path of dangers. Then he became a gypsy rogue, infiltrating an enemy territory and stalking its Dom-cat. He was a wild cat like Shamalat, hunting for his graille. Then, for a moment, he reverted to what he was, an immature feral bard out on his first Big Explore, and he became a little frightened and somewhat overwhelmed by the unlimited outward. A tingle of fear and uncertainty kept him very alert, and aware of his surroundings.

A full fourth of the darkfall was past before Solo finally stopped for rest. The sky was still canopied with branches and leaves, but the ground brush was thicker and more concealing. It was very dark, drabbing the forest colors into shades of sparkling black and deep blue, and the total silence aggravated the buzzing sounds in his ears. Adjusting his surround, Solo tried to mimic the rhythm of the forest and make himself unnoticeable to any creatures that might pass his way. His eyes closed, but not so much as a blade of grass could fall and escape his attention. No enemy would catch him napping this darkfall.

Feeling animal movement close by, Solo gathered in his surround and strained his eyes into the shadows. He held his breath and remained stone-still pending identification of the intruder. But it was only a rabbit kit, nibbling its way southward across his field of vision. Solo relaxed. He could tell from the kit's introverted, casual aura that it felt protected, and knew there must be a mother rabbit close by. According to the Legends, hoppits were fair game, and edible, but they were so gentle and shy that Solo simply couldn't think of them as graille. In any case, Solo wasn't hungry yet and needed to continue his journey. Flexing in stride, he eased silently back into the greyness.

The woods remained quiet, and Solo's initial state of alertness gradually gave way to a less taxing, yet still cautious watchfulness. He was far from his own territory now, farther than any of the Quorum felines generally went unless they, too, were on a major Explore. He sniffed at the evergreen thickets and flowerweed patches, studying and cataloging the animal life, and sharpened his foreclaws on brittle tree bark that had probably never felt a feline scratch.

Enjoying the expansive feeling of having no boundaries or limits, he practiced his jumps and turns. Running and flexing, he bounded through the forest, stretching himself out in near-flight. Solo rehearsed his various songs and calls, and even began arranging his personal life-fugue, the multipurpose, all-occasion Call that is a combination of a feline's history and philosophy. He wished that he never had to leave – but just the thought made him lonely and left him feeling vaguely guilty. His obligations lay elsewhere.

Solo didn't stop again until just before daybright. He was far westward now, and the ground had begun to slant upward. He was tired and needed graille and rest. Instinct told him there was no Owner Keep in the vicinity, and that brought him face-to-face with the inevitable – he was going to have to kill something. Daybright was just beginning to show through the trees as Solo slowed and lowered himself into a hunting stance. He wasn't sure yet exactly what he was hunting, but he was confident that he'd recognize it when he saw it.

Creeping into a thick stand of trees, Solo prepared himself for what might be a very long vigil. In the feline world, hunting and patience were synonymous. But it was not such a long wait after all. An adult blue crier was circling overhead, oblivious of the feral's camouflaged presence as he searched for a suitable landing site. Nervously Solo watched the bird as it landed about twenty cat-lengths from where he crouched.

He made no perceptible movement, but Solo's weight no longer rested on his belly. He slowly and very carefully extended his front lead-paw, pausing to check for any reaction from his prey before completing the step. The bird was intently pecking at the ground and had not noticed his approach. Encouraged, Solo inched forward, staying nearly flush with the grass. His tail flicked behind him, unseen, and the fur along his back stood out in excitement. Solo had practiced the stalk and capture many times, though not when graille depended on it.

He was now only ten or so cat-lengths from the crier, and soon the bird would feel his movement and take wing. Solo would have only a split second to spring before it left the ground. Solo slipped soundlessly through the weeds until he was six cat-lengths away. At this range he would have an excellent chance of catching the little crier. He raised his lead-paw slightly to step forward, but the bird felt him and froze. Before the crier could mobilize himself, Solo leapt out and came down, flattening the screeching thing under his chest and forelegs.

Solo hesitated. He had it now, and he knew what must be done. The thrill of the hunt was over. The blue crier had ceased struggling, and Solo knew it was now or never . . .

Afterward, Solo decided that the experience hadn't been so bad – his hunger was satisfied and he felt a certain sense of accomplishment, though he realized now that the trick was in getting the feathers off first. Carefully choosing an overgrown, secluded place to den, Solo circled out a spot and curled for sleep.

By the middle of the second darkfall, Solo was running out of new experiences. He had hunted a bird, climbed high into the trees, and had even laid down his first power gelt – he was not likely to insult or challenge anyone here; this territory was claimed by no feline, wild or feral. Boredom had begun to nip away at his purpose and resolve. He was a social creature, and needed to share his experiences with his friends. Imagine, he thought, being lonely in the middle of a feral paradise. As he looked around himself, Solo realized that he really was in the perfect feral environment; the hedges were thick and concealing, the air was clean, and predators seemed to be rare. Even graille was plentiful . . . such as it was.

Solo had decided that Selvyn was right – the field did go on forever. The ground went up for a while, then down, but basically it was all just fieldside, with more fieldside after that. How far did he need to go before he could accept that there was nothing more?

At last Solo lay down to rest in a patch of tall bristleweed. As he dozed, he constructed a fantasy: his feral Quorum was bravely carving out a new territory here in the wilds, facing dangers and living as felines were meant to live, led by the great Dom Solo . . .

Suddenly his thoughts shut down as he froze in total alert – there were animals approaching, rapidly and with deliberateness, and this time it was no hoppit kit. These were larger, and aware . . . of him. He tensed, but quickly aborted any idea of easy flight. Five animals seemed to be approaching. Solo flattened to the ground, wondering what creature traveled en masse. Whatever they were, they formed a circle around him, closing in as if for a collective attack. Frumped and bristling with fear, he felt for their positions, hoping to find an opening in their lines to dart through, but they were evenly spaced and moving in fast.

The first one broke through the brush, and Solo very nearly wet himself. It was a Wolfen-dog. Solo knew he could outrun a Wolfen, if he could get past it. But that would be the hard part, for Wolfens were not as flabby and clumsy as Tame-dogs, and were very fast. The others came into view, all silver-grey and very lean. They moved toward him with open, watering mouths. Solo crouched and turned, his heart pounding in his chest as he tried to keep them all visually covered. He was certain that he was about to die.

What appeared to be the lead Wolfen began a sort of wild, whining fugue, motioning with his head for the others to close in on their quarry. Solo braced and prepared to fight for his life, determined to hurt at least one of them before going to Shadowland.

Solo had frumped out and settled onto his hind-quarters when a huge white feline appeared from nowhere and jumped into the arena beside him. The Wolfens fell back in awkward confusion as they looked at the luminescent fog that took the shape of Speaker. He was larger than before and Solo could see the outline of the dogs and surrounding vegetation through his filmy, indefinite body. This time, Solo knew, it was no illusion of the starlight. He trembled with an eerie excitement as full realization dawned on him. The dogs had backed away but were beginning to collect themselves. Solo watched the shimmering prophet as he glared at the Wolfens in challenge.

'Run, Solo!' Speaker commanded, spitting and hiss-ing at the bewildered wild dogs. 'Run!'

'Speaker . . .' Solo began, hesitant and unsure. He couldn't just leave Speaker there to face the dogs alone . . .

'Solo! There's no time! Run!'

Solo leapt out between two of his surprised attackers and streaked away into the field southward. The trees and thickets were a fuzzy blur as he raced at top speed. Glancing back over his shoulder, he saw that Speaker had vanished, leaving the Wolfens to stare at the empty spot where he had been. Solo ran until his shallow, rapid breathing burned his lungs and his legs ached. He had just begun to slow a little when he saw the white bard again . . . ahead of him.

The excitement he felt at seeing Speaker gave him

new energy as he followed the Old One, knowing that that was what he was expected to do. Speaker would materialize ahead in the distant trees and then vanish, and Solo would correct his course and follow, no longer feeling tired or winded. He covered the ground at high speed, leaping over low objects, searching the forest ahead for glimpses of the ethereal feline. Just when he was afraid he had lost sight of him for good, Solo would catch a glimmer of white in the periphery.

'Speaker!' he called over and over. 'Wait for me!' But the white sage didn't answer and stayed well up ahead, seemingly without effort.

Intent upon following Speaker, Solo didn't consciously acknowledge the rack until it was quite strong and unmistakable. He slowed somewhat, twitching his nose. Finally he confirmed the impossible; there were greyrock and rauwulfen in the distance. How could this be? Greyrock and rauwulfen, here in the wilderness? Speaker was nowhere to be seen. Solo determined the rack's point of origin and moved toward it, perplexed and curious.

The rack was closer now, and more distinct. He could even hear the roaring from the rauwulfen, faint but clear, directly ahead, moving at high speed. His path took him up to the edge of a small rise, and looking down, he saw it all. There was a blackrock strip that was marked with white just below him, and many rauwulfen ran quickly along its length. It was what he saw beyond the blackrock, though, that held his attention.

Dominating the western sky was a mountain. It was so high that Solo had to tilt his head backward to see where the top of it disappeared into the clouds. Illuminated by the first light of early morning, it stood like some timeless majestic monument, awesome with its silent, powerful presence. Something from that mountain seemed to call out to Solo; something from deep within its shroud of dark browns and blues and greens stirred his heart like an old, forgotten dream or distant memory . . .

'Solo, go back. You're needed at home.'

Wheeling around toward the sound, Solo scanned the forest behind him, but the white specter was gone. The soft voice had sounded only a few cat-lengths away, and had instantly filled Solo with dread; Speaker would send him home like this only if something terrible had happened.

'Speaker!' called Solo, and his cry reverberated through the stillness and repeated itself over and over in dwindling waves. But there was no answer. 'Speaker! What's wrong?'

Confused and frightened, Solo confirmed the direction and headed eastward in a full run. He could condense two darkfalls' travel into one and a daybright if he didn't stop. By darkfall after next, he would be home.

10
The Fire

When Solo had first journeyed to this westward wilderness, he had been a kit on an Explore. Now he was a cat with a mission, and he was driven. He ran through the long daybright, stopping only when absolutely necessary, and then only for brief moments. Using the disciplined, evenly paced stride of one who has far to go, he settled into a steady run and concentrated on the motions of his body, hypnotized by the rhythm of his running, until it was nightfall. Several times Solo thought he saw a glimpse of shining white to his right or left, but the scenery moved around him like a garbled dream and he couldn't be sure. He drew strength from somewhere inside himself, and gradually the miles faded behind him and the forestland became more familiar.

Solo was still a good half-darkfall's run from the territorial boundaries when he first noticed the smell of smoke. The vague, acrid rack added to his sense of urgency and dread as he pushed himself even harder through the thinning foliage. When the sunstar had traveled the sky against him for the second time and the world was settling imperceptibly into shadow, he could see that in the distance, just about where the Dwelling should be, the air was darkened by a patchy, reddish-black fog that hung close to the ground like a low cloud. Was it a great storm? If so, it was like no storm he had ever seen, and he was afraid. Solo ran full-out without slowing until the ground beneath his paws was that of his own westward field. As he raced eastward, the sky gradually thickened with the smoke, and the air became progressively heavier and more difficult to breathe. When he was just within sight range of the central hedges, Solo saw what was making the red glow over the area – fire! He had never seen fire before, but the Legends told of its awesome, destructive power, how it devoured and burned the life out of all that lay in its path. Speaker had sent him home because of the fire!

The entire field was covered by a dense blanket of oppressive smoke, and flecks of ash, carried by the wind, made Solo tear and cough. A roar like constant thunder came from the Dwelling, and Solo could faintly hear the frantic voices of Owners calling out over the noise. Rauwulfen were moving along the greyrock, and there were wailing screams in the distance that Solo could not identify.

As he moved forward, the dark silhouettes of many Quorum ferals took shape in the greyness, and he could sense the panic and confusion in their surrounds. Solo could not see Spanno and the others, and a dull ache began to grow in the pit of his stomach. Eyes watering against the blackened air, the kit searched the field for his family.

Banda and Minit saw Solo approaching in the distance and rushed out to meet him, followed by several prills and younger bards. They looked truly frightened.

'Solo!' Banda cried. 'You're back! Look at the fire! It's all over the Dwelling . . . the Owners can't stop it!'

Even Minit was excited enough to speak out. 'You should see it, Solo! It's – '

'Where are Spanno and the rest?' Solo interrupted.

'Dom Spanno, Selvyn, and Ponder went to watch the burning,' said Mondy, pacing and obviously beside herself with worry, 'but Kitty-Kitty and Ditto have gone to bring them back . . .'

'They've been gone a long time,' added Rosen in a whine. 'Ponder – '

'They're over there? Close to the Dwelling?' An overwhelming sense of danger gripped the kit. Without waiting for a response, he streaked across the field, heading for the Great Fence.

As Solo skirted the hedges and neared the Wall, he could see red flames lapping out through the black cloud that poured up from inside the Owner dens. He had hoped to see Ponder and the others along the Great Fence ledge, but they were not there. Were they in the Woodstack? The wind blew waves of heat out into the field; Solo knew that something would have to be very wrong for them to still be here. Then he heard Kitty-Kitty's voice – screaming Spanno's name over and over.

Leaping to the ledge and looking down at the Woodstack, Solo was momentarily paralyzed with shock. Their home was in shambles; the tree slices had been knocked nearly flush with the ground and lay spread out haphazardly across the greyrock. Ponder, Ditto, and Kitty-Kitty were running wildly around the fallen logs with frantic helplessness.

'Ponder!' Solo cried. 'What's happening? Where are Spanno and Selvyn?'

Ponder glanced up at him briefly, wild-eyed. 'Solo! They're inside! A giant rauwulf hit the Woodstack . . . we all got out but Selvyn . . . Spanno went back in to help him . . . the wood kept falling! I couldn't get in! I couldn't stop him!'

'Spanno!' Solo screamed as he jumped to the greyrock beside Ponder. 'Selvyn!' There had to be a way to get them out. That's why Speaker had sent him home – *he* had to find a way to save them!

'Solo!' pleaded Kitty-Kitty. 'Do something! Help them!'

'We're in here!' came a voice from inside the Wood-stack. It was Selvyn, alive! Immediately everyone rushed to the place Selvyn had indicated; they could just see the smallest patch of orange fur between the logs.

'Spanno!' called Solo. 'Where are you?'

'I'm here,' came the reply, tight and choking, from behind Selvyn. 'I'm okay . . . we'll make it, Solo!'

'Push your way out!' yelled Ditto. 'We'll help from this side!'

Everyone began clawing and pulling against the logs. They needed to move them only a few inches, but they would have to hurry. The wood was already beginning to smolder in several places. Selvyn had found the broadest opening between two logs and tried to shove and squeeze his head through. Solo knew they would have to concentrate their combined strength in exactly the same place – the logs were as thick as a cat and it would take all their power to move them.

'All together, here!' Solo called, and they adjusted themselves beside the kit directly under Selvyn's position.

Soon the orange's singed, deeply scratched face worked its way through the opening. Ponder and Ditto grabbed hold of what little fur they could find and tried to drag him out while Solo and Kitty-Kitty scraped and fought against the heavy logs until their claws were torn and bleeding.

The Woodstack had started to burn on the topmost part.

'Harder!' shouted Solo. He could feel his own fur starting to singe and feared for Spanno. But the wood was moving and Selvyn was twisting and forcing his body through the tiny opening. His face and head were bleeding badly where Ponder and Ditto had tried to grip him.

'The wood's moving!' Kitty-Kitty cried as the logs shifted outward beneath their paws. 'Hold on, Spanno! It's working!'

Suddenly Selvyn was free. Ponder and Ditto pulled him out of the crack sideways and then went down under the sudden weight. Selvyn rose and faltered once, but within an instant they were all beside Solo and Kitty-Kitty to help free Spanno. He was bigger, and would need more room.

'We'll do it!' Ponder yelled. 'We'll get you out!'

'Spanno!' screamed Kitty-Kitty again and again. 'Please, Spanno! Hurry!'

Spanno tried to answer, but the heat and smoke stifled his voice. Breathing was almost impossible and came in painful gasps. But Selvyn had gotten out . . . Selvyn was safe.

They were encouraged and put their last bit of strength into fighting the wood that held Spanno captive. A fraction of an inch at a time, the wood was moving and making a passage for the calico.

Just then, the great log tore loose from their grasp and rolled back to its original position, undoing everything they had accomplished. Solo could still see Spanno's face, but he'd been driven back at least a half cat-length. He could not call out, but they could all hear him choking and pulling for air. Even Kitty-Kitty could no longer scream, and made only a broken, rasping whine-cry. Working now with broken or completely missing claws, they began again.

The incredible roaring from the Dwelling and moving rauwulfen added an unreal quality to what was happening, and from the sounds the Owners were making behind them, they were fighting their own battle for survival.

'Solo!' Kitty-Kitty said, her voice barely a whisper. 'It's moving!'

Spanno had once again begun to push his large head into the slender crack between the logs, and Solo shared everyone's optimism as more and more of the calico fur came into sight. Soon Ponder and Ditto would be able to pull him out as they had done Selvyn. They were so close!

They were all nearly blinded by the smoke now, and the heat was burning their faces. The flames were creeping steadily toward them, but they needed only another moment – Spanno was clawing and digging his way out and would soon be safe.

'Push!' Solo cried in a hoarse squeak. 'Spanno, push!'

The calico's head was almost through and everyone braced down shoulder to shoulder for one last, final heave against the logs. Spanno pushed and the others pulled, and they felt the wood finally giving way under their paws. But instead of providing an exit for Spanno, it moved too far and the remains of the Woodstack, now mostly in flames, collapsed completely and were engulfed. They were all forced backward as the burning wood slid down onto the greyrock.

'No!' Solo screamed. 'Spanno! No!' There was no way out now; the Woodstack was almost totally flattened against the ground. He had been too late.

Kitty-Kitty was screaming again, completely out of control, thrashing her head back and forth and calling Spanno's name over and over. Ponder, too, was screaming and lashing out against the logs in futile anguish. Injured and racked with spasms, Selvyn collapsed to his side, with Ditto close behind, looking as close to fey as any cat would ever see him.

Solo, cold as ice despite the fire, threw back his head and called out in an agony that penetrated the din of the flames and carried far into the field. 'Spanno!' he cried, and lunged wildly at the decimated Woodstack.

'No, Solo!' yelled Ponder as he grabbed the kit and jerked him down onto the greyrock. 'We can't help him now!' The smoke was too thick to see Ponder's eyes, but there was desperation in his breaking voice.

And then another cry echoed out into the darkness. It was Spanno, trapped and burning, and there was nothing more they could do. The calico screamed again, but his tortured call was cut off as the Woodstack shifted and settled to the ground, a blackened heap of burning wood.

After a time, Kitty-Kitty's cries faded to a silent sobbing, and the bards gathered around her, sharing the greatest loss any of them would ever know. It was only instinct that got them up and moving, and slowly they filed through the Great Fence and headed back into the field. One by one they veered away and went separately to mourn. Solo hid himself inside a stand of cottonweed and slipped into an exhausted, numbed sleep; he had to stop the pain, at least for a while. Ponder, several cat-lengths away, lost in his thoughts, kept a solitary vigil as the daybright came and went, fading into a new darkfall, and the last traces of smoke were cleared from the fieldside air.

When Solo finally roused himself and moved toward the thickets, he was not the same. His steps were purposeful and even, but lacked that little bounce of exuberance that had been there before, and his jaw was set firmly in the manner of one determined to go on, if only because there is no place else to go. As he walked forward to meet the others gathered just up ahead, he shed his kithood and accepted his place in an uncertain feral world where tragedy and death impinged upon life unannounced, and where survival was not so much a right as a privilege. He had been sheltered and protected, shielded from the harsher aspects of life both by circumstance and by those around him, but those days were gone.

Just west of the central hedges, Solo found the rest of the Gang of Six, now the Gang of Five, and they stood together in silence. The entire Quorum was gathered, unsure and confused in the aftermath of the disaster. Prills trembled and huddled in the hedge, feeling a terrible sense of loss, frightened for their futures. Looking to Solo and the others for direction and assurance, the younger bards milled and paced, speaking in low whispers among themselves. Solo knew that they looked to him now as their Speaker, and he knew that he needed to tell them something, but no words would come.

Banda, followed by little Minit, walked hesitantly toward them. 'What will we do now . . . Dom Solo?' Banda asked. Everyone turned to the kit, waiting for his response.

Solo realized that Banda was not just using the title of 'Dom' as a simple expression of respect. He faltered and looked around, completely stunned. 'No! I can't take . . . take Spanno's place! It should be Selvyn, or Ponder, or – '

Selvyn stepped up quickly. 'We've had a council, while you were . . . alone. Everyone has decided . . . we've all agreed. It's up to you to lead us now.'

'No! I'm too young! I've never been in a real battle! I've – '

'You do the figuring, Solo,' said Ponder softly, 'and Selvyn, Ditto, and I will do the fighting.'

'Solo,' Ditto added, 'in two more seasons you would outrank every cat in this Quorum. You were destined to be a Speaker since kithood.'

'We need you,' said Kitty-Kitty, her voice small and strained, 'and . . . and Spanno would want you to take care of us.'

The rest of the Quorum nodded in agreement. But Solo agonized over all that had happened. What could *he* do for the Quorum? He hadn't been able to help Spanno. And did he really outrank Selvyn, or Ponder? Even knowing as he did that rank was an inherent thing, not learned or earned, Solo couldn't think of himself in that light, even with time. He understood now that Speaker had handed down his office to Solo that strange night in the field, but he couldn't see himself in that way either – much less a Dom-cat. Or both Dom-cat *and* Speaker. Nothing in the Legends set a precedent for this. Overwhelmed, he turned away self-consciously and made his way into the deep hedge to be alone and gather his thoughts. Had this really fallen on him? Their territory was nearly destroyed and their leader and greatest warrior was dead. The prills were bloated with the kits inside them, and arrangements had to be made quickly, before birthing time. And now they would be led by a young, inexperienced kit . . .

'*Follow your path, Solo. Remember your dream.*'

Speaker's clear, soft words entered Solo's thoughts without warning – though Solo was not surprised. And the old Speaker's words gave Solo the peace and guidance he sought.

He *would* lead his little Quorum. He would lead them westward, into a wilderness paradise away from the Owners and territorial feuds, where they could be free, rather than 'feral' – half-domesticated. Their kits would be raised to know *true* feline pride and independence, living their life the way they were meant to do. They didn't need the Owners anymore.

Solo's stride was forceful and strong as he went back to the others. There was much he needed to tell them, much he needed to explain. Ponder, Kitty-Kitty, Selvyn,

11
The First Battle

The Quorum grieved over the loss of Spanno, and the sadness that held across the territory like a tangible shadow both bound them together and kept them apart; their relationships with the calico had been too deep, too abiding, to set aside so easily. They ate, and took water, and slept when they could, but the despair stayed with them, present in long, vacant gazes and in pointless daybright wanderings through the field that took them anywhere except close to the Wall and the remains of the Woodstack.

Six daybrights after the fire, an avalanche of strange new sounds came from across the Great Fence. Rauwulfen moved on the greyrock in greater and greater numbers, soon followed by loud, sharp bangings and buzzings and the call of Owner voices. The Owner dens were being rebuilt – they meant to put the Dwelling back together and go on as before. The Keep donations, relatively scarce for the last several darkfalls, gradually increased, and the small sections of field that had been blackened by spot fires began to sprout new green. The Quorum slowly roused from its lethargy; the prills began to put their own nests in order and the bards resumed their hunting games and halfhearted fighting. The watches and patrols were resumed and Solo took command, walking the ledge as had many Dom-cats before him, with Ponder always just slightly behind. The past gradually receded into its place – they would never forget, but the line between what had gone before and what lay ahead had finally been drawn.

One darkfall, Solo waited until Ponder left to silt before slipping out into the field alone. Ponder had always kept a close eye on him, but now that Solo was Dom and open to challenge, the big grey had become fanatic in his protectiveness. Even if Ponder were occupied elsewhere, he would see to it that Selvyn or Ditto stayed close beside the young Dom. But Solo was feeling the deep Calling need, at last, and he wanted to look for Pardie – without an escort. With nostrils flared, he read the fieldside air and searched for the white prill's delicate raksha. He hadn't gone far when he heard Kitty-Kitty's soft call of pain and distress. What was she doing out here alone? Was she hurt? He listened for the sound, and it came again, only much more faintly. With a start, Solo realized that he wasn't hearing the call at all – it was more of a vision, a sound echoing softly in his consciousness. As the sensation faded, the kit wheeled around and raced back to the others. Even if it were only a kind of vision, Solo knew it must have had a purpose.

In a few moments Solo located Ponder's surround; Selvyn and Ditto were with him, but not Kitty-Kitty. Solo could sense that they had been about to begin a search. Stomping through the weeds, Ponder bore down on him, wearing an irritated, slightly righteous expression, followed by the orange and Ditto.

'Where were you, Solo?' Ponder began. 'Don't you realize you're a walking target now?'

'Where's Kitty-Kitty?' Solo interrupted brusquely, and at the tone of his voice everyone's expression changed.

'I think she went northward, to be by herself,' answered Ditto. 'She's been restless and pacing all darkfall.'

'She wouldn't talk, either,' added Selvyn.

'Restless and pacing?' echoed Solo, and the way he said it communicated his fear to the others. 'The kits?'

'It's too soon, isn't it?' asked Selvyn, taxing his limited knowledge of such things.

'Kitty-Kitty said there wouldn't be kits for at least another quarter-circle,' muttered Ditto, trying to remember exactly when she'd made that statement.

'Kits?' asked Ponder, looking truly horrified. 'At a time like this?'

'I think I know where she might be,' said Solo, and quickly he turned to the north and struck out through the brush. The others exchanged glances and followed in nervous silence. Kitty-Kitty couldn't take another loss, not now.

Snaking silently through the cool shadow cover, the four bards extended their surrounds, trying to locate Kitty-Kitty, hoping to find her nearby . . . and alone. Solo headed for the far northern hedges, where his old den, abandoned for several seasons, was situated. He was almost certain she would be there.

As Solo approached the den, he located the prill's aura. The group halted uncertainly. Kitty-Kitty was not alone.

Solo lowered his head, eyes wide and nose quivering at the strange rack coming from the thicket. Thirping softly in his throat to announce his approach, he moved to the mouth of the nest.

'Solo?' answered the prill from well within the hedge. Her voice was laced with deep weariness.

'It's me, Kitty-Kitty. Are you . . . all right? Do you want me to stay out?'

'No!' she said quickly; and then, 'Oh, Solo! They're too small!'

Solo hesitated, and then moved carefully into the hedge, working his way through the intricate network of interlocking branches. Entering the small den, he saw Kitty-Kitty against the westward wall. She was on her side but her head was upright, her eyes round with worry. It was a moment before he saw the tiny movements beside her in the dark.

'Kitty-Kitty!' Solo breathed in amazement. Beside her were three tiny kits, one pure white, the other two multicolored orange. 'Are they . . . all right?' he asked in a whisper, staying back against the entrance. Solo couldn't imagine any kit that small surviving.

'I don't know, Solo,' Kitty-Kitty said. 'They should be bigger.'

Solo was unable to take his eyes away from the little kits. The calico ones, both bards, struggled and fought for their place at Kitty-Kitty's side, but the white one, a prill, moved more slowly and her head seemed to wobble more. 'They're beautiful,' Solo said gently.

Kitty-Kitty's eyes were slightly fogged, her breathing tense and quick, but she was not even close to fey. For the first time he could remember, Solo didn't know what to say to his friend. She saw the concern in his eyes.

'I'll be all right, Solo,' she said.

Solo stayed with Kitty-Kitty a little longer, and then at her request went to bring the others in to see her kits. Ponder had to be physically pushed into the hedge, and Selvyn was equally as reticent, but Solo understood that Kitty-Kitty wanted them to see her kits now, in case something happened. He also understood his friends' reluctance – they were bards, and not usually privileged to see such things. Solo was firm, though, and in they went, and thankfully Ditto's graciousness adequately covered for both Ponder's open fear of the fragile-looking kits and Selvyn's self-conscious silence.

Kitty-Kitty was left to rest and the bards camped outside the den, keeping watch over the prill, silently sharing the dark knowledge that these tiny, tiny felines would likely not survive.

'There will be kits all over the place soon,' mused Ditto, breaking the quiet. 'The hedge will be off limits for an entire circle.'

Selvyn had opened his mouth to speak, but his eyes grew wide as a thought struck him. He deliberately yawned and got up, stretching with exaggerated leisure. 'I'll be back later,' he said casually. 'I think I'll go check on the outwatch.'

Ponder, too, stood and tried to suppress his urgency with a long stretch. 'Good idea. I'll check southward.'

Ditto stayed down and winked at Solo. They both knew where Ponder and the orange were headed – Mondy and Rosen must be close to birthing time, and having seen Kitty-Kitty's babies, they wanted to be with their mates. After all, Spanno had said it was permissible for bards to 'recognize' their own kits.

Solo and Ditto settled each within himself, and were soon napping. They could hear Kitty-Kitty's soft purring and though it was directed toward her little ones, the older bards were soothed and lulled by the sound. Although they dozed, the slightest change in Kitty-Kitty's tone would bring them instantly alert.

But it wasn't Kitty-Kitty's purring that finally jerked them to their paws. A feral warning fugue had shattered the stillness, silencing even the fieldside insects with its primitive urgency. It was Ponder, and in top voice. His call was both a challenge and an alert that told them it was no intra-Quorum squabble. There was an enemy in the territory.

The call came from far westward of the prill-hedges and slightly to the south. Solo and Ditto, on full alert, quickly bounded off into the field, trying to gauge the magnitude of the crisis from Ponder's piercing fugue.

'This is serious,' said Ditto. There was real hatred in the grey's voice.

Solo pulled up sharply when they came to the edge of a clearing. The invader was Tanner. Bryndle's old nemesis was back – probably to try again for a take-over. Ditto stopped alongside the kit as they assessed the situation from the cover of the weeds.

With Selvyn beside him, Ponder stood in a semiclearing facing the white bard. The big grey was battle-frumped and had his claws unsheathed and splayed out on the ground. His head was down low and his lips were curled back in the inimitable fegin threat that was his trademark. Tanner stood arched, looking cool and unruffled. Behind him, Solo could now see, stood several tough-looking warriors. Tanner's timing was better than the last time he'd attacked their territory. The prill 'warriors' would be unable to do battle in this season, and the Quorum was in chaos after the fire and loss of their Dom. News must have reached Tanner that old Bryndle's territory was now held by a young bard not yet at full weight.

Solo watched and hesitated. Kitty-Kitty didn't need this, not now.

'Come on, Tanner,' Ponder hissed. 'Let's see how tough you really are.'

'Every time I come to visit, you get in my face,' Tanner sneered. 'Now, get out of my way. I'm here to challenge your Dom – directly.'

Solo felt empty inside. Tanner had the right, he knew, to challenge him, being a Dom in his own territory. But even Solo recognized that he was too young and inexperienced to battle a war-toughened veteran like Tanner. And Solo knew that Ponder would never let Tanner close to him, right or no right.

'You can challenge a rauwulf if you want to, Tanner,' spat Ponder, 'but you'll go through me first.'

'Then me,' added Selvyn, with just the right shade of indifference in his tone.

Ditto moved away from Solo into the clearing, adding his own silent presence with the others. Abalon and Babbot materialized from the weeds, as did Banda and Minit. Several lesser bards also joined the group. But Tanner was unintimidated. Most of the Quorum was present, though their Dom stayed crouched in the thicket, alone.

'Does this great Dom-Speaker-kit of yours *refuse* my challenge?' Tanner asked, an incredulous tint to his voice. Refusal of such a challenge was unheard-of in the feral world.

'I take care of the minor problems,' chided Ponder, trying to direct attention away from Solo.

'Are you sure it's not my turn, Ponder?' Selvyn snickered. 'We should save you for more important things.' The orange flipped an ear to show his disdain.

But Tanner didn't take up their challenge. He wanted a direct confrontation with the Dom-cat for control of the territory. And if they failed to produce their leader, he would initiate a free-for-all with the Enforcers and Quorum, drive them out, and bring in his own followers. Either way, he would finally have this territory for his own. He only wished he'd been able to take it from Bryndle, or even Spanno. This would be too easy.

Ponder bristled. 'Listen, silt-head. If my Dom-cat felt like looking at you, you'd be wearing him right now. Why don't you just – '

Ponder's words stopped in mid-sentence as all heads whipped around toward the movement in the eastward periphery – Solo was moving out of the brush.

No one, especially Tanner, was prepared to see the Dom Solo that walked toward them that darkfall. Approaching the gypsy in full stealth, he looked truly formidable. Fully battle-frumped and low to the ground, he seemed much heavier and more filled out. He carried his head down and level, and moved with a smooth confidence that usually radiates from only the most prepared. The grey-white of his shoulder scars glistened in the scant starlight, adding to the unexpected illusion of a seasoned warrior. Solo's movements were superbly controlled and confident, and a low warning fugue was building into a forceful call of challenge. Even Ditto stood openmouthed and gaping.

Solo had expected an argument or protest from Ponder and the others over his intent to fight, but was relieved to feel them fade back slightly out of the immediate arena. As a *true* Dom-cat, not one in name only, his decisions were Law, and as Enforcers they would not hinder that privilege – they would uphold it.

In his heart, however, Ponder knew how far he would let this thing go before stepping in.

Five or six cat-lengths from Tanner, Solo stopped and locked onto the gypsy's surround – he would have only moments to find a pattern, a weakness.

Tanner began to compose himself. He had heard the young Dom was but a kit, and would be a pushover in one-on-one combat. But this was no mere kit before him, to be disposed of with a swat. He would have to fight, and from the look of him, fight hard, and inflict deeper scars than the blond Dom carried now to put him down.

'You wanted me, Tanner?' Solo slipped suddenly out of fugue and into a strong, low, confident voice, hoping to take Tanner off guard. But the white barely raised a whisker.

'So this is the Speaker-kit this Quorum of Tame-cats calls Dom,' growled Tanner, staying cool. The correct ritual called for a long string of increasingly vile degradations to be flung at one another, but Solo didn't answer the insult as he continued to study the gypsy in silence.

'So you think you're ready, young Dom,' Tanner hissed as he widened his stance and lowered. They faced off, ready for battle.

A strained hush descended over the assembly. Solo's Enforcers watched him with wild apprehension, knowing what the kit was putting on the line with this fight. A Quorum cannot follow a defeated Dom. He would be banished as a gypsy, as Bryndle had been, followed only by those few still loyal to him; the fate of the territory would belong to the victor. There was no event in territorial life more important than a challenge for the leadership of the Quorum. Ponder suffered more than the rest of Solo's friends and Enforcers, torn between his habit of protecting the kit and his Quorum responsibility of serving his Dom.

Solo and Tanner edged closer, until they crouched less than four cat-lengths apart. Their low, rasping fugues gradually became clear, breathless notes of challenge intended to overwhelm the other's sensorium. They did not circle each other as was commonly done, each afraid of making any unnecessary movement. They studied each other with an intenseness unmatched in the animal world. Feline battle was like a form of physical chess – feints within feints, each alert for the smallest advantage over his opponent. It demanded intense concentration and control.

Tanner's flank muscles tensed slightly – a movement that was barely perceptible even to Solo. The kit readied himself to spring to the side should Tanner leap, staying in close enough to try a counterattack as Tanner landed.

'Clear your mind of all thoughts,' spoke a Voice inside Solo's head. 'Do not plan it, it will distract you.

Be receptive to all that you see and feel, and use your instincts.'

Was the voice Speaker's, or Spanno's? Or his own?

Solo stilled the inner dialogue in his mind and opened his senses to Tanner's mannerisms and movements, relying on his natural instincts to guide him. Never had he felt so feline. Any fear he had had was gone, replaced by a sense of control he had never before experienced. He could see Tanner's aura clearly, and he knew that slight variations in its hue or pattern would betray the white's intent before he struck.

The gypsy's eyes met Solo's. Tanner's concentration was fierce, but as a veteran of many battles, he leaned toward the more physical aspects of the fight. A dominant rogue, he followed the more brutal ways of the feral, feudal life. Compared with these cats, Solo's Quorum was incredibly civilized. Tanner's vast experience made him overconfident, however, and therefore more predictable. He would fight, Solo knew, in familiar patterns, ones that had worked for him in the past.

'Use your fugue, Solo,' the Voice advised. 'A good fugue can distract and intimidate. It can even mesmerize an opponent to a degree if used with precision.'

Solo lowered the volume of his call and let it rise again slowly, seeking that narrow range of sound that would irritate and distract Tanner. The white tensed slightly against the sound.

Arching his tail, Solo went into full fugue, collected, poised, ready. A sense of *déjà vu* spread over him, a feeling of power and confidence. It was an odd sensation, that of something old and long forgotten, but in a way intimately familiar.

'Draw from the Legends, kit. You carry the experience of every feline battle ever fought within your genes, within your memory.'

Solo sprang on impulse, with no detectable preparation, surprising everyone with such a decisive initiative. Tanner dropped and rolled, his claws upward, as Solo descended, giving Solo access to only the loose fur and hide of his side. Tanner slashed again and again at Solo's thick-coated underside, but was unable to penetrate the heavy fur and inflict any serious damage.

'If a round is a stalemate, be done with it,' the Voice cautioned. 'Do not weaken yourself with it.'

Solo lurched free and collected himself several cat-lengths away, always facing Tanner. He had learned much about Tanner's reflexes and fighting habits in the brief confrontation.

Tanner was instantly up and poised. The scuffle had taken nothing out of him. But he was determined to take the advantage this time. He lunged at Solo even before the battle calling had resumed, hoping to catch Solo by surprise; but the blond bard quickly side-stepped and leapt out over Tanner, curling around his head to avoid his sharp hind claws. The attack was good, and Solo brought Tanner down as he bit deeply into the white's neck. Jerking downward and tearing free, Tanner lunged instantly for Solo, without the slightest pause to collect himself. Solo met the attack head-on, and they locked together, poised on hind-paws, clawing each other viciously. Using his weight advantage, Tanner twisted Solo to the ground, but Solo managed a good cheek-hold and was doing damage to the white with his rear claws. Tanner was forced to back away and Solo used the moment to pull upward and back. Both Doms were bleeding, but the wounds were superficial and as yet unfelt.

They separated by several cat-lengths as they pulled themselves together and assessed the round. They were well-matched. Although Tanner fought from long experience and the confidence of many victories, Solo, drawing from instinct and cunning, had more than held his own. The other ferals had not moved since the battle began. The change in Solo held the Quorum spellbound; even Tanner's bards could sense that something more than a simple battle was taking place. Solo seemed to have the presence and mastery of a Great One of the Legends – even Tanner could see that in Solo he had found an opponent of frightening dimensions.

Solo began his fugue again, a pure and unbroken sound. He was perfectly tuned and focused; at the moment, nothing else existed other than the white bard who faced him. He could sense Tanner's readiness, and could feel the tension in the gypsy's tight muscles. Still confident and ready for more, Tanner had not yet considered the possibility of defeat. He began his own call in a high-pitched whining tone, deliberately clashing with Solo's fugue in an effort to break the young Dom's concentration.

But again Solo startled Tanner by abruptly leaping out at him in a motion so fast that several onlookers missed it. Tanner reacted in time, ducking down to come up under Solo as they met. Solo, however, landed with his hindquarters to the front and rabbit-punched Tanner with his back paws, knocking the white off balance. He twisted around hard to gain an ear-hold on the white that would have immobilized most cats.

Tanner, however, paused for only an instant before lurching back against Solo's grasp, sacrificing the ear. Pain scorched the side of his head. For the first time in the fight, Tanner began to think defensively. On impulse, he found traction and lunged free, but instead of falling back to gather himself for another round, he leapt over the blond in an immediate counterattack. Solo barely had time to drop with claws splayed upward as Tanner hit him with his full weight. The white was fighting wildly, trying to wound Solo as badly as he himself had been wounded.

'Now, Solo – it has to be now!' the Voice within him said.

Solo clamped down on Tanner's chest fur with his teeth as he lashed out viciously with his claws. The white tried to bite the top of Solo's head, but was too far forward for a strong hold. Solo continued to slash at Tanner's underside, while gradually trying to work his teeth up to a throat-hold. He knew instinctively that that would be the only way to stop the white. Feeling Tanner falter slightly, Solo seized the slight advantage and came up hard, throwing him over sideways and gaining the topmost position. The gypsy was on his side, unable to use his claws. As Tanner turned his face upward, Solo clamped down tightly over the white's cheek and eye. Tanner screamed and tore wildly free, paralyzed with pain. He sidestepped clumsily and nearly fell, partially blinded by blood. The entire left side of his head was soaked. Dazed and gagging, Tanner sank back down on his haunches, belly-to-the-ground in defeat.

The fight had taken only three rounds.

For a moment the Quorum remained still and tense, silently staring from the outer circle. Ponder, of course, had his face in the dirt, unsure what expression was appropriate. Selvyn and Ditto stood together, openly awed at the young Dom they had recently called 'kit.'

Tanner wiped at his face and looked down at the ground. There was a subtle change to the gypsy's aura, and Solo knew at once that the white Dom was no longer an enemy. Tanner rose and his bards grouped uncertainly around him. Together they headed back northward into the field, tails tucked under in submission.

Solo's entire Quorum was gathered; even the prills had come out into the open, admiration and respect for their Dom in their faces. Solo was uncomfortable in the long silence, but Ponder soon took care of that. Rolling over on the ground, lying full-out on his back and looking deeply satisfied with life, Ponder closed his eyes and stretched himself out, saying, 'Bring on the dogs! Bring on the gypsies and giant wildcats. Silt, bring on the Owners! We are *invincible*!'

As the Quorum burst into giggles, Ditto proudly moved beside Solo and shook his head with relieved weariness. They had all, in their hearts, fought that battle with Solo, and they felt it.

'I guess we'd better tell Kitty-Kitty,' Solo said simply. 'She's undoubtedly heard the ruckus.'

'I'll go,' offered several feline voices.

'We'll all go,' said Solo, straightening his coat to hide the scratches and cuts. He needed to get away from the battlefield, and was embarrassed by the way the Quorum ferals all looked at him. It was the way they once had looked at Bryndle and Spanno. And even Speaker.

Solo turned abruptly and headed northward along the hedge. Ditto, Ponder, and Selvyn followed closely behind him, their heads held high, their step lighter than in many days. Kitty-Kitty called out to them while they were still several cat-lengths from her den.

'Solo? Ponder? What happened? Is Solo . . . ?'

'The twit's just fine,' called Ponder, grinning as they nosed their way just inside the hedge. 'Barely a scratch on him.'

'You let him fight?' shrieked the prill. 'Ponder! You silt-head!'

'How are the kits?' interrupted Solo. 'Are they still . . . all right?'

Kitty-Kitty paused in her tirade against Ponder and

looked around at her little ones. 'They're fine. There's been no change.' She hesitated and turned back to Solo. 'You're okay? You're not hurt?'

'Believe me, Kitty-Kitty,' Ditto laughed, 'Solo didn't even need our help. He took care of that gypsy in style.'

'He stomped him bald,' added Ponder reverently.

'But, Solo,' Kitty-Kitty insisted, 'you could have been hurt, and . . . we need you.'

'I'm fine.' Solo smiled. 'I'm not a kit anymore. Please don't worry about me. You need to rest.'

Kitty-Kitty relaxed and smiled, but smelling Solo's blood, she had barely subdued an urge to go to him and help clean his wounds. But he *wasn't* a kit anymore, and she knew she could no longer do such things for him.

The bards backed out of the thicket and wearily made their way southward. Solo was hoping they wouldn't want to discuss the fight throughout the remainder of the darkfall.

'Droud, kit,' said Selvyn at length. 'I've never seen any cat handle himself like that in his first fight – or in any fight, for that matter.'

'Well,' drawled Ponder, 'he had good teachers. I personally remember showing him that rabbit kick . . .'

'You fought well, Solo,' said Ditto, 'but you didn't have to fight. You took a big chance, you know.'

'It wasn't that much of a fight,' Solo said self-consciously. 'And I *did* have to fight, Ditto. I am the Dom.'

Suddenly the four stopped dead in their tracks. A sweet, musky female gelt floated through the cool night air.

'Raksha!' Selvyn said, flaring his nostrils. 'I wonder who it is?'

'It's Pardie.' Ponder smiled, glancing at Solo. Everyone had seen how the kit looked at her.

'I think she's waiting for you,' chided Ditto as he nudged the young Dom.

'Me?' stammered Solo, feeling his shyness returning.

'You're the Dom. And a hero on top of that,' Selvyn said, trying to sound very serious.

'But the watch . . .' Solo said lamely, glancing from one to another.

'I'll post the watches,' offered Ponder. 'That's what Enforcers *do*, remember? And Selvyn and Ditto will stay by Kitty-Kitty. Now, go on out there and find her.'

Solo cleared his throat and hastily smoothed out his coat. Moving away from the others, he ventured a low, unsure Call. Pardie's delicate thirping reached back to him and Solo edged through the weeds toward the soft, alluring sound. Pardie's white coat, partially hidden in the brush, sparkled in the starlight as she watched him coming. Her heavy perfume went to Solo's head and a subtle fire began to spread inside him. She was beautiful. And she was waiting for him.

It was close to daybright when Solo returned to the thickets. He circled out a place just far enough away from the others to be alone. This had been an eventful darkfall for the young Dom, and more than anything else right then, he needed solitude.

The sun-star was halfway across the sky when Kitty-Kitty's anguished moaning woke the four bards who kept watch in the thickets. Solo rose and went in to her while Ponder, Selvyn, and Ditto waited silently outside the den entrance. The little white prill-kit had died. Kitty-Kitty turned her head away as Solo gently, hesitantly grasped it between his teeth and carried it outward, much as Dom Spanno had done for her long ago. The fire continued to take its toll.

Kitty-Kitty curled protectively around her two remaining kits, her legacy from Spanno. They were active and strong; she would be able to keep these little ones, she knew, and they would grow feral and proud . . .

Dom Solo carried the tiny kit westward past the hedges and laid it close to Speaker's death place. Several Quorum members watched silently from within the brush. Solo had proved his bardhood and his fierceness, but this gentle act bound them more closely together than his fighting power ever could have.

For a long time Solo sat alone and gazed into the westward sky. His life had changed so completely – he was now responsible for so much. Could he live up to the Quorum's expectations – and to those who had gone before him?

Feeling Ponder moving in the weeds, Solo rose and turned back. So far he'd been unable to bring himself to lay down his gelt over Dom Spanno's. But as soon as it was darkfall, he would have to begin marking out his territory.

12
Exodus

Ditto had been right: by early spring there were new kits everywhere in the hedge. Ponder complained to Solo that the whole territory was 'crummy with the little twerps.' Mondy had given birth to three orange kits, and Rosen was the mother of two little greys, and every other conceivable combination of feline colors was represented in the Quorum. Kitty-Kitty's tiny calicos, Carver and Justin, had already grown pesky and strong, fond of torturing the elder bards during daybright, and had developed an unerring instinct for finding the most sensitive parts of the body to attack and chew on.

Few of the other prills were as relaxed as Kitty-Kitty about having bards around their new kits, but Ponder was occasionally seen sneaking into Rosen's den, and Selvyn often came home from 'patrol' with kit-rack clinging to his orange fur.

The general activity of the Quorum had gradually shifted to the far side of the main thicket. The Owner commotion across the greyrock, as they put the Dwelling back together, was overwhelming and the cats tried to keep as much distance between them as possible. Before the fire, Owners seldom seemed to even notice the ferals, but now, as they bustled about the outside of the Dwelling making repairs, it became more and more frequent to have a Quorum member report being chased back to fieldside or having rocks thrown at him by the giant creatures. Once, during an early-morning forage to the Keep, several ferals had been nearly frightened to death when an Owner took a large object and banged loudly on the walls. They had scrabbled over the far side and escaped unhurt, but the new attitude the Owners seemed to have about the ferals greatly worried Solo. He issued orders that the greyrock was off limits to the ferals, except at mid-darkfall when they went to the Keep for graille. Perhaps, he thought, the situation would get back to normal when the Owners had finished with their Dwelling. Already it looked much as it had before. The burned Woodstack, finally, had been taken away. Except for the change in the Owners, a semblance of normality had returned to the territory.

Except, perhaps, for Elrod.

Elrod, a Tame-cat recently abandoned by his Owners, wasn't adjusting well to Quorum life. He had attached himself to one spot at the base of the Great Fence, and hadn't moved for three darkfalls.

'Elrod!' Solo tried to reason with him, 'Ferals don't need Owners to live! Come on back with me!' But Elrod was disconsolate and no amount of logic or pleading would budge him. Born in an Owner Dwelling to a prill who herself had never gone outward, Elrod simply couldn't imagine another way of life. Even his knowledge of the Legends was sketchy and translated within the narrow boundaries of Owner confinement. Ponder, too, felt sorry for the Tame-cat and took him graille once when he thought no one was around, but Solo had begun to lose patience. That one of his feline brothers should be reduced to such dependency! The next time one of the Quorum cats asked him why he was so insistent that they move westward away from the Owners, he would just trot him past Elrod and save himself any further explanation.

One darkfall, as Solo sat by the Great Fence talking with Elrod about his situation, a great owl came to hunt in the field. Most of the other bards were on patrol and Ponder had gone to make a quick check on the watches. Rosen was out by the central thickets with several other prills, beaming with pride as she supervised her young ones' first venture from their nest. By the time she caught the movement overhead, and realized what it was, it was already too late. Dubby, the smaller of her kits, was several cat-lengths out into the clearing alone and the giant yellow-eyed bird was bearing down fast on its defenseless prey. The prill screamed just as the owl struck the ground, missing the tiny kit by inches as Dubby scooted haltingly toward the far brush. Rosen leapt out but the bird had already turned and was making another pass. Selvyn materialized from the other side of the clearing and raced toward the kit, knowing as he ran that he could never make it in time. Within an instant the great owl dove, snatched up the little feline, and recovering its balance with a great flapping of wings, began to rise. Solo, alerted by Rosen's first cry, hit the edge of the clearing just in time to see a sparkling white figure leap straight upward from the weeds.

'Speaker!' breathed Solo, frozen in his tracks.

The white feline appeared airborne himself as he collided with the owl a full four cat-lengths from the ground. Knocked roughly from the bird's deadly grasp, Dubby landed and rolled twice, curling into a very fey little ball. The huge owl screeched and clamored away as the white cat landed on all fours and collected himself in the grass.

Rosen, frightened nearly to fey herself, grabbed her kit and rushed it back toward the hedges and the kit she'd left behind.

'Speaker?' Solo whispered again, but the feline who turned to face him was not Speaker – it was Tanner.

Just then, Ponder stormed into the clearing, rage in his eyes and voice. '*You!*' he growled at Tanner, barely in control. 'How did you get in here?' The big grey moved toward Tanner threateningly.

'Wait,' said Solo. 'He saved Rosen's kit from a night-bird. Let him settle.'

Ponder looked quickly to Rosen and saw her fretting over the two kits. He was momentarily torn between a desire to go to Rosen and his duty to the Quorum as Enforcer, but of course his responsibilities came first, especially since neither kit seemed to be injured. He looked at Tanner questioningly.

'How *did* you get in here?' Solo asked, knowing that the borders should have been fully guarded at this time of darkfall.

'I just slipped in through a gap in your patrols,' Tanner answered, shrugging his shoulders self-consciously. 'You got a couple of real amateurs out there. I wanted to get to Dom Solo – ' Tanner was cut off by warning growls from both Selvyn and Ponder.

'The Dom got to *you* already,' hissed the grey. 'Don't you ever learn?'

'You don't understand,' Tanner continued quickly. 'I wanted to see your Dom without having to fight my way in. I hoped I could catch him alone on patrol – '

'Why?' Selvyn asked, confused.

Tanner looked directly at Solo for a moment, then back to the ground, hesitating before launching into his story. 'My Quorum . . .the North Quorum . . . has been decimated. There are only a few of us left – just a couple of prills and their kits and two of my Enforcers. The Owners have been trying to run us out for several seasons; four darkfalls ago they set traps . . . many were captured and taken away, some died. Graille has been scarce too. The Owners have started covering the food containers so tightly we couldn't get in them – we've been having to raid neighboring territories. Two daybrights ago some of the Owners put out graille in several places, but it had a bad rack ... I told everyone not to eat it. But they were so hungry that many of them did anyway. By darkfall they were dead. Most of those who remained have left in search of other homes ... but I thought that maybe you might be able to use another Enforcer. After all, I couldn't beat you, I guess I might as well ... join you.' Tanner looked relieved to have it all out, and continued in a torrent, 'I've got a few rough edges, I know, but I'm strong and not afraid of much, and – '

'He wants to join us?' Selvyn said in a shocked tone.

'Solo!' said Ponder, equally shocked. 'Don't trust him! He's challenged every Dom this Quorum has had for control of the territory!'

'It's a trap,' Selvyn agreed. 'He wanted to kill you before!'

Solo saw the weary expression on Tanner's scarred face. There was sincerity in his surround, they could all see that, but the Quorum cats had spent too much time protecting themselves from Tanner to trust him so quickly.

'Who killed the kit in the field when you invaded the territory and challenged Bryndle several seasons ago?' Kitty-Kitty asked, seemingly without emotion. She stepped into the growing group of felines and looked into Tanner's startled eyes.

Tanner looked around in amazement before he realized that the bards were allowing a prill the right to interrupt at council. He recognized her as the warrior-prill leader he had seen that darkfall so long ago. 'The bard's name was Cutter ... he wasn't really one of mine, just a gypsy who joined us for the fight.' Tanner was almost stuttering. 'He's long empty now. I never condoned killing kits ...'

'He saved my Dubby,' Rosen offered from the edge

of the clearing, referring to Tanner. 'He knocked a bird right out of the air.'

Sitting back, Kitty-Kitty remained quiet, apparently satisfied with Tanner's answer.

Selvyn and Ponder continued to argue among themselves over Tanner's request to join the Quorum, but Solo was thinking about what Tanner had told them of the Owner persecutions. Could the Owners here turn against the ferals as they had in Tanner's territory? Had they only been fortunate in living in relative peace this long? The Legends said that Owners were unpredictable and never to be trusted – and Tanner's report more than confirmed this. Solo was suddenly filled with a sense of danger and dread.

He stood and walked up to Tanner, silencing the Quorum. 'Tanner, I give you sanctuary in our territory, and any that want to come with you.' It was a decree, and would be accepted as final. Sanctuary, as all the ferals knew, was substantially different from complete acceptance. Tanner had more or less been placed on probationary status – his rank and place within the Quorum would have to be established.

Taking his cue from Solo, Tanner left the Quorum bards alone to discuss the situation, moving out of the circle and off into the field. There was something else he'd wanted to say to Solo, his biggest reason for coming here. He was almost sure that Solo was one of the Great Ones spoken of in the Legends, ones that would come someday and lead felines out of Owner bondage. He'd seen something in Solo's aura the darkfall of the battle that he'd never seen before in any feline, something powerful and eerie, and majestic. And if he was right, Tanner thought, this was something bigger than his own pride, and he wanted to be a part of it.

'I'll be watching you, silt-head,' Ponder called as

Tanner moved away. 'One wrong move and you're mine!' Tanner winced, but held himself in check, walking away with quiet dignity.

Everyone supported Solo's decision to give Tanner sanctuary, although Ponder continued to grumble. It wasn't easy for a fighter, an Enforcer like Ponder, to embrace a former enemy and accept him into their feral community so quickly. Nonetheless, even the grey couldn't deny that Tanner had saved Rosen's – and his – kit. And in the end, that act of heroism was the deciding factor in Tanner's acceptance.

The prills that Tanner had spoken of refused to move their kits and stayed in their old territory, and the two Enforcers had simply disappeared, presumably to follow the gypsy life on their own. So Tanner wound up joining Solo's Quorum alone, and the next several days were hard ones for him. He didn't fit in right away – it would be quite a while before he did. He seemed uncomfortable, as if he were playing a part, restraining his opinions and acting in a circumspect manner. Accustomed to holding highest rank, he had held himself second to very few felines since kithood. The only cat he had ever respected was the old dark Speaker who had been with his Quorum before the Owners had declared out-and-out war on the ferals. It was not easy to suppress his desire to assert his rank and claim a place within Solo's hierarchy. But Tanner had patience and a force of purpose; he was determined to endure the wary looks from the bards and frightened scurrying of prills and kits as he passed. Eventually he would work his way within Solo's inner circle. If the Dom-kit was the leader he hoped he was, if the magic he'd felt in Solo's surround represented what he thought it did, he would walk behind this young one. If not he would kill him.

* * *

Ditto came home the following darkfall from a minor Explore and ran across Tanner in the field. He had sounded a general alarm and had the entire Quorum ready to wage full-scale war before he could be convinced that the Quorum's favorite enemy was now its newest member. After he had accepted the situation, he viewed it from his usual practical viewpoint.

'You realize, Solo,' he said solemnly, 'that you've taken all the joy out of field-watch. And what will the prills threaten their kits with? They can't say "Tanner will come and carry you off if you're naughty" when Tanner lives in the same hedge.'

Everyone appreciated the humor, even Tanner, but Ponder was sullen. He'd hoped for support in his campaign against the white, although the other bards seemed to be taking Tanner's acceptance into the Quorum in stride. Realizing that big trouble was surely brewing between Ponder and Tanner, Solo resolved to have a talk with the grey at the first opportunity.

But something happened early the next daybright that overshadowed every other concern they might have had. Not long after the Quorum had settled down for sleep, the loud, roaring sound of a rauwulf woke them, coming from the direction of the southern border. There was a rauwulf in the field! Quickly Solo, Ponder, Selvyn, and Ditto rose and crept warily through the weeds until they were within sight range. The rauwulf was unlike any they had ever seen before: it was larger and shaped differently, and smelled strongly of fire. Two Owners walked beside it. As Solo watched, he began to tremble inside. Occasionally an Owner or Owner kit would come into the field, but never in his memory or in any story he had ever heard had a rauwulf invaded their territory. They had brought the rauwulf right through the hedges that lined the south border and left it twenty or so cat-lengths into

215

the field. The Owners stayed in the field for a long time as Solo and the others watched in silence, and before the giant creatures left, they drove short sticks into the ground that had thin, brightly colored strips of cloth attached to them. But they didn't take the rauwulf. It waited silently, ominously, in the southern field.

'What do you think it means?' asked Selvyn as the four made their way back toward the hedges.

'I don't know,' answered the young Dom. 'But I don't think it's good, whatever it is. Ponder, post a watch on that rauwulf, darkfall and daybrights too. The Owners wouldn't have left it there if they weren't coming back.'

Ditto volunteered for the first watch, but there was no further conversation about it. Owner activity, they all knew, was inexplicable and far beyond their understanding.

The southern part of the field, with its mysterious Owner markers, was pronounced off limits to the ferals, just as the greyrock had been, and the Quorum became progressively more nervous and jittery. The silent presence of the rauwulf in their field infected them all with a sense of imminent danger, and Solo was deeply concerned. He remembered Speaker's cryptic words about sensing danger himself, and couldn't shake the feeling that something terrible was about to happen. Ponder, however, was obsessed by Tanner's presence within the Quorum, and Solo was concerned that if a crisis should strike, the two would not be able to function together effectively. That darkfall, on rounds, Solo decided to speak with the grey.

'Ponder,' Solo began firmly, 'I think we need to discuss Tanner.'

Ponder remained silent.

'If Tanner's going to remain with our Quorum, we have to accept him, trust him, and respect his rank – '

'*If* he's going to stay? You mean there's a choice? Well – '

'Ponder!' sighed Solo, frustrated. 'Why can't you give him a chance? It's important that we all work together, especially now. I don't know what the Owners are up to, but . . .'

Solo stopped talking suddenly, becoming stock-still and focusing on something in the air just ahead that Ponder couldn't see.

Speaker had appeared before him, and this time there was no question who it was. The prophet looked much as he had during the Wolfen attack – shimmery and semitransparent, like a fading afterimage of himself against the darkened background. What Solo 'saw' might be only an image in his mind, but he knew that Speaker was really there.

'Great changes are coming to the territory, Solo, and great danger. Move the Quorum now, or the field will run red with feral blood by mid-daybright. Hurry, little one. After tomorrow this territory will be no more.'

'Speaker,' Solo said, but even as he called to the Old One the vision faded to a single point of light and then disappeared altogether. 'Speaker, wait!'

The prophet's words echoed over and over in his mind, though he had not yet grasped their full impact. Still round-eyed and shaken, he turned and looked for Ponder. The grey had backed away several paces when Solo called out Speaker's name, not understanding what had happened. He had seen nothing in the stillness of the darkfall.

'Solo?' Ponder ventured in a small voice. 'Who . . . who were you talking to? Are you okay?'

'I'm all right, Ponder,' Solo said absently, still a little disoriented and confused. 'Speaker was here . . . he says we're in great danger and have to move the Quorum.'

Ponder looked stunned. 'I didn't see anybody . . . and what are you talking about? Move the Quorum? Where? When?'

Solo was collecting himself. 'Now. Tonight. I'm not sure where, yet. But we've got to get everyone out of here before daybright. Speaker says if we're still here tomorrow, the field will run red . . . with our blood.'

Ponder was silent for a moment, looking intently at Solo. Finally he said, 'Are you sure, Solo? Really sure? Do you realize what it will mean to move the entire Quorum?'

'I'm sure, Ponder. But we've got to hurry. We only have until daybright.'

'Oh, droud,' Ponder said softly. 'Oh, droud.'

From a small rise to the southwest, Tanner listened and felt the excitement building in his chest. He had been right about Solo. Even if the others couldn't see it, a Great One had come to lead them out of Owner bondage. This kit was truly a prophet, and the prophecy was falling into place.

Solo didn't say another word on the way back to the hedges and Ponder didn't press him. He didn't pretend to understand such things, but he trusted Solo implicitly. Would the *others* trust the young Dom enough to follow him in this? That would be the question. Solo's mind was racing as he realized the magnitude of what must be done. And with so little time!

Feeling Tanner approaching from behind, Solo paused and turned as the white caught up with them.

'Tanner, I'm glad you're here. Listen, find Selvyn and Ditto and have them help you round up the entire Quorum – and I mean everybody, kits, prills, and bards

'– as fast as you can. We'll all meet at the main hedge. Hurry – I'll explain later.'

Tanner wheeled around to the west and was gone without hesitation. Solo thought it was odd that the white hadn't asked a lot of questions, but didn't have time to dwell on it.

'I could've done that,' muttered Ponder, unnoticed by Solo.

They found Kitty-Kitty in the south hedge and Solo hastily explained his vision of Speaker and what the prophet had said.

Shocked, the prill sat back and shook her head. She looked down at her kits, then back to Solo. 'Solo! How can we move an entire Quorum? And with so many kits! Do you know what you're asking? Are you sure about this?'

'Yes, Kitty-Kitty, I'm sure. Right now I wish I wasn't.'

'All right,' Kitty-Kitty said after a moment. 'What can I do?'

'Get the prills and kits to the clearing at the main hedge – tell them anything you have to. We'll all meet there in a few minutes. Hurry, Kitty-Kitty. Half the darkfall's gone and we only have until mid-daybright.'

'I'll get them together, Solo.'

Kitty-Kitty, frightened at the urgency in Solo's voice, began a thirping call to the other prills as Solo and Ponder left.

'Where to now?' asked Ponder, feeling a little useless.

'We've got to get Elrod away from the Great Fence. We can't leave him behind.'

Ponder suppressed an urge to ask why not. 'Good luck, kit. The little wall-hugger hasn't moved for a quarter-circle. Something's not right with that cat, Solo.'

They had no trouble locating Elrod. Walking up very

close to the little bard, Solo looked directly into his green eyes.

'Elrod, unless you want to die here, you're coming with me. I don't have time to explain or argue. If I have to, I'll have you dragged, carried, or pushed. Ponder here will be happy to accommodate.'

Elrod blinked in surprise, cringing back from the big grey. 'Okay,' he squeaked, 'if I have to . . .'

'You have to,' Solo answered. 'Now, let's go.'

The two elder bards herded the trembling Tame-cat through the Great Fence and out into the field. In the distance, calls of general alarm carried through the night as Ditto, Selvyn, and Tanner gathered the others of the Quorum as instructed. It was going to be quite a council.

At the meeting site, Elrod was left in the care of Banda and Minit, who were more likely to put up with him than anyone else. Kitty-Kitty had assembled all the prills and was helping them contain the kits in one area where they could be watched. The kits, of course, thought it was playtime and were giving the prills a good run. These kits, Solo realized, would be their single greatest difficulty – getting all of them safely moved in time.

As the bards arrived they talked excitedly among themselves, trying to guess at the reason for this unusual meeting. Before long all the ferals would be gathered together, and Solo still wasn't sure what he would say, how he would explain his vision and convince them of the danger they would face if they weren't gone by daybright.

Selvyn, Ditto, and Tanner came in with the last of the bards, anxious excitement on their faces.

'What's happening?' Ditto asked, walking quickly over to Solo. 'Tanner told us to get everybody, even the patrols . . .'

'This leaves the entire territory unprotected,' added Selvyn, pacing and nervous. 'What's going on, kit?'

'We've got to leave the territory,' Solo answered, braced for their response. 'And we have to do it this darkfall.'

'What?' Ditto said. 'What are you talking about?' He looked in amazement at Selvyn and several of the others, whose surprise was clearly evident in their own shocked expressions.

'Why?' asked Selvyn simply, confusion in his face.

Solo looked away for a moment, gathering his thoughts. He didn't want to have to repeat what Speaker had told him more often than necessary. 'Just give me a few minutes, Selvyn, and I'll explain everything.'

The entire Quorum was now assembled – fourteen bards, eight prills, and seventeen young kits. Solo was worried – there were almost more kits than adults. Moving them to another territory at such a young age would be dangerous – and slow.

Solo went to the center of the clearing to address the Quorum. Did they trust him to this extent? Somehow, he knew, he had to convince them to follow him.

'I have seen our Speaker,' Solo began, 'and he issued a grave warning to our Quorum. He said that a great danger comes with the daybright and that many of us will die if we don't leave here – now. Speaker said that after the coming daybright this territory will not even exist anymore. Our only hope is to move the Quorum before the darkfall is gone.'

No one moved or spoke.

Solo continued. 'I can only guess that this great danger involves the Owners in some way. We've all seen how they've changed toward us since the fire, and there's even a rauwulf in the field. And Tanner has told us what happened in his own territory. We have to move the Quorum westward; anyone who stays behind will be in great peril.'

There was a soft explosion of low murmurs through the assembly as Dom Solo gave them time to assimilate what he'd said. The bards were shocked and confused, but the prills were openly frightened.

'But our kits!' called Trivet, speaking to Solo but looking at the other prills. 'How far must we go? These kits can't travel fast enough to clear this *field* by daybright.'

'Trivet's right,' agreed Sondle. 'How will we move our kits?'

'We'll have to go as far as we can before daybright,' said Solo. 'The bards will help carry the kits . . . there are enough of us.'

Bards carry kits? The prills were horrified. The bards had very much the same reaction.

Time was against them, however, and Solo had no time to waste on a long, persuasive argument. In an authoritative voice he issued his orders for the Quorum. 'We will have to move quickly. Any kit that is not carried will be left behind. And anyone who stays behind will likely not be alive by next darkfall.' Although Solo felt very cold and heartless in issuing such an order, he had no choice. Lives were at stake.

'We can show the bards how to carry them,' offered Kitty-Kitty. 'I think it's the only way.'

'But where will we go?' came a voice from within the crowd.

'We'll go westward, away from the Owners. We don't need them to live.'

The Quorum was hushed. The prills began to scan the bards, deciding which of them would be allowed to touch their young ones. The grumbling from the bards had increased, however.

'I'm not carrying any kit!' said one young bard. 'And

I'm not leaving this territory because of any vision. You all can leave if you want to, but I'm staying.'

Before Solo could answer, Ponder had stepped out beside him. 'Any bard who disagrees with any of Dom Solo's orders is invited to step behind the hedge for a little chat with me.' The grey felt useful again.

The bard who had spoken out quickly left in the direction of the Great Fence, evidently firm in his decision to stay behind. Ponder had started out after him, but Solo signaled the grey to let him go. He would not force anyone to follow him. One older prill with a single kit also refused to leave, and went deep into the hedge, refusing even Kitty-Kitty's urging to come out. The rest of the Quorum, trusting in Solo's vision and in his wisdom, made ready to follow him into the westward wilderness.

Solo began issuing rapid-fire instructions. 'Kitty-Kitty, get the prills organized and ready to move out. Ditto, Selvyn, start matching up kits and bards. You'll take flank positions when we're ready – you'll still have to carry, though. Ponder and Tanner, neither of you will carry kits – you'll act as front scouts up ahead to warn of danger. Weldon and Sessel, you have rear-watch; both of you will carry. Elrod won't carry a kit – he'll do well to bring himself.'

Elrod sat between Banda and Minit, completely fey.

Ponder cleared his throat and moved a little closer to Solo. Solo knew what was coming.

'Uh, Solo? Why not have Ditto or Selvyn take front-scout with me . . . we're used to working together, and – '

'Take Tanner, Ponder. You should be in position already.'

Although Ponder didn't understand Solo's logic, Solo knew that no prill would let Tanner carry her kit. And there was something else. The two strongest bards in the Quorum, Ponder and Tanner, wouldn't really be effective until they learned to live with each other.

The grey sulked but headed grudgingly westward with Tanner to keep watch until the exodus began. The ferals quickly set to their tasks amid a flurry of minor disputes about which bard would carry which kit. Kitty-Kitty oversaw the process, showing the bards how to safely pick up and carry a kit. All in all, the bards took to the task very well. Solo urged them to move quickly – already he sensed that time was running out.

Finally, every bard except Tanner, Ponder, and Elrod held a squirming kit in his jaws. Solo and Kitty-Kitty moved to the front of the restless Quorum.

'It's time,' Solo said simply. 'Let's head out. Go easy and pace yourself. We'll stop often.' He looked at Kitty-Kitty, then picked up little Carver and took the first step. The white prill took Justin, and the great journey began.

Ponder had been given their direction – due west.

Carrying kits, the bards discovered, was not as simple as the prills made it appear. They couldn't just grab them up by the fur or hide – they had to fit their whole mouth around the little wiggling bodies, keeping just enough pressure to hold them in, but not enough to hurt them. After only a few minutes their jaws began to ache. To some of the bards it felt like having their mouths lock open during an enormous yawn and not being able to get them closed again. The kits whined constantly about being uncomfortable, tired, or thirsty. The bards rapidly developed new respect for the prills.

Tension was thick among the Quorum. Not only was Solo urging them forward, the fear almost palpable in his voice, but the ferals were headed into unknown territory, away from the home they had grown up in. None of them knew what lay ahead. The going was agonizingly slow. Moving in such a large group and carrying kits as they were, anything over a steady walk was impossible. Conversation was, of course, out of the question, and they all silently grieved over the loss of their home.

They traveled the first several hundred cat-lengths without incident, not stopping to rest until they were well out of the territory proper. Solo had a goal in mind, a place he remembered from his Explore that he wanted to reach before daybright. A bard alone could have made it in less than an hour's run, but at this rate they would be lucky to get there by the end of the darkfall.

Solo called a halt to the group to allow them to rest and regroup. Suddenly a hush fell over the Quorum as two feline battle calls and fugues built quickly into fegin-sounding screeches. It was the sound Solo had been dreading. Far up ahead, Ponder and Tanner were fighting. Selvyn and Ditto were instantly up and anxious to watch, but Solo signaled them to remain at their posts. This was a private matter, and needed no spectators. Inevitable as it had been, it was painful to listen to.

'Solo!' cried Kitty-Kitty when she could stand it no longer. 'They'll kill each other – go out there and stop them!'

'They'll be fine,' soothed Solo, barely managing to hold himself back. 'You know Ponder, he thinks fighting is fun.'

'But listen to them!' she pleaded. 'It doesn't sound like they're having fun to me!'

The battle raged and Solo paced, trying to look unconcerned. He really wasn't worried about Ponder. After all, he himself had fought Tanner and won, hadn't he?

Out in the forest beyond, the two lifelong enemies

were hard at it. They clawed and scratched and bit and gouged; it was a real no-holds-barred brawl. Fighting in one long, continuous round, they felt completely free to use every dirty trick they knew, and they knew a lot. There were no stakes other than feline pride and personal animosity. Locked in a ball of grey-and-white fur, they rolled over and over through the dirt and leaves, spitting blood and loose hair through a cloud of dust. They fought until exhaustion slowed their reflexes and made them pant for air, and still neither was close to a decisive victory. They had slowly begun to wear each other out. Their movements slowed further, and finally the great warriors simply lay side by side scratching weakly at each other.

Suddenly Tanner started to giggle.

'What's so funny, silt-head?' demanded the grey, gasping for breath.

Still giggling, Tanner rolled over on his back without answering. Soon he was laughing out loud, and Ponder himself was finding it hard not to smile.

'What's wrong with you, Tanner?' Ponder asked, giggling a little himself. 'I thought we were having a fight here . . .'

Tanner looked over at the grey, nearly in convulsions. 'You should see yourself! Do I look as bad as you?'

Ponder looked at his own dirt-and-leaf-encrusted coat. It was pretty grim. 'Well, who won?' he asked, now as hysterical as Tanner.

'Tell it any way you want to, Pon,' answered Tanner, trying to straighten his face. 'In any case, it was worth it. You fight like a true gypsy!'

'You didn't do too bad yourself,' Ponder allowed. 'For a gypsy, that is.'

Within a few minutes they had pulled themselves together and cleaned themselves perfunctorily. Side by side they trotted eastward to rejoin the Quorum. Surely everyone had heard the commotion.

As they approached, Solo, Kitty-Kitty, Selvyn, and Ditto, along with half the other bards, dashed out to meet them.

'Well, did you get it over with?' asked Solo, trying to sound gruff, as Ponder and Tanner stopped in front of him. The grey and the white looked at each other innocently.

'I guess you heard it, huh?' Ponder smiled. 'We were just . . . just . . .'

'Sparring,' put in Tanner. 'Testing our reflexes.'

'Yeah, that's it,' Ponder agreed enthusiastically. 'No problem at all.'

'Sparring, my hindpaw,' grumped Ditto sourly.

'They look like they've been dragged through a mudhole,' said Selvyn.

Kitty-Kitty flipped her ears in disgust and walked back toward the kits. For this she had worried?

'Are you two all right for patrol?' Solo asked. He was greatly relieved that the two had resolved their differences with minimal damage.

'Oh, sure.' Ponder beamed. 'Ready, willing, and able.'

'Okay, then. Head on out!'

Tanner nodded at Solo, then bounded back westward to his position. The fight had marked a change in Tanner's status. He belonged with them now; he had established his place.

Solo turned back to his Quorum. They had lost precious time and would have to march long and hard to make up for it. But at least Ponder and Tanner would be working together now, and not against each other.

'Let's move out!' called Solo. The Quorum scrambled to their places and were soon headed out into the darkfall.

The trail was much as Solo remembered it, except that the forest had grown denser with the new green of spring and the earth was warmer under his paws. The journey, a first major Explore for many of them, would have been an adventure under any other circumstances. But despite their apprehension, many of the ferals remained curious about the unknown that lay around and ahead of them. It was the dangerous unknown behind them, however, that pushed them forward.

By the time the first faint traces of daybright began to lighten the forest shadows, the ferals were far into the wilderness. The kits, bruised and sore, were exhausted, as were the adults who carried them. But Solo felt confident that they'd come far enough from the territory to be safe. Stopping in a natural shelter thick with foliage and dark with tree cover, the prills found suitable places and nested with the hungry kits, while Solo and the bards posted watches and held council.

As the light grew stronger, Solo's thoughts were on the home they had all left behind. What was happening there? Would they be able to return later, or were they truly homeless refugees? If they couldn't go back again, where would they go? Solo wasn't sure of the answers to these questions, and he, like the others, waited.

The rumbling began after the first watch, when Solo had finally circled out a place to rest. Although it couldn't be heard, the ferals could feel it through their sensitive footpads. The tremors were intermittent and heavy, and unlike anything they had ever felt before.

'Is this . . . it?' Selvyn asked excitedly, working his way through the brush to a position beside Solo.

'I don't know, Selvyn,' answered Solo quietly. 'It's definitely coming from the territory, though.'

Moving out into the open, they saw Kitty-Kitty standing under a great tree, her footpads at its base. Even vibrations from great distances would be magnified there. Ponder and Ditto came in from watch and stood with Solo and the rest of the Quorum, trying to read meanings into the subtle sensations, but they fit no known pattern. They were anxious and frustrated; they needed to know what was happening at home.

Soon there was another vibration under their paws. It was a single cat, running hard toward them from the east. Slowly the rapid footfalls of the lone runner became stronger, until it was difficult to distinguish the ground echoes from the actual sound. A few moments later Tanner burst into sight. The white bard skidded to a stop, dangerously exhausted, and flopped belly-to-the-ground in front of the paralyzed group.

'Tanner!' Solo exclaimed. 'Where have you been? Did you go back . . .?'

'It's happening, Solo,' panted Tanner, barely able to speak. 'I went back . . . I saw it! We could never have gotten away in time.'

A tight, choking dread squeezed at Solo's throat. He could hardly manage a whisper as he asked, 'What's happening? What did you see?'

Tanner looked up at Solo, still pulling for air. 'The Great Fence . . . they're breaking down the Great Fence.'

'The Wall?' stammered Ponder. 'But . . . how? Why . . .?'

'Let him catch his breath,' said Solo. He could tell from Tanner's expression that there was more.

The Quorum waited in numbed quiet as Tanner fought to collect himself. He glanced around at them, then back to Solo. 'Giant rauwulfen are in the field . . . they're turning the ground over! The hedges are

229

already gone . . . nothing left but dirt . . . all empty and flat.'

There was a collective gasp from the prills. The adults might have found a way to safety, but the kits . . .

Hesitantly Tanner continued. 'The prill who stayed behind . . . I heard a scream . . . she didn't get out.'

Solo closed his eyes. He should have found a way to force her to come with them.

'They were trying to kill us all!' Kitty-Kitty said, interrupting his thoughts. She was obviously deeply shocked.

'I don't think so,' Solo said, without looking up. 'We were just in their path.'

'*Why* are they destroying the Wall . . . and the field? That place was *ours*!' Even as he asked it, Selvyn realized the futility of his own question.

Suddenly everyone began talking at once. They had left the territory because they trusted Solo's prophetic knowledge, but they had not been prepared for this. Solo sat behind closed eyes as the Quorum tightened around him.

Tanner went over on his side. He would need rest before he could travel again, but it had been worth it to him to bring this news to his Dom.

'Solo,' whispered Trivet, as she stood over her kits, 'our babies – you saved our babies.'

'You did it, little Speaker,' Ditto agreed. 'You really did it.'

It was subdued chaos. They had not really had time to recover from the fire, and now here was an even bigger catastrophe. The ferals hovered in confusion around their only anchor – Dom Solo.

Solo had his head down, embarrassed by the display of emotion. Ponder, seeing Solo at a loss for words, took command in his role as Enforcer, raising his voice above the others. 'Okay, everybody. It's over, and we're all safe. There are watches to keep. The rest of you, go back to your dens and get some rest. The Dom's got figuring to do here, and he needs a little quiet.'

Ditto turned away with the others. 'Figuring,' Ponder had called it. The ultimate application of wisdom.

Solo stayed down where he was, thinking. He knew their journey had just begun. They were homeless now; even the hedges of his birth no longer existed. They had kits too young to be out of the nest and prills who had never ventured beyond the territorial boundaries – an unlikely crew to be suddenly in the wilderness without a home.

After a time the young Dom retreated into the cover of the near briars. He remained there, quiet and subdued, throughout the rest of the daybright, pondering their next move. The others looked to him, more than ever, as if he were a 'prophet' or 'Great One' of the Legends, yet the Voice he sometimes heard in his head was not his own; he could neither control nor summon it. And it was Speaker who had warned him and saved the Quorum. None of it was Solo's own doing. Great Ones, according to the Legends, were supposed to see clearly into the future and create changes. What could *Solo* do? He'd created no changes; at best he'd only helped them to flee an unknown danger.

Then the Voice sounded through his self-doubt. 'But the bards carried kits alongside the prills, and the prills allowed it, making an organized exodus from a place they had chosen and marked as their own. All this in defiance of deep instinct and custom. These are changes, Solo – changes *in* the Legends, according *to* the Legends.'

Solo held his breath and listened, but the Voice was gone.

13
The Journey

Sleep, for everyone, had been sporadic and fitful, and even before the bright light-paths that streaked through the forest canopy had gentled into shadow, the Quorum ferals were outward and gathering in small groups. Solo had called for a council at darkfall, and they all knew it would be a High Council, formal and structured. The things to be discussed and decided were of greater importance than in any High Council in their memory. The decisions at hand could not be made by any one of them alone, even the Dom. Solo could present the options and alternatives, but every feline had the right to decide for himself the course of his immediate future.

The ferals reacted to all that had happened, each according to the bent of his personality. Ponder had silenced his mind by filling it with practical necessities – watches and patrols and hunting assignments. There was the question of food, now that they could no longer depend on the Keep for graille. For Ditto, the retreat the darkfall before had been dangerous and inconvenient, but to his mind, they had changed location, nothing more, and he was used to that. Selvyn's reaction was the most uncharacteristic. He was furious at the destruction the Owners had wrought. Many creatures and their young had called the territory home – how many had the Owners killed at daybright? Such premeditated violence staggered him. Were the Owners inherently evil? The destruction of the field was incomprehensible to him.

Kitty-Kitty, though she tried to hide it, was as shaken

as the rest of the prills. She had kits to raise, and the steady source of graille, fresh water, and the relative safety of the hedges all meant security to her. Who knew what dangers lurked before them?

Solo rose and went outward to meet his friends. Carver and Justin stayed quietly beside their mother, obviously infected with the disoriented calm of the elders.

'Tanner, Babbot, and Abalon have taken the watch,' reported Ponder as Solo joined them. 'Everyone's ready when you are.'

'They await your Domship under the great tree southward,' added Ditto, managing a smile.

'They think you've had another vision, and will present us with a great plan,' Selvyn said, looking at the kit intently.

'You haven't, have you?' asked Kitty-Kitty. 'I mean, had another vision, and decided what we should do?'

'No, Kitty-Kitty,' answered Solo uncomfortably. 'No visions. We'll have to figure this one out on our own.' He forced a smile and added, 'Come on. It's time for the council.'

It was a relatively large Quorum, counting the kits. Its members grouped loosely under the giant tree, nearly invisible within its shadow. The strain and tension were evident, and Solo felt small and uncertain under their collective gaze. When he finally spoke, however, the words came easily and from his heart.

'There are many paths we can take from this place,' he began as the Quorum became quiet, 'and none of those paths would be wrong. We are feline, and will live in dignity no matter where we go. First of all, we could stay here. This is not a bad place. Cover is good, and graille plentiful, and there is water close by in the ground.'

There was silence as they looked around themselves.

There were trees higher than most had ever seen, no glare of Owner lights to spoil the shadows, and the air was clear and clean-smelling.

'This is where I came on my Explore,' Solo said to them, 'here, and much farther. Two darkfalls' run to the west, the forest is broken from north to south by a wide blackrock strip, filled with many rauwulfen. But beyond it I saw a wilderness much bigger than this forest, and giant hills reaching into the sky, nearly touching the clouds. I don't think there are any Owners there – it might be a good place for a . . . new territory.' Solo had wanted to say 'wild' territory, but thought better of it.

He stopped and waited for their reaction. It was difficult not to say more, to tell them about his lifelong dream of real feline freedom, and the yearning that pulled his heart toward those hills.

'It took us a half-darkfall just to get this far,' said Weldon. 'How long would it take us to get *there*, carrying kits?'

'And we would have to carry our kits across blackrock,' Trivet said nervously. 'We all know how dangerous a blackrock strip is, even if you're alone, and running!'

Solo knew this would be the greatest hurdle. 'We could get across it, if we're careful. But the journey would be slow, perhaps even a half-circle.'

'Dom Solo,' asked Mondy shyly, 'what are you and Selvyn and the others going to do? If all of you go westward, anyone who stays behind will be . . . well, alone. We'd have no Dom, and no Speaker . . .'

'Mondy's right,' agreed Sondle. 'I'm going wherever Dom Solo goes. He's always been right, so far.'

Solo didn't want them to go west just to follow him. He wanted them to make the journey because they believed in it. 'If the greatest part of our Quorum decides to stay here, then that's what we'll all do. We're a *Quorum*, and we'll not be divided.'

'Well, I'm certainly not excited about carrying *kits* for a half-circle,' said Murdok. 'That's asking a bit much – '

'Watch your mouth, silt-head,' snapped the grey. 'You'll trot all the way on two paws if Dom Solo says so – '

'It's all right, Ponder,' Solo said quickly. 'Let them say what they feel. I'm not Bryndle.'

'Let them also watch the way they say it,' added Selvyn, looking at Murdok. The little bard had been properly rebuked.

Kitty-Kitty finally spoke out. 'We won't be as . . . rushed now, and the kits could walk most of the time. There wouldn't be as much carrying.'

'It would be worth it,' said Rosen in her tiny voice, 'to all be together, and have a Quorum in a place like that, far from Owners.'

Several prills raised their voices in agreement. Few among them had not lost a kit to a speeding rauwulf at some time in their lives.

'I don't ever want to live beside Owners again,' said Abalon. 'Most of us have suffered in some way at their hands, even the Tame-cats . . . just look at Banda. And Minit would be dead now from choking if it wasn't for Solo.'

'That's right,' agreed Banda self-consciously. 'I'll follow Solo westward – I wish I'd never seen an Owner and I hope never to see one again.' Minit, well within Banda's shadow, nodded his agreement enthusiastically, but didn't speak. Elrod, well within Minit's shadow, remained silent, as if he were sleeping with his eyes open.

'When *my* kits come, I want them to grow up free and . . .' Pardie hesitated, unable to find the word she needed. 'I don't think we really belong beside an Owner dwelling . . .'

Solo was pleased – so Pardie *had* 'settled.'

Soon everyone was talking at once, recounting personal stories of Owner cruelty or neglect. They had stayed because they felt dependent on Owners, but now the pent-up hatred and distrust came out in torrents.

Solo called for order, then closed the council. 'No decision has to be made right now. Think carefully on these things, and whether we stay here, or travel to the hills beyond – '

'You're talking about Morgalian's Mountain.'

Every head whipped around toward the strange voice that came from the eastern edge of the group. Reflexively Ponder jumped out over Solo and landed five cat-lengths in front of what had to be the oldest, thinnest bard any of them had ever seen.

'Where in silt did *you* come from?' The grey arched in full defensive stance, but his posture quickly relaxed as he noticed the complete defenselessness of the ancient feline before him. The Old One was mottled black, with huge sunken eyes and legs that looked too frail to support even his own meager weight.

Suddenly Tanner, who had felt the disruption from his watch position, burst into the circle from the north. Ponder, Selvyn, and Ditto had the elderly cat surrounded, and Tanner moved quickly beside them, looking a little sheepish and embarrassed. How could another feline have gotten past him so easily? The rest of the Quorum stared in silence at the newcomer, unsure how to react.

It took Solo a moment to recover from his own surprise before he rose and approached the elder. The young Dom's surround mingled with the Old One's, and in it he read wisdom, and kindness, and that eerie, secret sadness of an Old Speaker. Later, he would assure his Enforcers that no power known to the ferals could have prevented the stranger from coming to this place if that had been his intended purpose.

'Please,' said Solo reverently, 'sit and speak with us.' Ponder and the others took their cue from Solo and backed away to give them room.

'Thank you,' answered the old black as he lowered his fragile body into a full sit. There was a flicker of mild amusement in his eyes as he glanced at the questioning faces around him. 'My journey has been long, and I am weary.'

'Our cover is yours,' Solo said formally. When the Speaker had adjusted into his spot, the kit asked, 'What did you say a moment ago . . . about the mountain? Do you mean the hills to the west? Do you know of this place?'

'It is my home,' answered the Speaker simply. 'I left it only to make this, my Final Journey.' Everyone understood his meaning, and Solo waited a respectful moment before continuing.

'You mean there are others there? Is it . . . held as a territory?' Solo tried to control his excitement.

'It's a territory – the black smiled – 'but probably unlike any other territory in the world. If you have the time, I'd like to tell you a story . . .'

'Please,' encouraged Solo, 'continue.' All were riveted to the Speaker's voice as he closed his eyes for a moment, and then began.

'Many seasons ago, when I was just a young bard, a Dominant Tame-cat named Morgalian gathered together a small Quorum from several Owner-based territories far southward. He led them into the westward high country, and they followed because Morgalian had had a great Vision, and they shared in his dream. He believed that a Great One was coming,

237

someone he called the Only One, to lead the feline race out of bondage. And he believed that this Great One would come to those westward hills. Morgalian has waited many seasons and grown very old with the waiting, hoping to see his vision come true before his life is done. I, too, have waited, but my Final Journey is now upon me.' The Speaker was silent for a long moment, and then continued. 'Morgalian's Quorum grew, and he was joined by many others, some who had also seen the great prophecy, and even more who felt only a dream in their hearts. They live there yet, free and wild within the dense trees and thickets of the high forest . . .'

The Old One's eyes were far away as he told them of his home. He spoke of sparkling clear water paths that wound their way down gentle slopes into quiet valleys below, and of soft, thick, damp places that were heavy with shadows and secrets. He told of high trees for climbing and looking down on an unspoiled world, and of good hunting and plentiful graille. The old Speaker's words wove a spell around Solo and his band of ferals, a spell of magic and of the Legends, and of the possibility of finding a feral paradise.

Solo was overwhelmed. So there were others, many others, who felt the same things he did! Ever since he was a kit he'd felt this deep call within him. At last he had some idea as to its meaning.

Suddenly there was a flurry of questions, with everyone talking at once. Ponder wanted to know how Morgalian felt about newcomers, and how many Enforcers he had; Selvyn wanted to know if there was good, therapeutic grass up that high; and Kitty-Kitty asked about the status of prills in the Quorum hierarchy. Each asked his questions, and finally the old black bard rose, shaking his head and smiling. 'You will all be welcome on Morgalian's Mountain, and you'll be happy there. I was. I have done what I wanted to do in my life, and seen what I wanted to see, and now I am going back to my birthplace. I wish us both a safe journey.'

The Speaker was looking directly at Solo, but the young Dom was a little confused at his parting words, and thought that the Old One had somehow contradicted himself. Solo didn't mention it, however, and quickly urged the Speaker to stay with them until he was rested.

'My journey is long and my legs are old,' said the black, 'and I hope to be far eastward before daybright.'

'Safe journey to you, then,' called Solo as the Speaker turned and was gone as quickly and soundlessly as he had come. Solo watched him go, wondering if his visit had really been the 'accident' it seemed to be. For that matter, had anything that had happened to him been an accident?

Later, after Ponder and Selvyn posted the watches, Solo and Kitty-Kitty sat together in a small clearing, watching Carver and Justin playing war games with several of the other kits.

'With this Morgalian there,' asked Kitty-Kitty at length, 'does it mean you won't be ... our Dom anymore?'

Solo honestly hadn't thought about it. 'Kitty-Kitty,' he said with a sigh, 'that just might be the best part of this.' The white prill busied herself with some much-needed preening, and said nothing.

During the darkfall and daybright that followed, each and every Quorum member came to Solo with his or her decision. There would be no need for another council – they were going west, all the way to Morgalian's Mountain, to live in a new feline territory and wait for the Great One of the vision. In the typical under-stated feline way, they had committed to a new destiny and shared in Solo's dream, a dream that was very nearly upon them.

The march was slower and more difficult than any of them had imagined. The days and nights of maintaining a forced state of maximum alert, and alternately herding and carrying the tired, complaining kits, had taken their toll. They were dirty and their fur was matted, but they were lean and strong and found their instincts well fitted to their quest. They were, after all, *feline*, and their pride in themselves stretched proportion-ately with their endurance. The closest they'd come to a casualty was Selvyn – for three days straight he'd suffered through the worst case of indigestion in memory, earning himself a place as rear patrol, *far* rear, until he was well.

By the end of the tenth darkfall, they could hear and feel the noise from the rauwulfen on the blackrock strip in the distance. At the end of the twelfth, the sounds were stronger, and Solo could see the rise that overlooked the blackrock strip just ahead. The exhausted felines readily agreed to rest throughout the coming daybright, giving them time to plan for the crossing. With prills and kits, it would not be an easy task.

Everyone wanted to see what they'd be facing come the new darkfall, however, and soon they were up the little incline and crouched single file in the weeds that lined the crest of the overlook.

Up there, the intermittent roar of running rauwulfen was deafening. Even at twenty cat-lengths the wind from their passing was strong enough to blow a cat's ears back, and the familiar, burned-smelling smoke they made was nauseating. The blackrock strip was big

– bigger than even Solo remembered. Four rauwulfen could easily race side by side down its length. It was a place of extreme danger, but it was also fascinating and even strangely beautiful, the way the blinding rauwulf lights grew larger and fused into a solid streak of white against the blackness before passing, their tails a fuzzy red swatch of light as they sped away into the darkfall. They traveled in loose bunches, with an occasional lone runner, but there was easily enough room between them for crossing if it was done one at a time and quickly. There was a thin grassy strip down the center of the blackrock, a neutral space where the rauwulfen did not go; if necessary, they could cross the blackrock half at a time and pause in the middle. Solo was both encouraged and apprehensive. With care and planning it could be done, but it would draw heavily on the courage of them all, especially the prills.

The Quorum stared in silent wonder and trepidation at the blackrock below, but soon shifted their gaze farther westward to the outline of the hills beyond, which stood clearly against the deep black sky. They were not as tall as they had been in Solo's memory, but they were broader, filling the horizon. They seemed to emanate the same feeling of durability and strength present in very old trees or giant rocks, a comforting sense of permanence and invulnerability.

'Is that where we're going?' Ponder asked, distracting Solo from his thoughts.

'Yes,' Solo said with a smile. 'Those are the mountains.'

'I thought they would be farther away, Solo,' said Kitty-Kitty. He could tell from her tone that the hills affected her much as they did him. 'We could *be* there in another darkfall or two – once we get past the blackrock.' The fear in her voice once again gave away her feelings.

'Nothing simpler,' Selvyn said confidently. 'We could cross that blackrock running in circles.'

Ditto gave the orange a sour look. 'Easy for *you* to say; you're the fastest cat in the Quorum.'

'Don't worry,' said Tanner. 'I used to play dodge-the-rauwulf for *fun*, back in my hoodlum days when I was younger.'

Several of the prills were huddled together, talking in low voices. Solo could tell that they were worried, and he didn't know what to say to them.

'Will we have to cross it ... alone?' asked Pardie, evidently speaking for all of them. She had looked up suddenly and caught the young Dom looking at her group of prills. 'I'm not sure I can do it by myself ...'

Selvyn answered for Solo. 'Sure you can. Just watch this!'

Before Solo realized what he was up to, the orange streaked down the embankment.

'Selvyn, don't!' Solo said quickly, but it was too late. Selvyn had reached the edge of the blackrock. He turned and grinned up at the Quorum.

'Take a lesson, everyone! There's nothing to worry about!'

'I'm gonna kill him,' growled Ponder as they crouched and watched the orange. There was no way to stop him. Selvyn turned back toward the racing rauwulfen and assumed an exaggerated full-stealth posture. A flurry of rauwulfen sped past, ruffling the orange fur, followed by one more, and then Selvyn made his move. He leapt out onto the blackrock, hesitated briefly while glancing both ways, then broke into a flamboyant, high-leaping run, as if he were jumping through tall grass.

'Don't get cocky,' muttered Solo to himself. What was Selvyn trying to prove? This was very out of character for the orange.

Selvyn reached the median grass strip well before the next rauwulf whizzed past, immediately turning around to return. Checking for rauwulfen again, he moved back onto the blackrock, more slowly this time, then crossed back to the others – running in tight, elongated circles.

'Sweet silt in the grass,' Ditto moaned. 'I do not believe this one.'

'At least he makes it *look* easy,' added Tanner with a mixture of respect and concern in his voice.

'Solo!' whispered Kitty-Kitty. 'That's exactly what he's doing! Trying to make it look easy so the prills won't be so worried!'

Solo knew that, but was too busy watching Selvyn to answer. The orange was over halfway back, and seemed to have room to spare.

'I'm still gonna kill him,' Ponder muttered.

Seconds later, Selvyn was across and running up to meet them, a little out of breath, but unharmed.

'Finished, are you?' asked Solo as Selvyn trotted back to his place. 'Or would you like to roll across, for your next trick?'

Selvyn grinned, but didn't answer, and Solo didn't push it. The orange seemed to have accomplished his purpose, though. The prills looked a little less anxious, and many of them quite impressed.

The Quorum moved back into the forest to sleep and wait for darkfall; their spirits, under the circumstances, were high. The shadow of Morgalian's Mountain served as a constant reminder that the journey and the dangers were not in vain.

Solo, the Enforcers, and several of the other bards stayed in council throughout most of the daybright; well before the evening shadows came, they were ready. Everything had been carefully outlined and rehearsed. Solo would be the first across, and he knew very well that Selvyn's seemingly easy crossing had been deceptive. There was great danger in what they did, and the least hesitation could cost a life. The bards would probably do well enough, but the prills would be badly frightened. And then there was the complication of the kits. Even Selvyn would be considerably slowed with a kit in his mouth.

After Solo crossed with Justin, Kitty-Kitty would follow with Carver. Solo would help coordinate the crossings from the far side, and the prill would be there to hold on to any extra kits that the bards brought over until their mothers were across. Selvyn would be next, and would go on ahead to the westward forest and keep watch over the ferals as they gathered. Ponder, of course, would be last, to act as an encouragement to the faint of heart. The prills seemed willing enough now, but there would be hesitation when the time was at hand. And then there was Elrod. He would probably have to be dragged across. Ditto and Tanner would hang back and make the crossing with anyone who might need help; then they would cross just ahead of Ponder. It was a good strategy. The main thing for them to remember, Solo warned, was *not* to look directly into the rauwulfen lights – they could hypnotize and dazzle to the point of fey.

Soon full dark was upon them, and it was time. Subdued and quiet, the entire Quorum moved to the top of the incline.

'I guess we're ready,' said the young Dom. 'Let's go.' He picked up Justin and crept slowly down the embankment, followed by Kitty-Kitty with Carver and the big grey.

Ponder and the white prill stopped a few paces back; Solo went straight to the edge of the blackrock. Here, the roaring from the blurred rauwulfen was very loud, and the wind from them was so strong that Solo gripped Justin even more tightly, afraid the small calico would be blown from his grasp. It was like standing in the path of a tornado.

'Careful, Solo,' called Kitty-Kitty. 'Don't drop my baby!' There was far more seriousness in her tone than she had meant to imply. The others waited up above, straining their eyes into the darkness. If there was ever a time for second thoughts, it was now.

Crouching, Solo braced against the wind currents. The rauwulfen were moving fast, faster than any he'd seen in the home territory. A group of the smoking monsters thundered past, spraying the blond bard with their white light; then several more whizzed by, more widely spaced. The next lights were but small dots in the distance, and Solo sprang out onto the hard black ground. He had picked his time well, and did not look right or left as he ran in a low, controlled lope. His ears kept track of the growing sounds from the rauwulfen. Only halfway to the grass strip he realized just how fast the rauwulfen were moving – they had already covered half the distance to him. Justin was frightened and rigid, but did not struggle or cry. Solo made a final leap, landing in the grass, and seconds later a wave of rauwulfen sped past behind him. Flattened to the ground, he tried to control his ragged breathing, wishing for higher grass – or at least a darker coat. He knew he made quite a target out in the open and with a kit in his mouth. Solo wormed belly-down to the far side of the grass strip. The rauwulfen came from the north now, and he waited as seven or eight of them whizzed past, running tightly together. Then the blackrock was clear for a safe margin and Solo bounded out and across, reaching the west side with time to spare. Safely away from the edge, he turned and placed Justin securely under a front paw.

'Nothing to it!' Solo called to Ponder and the prill

across the expanse of blackrock. 'Cross when you're ready, Kitty-Kitty, and don't stop on the blackrock!'

Kitty-Kitty didn't answer. She had already moved to her starting position, Carver firmly between her teeth and Ponder protectively behind her. Her eyes were round with fear but she did not hesitate. For a few seconds Solo's side of the blackrock was busy with rauwulfen, and when his view was clear again, the prill was nearly to the middle grass. She had cut it a little fine, thought Solo, as several rauwulfen closed in behind her, but still with a margin of safety.

'Be careful, Kitty-Kitty,' Solo called. 'They're going faster than they look!'

Crouching low, Kitty-Kitty crept across the neutral area. One rauwulf was close in the north, but the blackrock was clear behind it. She had not stopped in the grass, though, and already had one paw on the blackrock to cross. She was going to try it.

'No, not now! Wait!' Solo cried, realizing that the white prill was far more frightened than he'd thought she would be.

She pulled her paw back and the screaming rauwulf flew past. Solo could see her fur flatten with the wind that it made.

'Now!' called Solo. 'Run now!'

Kitty-Kitty jumped out and sped across the blackrock without looking, trusting to Solo's judgment, her eyes locked on Solo's. Well before the next group of rauwulfen, she was beside him, trembling and exhausted. Justin scooted over to her, and Kitty-Kitty put Carver down next to him, standing protectively over her frightened kittens.

'You did it, Kitty-Kitty,' said Solo, relieved. 'You were wonderful.'

'I was so afraid, Solo. I didn't think I would be, but I was.' Her surround tingled with excitement.

Solo looked at her and smiled. 'So was I. Now, let's get the rest of them over and make an end to this journey.'

Selvyn had already started across, but not as theatrically as he had done the darkfall before. He carried a small orange kit in his mouth this time, and there were considerably more rauwulfen. He judged the distances carefully, pausing on the grass strip before bolting across to join Solo and Kitty-Kitty.

'I told you it would be easy.' The orange grinned when he'd deposited his kit with Kitty-Kitty. He wasn't even winded.

Solo shook his head but did not answer. Ponder had Mondy in position on the other side, and she, too, carried an orange kit.

Her aura sparkling with panic, Mondy crouched and listened to Ponder's last-minute instructions. He moved up beside the little prill, gaining a clear view of the blackrock in both directions to help her gauge her run. When the rauwulfen cleared and Ponder felt that it was time, he nudged her from behind and she started across, eyes fixed straight ahead in heed of his warnings. But she was not running. She crept out onto the blackrock in an agonizingly slow stalk-type gait.

'Solo!' breathed Kitty-Kitty. 'She'll never make it! She's going too slow . . .'

'She can make it if she doesn't stop,' answered Solo as he tried to calculate how quickly the lights approached her.

Selvyn, straining forward at the edge of the blackrock, cried, 'Hurry, Mondy. Oh, please hurry!'

Mondy was halfway to the grass, moving slowly but steadily forward; she looked like she was walking in a trance, stiff and unblinking. A rauwulf, coming from the south, would reach her before she got to the median strip, but whether she was directly in its path was impossible to tell. Selvyn nearly ran out to help her, but it was too late even for that. Mondy had a good four cat-lengths to go when the raging rauwulf reached her, but it flew past behind her to the eastern side, missing her by several cat-lengths. The wind it created was so strong that Mondy was pushed slightly off her course, but she kept moving. Finally she was on the grass, safe for the moment. All three cats on the western side released their breath in unison. It had been close, very close. And she was only the second prill to cross. They had a long way to go.

'Mondy!' Selvyn called. 'This time, *run*! You've got to *run* across!'

The orange prill gave no indication that she heard. Like Kitty-Kitty, she crawled straight across the grass strip without hesitating, and stepped down onto the blackrock.

'Silt!' Selvyn gasped. 'She's coming straight over!'

Solo and Kitty-Kitty stared in horror. A rauwulf suddenly whipped by in front of Mondy, and still she moved forward. But at last the blackrock was clear, and even at her painfully slow pace, she could get safely across. Selvyn went out a few steps to meet her, and together they walked into the sparse weed cover that lined the blackrock.

Solo closed his eyes for a moment. Would all the prills be like Mondy? How many would die tonight, so close to their journey's end?

Selvyn was licking Mondy's ears, trying to soothe her. 'You made it, Mondy – you were just wonderful. I knew you could do it.'

Solo and Kitty-Kitty exchanged glances, and turned back to the blackrock. Abalon was ready to cross, Mondy's remaining kit with him.

'Here we go again,' sighed Solo, prepared for another ordeal. But Abalon kept his head, and after

248

checking carefully for rauwulfen, moved quickly and confidently out and across. He made it over the black-rock without incident, and went to Solo's side looking very pleased with himself.

'Good job, Abalon,' Solo praised. 'I hope the others do as well.'

The bard joined Selvyn and Mondy. Carrying the three kits, they moved out into the darkfall, headed for deeper cover to wait for the others.

Murdok and Sessel crossed over next, both carrying one of Trivet's kits, and made their runs beautifully. Trivet herself crossed as well as any bard, and that group of three adults and three young ones was sent on to Selvyn. Solo and Kitty-Kitty began to relax. The crossing was going very well now, and they were both encouraged.

Lundy's turn came next. When he had reached the central grassy area, Solo called out to him to stay there. The young Dom had decided that someone needed to keep that position in case any more of the ferals 'forgot' to stop and look for rauwulfen. Fortunately, Lundy had a dark grey coat that wouldn't show up well in the lights. He should have made this part of the original planning, Solo thought to himself.

Banda and then Minit came over, each with one of Rosen's grey kits, and both crossed without incident. Solo had been worried about Minit, and was impressed with the little bard's courage. Across the blackrock, Rosen was huddled beside Ponder, and Solo could tell from the grey's anxious expression that she was going to be a problem.

Several adequate spaces between rauwulfen came and went, and still Rosen remained crouched against Ponder's side.

'Someone will have to go with her,' said Kitty-Kitty over the din of passing rauwulfen. Solo agreed, and was just about to call to Ponder to have Ditto or Tanner help her over when he saw the grey reach back behind Rosen. Whether he pushed her or actually nipped her behind, she darted out onto the blackrock. The timing was excellent, with no rauwulfen in sight to the south at all. Rosen started off in a run, but quickly lost momentum and slowed to a sort of hesitant creeping walk. She could still make it, if she kept going – she was over halfway across the east side, and no rauwulfen were close. And then she stopped, frozen on the blackrock. Solo could tell from her surround that she was fey.

Ponder realized it too, screaming at her from the edge. When she did not respond, the grey immediately bounded out to help her. Several rauwulfen were coming up rapidly from the south now – he woud have to be fast. Solo wanted to call out to Ponder, but kept his silence, afraid of breaking the grey's concentration. Kitty-Kitty stood over her kits beside Solo, horrified.

Ponder leapt to Rosen's side and was frantically trying to get her up and moving again, but she was paralyzed with fear and would not budge. The rauwulfen were getting dangerously close now, spread out across the width of the blackrock.

'Rosen!' Ponder screamed. 'Run! Get up and run!' Rosen gave no response. Grabbing hold of the prill's neck fur, the grey started to drag her across, but Solo knew as he watched that Ponder could never pull her to safety in time.

Looking to the south, Ponder realized that he had only seconds before the glaring rauwulfen would be upon them. He held on to Rosen's neck, and turned to face the bright lights.

'No, Ponder!' Solo cried. 'Get out of the way! You'll both be killed!' But even as he screamed, the rauwulfen thundered toward the two ferals.

Judging his timing and position carefully, Ponder jerked Rosen over to the left at the last possible moment, throwing both of them into the slender space between two flying rauwulfen. They sped past with incredible speed, missing the two ferals by inches. Several other rauwulfen followed closely in rapid succession, and one of them had to swerve wildly to avoid hitting the stranded felines. Then it was clear, and Solo could see Ponder once again working to mobilize Rosen. Inch by inch, the big grey pushed and pulled the prill toward the grass. In three or four more cat-lengths, they would be safe. But more rauwulfen were coming, fast, and it was going to be close.

'Hurry, Ponder,' Solo called out in panic, but the grey could move her no faster. They were nearly to the grass when a lone rauwulf raced past them, missing the two by three cat-lengths; the wind from it literally blew Ponder and Rosen up onto the neutral strip.

'They made it! They made it!' Solo cheered, but Kitty-Kitty was down with her face between her paws, and Solo could see that she was trembling.

The battle was only partly won. Somehow, they had to get Rosen across the other half of the blackrock. Both Ponder and Lundy stood over the prill, trying to coax her out of her fey. Attempting to drag her over wouldn't work, it would be too slow. They had to get Rosen up and traveling under her own power. Solo was grateful that she was not carrying a kit. Then, in a flash, it hit him. Her kits! Why hadn't he thought of it sooner?

'Banda,' Solo called without turning his head. 'Bite Rosen's kit!'

'What?' stammered the little bard, confused.

'I don't have time to explain! Bite that kit, hard!'

Banda looked down at the tiny kit in his charge, unable to understand what Solo had in mind. Finally

251

Solo reached back himself and bit the kit's shoulder. It cried out sharply. Kitty-Kitty's expression changed from disbelief to understanding as Solo nipped the kit again. It began to mew loudly for its mother.

Rosen looked up in alarm from across the blackrock, quickly coming out of her fey at the sound of her kit in distress. Her eyes cleared a little as she looked for her baby – someone was hurting her kit!

'Rosen!' Ponder encouraged her. 'It's your kit! You've got to get over to your – '

Rosen lurched up out of the grass, ready to run for her kit. She was still confused and dazed, responding only to a deep instinct. Ponder had to hold her back until there was enough time between rauwulfen to cross. Standing directly in front of her, Lundy and Ponder waited as several of the huge monsters went past; there was a large enough opening, and they simply stepped aside and let her go. Rosen dashed across the hard surface toward Solo and her kit, crossing the blackrock with ease. Kitty-Kitty took charge immediately, calming her down and explaining that her baby was unharmed.

'You mean it's over?' Rosen asked when she'd begun to regain her composure. 'I'm across?'

Solo reassured her that the ordeal was over, and at last sent her with Banda and Minit to join Selvyn and the others. Ponder went back over to the far east side of the blackrock, looking emotionally exhausted. There were eleven more felines to cross, not counting kits. There was still a lot of work ahead of them.

Weldon, Babbot, and Alfa came over with their assigned kits without incident, followed by Sondle, who had a hard time taking the first step or two, but finally crossed without mishap. Pardie made her crossing well too, determined not to make Solo ashamed of her. The last of the prills was Chelsea, and she was so frightened that Ditto made the crossing with her to avoid a repeat of what had happened with Rosen. With all the females safely over the blackrock, Lundy relinquished his post on the median strip and went with Chelsea to meet Selvyn. The only remaining ferals on the far side were Ponder, Tanner, and Elrod.

It was Elrod's moment of truth. Tanner and Ponder led the shy young bard to the edge of the blackrock, and looked at each other uncertainly.

'Elrod,' Ponder said with a weary edge to his voice, 'the way I see it is this: either you pull your head out and cross that blackrock like a bard, or we try dragging you over it and take a chance on us *all* getting hit. Or we can leave your worthless hide here to rot. Personally, I prefer the last plan. What do you think, Tanner?'

Elrod looked hopefully up at Tanner, wishing for other options.

'I think you summed it up pretty well, Pon,' answered the white slyly. 'But we could always stomp the silt out of him and *then* leave him to rot.' Tanner began to settle back, as if for a face-off.

It took Elrod only a few moments to make his choice. Taking a deep breath, he inched to the blackrock, buffeted by the wind as the rauwulfen stormed past. The way was now clear, but Elrod hesitated.

'Let me at him!' growled Ponder with feigned viciousness.

Elrod dashed out, actually making it to the grass strip before his courage failed him. Crouching tightly down in the thin grass, he listened to the roaring of the rauwulfen; the sound grew louder and louder in his ears, becoming the focal point of his attention. Elrod's mind began to block out the overwhelming sights and sounds, turning inward until the only thing he was conscious of was a deep desire to sleep here in this peaceful place . . .

'I'm gonna kill you, Elrod!' Ponder screamed, bringing the little bard out of his malaise and quickly back to full consciousness. Opening his eyes, Elrod saw the grey standing beside him, a white kit held under his lead-paw. Ponder's expression was ugly.

'You worthless twit. Get up and move before I stomp you faceless!'

Elrod jumped to his paws, backing away from Ponder. From the other side Solo watched, suppressing a grin. Ponder could be so persuasive. Caught between the grey and a blackrock full of raging rauwulfen, the choice was simple. Elrod spotted an opening and raced out to the relative safety of the blackrock.

'Great going, Elrod!' called Solo as the young bard ran to his side. 'I knew you had it in you!'

Smiling broadly, Elrod squared his shoulders and gave his head a little toss, then stepped proudly into the weeds, heading toward Selvyn's group.

'We may make a real feral out of him yet.' Kitty-Kitty smiled. She, like Solo, felt a flood of relief – an entire Quorum had crossed the blackrock, and without casualty.

Ponder and Tanner brought over the last two kits, and for a long moment they stood together looking out over the dangerous black ribbon in silence.

'We did it,' said Solo simply. He felt as if they had crossed over into another world.

14
Morgalian's Mountain

Solo, with Kitty-Kitty, Ponder, Ditto, and Tanner, joined Selvyn and the rest of the Quorum in a clearing about fifty cat-lengths from the blackrock. The restless kits were turned loose on each other while the prills and bards looked on. The mood was relaxed and almost festive; the successful crossing of the blackrock had marked a milestone, although none of them could have put it into words. They had slipped the shackles of domestication and were ready to claim their place, apart from Owners, high on Morgalian's Mountain. Already they noticed that the ground sloped slightly upward. Soon, probably within the next darkfall's travel, they would reach the borders of the new territory.

Kitty-Kitty looked upward at the hills that were obscured by darkness. 'We're almost there,' she said. 'We made it.'

Ditto took a deep breath and shook his head. 'You know, I can even *feel* a difference in this place. There's a kind of peace here.'

'I feel it too,' agreed Selvyn. 'It's like this is where we belong.'

'We're not up the mountain yet,' said Ponder. 'I want to get a look at this Morgalian and see what kind of outfit he's running up there.'

'What about the Great One they're supposed to be waiting for?' said Tanner. 'Do you think it's true? Do you think there is such a Great One – and that he would come to these hills?'

Solo was thoughtful for a moment before answering.

'Yes, I think it's true. Our old Speaker used to talk about such things to me when I was a kit. And there are Great Ones in the Legends.'

'If only . . . if only Spanno could be with us now,' sighed Kitty-Kitty.

After an uncomfortable silence, Ponder coughed for attention. 'Well, at this rate we'll never get up the mountain. There's plenty of darkfall left; we could probably find the territorial markers before daybright, or at least get close. What do you think, Solo?'

'I think you're right, Ponder.' Their young Dom smiled. 'Let's go find us a home.'

Just before daybright, and a little better than halfway up the uneven slope, Ponder froze in his forward position, listening.

'I think we got company,' the grey whispered over his shoulder.

Solo released the kit he carried to Kitty-Kitty's care and moved up beside his tense Enforcer. 'We're the company here,' he said, trying to see through the low, dense foliage before them. His voice betrayed his anxiousness and uncertainty. He warned them to follow protocol – after all, they were intruders in someone else's territory.

'Selvyn, Ditto . . . come on up ahead with me and Ponder. Tanner – '

'I understand, Solo. I'll stay with the others. We'll wait for your signal.'

Kitty-Kitty and Pardie herded their kits back into the main group as the four bards assumed a loose shoulder-to-shoulder formation. Without another word they continued the gradual climb up the slope, extending their surrounds far ahead of them. There was a group of felines not fifty cat-lengths ahead. Already Solo could feel the alien, powerful aura probing his own. It must be Morgalian himself, thought Solo. Why would the great Dom-cat come down to meet him this way? But then, how often did an entire Quorum enter his territory? His outwatch had probably been following their progress up the mountain since sometime after they'd crossed the blackrock. It must be obvious to them that Solo's Quorum was not here to challenge Morgalian, carrying kits as they were. Solo hoped he'd judged Morgalian's number correctly – it would be unseemly to approach with more Enforcers than Morgalian had brought with him.

The ground leveled abruptly into a bare, rocky jut and suddenly Solo saw them. It was Morgalian – it could be no other – surrounded by six able-looking warriors. Morgalian looked virtually identical to Dom Bryndle. Solo felt a collective ripple of shock in his own group as they registered the same impression. It was like looking backward into time.

Quickly recovering composure, Solo moved to within a half-dozen cat-lengths; following the required form, the others remained slightly behind, still and silent. Deliberately emptying his mind and relaxing his body, Solo left himself open and vulnerable to those he faced. In this manner he clarified his intentions, proffered his allegiance, and acknowledged Morgalian's right of Domship over himself and those who waited behind him.

'You are ...?' said the giant black feline as he stepped closer to look into the young blond bard's eyes.

'I am Solo,' answered the kit quickly, realizing that he should have offered his name on first approach. 'My ... our Quorum waits below. We have come for sanctuary in your territory.'

The hint of a guileless smile played on Morgalian's

face. Although he was physically Bryndle's twin, mottled and dark and scarred, there the resemblance stopped. The presence he radiated was neither affected nor manipulative; he led because he was a leader, and did not lose respect for those who followed. Solo felt from him the same straightforwardness and gentleness he'd admired in Speaker, and the kind of quiet humility that always accompanies deep wisdom.

'You have sanctuary, young Dom,' said Morgalian simply. 'You and any who follow you are welcome on this mountain.'

Solo hesitated. There had been so much he'd planned to say, speeches he'd rehearsed in his head for this moment. All those words left him now that their time had come. Morgalian reached out to Solo and they exchanged the breath of their life; the perfection of that moment was marred only by the calico shadow that still lay over Solo's heart. Spanno should have been here standing in his place.

At a glance from Solo, Ponder turned and called a throaty signal to Tanner and the others below. Selvyn and Ditto silently went back to help with the kits, wondering at the emotion that had passed between their Dom and the black. Something more than a simple first meeting had taken place in those few moments. Ponder remained with Solo, masking his confusion at the preceding events with a careful evaluation of Morgalian's Enforcers. He realized that no amateurs stood beside this leader.

Morgalian sat back on his haunches, as if releasing a deep weariness long held at bay. He opened his mouth to speak, but the words died in his throat as Solo's Quorum came up the rocky promontory by twos and threes. Morgalian realized for the first time that Solo's group really was an entire Quorum, thin and bedraggled from travel, but over two dozen strong. And kits! There were nearly as many kits as adults; they had migrated en masse across a vast distance carrying their kits! Virtually every one of them, bards as well as prills, carried a babe in his or her mouth. And the bards didn't seem to be shamed or lessened at this task – their heads were high and their stride full of feline pride as they gathered behind the Dom-kit who had led them here. Morgalian's bards were open-mouthed at the sight – they had received reports, of course, but actually to see a bard carrying a kit was a shock. What magic did this young Dom wield, what force of personality was responsible for such a twisting of instinct in the face of common need?

As the last of Solo's Quorum emerged from the hillside brush and waited, Morgalian slowly stood. 'Follow us,' he said softly, his voice nearly faltering. 'The Main is up ahead.'

Solo and his Enforcers exchanged wondering glances before following Morgalian and climbing what was left of the mountain. Solo and the elder black walked side by side in quiet conversation, their combined Enforcers fanned out around the tightly grouped Quorum. Before long, the ferals of Morgalian's territory began poking their heads out of bushes and briars, one by one joining Solo's group and falling into place as they marched up the incline. Soon the original thirty-odd adults had swelled to forty, then fifty and more, and still they came. They grew into a silent feline army that seemed to number in the hundreds, and every one of them watched Solo with something very near reverence. Solo choked down a lump in his throat. They were home.

Solo's group came over one last steep rise and broke through the weeds onto nearly level ground. There was a collective intaking of breath as Solo and his gypsies looked out at the landscape that lay before them. This was, Morgalian told them, the Main, the very crest of the mountain and the heart of the feral territory. Many times the size of the old home field, the Main was a circular meadow of tall yellow-green grass and dark, newly flowered mustard-weed. It was spattered generously with tight growths of an unfamiliar thicket brush, and dotted here and there with straight white-barked trees. Bordered by the timberline and thick forest growth all around its uneven edge, it was both vast and hidden, secret and expansively open at the same time. A few giant boulders formed a semicave and natural archway just to the north, and the sound of running water carried up to them from somewhere down the opposite side of the mountain. The cries of distant wild birds in the very early dawn completed the picture of pristine perfection – it was, to Solo and his band, a paradise.

Ponder inched out ahead of the others. 'Kinda makes you want to clean up, just being here.'

There was a general chuckle, relieving the serious mood of the Quorum. Morgalian turned to Solo, smiling. 'It took us a while to get used to it too.'

'It's . . . wonderful,' Solo said, looking around. 'Does your territory include the entire mountain?' As tired as Solo was, he felt an urge to conduct at least a cursory Explore of this fascinating new place.

'Yes, and into the valley southward, right up to a distant Owner complex . . . but we never go there.' The way the big black had said 'Owner complex' told Solo many things about the way Morgalian felt about Owners.

'But it's daybright and you need to rest. There will be plenty of time for talk at darkfall.'

Morgalian turned to a sleek orange that seemed to

be his first lieutenant. 'Slade, see that they find places to den. And, Solo, the watch is well kept here. You can all rest easy.'

Ponder and the others seemed to accept this without question – it would be the first time in many days that they had all rested without constantly being on alert. Before Solo could say anything further, Morgalian had turned and headed south into the brush, evidently to his own quarters, followed by his bards. Solo's Quorum grouped in and followed Slade out into the Main. Most of them were exhausted, and some of the kits slept even while being carried.

'I wonder if everyone gets a reception like this?' asked Kitty-Kitty as she nipped and prodded Justin and Carver to keep them moving.

'Well, I guess it's not often an entire Quorum seeks sanctuary.' Solo smiled as he walked.

'Compared with their number, we're just a few stragglers,' said Selvyn, shaking his head. 'There must be at least . . . at least – '

'More than any of us could count,' interrupted Ditto.

Tanner looked back at the horde still behind them. 'I'm just glad they're friendly. Imagine having to fight them.'

'Friendly?' Ponder echoed. 'This goes way beyond friendly. Silt, they did everything but *carry* us up here.'

Slade had gone out ahead and was waiting beside a large rock pile for them to catch up. With a manner that was a curious mixture of deference and curtness, he showed them a hedge that would be comfortable for the prills and kits, while inviting the bards to den anywhere they found suitable. Slade covered his surprise well when Kitty-Kitty and her two calico kits followed Solo and the other bards into the rocks. He realized that she was a rarity, a dominant-ranking female. He discreetly took his leave and was barely out of sight before the Quorum members had circled out a spot and were down.

'Can you believe this place?' Ponder yawned, scratching at an ear. 'This is really something! I bet the rats here are so big – '

'Shut up, Ponder,' said Selvyn, his eyes already closed. Everyone else was asleep.

Solo slept lightly and woke often. He was not relaxed in such new surroundings. The vibrations were foreign and did not blend with his own; it would be at least a half-circle before his inner rhythms altered and harmonized with his new territory. The others must feel the same, Solo knew, and he stayed down and quiet to let them sleep as long as they could. It was not yet full darkfall.

Solo could sense the presence of many others scattered throughout the rock caverns; some he knew and some were still strangers. He had not dreamed there would be this many. It was a true refuge for his kind, perhaps the only one in the world, and they had found it. This thought was followed by an immediate sense of guilt – there were many, many more who hadn't.

Sensing a slight change in Ditto's breathing, Solo realized that he, too, was awake and remaining quiet so the others could rest. Within moments, however, they were all awake.

'Are we just going to lie around here all darkfall?' Solo laughed, raising his head. Immediately, the others were up, stretching and grooming. Ponder carefully disengaged himself from the two little kits that had curled up beside him.

Selvyn yawned. 'Well, what now?'

Tanner answered him. 'I don't know about you, but I'm starved.'

There was a chorus of agreement. Kitty-Kitty chose to stay in the den with her kits – the mountain was too new yet to even think of leaving her babes alone. That sense of security could come only with time. Selvyn, Tanner, Ponder, and Solo left alone.

Once outside the rock caves, however, Solo saw Slade and a smallish grey waiting a respectful twenty cat-lengths southward across the Main. Solo understood immediately that they were waiting to take him to Morgalian.

'I'll go with you,' said Ponder without hesitation. He had guarded Solo so long it had become habit.

'I'll go alone,' Solo said firmly. 'I'm not in danger here – none of us are. And I'm not Dom anymore, Ponder. I have nothing that anyone would want to fight me for.'

Ponder and the others reluctantly turned northward to begin their assessment of the territory. Solo went with Slade and his companion. For the first time, Solo wondered just how his ranking bards *would* fit into this new system. Ditto and Kitty-Kitty might accept relative anonymity, but Ponder, Tanner, and even Selvyn would expect to assert their rank and be recognized as Enforcers. Perhaps that explained Slade's reserved attitude – he would, of course, be threatened.

It was full darkfall as they moved deep within the southern brush. Morgalian's gelt was strong and pervasive as they approached a heavy stand of barbed thicket that was the Dom's den-quarters. Slade and the grey, called Tuner, waited outside the entrance with several others while Solo went in alone, coughing to announce his presence.

'Young Solo!' called Morgalian. 'Come and sit with me. I've been waiting for you. You are rested?' The Dom was obviously trying to put Solo at his ease.

'Well-rested, Dom Morgalian,' Solo answered, although that wasn't quite true. 'We thank you for your – '

'Solo, there's no need to be so formal. Sit and relax. I can tell your journey has been long, and I'm anxious to hear of it. What . . . brought you to our territory?'

Solo took a deep breath. He had no idea where to start. Everything had brought them here. Deciding that his first Explore had been the turning point, he launched into his story, telling Morgalian about Spanno, and the fire, and Speaker, and his warning vision. Morgalian listened carefully as Solo spoke, but when the young bard related his meeting with the old black Speaker in the forest, the Dom looked shaken.

'When . . . did you see our Speaker, Solo?' the black asked, trying to control his voice.

Solo was confused. Had he said something wrong? 'About a half-circle ago, eastward in the forest. He said he was making his . . . Final Journey.'

The old black's eyes searched Solo's face with an intenseness that made the young bard uncomfortable. After a moment he said, 'Our Speaker has been empty for more than two seasons. We found his body on the northern slope . . .'

Solo hesitated. Had he seen an apparition? But *everyone* had seen him. 'Maybe the Speaker we saw was someone else . . .' Solo's words trailed away. He knew it had been no other.

'Solo, listen to me. There is much I need to tell you, so many things about this mountain that you must learn. We have a few enemies here; it is only our number that keeps us safe from some of them . . .'

Morgalian told of the occasional band of Wolfens that came to hunt in the high ground, and of the Owners who came in twos or threes in certain seasons to kill hoppits and deer. He explained how the ferals' hunting was rotated around the mountain to ensure that graille was always plentiful. The old Dom continued, sharing the details of Quorum structure and life, until well into mid-darkfall. There was a sense of urgency in Morgalian's tone and manner that was vaguely unsettling to Solo, and when the young bard finally took his leave, it was with the uneasy suspicion that there had been more to this meeting than a simple exchange of information.

Watching Solo go, Morgalian shook his head in silent wonder. He hadn't expected a bard not much past kithood, but once he'd seen Solo, he was sure. He was the one to bring purpose to the mountain, to end the comfortable stagnation of their day-to-day life. What that purpose might be, Morgalian didn't know, but he had lived to see a dream come into reality. Whatever would happen would take its course despite Solo's ignorance of why he had been directed to this place. A destiny cannot be denied.

Halfway back to the rock cave, Solo felt the ground echoes of a heavy cat coming toward him.

'Solo! Solo, there you are! Come on, quick! You've gotta see this!'

It was Ponder, nearly in a frenzy. Behind him were Tanner and Selvyn, just as excited.

'Where's Ditto?' asked Solo.

Ponder was huffing. 'Off counting prills or something. Come to the southern slope. You won't believe it!'

Solo fought down impatience with the big grey. 'Believe *what*, Ponder?'

'Water hunting!' Selvyn answered, already wheeling to lead Solo back to the south. 'They've got something here called water hunting!'

'Hunting for water?' Solo asked. 'What are you talking about?'

'There's no way to explain it, you just have to see it for yourself. Come on!' Even Tanner was infected with the mild hysteria.

Solo ran with them across the open Main and into the brush. After traveling a good third of the way down the slope, they slowed their pace.

'Quiet, now. You'll break their concentration.' Ponder lowered his head and led the small group through the weeds. Solo could hear the sound of moving water and sensed several felines just ahead. In the dim starbright he could make out three ferals, crouched and stock-still, beside a shining water path.

'What are they doing?' Solo asked, becoming curious himself now.

'Shhh. Move up close. You'll see.' Ponder was enjoying Solo's confusion.

Solo moved up silently beside one of the poised cats. Suddenly a lightning-fast paw flashed into the pooled water and emerged with a silvery, dripping creature securely hooked by the cat's claws. The bard quickly slapped it down onto the ground, sniffing at it as it flopped wildly in the grass. It was scarcely more than a paw's-breadth long, but its rack was delicate and delicious, and obviously edible.

'Try it,' offered the stranger, backing away a pace in the manner of one deferring to rank. 'They're good, and there are many more in the water path.'

Solo waited until the creature was still before venturing a taste. He had never eaten anything quite like it – this was graille of the highest order. Ponder, Tanner, and Selvyn sat grinning, waiting for his reaction.

'Well?' asked Selvyn. 'What do you think? Not bad, huh?'

'I think,' Solo answered, 'that we need to learn water hunting.'

Before much time had passed they had mastered the technique of catching the creatures, and had eaten their fill. They carried a few extras in their mouths for Kitty-Kitty, and lumbered back toward the Main. Solo had not seen his friends this relaxed in many darkfalls, and allowed himself a moment of pride and satisfaction. He had brought them to a safe sanctuary – the journey had not been a mistake.

The rest of the darkfall was given over to exploring. Ditto found them, and together the five bards covered a large part of the new territory, and began to get a sense of the geography and terrain. They learned that roughly twenty ferals were kept on patrol at all times, and the watches were well placed and alert. The prills were largely segregated in the center of the Main with their kits. Kitty-Kitty – Solo smiled to himself – would find much to do here in the way of improving the status of the prills. And there was a special grass on the mountain called 'onion-weed' that all the ferals ate religiously; it gave a certain rack to the skin that helped to repel fleas, ticks, and other fur vermin. Ponder hoped it might help rid him of his insufferable ear-grunge.

The territory didn't feel as crowded to Solo as he had first thought it might; the mountain was large and could accommodate many more without infringing on the privacy needed by all felines. The ferals that Solo and his companions met seemed accepting and hospitable, if just a little distant, and Solo could see that the old ways of feral life had at least been partially abandoned – ferals of different rank and class grouped together openly, and the prills did not seem to fear the bards. Rank, of course, was still recognized and respected.

The darkfalls that followed were filled with Explores and rest and getting to know their new Quorum brothers. Solo found time for long walks with Pardie, and Kitty-Kitty began to stay more and more in the company of the other prills, eagerly telling them of the changes she had helped bring about for prills in the

267

old home territory. Ponder, Selvyn, Ditto, and Tanner had been asked to join the watch rounds, and life was quickly becoming routine, something they all needed after the upheaval that had been their lot for so long. There had been a few inevitable halfhearted scuffles as the two Quorums blended into one, but nothing of any proportion or lasting concern. The chief rivalry lay between Selvyn and Slade; not so much as an impolite word had passed between them, but the tension was thick and tangible when the two were together. But, Solo thought, the resolution would likely be a contest rather than a battle – such was the way on Morgalian's Mountain. And that kind of competition usually ended in friendship and mutual respect.

It was Solo who was most unsure of his place. The young ones insisted on calling him Speaker, and although he didn't really feel like one, Solo accepted the title just as he was gradually beginning to accept that part of himself.

At dusk of the eighth darkfall, Solo awoke and immediately felt a great gathering outward. Had a council been called? he wondered. As he stirred, Ditto and Tanner also woke. Selvyn and Ponder had drawn the early watch and were gone.

'I think every cat in the territory is out there,' grumbled Ditto, shaking himself awake.

'It may be a council,' Tanner said. 'Can you picture this many ferals together in council?'

'Something's wrong,' Solo whispered as he got up, his ears cocked. 'It's too quiet.'

Cautiously Solo eased his way out of the rock cover and glanced around. Almost every Quorum member's eyes were on him. Solo felt his insides tightening – something definitely was wrong. The three bards walked boldly out into the open to face the crowd. Solo spotted Kitty-Kitty, sitting with a small group of prills. She avoided his eyes when he looked at her. He couldn't find Ponder or Selvyn yet. Slade rose and walked hesitantly toward them. It was then that Solo noticed that Morgalian was conspicuously absent. Solo sat back abruptly. He knew exactly what had happened.

'Morgalian has . . . gone,' Slade began haltingly as he stopped in front of Solo. 'He left last daybright. He said . . . he said it was his . . . time. He said that you should . . . that you were to be the Dom now, and that you were . . .' He faltered and fell silent, turning his head away. He had obviously loved the old black very much.

Solo was speechless. He looked out at the sea of faces around him. They wanted *him* as Dom? Yet he knew beyond a doubt that this was expected – Morgalian had passed the mantle of leadership on to him. Ponder and Selvyn had appeared from somewhere and stood with Ditto and Tanner, but none of them spoke. Solo opened his mouth, only to close it again, shaking his head before wheeling around and disappearing into the rocks.

Alone in the cool, dark privacy of the little cave, Solo put his head between his paws and closed his eyes. Why did others always read into him more than was there? He felt like an unwitting impostor, for the second time forced into a role not of his own choosing. There was a note of indulgent self-pity in his thoughts as well – he felt robbed and cheated of the unburdened youth that should have been his. It was Kitty-Kitty who finally came in to sit beside him.

'Solo, there are well over a hundred ferals out there waiting for you to speak.'

'I'm *not* who they think I am!' Solo said, his head still down. 'I'm not *what* they think I am! I didn't bring us here to be Dom . . . I don't want to be the Dom. I don't have the right to lead this Quorum.'

'Maybe,' Kitty-Kitty said softly, 'maybe you do.'

Solo looked up at the white prill in surprise. She was his friend, at times his mother. She knew him perhaps better than anyone else. Before he could reply, Kitty-Kitty stood and assumed a stern look.

'You can only throw this Quorum into chaos if you refuse. Morgalian had told them to follow you, and that's what they are prepared to do. Now, straighten out that coat. It's time to go.'

The formal ceremony took half the darkfall. Felines of every rank, color, size, and description came forward to offer their loyalty and allegiance, accepting Solo as their leader as well as their Speaker. Even Morgalian's close group of Enforcers enlisted in Solo's 'service,' seemingly without reservation. Slade was the only one who seemed to have mixed emotions, but it was obvious that he harbored no desire to lead this Quorum himself – he was a captain in the same sense that Ponder was, born to guard and enforce the leadership of another, and comfortable in his place. Morgalian had charged him to walk behind this new young Dom and that's what he would do, even though he would rather have followed the old black on his Final Journey.

The mood was solemn throughout the long affair. The great Dom Morgalian would be long remembered and sorely missed. He had founded the territory and held it well in trust for another, and now, Solo thought, that trust, and the wait, had been passed on to him. By choice or not, he was now the leader of what was most likely the largest territory in the world, and he was frightened.

When it was finally over, Ponder, Slade, and Tanner went off to set the watches and Kitty-Kitty returned to the central briars to tend her kits. Selvyn and Ditto sat with Solo in merciful silence, watching the flickers of starlights in the cloudless darkfall sky.

'It's like sitting on top of the world,' said Ditto, unaware that he spoke out loud.

'If the world has a top, this must surely be it,' agreed Solo, mesmerized by the giant round night-star that dominated the far horizon. In his heart, though, the young bard realized just how badly he missed his first home, and understood why felines were so often drawn back to the place of their beginnings when their final days were near.

'You can do it, kit,' Selvyn said gently, misinterpreting Solo's mood. The orange watched Solo, remembering the skinny, wet-bottomed kit he, Ponder, and Spanno had first found at the Keep so many seasons ago. He wondered at how far they'd come. 'After all, you have *us*, you know.'

Solo closed his eyes. Sometimes, he discovered, you could feel so much love for another that it hurt.

The next half-circle was a busy time. Solo had a lot of territory to mark, but he laid down his gelt more from necessity than from any pride in his new rank. Morgalian's rack was fading and the parameters of the territory must be clearly delineated to warn enemies that it was well-defended. Solo, as the Dom, was final arbiter of all disputes, solver of a myriad of minor problems, as well as teacher of the Legends as the Speaker. He quickly gained the respect of the entire Quorum for his fairness and wisdom and his unerring instinct for when to make a Law and when to step aside and let a battle take its course.

It didn't take a Speaker, however, to know that trouble was festering between Selvyn and Slade. There didn't seem to be any real cause for animosity, but they were well-matched and needed to test each other, just as Tanner and Ponder had once done. It was out of character for Selvyn to assert himself this way, and when asked about it he would say only that Slade got on his nerves. Ponder advised Selvyn to just 'stomp him bald and get done with it,' even though he himself had accepted Slade as an equal. But then, that was Ponder's solution to just about everything.

The situation came to a head less than a circle after their arrival on Morgalian's Mountain. Solo was walking with Pardie in the north border area when Tuner brought the news that the two orange bards were close to a face-off near the widest part of the water path on the west slope. By the time Solo arrived on the scene, a large part of the Quorum was gathering excitedly, and the would-be warriors were well into full fugue.

'Solo!' said Kitty-Kitty, making her way to Solo's side. 'Put a stop to this nonsense! They're acting like a couple of immature kits! What if they actually hurt each other?'

'Oh, let them get it over with,' Ponder said, rolling his eyes. To him, fighting was a birthright. Even Tanner looked eager to see the battle.

Solo thought for a moment before moving in between Slade and Selvyn, cutting off both cats in mid-chorus.

'Listen, both of you. I'll not have my Enforcers fighting each other. I have a better idea. You both pride yourselves on your speed – why not have a race, all the way to the Owner complex below and back again. That would be a test of both speed and endurance.'

'I can run rings around that ragtail,' said Selvyn, obviously warming to the idea, 'and everybody knows it.'

'This is your chance to prove it, Selvyn.' Solo was

hoping Slade would take the bait. Slade, too, had a reputation for incredible speed.

'Anytime you're ready, silt-head,' said Slade with a confident smirk. 'Just pick the time and place.'

'Now's as good a time as any,' Solo said quickly. 'You can start from the edge of the water path and use the old dead tree at the far southern border as a turn-around point. And no matter which of you gets back first, let it be an end to this thing. I'll not have two of our best warriors wasting time on pointless bickering.'

The subtle flattery in Solo's remark was not missed by Slade. He had never felt quite secure in his position with the new Dom. Selvyn went to take water and then left briefly for siltaa, and Slade did the same. It would be a long race and there would be no time for such necessities until its end.

A festive spirit quickly infected the Quorum as the two made ready; the cats seemed equally divided as to the winner. At last the two orange bards stood poised at the edge of the water, ready to begin. A hush fell over the huge assembly as Selvyn and Slade lowered themselves, ears well back, and lead-paws forward. Solo's shout rang out – 'Now!' – and the two flew off their marks over the water path, disappearing into the mountain forest in a cloud of dust and dried summer leaves. The Quorum erupted into shouts of encourage-ment and general revelry, each cheering his or her champion on to victory. 'If Selvyn loses, he'll pout for an entire season,' grumbled Ponder when the activity had died down.

'He won't lose,' said a small feminine voice from just behind them. 'Selvyn is the fastest feral anywhere.' Mondy stood with her tiny orange carbon copies of Selvyn, her faith in her bard unshakable. Kitty-Kitty smiled at the little prill with understanding. She knew what it was to have such deep feeling for a bard.

The wait seemed interminable. Tanner and Ditto had reluctantly left for patrol, but were promised word immediately on the winner's arrival. Solo, Kitty-Kitty, and Ponder paced and listened while the rest of the Quorum milled about expectantly. It seemed like an eternity, but finally everyone quieted as faint ground tremors reached them. Solo realized with a start that only one feline approached – he had been certain the race would be close.

'It's just one!' Kitty-Kitty whispered, trying to discern who it was from the pattern of the footfalls.

'I know,' said Solo, and as the ground echoes grew stronger he recognized their origin. So did everyone else. At least half of them were cheering in elation. Soon the approach was audible, and at last the orange crashed through the foliage. Slade leapt the water path and braked to a stop in front of Solo, winded and panting but exuberant.

Slade's supporters smiled happily, but Solo had begun to be concerned, as had Kitty-Kitty and Ponder. Selvyn was very fast, and he shouldn't have been this far behind.

Solo waited until Slade could catch his breath enough to talk. 'What happened to Selvyn?'

'We hit the turnaround just about the same time,' panted Slade, 'then he veered off to the east. I thought he was looking for a clearer way. We were side by side till then . . .'

Splaying out their toes against the ground, Solo and Ponder felt for Selvyn's vibrations, but there was nothing. Gradually everyone grew quiet. After a few more moments Solo turned to Ponder.

'Let's go,' he said simply. Tanner had been alerted and came in from watch with Ditto at his side. Tuner was left to attend to the patrols, and the Five struck out rapidly down the hill to search for their friend, followed by several other Quorum bards. Mondy, beside herself with worry, stayed behind with the kits.

Wordlessly the ferals made their way down through the forest, each alert for any sign or sound of Selvyn. The race had meant too much to him – something had to be very wrong. They were almost to the bottom of the mountain when they heard Selvyn's call. The orange had felt their coming and was signaling to them. Was he disabled? Solo thought. Quickly the ferals turned toward the sound, and soon they saw the bright orange fur shining in the starbright. Selvyn was upright, but a dark, still form lay in front of him.

As Solo and the others approached, they could tell that Selvyn was uninjured, but the dark shape beside him literally took their breath away. It was a cat – and it was dying. No one spoke as they looked down at the pitiful bard who lay gasping for what had to be his last breaths. The outline of his bones was plainly visible through the little fur he had left. He had obviously been starved for weeks. There were large sores over his body, and his eyes were matted and crusted over. A thin metal object had been clipped through the flap of his left ear, with markings that were clearly of Owner design. The emaciated feline's breathing was rattled and wet-sounding; he carried an acrid, pungent rack that was heavy with the smell of death. Even Kitty-Kitty, normally so strong, had to turn her head away.

'I found him like this,' Selvyn began, looking helplessly from one to another. 'He was trying to . . . crawl up the slope. I couldn't just leave him . . .'

Solo bent close to the barely conscious bard. 'What happened? Who did this to you? Can you talk?'

'Have I found it?' he croaked, barely able to whisper. 'Did I make it? Is this Morgalian's Mountain?'

Solo nodded. 'Yes, you found it, little brother. You found the mountain, and you'll be all right now. We'll

275

15
The Mission

'Solo, you can't be serious!' Kitty-Kitty gasped, looking at the young Dom. 'You saw what they did to that cat!'

'How could we even find it?' added Ditto. 'And if we did, what then?'

Solo kept walking and didn't answer.

'If the kit says we're going to get them out, then we'll get them out. Let him worry about how,' Ponder said. After a moment he added, 'Uh, how *are* we going to do it, kit?'

'I don't know yet. We'll have to see it first.'

Selvyn finally spoke out. 'You know I'm with you, Solo, but in order to see it we've got to know where it is.'

'The feel and smell of that place was all over . . . him,' Solo said, still walking. He was oddly disturbed that he did not know the bard's name. 'I don't think I could forget it if I tried. I'll find it.'

The others exchanged glances, but knew that there was nothing more to be said.

There was no need to call a council when they reached the Main. Everyone was already gathered and waiting for news of Selvyn. In controlled tones Solo told the Quorum about finding the gypsy bard at the base of the mountain, and what they'd learned from him. A gentle murmuring rippled over the assembly as they reacted to yet another Owner horror story. When Solo told them of his plan to find the place and free whatever felines might still be alive, an unbelieving hush descended on the Quorum. Nothing like this had ever been attempted – even in the Legends. Solo thought of many things he wanted to tell them in order to make them see what he was beginning to feel – that living here in ease and plenty was not enough when there were so many left behind in bondage, and that they could not truly call themselves warriors when all they battled were themselves. He was beginning to feel a sense of purpose he had never felt before, and once that purpose had reared its head, it would not be ignored. The words spilled out of him, and as he finished he said, 'If anyone chooses to come with me, I'll be leaving at the new darkfall.'

For long moments Solo waited in the silence, but not one feral offered his voice or stepped forward. He nodded his understanding and turned away, headed for the rock caverns. Who could blame them? Most of them had fled here to escape Owner tyranny.

He had taken only two or three steps when he heard a massive rumbling behind him. Turning around, Solo saw that every feral, prills included, had risen from his or her place and moved that symbolic pace or two forward. There were a hundred volunteers; a little nervous, and not completely sure, but perhaps that was the best sign of all. They were willing to go anyway.

Grinning and scratching at an ear, Ponder said, 'Kit, it's gonna be real hard to sneak up on this place with this many cats on the mission. I think we'd better cut it back a little.'

By daybright Solo had 'cut it back' to a group of eleven. Kitty-Kitty would have to stay behind, because of her kits, and Selvyn was to remain and assume responsibility for the Quorum. The great danger in what they were attempting was obvious, and Solo could not ignore the possibility that he might not return. Selvyn understood why he had been chosen to stay, and did his best to conceal his disappointment. Ponder, Ditto, Tanner, and Slade could not have been held back, and Tuner, Morgalian's second lieutenant, also volunteered, and had recommended Grover and Marley as good fighters. Abalon, Sessel, and Babbot completed the company. Banda and Minit, and several prills, had begged to be included, but were diplomatically told that they were needed to help guard the Quorum in the absence of so many of the warriors.

There were really no other plans to be made, and no one pressed Solo for any details. Slade said that he knew the area as far southward as one darkfall's hard run, but other than that they were walking into a total unknown. It would have to be taken one step at a time.

As the bright sun-star rose and stole what was left of the shadows, each of the ferals chosen for the mission lay in his place and took what rest he could. It would likely be a very long darkfall.

They left early and without fanfare while it was still dusk. Fanned out loosely, they made their way down the mountain with Solo and Slade in the lead. The bard had said he came two darkfalls from the south, but south covered a lot of territory. And at what rate had he traveled? Recalling the faint, ebbing rhythm he'd felt from the dying gypsy, Solo tried to correlate it with his own; there had been more of a westward pull, and he altered the course slightly. Much of the journey would be passed in silence this way, with Solo comparing the vibrations from the empty bard with the feel of their present position and making appropriate adjustments in direction. It was a difficult way to navigate and could be deceptive, especially where the earth's north or south pull was very strong, but Solo's instincts were good, and he was sensitive to the slight feeling of imbalance when they veered off course.

In addition to the Owner complex at the base of the mountain, Slade warned them of a cluster of smaller

Dwellings that they should avoid. Past that, he said, they would find forest again for at least two darkfalls, maybe more. Solo supposed that whatever their target was, it would lie within that area. Slade, watching the young Dom carefully, realized almost against his will that he liked Solo. He didn't want to like him; it seemed to imply a disloyalty to Morgalian. And this mission! Logically, what they attempted was an impossibility, but listening to Solo, walking beside him, made anything easy to believe.

Soundlessly they snaked through the dark wilderness, weaving through the night like intangible shadows. They were part of the darkfall, each one fine-tuned and in his element. Solo rarely spoke. Having to skirt far out of the way around the Owner places made it difficult to locate the direction again, and it was time-consuming. As long as he stayed directly south, the vibrations slowly but surely began to resemble those the dead bard had carried, but the connection was very fragile and Solo knew that if he ever completely lost it their quest was doomed.

Traveling rapidly and steadily for extended periods, a feral gradually begins to lose his sense of time, a phenomenon that enables the species to cover long distances in a state of maximum alertness with little or no fatigue. The instincts take over and the body finds an inherent rate and rhythm, the mind almost sleeping. Following Solo, the bards lapsed back into themselves, silent ripples within the flowing darkfall. Solo kept his silence and led them forward.

They were all surprised when the grey of first dawn found them still running.

Finally coming to a halt in dense forest, they remained quiet, reluctant to break the mood. After a few moments Slade turned and looked evenly at Solo.

'We went well,' he said simply. It was as close as he

could come to telling Solo his feelings. Just running beside this young Speaker created a sense of being special, of being part of something that was important.

Solo was still. 'We're very close. I think if there was wind, the rack would carry this far. I wish we had more darkfall.'

Tanner, still mentally excited from the running, said, 'I'll take first watch. We'll have darkfall soon enough, I think, once we get down and settled.'

'I'll go with you,' offered the grey. Tuner and Marley also made ready as if to go.

'If everyone's on patrol, whom will we be guarding?' Solo smiled. 'We'd better get a little rest – I have a feeling the easy part is behind us.'

Everyone wanted to ask what the darkfall would bring, but they all knew that the question would have to answer itself when night came again.

Solo, resting apart from the others, was filled with second thoughts about the mission. He led them into danger, he knew. Would the quest be worth the danger? But the memory of the bard who lay empty at the base of their mountain overshadowed his trepidation. What they were attempting was important, even if they brought out but one captive feline. O Speaker, he thought, closing his eyes, how I'm going to need you this time!

The daybright seemed to last forever, but darkfall finally came. Not a word was spoken as the bards made their preparations and headed off once again into the southward wilderness. They walked steadily and deliberately now, searching the air for any rack or sound that might indicate their target. They had traveled only a short way before the first wisps of a strange rack reached them. There was no scent in any of their memories to compare with it; sharp and stinging, it fairly screamed of Owners. Mixed with it was the heavy, burned odor of rauwulfen and other inexplicable racks so indigenous to an Owner place. If this was their target, Solo thought, they would soon be picking up feline emanations, especially if those cats were in the distress he supposed they were.

'*Now* we get down to it,' Solo said to himself, as the sounds of a moving rauwulf (obviously a big one) and the choppy rumble of Owner voices reached them and became increasingly distinct. There was still no trace of felines – could he have made a terrible error?

The others followed behind Solo, jaws set, muscles tense with readiness. The Owner atmosphere made them nervous and wary.

Seeing an abrupt end to the dense forest just ahead, they slowed, inching forward until they were covered by little more than tall grass and weeds. At last they could see the Dwellings.

'Droud,' breathed Ponder, 'what is this place?'

The feel of death hung over the place like a fog. Two structures were situated fifty to sixty cat-lengths into the clearing, well-lit and brightly outlined from both within and without. One of the Dwellings was fairly large, as long as ten rauwulfen end to end, but the other one was much smaller and resembled one of the miniature Dwellings they had passed on the journey. They were separated by a good forty cat-lengths. In front of the large structure sat two silent, waiting rauwulfen, white-colored and very large. Along their sides were the cryptic markings that Owners put on so many of their objects – Solo wished he could decipher their meaning; what secrets might they reveal about their creators?

The largest structure was high, although not nearly as high as the Dwelling in the old territory, and its sides had no see-through squares, at least from this angle. The main entranceway was huge; bright light escaped from its loose-fitting edges. Solo could feel the activity of three or four Owners from inside. Isolated a little way left of the two Dwellings was an object most of the ferals instantly recognized – a medium-size green Keep.

'We'll circle around back later to see if there's a way in from behind it. We'll have to wait awhile, though. Owners take their rest during darkfall. They may den elsewhere, and be leaving soon.' Solo's knowledge and logic struck the others as nothing short of inspired.

Crouched low in the scant cover, they waited. They were all nervous, though not from fear, but uncertainty. It wasn't very long before two of the Owners came out of the largest structure and headed directly for the nearest white rauwulf. Solo had been right – they were leaving. The hidden ferals braced against the explosive noise that always preceded a rauwulf's movement, and watched as the thing lurched forward and lumbered away eastward. It did not run on blackrock, but on a wide, cleared path covered with small rocks. Seconds later, a third Owner came out through the entranceway, carefully closing it behind itself and pausing, as if to adjust something at the closure.

'It's going to the small Dwelling,' whispered Ditto, as the giant creature quickly strode away to the right and disappeared into the little structure.

There was no longer any light coming from the large Dwelling. The ferals watched Solo, waiting for directions. Solo, too, waited – for word from Speaker. But none came.

'We need to get back behind that place,' Solo began, as if thinking out loud. 'I don't see any way of getting in from this side. Tuner, you and Grover stop and take cover in those bushes between the Dwellings – you can signal if the Owner comes out again. Ponder, Tanner, Ditto, and Slade will come with me around the

Dwelling. The rest of you stay here. If there are any cats in there and we get them out, we'll need someone to direct them away from the Dwelling. I guess we're ready – let's go.'

The seven ferals moved swiftly and silently into the open, moving across the pebble-covered path without so much as disturbing a stone. Halfway to the bush cover, Solo sensed what he'd been hoping for, and knew the others had felt it as well. There were felines inside, many felines, but their emanations were thin and ragged, and they did not seem to detect Solo's group at all.

The closer they crept toward the Dwelling, the more stifling the peculiar rack became. Soon Solo and the others found themselves breathing in shallow, quick breaths to avoid the scent. When they reached the small clump of bushes between the two Dwellings, Tuner and Grover remained behind, taking cover beneath it. Solo and the other four hurried back around into the shadows behind the Dwelling.

The back was much like the front, except there was no entranceway. But there were two see-through squares about Owner height at each end. No light came from them.

'It's so quiet, Solo,' Tanner said in hushed tones. They had all noticed it. That many cats held in captivity should have been more than just audible.

Solo didn't answer. He was looking intently at the transparent squares. He had seen them being raised at the Dwelling back at the old territory, but had no idea how it was done. And he could see no other possible way to enter.

For a long moment Solo studied the dark squares; taking a step backward, he jumped and landed up on the thin ledge that bordered it. Ponder was instantly beside him, balancing his ample weight as the rest kept watch below.

Sniffing along its edges, Solo found no clue to help them get inside. He was becoming frustrated – there *had* to be *some* way in.

'I could probably break it, kit. It looks . . . thin.'

After considering for a minute, Solo said, 'I don't think we could risk the noise. The Owner would be sure to come.' Solo realized that they would have to chance going back around to the front and look for access there. It seemed hopeless from this side.

Jumping lightly back down to the ground, the young Dom tried to disguise his discouragement and concern. Nonetheless, he could tell that the others were losing faith in the mission. Even Ponder avoided his eyes as he leapt from the ledge and stood beside him.

'There might be a way to get in from the other side,' Solo said to them. 'But be careful. At the first sign of an Owner, run straight for the forest.'

Following the shadow of the structure, the ferals eased around the east side and worked their way to the large opening place at the front. They sniffed it and inspected it, pushing against it, but could find no way to gain entry. They couldn't even dig their way under the entrance – there was a kind of greyrock beneath it.

Solo was truly concerned now. Had the mission been for nothing? His mind kept going back to the squares on the other side. Could they have missed something? He couldn't shake the feeling that those closed squares held the key.

'Let's try the back side one more time,' Solo said to them. 'Maybe we can find some way – '

'Solo,' Ditto began, looking at the ground, 'we're not going to get in from the back. Maybe we should – '

'Let's just look at it one more time.' Solo started back around the Dwelling and the others followed. This would be his last chance, he knew, before they would be forced to abandon the mission. Moments later Solo stood beneath the see-through squares, wondering how the Owners managed to get them open.

'You're gonna have to let me try to break it, Solo. It's that or we'll have to give up.' Ponder and the others were obviously getting jittery.

It was surely their only hope, and Solo found himself tempted to the point of wondering how much of the sound would carry to the smaller structure where the Owner was denned. But even as he considered it, he knew they could not chance it. In frustration, Solo rose with his forepaws against the upper part of the square, straining to see into the blackness on the other side. Suddenly the upper part of the square rotated smoothly inward, while the lower edge went outward, leaving Solo balanced on the now horizontal square. Surprised, he leapt quickly back down to the ground below. Glancing back up at the newly created entrance, Solo trembled with excitement. It was open! The others were staring at the square with open mouths.

'What now, kit?' Ponder asked, trying to sound nonchalant.

Solo took a deep breath and recovered his composure. 'Now we go in. I don't know what's in there, so be careful.'

Solo was first up, and one by one they leapt to the ledge and dropped silently down inside the Dwelling. It was very dark, but when their eyes adjusted, what they saw made them want to run.

They were standing in the middle of a waking nightmare. Row upon row of metal traps lined three of the walls, in some places as high as four deep, a single cat in almost every one. There were well over twenty of them, and very few had even raised their heads when

Solo's group came through the opening. The bards remained where they landed, trying to assimilate what they were seeing, breathing in the despair, sickness, and the hideous artificial rack that seemed to permeate even the ground on which they stood. The stench of uncovered silt, too, was thick and nauseating.

Most of the caged felines lay flat on their sides, weak and panting, some purring in the ragged, low rumble of grave illness. They all looked starved – Solo could see no form of graille or water in any of the enclosures. Some, perhaps those who had been here the least amount of time, had their heads upright, but even these had the glazed eyes and vacant stare of deep, deep fey. These cats had not just given up, they were *trying* to die, and Solo knew that a great many of them would never walk again.

Looking around, Solo forced himself to speak. 'Is anyone here called Rainey?' A moment passed and no one answered. 'Rainey? Does anyone know a prill named Rainey?'

'Here,' came a faint rasp from the east wall.

Solo followed the sound toward a small orange prill who was huddled in one of the second-level traps. She looked at him through matted but lucid eyes. 'I'm Rainey . . . how did you know . . .?'

Solo hesitated. 'A bard came to us . . . to our mountain. He's the one who told us about this . . . place. He spoke your name.'

'Harker? He escaped? He lives?'

Solo's silence answered her question and she laid her head back down. They must have been pair-bonded, as Kitty-Kitty and Spanno had been.

'Your bard was strong and brave. If it hadn't been for him we couldn't be here. Be proud of him, Rainey. Now, make him proud of you.'

The little prill looked at Solo, and he knew he would count her among the survivors.

Turning away from her, Solo saw an open archway on the empty wall and quickly went to see if the area beyond it housed even more confined felines. He stopped halfway through it, unable to understand what he saw. There *were* cats in there, empty ones. On raised four-legged platforms stood lines of stiffened, grotesquely displayed felines, obviously filled with whatever caused that ever-present acrid rack and encased in thin, transparent coverings. Every one of them had a flat, narrow object fastened to an ear. Their legs were splayed out at unnatural angles as they lay on their backs, mouths open wide and lips curled far back, as if forever frozen in a silent scream. Swallowing down his own vomit, Solo turned away – no one else must see this.

'There's no one in that section,' he said stiffly, realizing the others were looking at him and waiting for directions. 'Check out each of these traps and see who's able to travel. I'll work on figuring out a way to open these things.'

His words seemed to jar them into action, and silently they got to their work. Solo began to inspect one of the traps closely. He could see no obvious way to open it. He did, however, notice that one particular area on the bottom right carried slightly more Owner rack than any other part, and there was an extra metal tablike object that seemed to fold up from under the enclosure. Owners had to get these cats in and out somehow, and it must have something to do with this area. Part of his head was secretly listening for whispered instructions from Speaker, but he was beginning to realize that they were on their own. All he heard was the others moving from cage to cage, taking their grim inventory, and the sounds of the captured cats and their misery. Solo pawed at the place on the cage experimentally. He even tried to push it from side to side with his nose. It wouldn't budge. He had started to try pulling at the tab with his teeth when he heard a horrified gasp behind him. Had someone gone into the other area?

Wheeling around, Solo saw that it was Ditto, shaking his head back and forth and making a desperate, almost sobbing noise as he stood in front of a trap. Looking inside, Solo saw a small slate-colored prill. She was tailless.

'Doeby,' Ditto soothed as he pulled himself together, 'I'm here. We'll get you out . . . you'll be all right. Hold on, little one, I'm here now.'

The prill's eyes cleared a little. 'You came . . . I dreamed you would . . .' She could barely speak, but Solo realized with relief that she was better off than most and would likely make it out of here. Ditto tried to touch her through the trap bars.

'How did you get here, Doeby? How long . . .? No, I'm sorry. Don't try to talk.' Ditto hurried over to Solo. 'It's Doeby!'

'I know,' said Solo gently, and turned back to his task. Tanner appeared at his side, his eyes wild.

'I don't think that more than ten can make it. We'll have to leave the others . . . some of them aren't conscious – '

'We're not leaving anyone,' Ponder hissed from across the room, and they all understood him completely.

Solo took hold of the slick metal tab with his teeth and pulled. It was tight, but suddenly it gave way and came loose with a snap, surprising Solo and nearly causing him to lose his balance. The others came close to see how it had been done.

'You grab it from the top and pull down hard,' the

289

kit explained hurriedly. 'Now, let's get them all open and get these cats out.'

The highest cages were the most difficult – they had to be opened while hanging on to the side of the enclosure. More than one claw was sacrificed to the task, but in the end, all the traps stood open wide.

Ponder and Tanner were immediately busy with another project. They were pushing a large square brown box that was made of some lightweight material to a spot directly under the open square. This would be a necessity, as none of the freed felines would be capable of the jump needed to reach the outside without an intermediate step.

Doeby could walk, but not upright. The enclosures had been too shallow and she probably had not stood for many darkfalls. Several others were only able to crawl, and it was hard to watch them having to painfully stretch contractured muscles just to move. Getting them up to the escape-way was going to be very difficult. Some that had been pulled out of the traps were not even able to crawl, and the final count of possible rescues was thirteen.

Thirteen out of more than twenty.

'Slade, Tanner – go out and wait below. Try to break their fall if they can't land correctly. Ponder, you and Ditto help me get them up onto this box. We need to hurry – we've been in here too long already.'

One after another the imprisoned cats were pushed, shoved, and hauled up onto the flimsy box. Doeby made her try for the opening first, but after two unsuccessful attempts at jumping, finally just shimmied up the wall with Ponder pushing from beneath her until she could reach the ledge with her forepaws. She barely found the strength to pull herself over. Ditto stood below, mentally urging her on. In more of a controlled fall than a true leap, she hit the ground outward on all fours, braced up by Slade and Tanner.

This proved to be the pattern for the rest of them, as well. Only one, a large young bard, was able to actually jump up and out under his own power. But all thirteen made it outward.

'Take them to the shadows,' Solo called down as the last one left the ledge. 'We'll be out in a few minutes.'

Inspired by Ponder's gentle act of violence with the bard called Harker who had sent them here, Solo went back inside to assist the grey and Ditto in an act of mercy that would leave not one feline for the Owners to torture a moment more. Solo laid his body over one after another, quickly snuffing out the little life they had left. Solo, as well as the others, knew he would be haunted by this night until the darkfall he took his own last breaths. Finally it was over, and the three left that place of horror, forever changed.

The fugitives were ferried one by one around the Dwelling and across the clearing, with escorts to prod and push or even just give them something to lean against as they made their way slowly toward the forest. Grover, Tuner, and the others were called to help, and Solo and Ponder both returned and made an extra trip with the last two. Once under adequate cover, the weakened felines were allowed to rest – the exertion for most of them had been unbelievable, and they were all in shock.

Ditto stayed beside Doeby constantly, determined that she would make it even if he had to pull and drag her all the way to Morgalian's Mountain. Her once beautiful coat was scraggly and crusted, and she was thin beyond belief, but in Ditto's eyes she had not lost the great beauty he'd first seen at the old territory Dwelling. She was changed in another way that Ditto did recognize, however. Sometime in the not very distant past there had been kits.

'There's a water place not too far westward,' Solo said when he felt they were ready to move. 'Let's get them there – they will need both water and graille before we can start back for the mountain.'

Slade sniffed the air and caught no rack of water, but had no doubt that it was there somewhere. 'How does he know these things?' he asked, looking at Ponder and several of the others.

'You'll get used to it,' Ponder answered matter-of-factly.

They found water a short time later. Due to the exhaustion of the liberated cats, they stayed beside the water path for two darkfalls, secluded in good cover and surrounded by plentiful graille. The starved felines were at first able to eat very little at a time, but quickly they regained strength as well as spirit. Two of them were very ill, however, and Solo feared that they might not make it home.

Whether from an unconscious reluctance to hear it or from some innate sense of feral protocol, none of the tormented felines was pressed for details about what had happened to them. *What*, after all, was obvious. It was the *why* that hung heavy on their minds as they watched the broken felines gradually try to recover. Slowly, unbidden, one by one, their stories emerged like jagged thorns torn from a sensitive paw, followed by an emotional bleed that drained them all, captive and rescuer alike.

Doeby lay next to Ditto, trying to take some of the food he had brought for her, when she suddenly began to talk. It was as if she had just remembered, and needed to tell it out loud before she forgot it again.

'It was the darkfall that the great fire came to our den. That's when it all started.' She spoke to Ditto, but her eyes were focused on an empty spot in the air in front of her. 'The fire and smoke were everywhere, coming through the top of the Dwelling. My Owners were running and screaming and taking things outward . . . they were so afraid, so *helpless* . . . and that scared me more than anything! I tried to hide, but they found me. Then everything is all fuzzy and jumbled up, but I know we were in a rauwulf and it was like the whole world was flying past, faster and faster. I cried out as loud as I could and looked for a way to get free, but I couldn't find an opening! My Owners were yelling and making fear noises, especially the young ones, and then I remember one of them grabbing me and I clawed and scratched to get loose . . . the big Owner jerked me up by my neck and kept shaking me and shaking me . . . then I was outward and on the black-rock, and the rauwulf was gone. I ran and hid for a long time, I don't know how long. At first I was relieved to be away from the rauwulf, but then I realized that this place didn't feel anything like home – I must be a long way from the den, and I didn't know how to get back again. And even if I could, there was the fire . . . Then I remembered you, Ditto. I knew I had to find you! I started walking, and I walked for a long, long time, but I couldn't get my direction. I was lost, but I kept going because I didn't know what else to do. Oh, Ditto! I went like that for two darkfalls . . . or was it three? I was hungry and I didn't know how to get graille, and I was so ashamed. But I finally did find food. I smelled it and followed the rack to a little alcove inside some bushes . . . but as soon as I was near enough to get to it there was a great crash behind me. It was a trap, Ditto! I had walked into an Owner trap! I couldn't even fight it, I just lay down and . . . waited. I kept telling myself that maybe I'd just be taken to

293

another Owner den and have a new home – now I don't know if I really even believed that.

'Finally, at the new daybright, two Owners came and opened the trap, but before I could run, they threw something over me and pulled me out. I was carried that way for a while, then they shoved me into a dark place . . . I couldn't see anything but there were dogs there too, barking and whining all around me! Then the whole place started shaking and bumping and I could tell from the noise that I was in another rauwulf. I think I went fey then, because I don't remember anything else until they took me back out of the dark place. I was still in a cage but I could see out of it, and they carried me inside a great Dwelling . . . there were so many creatures there, all in traps like mine . . . the sounds they made were horrible . . . mothers crying for their kits . . . the rack of fear . . . that terrible, constant barking of the dogs . . . the smell of silt everywhere . . .'

Doeby was breaking down, and Ditto was not far from it. 'But we found you, Doeby. You're free now. We got you out.'

'No,' Doeby said, her voice filled with pain, 'you don't understand! That wasn't the place where you found me! The Owners there were . . . gentle, and there was graille and water. I don't know how long I stayed in that place, I could never tell if it was darkfall or daybright for sure . . . after a while it was all like a dream. Owners would come and stare at us, and sometimes they would take one of us away, I don't know where. Finally I thought I understood . . . this must be where Owners came to choose their Dwelling felines! I preened my coat and purred when they stopped in front of my cage, hoping to be chosen and taken away. And eventually I *was* taken away. How happy I was when they lifted me out of the trap at last

– some kind Owner must have picked me from all the rest, and the nightmare would soon be over! I would try so hard to please them, I thought, and be very careful not to scratch or nip even in play . . . but it was all just a fantasy. I, and at least ten others, were shoved roughly back into covered cages and after much bouncing and crashing around I realized I was back in another rauwulf, and we stayed inside the thing for a very, very long time. When we finally stopped and were taken out again, I smelled death, *my* death. We were brought inside that Owner Dwelling and put singly into tiny, low enclosures. This time there was no graille or water or gentle Owners, it was a place of horror.

'We were all silent after the first darkfall or two . . . we knew there was no escape, no hope. We were standing at the threshold of Shadowland, afraid of an unknown death and just as afraid of living long enough to die slowly. And many died slowly in the time that I was there. Starvation, lack of water, illness, despair – these were the slow killers. I suppose it was the . . . lucky ones that died by Owner hands. Many times throughout the daybrights that came and went an Owner would go to one of the traps, open it, and reach inside. There would be no sound, no struggle, no cry of pain, but when the great being turned and left, it would be carrying the limp, empty form of a feline. I don't know how it was done. But I could see into the other place where they took them, Ditto. I could see what they were doing to the bodies! I learned not to look, not to listen . . . I just waited, waited until the time the Owner came to stand in front of my cage. I didn't want to die like that, Ditto! I didn't want them to take me and – '

Doeby was cut off by a blood-chilling war cry. Ponder was up and in full, wild fugue. His head was thrown back and his eyes were totally fegin and unfocused. Suddenly the huge grey leapt out and ran crashing through the leaves and brush, headed eastward toward the Owner place. Solo shot a frantic look at Tanner and Slade, and together they streaked away in pursuit. Ponder was not the fastest among them, but he was driven by an insane vengeance, and they had covered nearly half the distance through the forest before they caught up with him.

'Ponder!' Solo screamed. 'No! There's nothing you can do!'

They were running at Ponder's side but were unable to stop or even turn him. The great grey giant had found his breaking point. Tanner jumped on top of Ponder, but barely slowed him. Slade, too, tried to topple the grey, and Solo added his own weight, but Ponder kept lunging forward, dragging the three smaller bards as he went. Finally Ponder was moving slowly enough for Tanner to find traction against something and heave hard over sideways, at last bringing him down. Screaming out into the night, Ponder regained his footing and was upright, trying to shake off the other three. Slade pulled back a little and hit the grey with his full weight, knocking him down again. Tanner and Solo threw themselves across the thrashing bard, holding on to him with their teeth and tasting blood.

'Ponder,' Solo gasped, 'don't do this! You'll only get yourself killed! Please, listen to me!'

Slowly Ponder's violent struggles faded into an unashamed trembling. Solo, Tanner, and Slade backed away, panting and exhausted, watching helplessly as their great friend quietly came apart.

The journey back to Morgalian's Mountain covered four and a half darkfalls. One little dark prill was lost along the way – she lay down to rest on the second daybright and never got up again. It was a real struggle for the rest, weakened as they were, but they made it. Ponder gradually pulled himself together and covered his emotions with the tasks of advance guard and wide patrols, and they all respected his need for solitude.

Doeby did well, as did little Rainey, even through her sadness. Solo made sure that their path up the mountain would take them well away from Harker's empty body, and not just for Rainey's sake. They had all seen enough death.

Selvyn's outwatch had reported the return even before they'd reached the mountain's base. Haggard from worry, the orange, Kitty-Kitty, and three other Quorum bards hurried down to meet them.

'Solo!' Selvyn called when just within sight range. 'What happened? We were getting ready to go and look for you! A quarter-circle almost. Why – '

Selvyn and Kitty-Kitty stopped cold as they took in the twelve new additions to Solo's party, wide-eyed in horrified silence.

'Sweet silt, you did it,' whispered Selvyn, inching closer. 'I don't know how you got them here, but droud, kit, you did it.'

After a few moments, Kitty-Kitty recovered her composure.

'Well, let's not just stand here. We've got to get these poor things up this mountain! They're going to need decent graille and plenty of rest.'

Solo watched while Kitty-Kitty gave orders and got them organized and moving up the slope – her way of disguising her own shock at the condition of the newcomers. It was a near-miracle that they were here, but Solo realized that these twelve would be just the first of many.

* * *

'I guess this means we shouldn't count on Ditto for watch patrol for a while,' Selvyn grumbled as he circled out a place inside the rock den. He looked as weary as any of the triumphant warriors. It had been hard on him too.

Ponder yawned expansively. 'Yep, the bare butt will be worthless for at least a circle. Grimit will have to take his rounds. I've never seen a bard . . . *grovel* like that over a prill.'

'Oh, *I* have.' Solo smiled. 'I seem to remember a little black-and-white prill that "someone" nearly went to battle for not too long ago.'

'That was different,' Ponder snapped. 'I'd been looking for an excuse to stomp on Rivalle for a long time.'

Tanner looked up and grinned. 'Right, Pon. That's why we've got a bunch of shaggy grey kits twerping around all over the Main.'

Solo lay quietly listening to them bicker, but he knew that they were all very happy for Ditto. The tailless little bard had been lonely for as long as any of them had known him, and he well deserved this joy.

Kitty-Kitty had gone to help settle the new prills and Slade was seeing to the bards. They would have to be kept at least semisegregated until their health had improved and the fur vermin they carried were gone, but Solo knew they suffered not so much from true illness as from simple debilitation. Selvyn was convinced that there was absolutely nothing that a steady diet of onion-weed and the silvery, legless watercrawlies couldn't cure – after all, the orange himself hadn't had a single attack of indigestion since he'd come to Morgalian's Mountain. Of course, Ditto would remain beside Doeby constantly. Not only was she the victim of long deprivation, but a Tame-cat as well, and she would need him.

Slade entered the rock cave and settled in front of

Solo. It was still darkfall, but they were all exhausted. Traveling at a snail's pace for four nights had been much more tiring than a longer journey would have been at a full run. Slade had his head down between his paws even as he made his report to Solo.

'Everyone's settled and we've set the patrols. Grover has outwatch . . . he's young, but he's good and I think he can handle things.' Slade hesitated and looked up at Solo.

'Is there something else? Anything wrong?' the young Dom asked, sensing a tinge of reluctance in Slade's tone.

'Oh, no, Solo. Everything's fine. It's just the Quorum . . . they're so excited over everything. I've never seen them like this. They want to council . . . they want to hear all about the mission . . . from you.'

'A council? Now? You must be kidding – '

Solo was interrupted by a very grumpy-sounding Ponder. 'Well, you can council without me, if you do. Wild Wolfens couldn't get me out of this spot.'

Selvyn rolled over on his back and stretched out long. 'Just tell them that his Greatship has to sleep like everyone else.'

'Some of them escaped from . . . bad places to come here,' Slade said softly, avoiding Solo's eyes. 'Now they think you'll find a way to go back and get those they left behind.'

'Oh, silt,' moaned Ponder, rolling his eyes. 'I think we've just been volunteered for a life's work.' Tanner kept his silence and waited for Solo's reaction.

Sighing, Solo rubbed his eyes against his forepaws. He had expected this, and was not really surprised. And he knew that even if it wasn't spoken of out loud, this Quorum believed that he was the 'Great One' of Morgalian's vision. Selvyn interrupted his thoughts.

'If you do go out again, I'm not staying behind. You

can't make me stay behind again. That was the longest stretch of darkfalls of my life. Next time, *I* go too.'

'I don't think we should council over this. The ones we brought back can tell their own stories in their own way, *if* they want to – they shouldn't be put on display. The Quorum will understand that. As for more missions . . . let's get over this one first.'

Solo's tone carried finality, and the subject was closed. Gratefully the bards curled and made ready for sleep. The kit, though, lay awake for a long time before rest came to him, haunted by something he'd come to realize as they'd brought the twelve up the hill – 'just the first of many.'

By the time a circle had passed, it was hard to tell the rescued Tame-cats from the regular Quorum members. They gained weight and strength quickly, and their wounds healed and became invisible beneath new growths of healthy fur. The outward signs of their ordeal were fading, but the inner scars were mirrored clearly in their eyes. None of them, though, was more determined to become truly feral than little Doeby. Most of these new ones had led sheltered, artificial lives, but the dark tailless prill was a veritable cripple, her instincts almost completely atrophied. She had never hunted, or eaten grass, or learned to find water by the feel of the air. She could not distinguish the natural sounds of peace and order from those of danger, and her surround was limited in effectiveness to less than four or five cat-lengths. But Ditto was endlessly patient and constantly encouraging, and she learned quickly, spurred on as much by her bard's faith and love as by her own newfound pride in herself. Even Kitty-Kitty came to like and respect her, realizing that she was no longer the haughty, aloof Tame-cat of so many circles ago.

Rainey, too, adjusted well. She and Harker had been with a feral Quorum before their capture and she fell easily back into the routines of community life, handicapped only by occasional relapses of despair that took her into the dark forest to mourn. Solo had at first thought that she and Kitty-Kitty might become friends, having such deep pain in common, but they reminded each other too much of their loss and it was something that neither of them could talk about.

One of the new bards, a large young black, was of the Enforcer class and would soon be ready to take his place among the ranking bards. The sudden appearance of so many new prills without kits (and therefore due to Perrl at any time) had the young bards already practicing their Calls and fugues. Overall, they were a good, strong group, and Solo was pleased. He was surprised, though, to learn that several of them had heard of Morgalian's Mountain before, most regarding the story more as a tale than fact. Harker *had* believed, and invested his last reserve of strength to find it and the great leader that was supposed to reside there, hoping to save his Rainey.

Solo knew the uselessness of trying to convince the Quorum that he was not the Great One. He finally handled the problem by being careful to act extraordinarily ordinary. He scratched his ears just like the other ferals, ate the same graille, mingled with all of them regardless of rank, rolled in the dirt occasionally (when Kitty-Kitty wasn't looking), and played openly with the kits on the Main. His strategy seemed to work. It's difficult to overtly worship someone who walks on the ground with you like a mere mortal. They might still *think* of him as an incarnate figure from the Legends, but at least he was spared all but the usual amount of respect and deference due any Dom-cat. Solo could have happily lived without that as well.

301

In the darkfalls that followed their return, Solo would invariably wake and leave the rock hill to find one or more of the Quorum ferals waiting for him. He would listen as they told of places they'd been and things that they'd seen, takes of incredible suffering and degradations. It was difficult to hear these things with a critical, unemotional ear, sifting through facts blurred by the passage of time and details exaggerated or lost in painful memories, separating the possible from the impossible. But throughout it all, one thing emerged clear to everyone, that no matter what direction they might travel, or how far they might go, they would find felines in bondage, most of them unaware of any other way of life. Rescuing them would be a worthy task, but not one that Solo or any of them contemplated lightly. It was a path filled with danger. Nonetheless, the importance of such a mission was so big that it overshadowed all reservation. They were feral, and they were warriors, and now they had *purpose* as well. Solo knew there would be many missions in the seasons that followed.

'You know, you can't save the entire feline species,' Kitty-Kitty remarked one darkfall as she and Solo sat together watching Justin and Carver play on the central Main.

'No.' Solo smiled. 'I thought we'd just save part of it, and let someone else take care of the rest.' He knew that the white prill was as committed as any of them, but felt it was her duty to protest everything.

'This mountain will support only so many cats. I don't suppose you've thought about that, have you?'

'There's lots of mountains, Kitty-Kitty. The last time I looked, the hills in the west hadn't been moved yet.'

Involuntarily Kitty-Kitty looked westward at the vague outline of the giant hills beyond, some of them reaching so high that they dwarfed the 'hill' they called home. She relented and fell silent, giving over to the unbelievable sense of peace and security that held across the Main. Gradually Solo's breathing slowed and became regular, and Kitty-Kitty realized that he was actually napping out here in the open. And why not? With cats like Ponder, Selvyn, and the others on watch in the timberline below, they couldn't be better protected.

'So this is happiness,' Kitty-Kitty whispered to herself as she, too, slipped quietly into sleep.

Epilogue

The Dom-cat moved confidently across the Main, his large, heavy body rippling with the kind of strength and power that comes only with age and a long feral life. He entered the thick brush and descended the west slope, finally settling into his favorite place out on a rocky prominence, scanning the valley below. Selvyn was due in from his West Territory any darkfall now. The new Quorum was flourishing, from all reports.

Tanner would soon be leaving with thirty or so young warriors and prills to start his own territory, and if cats kept arriving (and kits), Slade would eventually do the same. Ponder, of course, could not be budged. Solo called it laziness, but knew very well that it was something else. The grey said it was to 'properly train' the calico bards he had to 'wear like a second fur,' but Carver and Justin were well into adulthood now and eventually destined to lead Quorums of their own. They already commanded most of the raids into Owner-centered territories, under Ponder's watchful eye, and last circle alone had brought another ten felines up the mountain. There was much of Spanno in them, and Kitty-Kitty did a poor job of hiding her pride. She had never accepted another bard, and probably never would.

Solo, of course, still waited for that 'Great One' to come to Morgalian's Mountain. Ditto had long since given up trying to tell him that he'd already arrived, many, many circles ago.